10 BILLION DAYS & 100 BILLION NIGHTS

RYU MITSUSE

10 BILLION DAYS & 100 BILLION NIGHTS

RYU MITSUSE

Translated by **Alexander O. Smith** and **Elye J. Alexander**

HAIKA SORU

**TEN BILLION DAYS AND
ONE HUNDRED BILLION NIGHTS**
© 1967 Ryu Mitsuse
Originally published in Japan by
Hayakawa Publishing, Inc.

English translation © 2011 VIZ Media, LLC
Cover and interior design by Fawn Lau

HAIKASORU
Published by
VIZ Media, LLC
295 Bay Street
San Francisco, CA 94133

www.haikasoru.com

Library of Congress Cataloging-in-
Publication Data

Mitsuse, Ryu.
    [Hyakuoku no hiru to sen'oku no yoru.
English]
    Ten billion days and one hundred
    billion nights / Ryu Mitsuse ; translated
    by Alexander O. Smith and Elye J.
    Alexander.
        p.   cm.
    ISBN 978-1-4215-3904-1 (hardback)
    I. Smith Alexander O.   II. Alexander,
    Elye J.   III. Title.
    PL856.I738H9313   2011
    895.6'35—dc23   2011030464

The rights of the author of the work in this
publication to be so identified have been
asserted in accordance with the Copyright,
Designs and Patents Act 1988. A CIP
catalogue record of this book is available
from the British library.

Printed in the U.S.A.
First paperback printing, November 2012

For ten billion days and one hundred billion nights—
Only dreams.
- *R.M.*

TABLE OF
CONTENTS

Surging and receding . . .

Surging and receding . . .

The sound of the waves rolling in and rolling back out has echoed across this world for hundreds of millions of years, a long reach toward eternity.

Not once in that span has it ceased rocking and crossing this blue world, sometimes gently, sometimes powerfully; stormy as the morning, calm as the deep of night.

Surging and receding . . .

Surging and receding . . .

The sea rolls in and rolls back out. One hundred billion shimmering stars rise between the wave crests, only to sink back into the vastness of the waves with the first dim light of dawn.

On a night of exceptional darkness, a faint shooting star cuts across the void, trailing a long tail of light, then falls behind the nacreous line of the horizon, its glow becoming an unfading scar—a memory in the space between the stars.

Gradually, the constellations change their shapes; white stars take the place of blue stars, red stars take the place of orange, each making way for the next as they slide past each other to weave new shapes in the sky.

Surging and receding . . .

Surging and receding . . .

Time that knows no haste flows over the waves as they roll in and roll back out, through night and into day and into night again.

●

The vast flow of time leaves traces of its passage across everything without exception. It moves within everything that is, mischievously touching, changing—sometimes destroying. Not even the sea is spared, for over one hundred billion days and nights, the starlight that falls upon its surface, the wind and rain that blow across it, the brilliance of the burning sun that warms it, and the snow that whirls in eddies around its frozen waves, all are absorbed and reduced into individual molecules, tiny motes that show no hint of their vast history. In the bottomless sediments only a vague memory remains.

The sea: it contains within itself the long, long story of time, a perpetual record of shapes that will never be seen again.

Of wind and cloud and wave, of bright days and dark nights.

The sea has always been time's closest confidant.

Surging and receding . . .

Surging and receding . . .

Hundreds of billions of days and nights roll in and roll back out again. All the while the waves sound ceaselessly, rolling and roiling in unending motion.

●

And yet, there was a time before the waves. In those far and distant days, when the planet still boiled with accretion heat and the furious energy spewed forth by the molten rock and metal beneath its surface, hydrogen and oxygen swirled in wild clouds of incandescent gas, having yet to combine into the new substance they would one day become. The great sphere's surface was crisscrossed with fissures; explosive gas and molten lava gushed high into the sky like crashing waves, there to twist and scatter. Primal mountains and hills reared up, only to sink once again into the lava. Sheets of flame like waterfalls bloomed across half of the planet.

The orange sun that dominated this solar system with its strong magnetic field ceaselessly blasted the landscape with precise quanta of radiation and heat, triggering minute physical and chemical changes in the planet's depths and across its surface.

The result of two billion years of long, long toil was about to make itself apparent.

Thick, thick clouds filled the sky, barring the sun from reaching a surface still ravaged by wild flames. Through the ashen shadows, glowing lava flows rushed like rapids, colliding with other similar streams to send forth hundreds of thousands of sparks that rose and fell like a burning ocean. The undersides of the clouds were lit eerily by the light of those explosions, and the fiery slag of the surface seemed capable of destroying the very planet that birthed it.

Bursts of lightning flashed inside the thick cloud layer, sending occasional pillars of electricity shooting up toward the tops of the clouds. Meteor showers rained down again and again, puncturing the savagely swirling atmosphere. Many of the descending fragments scored direct hits on the fiery mud below. The giant conflagrations that lit the thick, dark clouds and the firestorms that followed made this world a thing of terrible beauty, though there were none to see it.

The grand gala of creation was approaching its conclusion. The stage for the next event was already prepared beneath the sea of flame that covered the planet's surface.

Yet it would be another long, long time before the true lead players arrived.

●

It all began eons earlier still, as tiny particles of interstellar matter were pushed by the faint waves of light radiating from distant stars, gathering one by one in this region that had been mere empty space. Objects as small as one hundred millionth of a millimeter cannot move far in an hour propelled only by weightless light; yet they had come, slowly but steadily, from the far corners of the almost-void. After an impossibly long time, this collection of interstellar matter had gradually formed into a dense cloud of floating gas.

This frigid cloud—close to minus 160 degrees Celsius—hung like a veil between the stars, receiving their energy, becoming a cloud of light—an emission nebula, streaming a vast luminescence of its own. And still the various particles in this veil of brightness continued to pull at each other, the greater absorbing the lesser, forming innumerable tiny masses. Smaller masses spun into larger masses, and larger masses grew larger yet. Eventually, the largest accretion came to control the gravitational field of the entire system. This great monarch of matter had already begun to breathe—its hydrogen fusion reaction the very essence of power. The other, lesser bodies were swept into place by that shining nuclear power to form a solar system.

The orange star at its center consumed an entire 564 million tons of hydrogen every second, creating 560 million tons of helium. The remaining four million tons of matter were converted into a stupendous amount of energy that spread throughout the surrounding space.

This particular sun held ten planets within its grasp. The closest kept a distance of fifty-seven million kilometers from the star; the planet in the farthest orbit kept an average distance of roughly sixty billion kilometers.

The third planet from the system's center had a diameter of twelve thousand kilometers and completed a full circuit of the sun in about 365 days. The long, long flow of time brought tremendous change to the substance of this planet. Its own gravitational field caused it to contract, creating tens of thousands of degrees of accretion heat in its core. This sum of fire was compounded by heat released from radioactive particles over their long decay. Together these two energy sources melted and scorched the crust that had begun to form over the planet's surface.

The process of transformation was accelerated when the planet began to release the incredible heat that had built up within its core. The lava that spewed forth changed the chemical composition of the surface, creating countless new compounds and releasing even more complex chemicals into the air to become part of the atmosphere.

At long last, water steam shot from the heated mantle, roiling beneath the thick clouds, glowing like fragments of a crimson mirror.

After countless years, this water steam became a fog that dropped back down toward the surface. Still, pillars of flame reached into the sky, and scalding hot winds scoured the surface. Incandescent lava moved in great rivers of fire, scorching the barren terrain. Heated clouds burst, sending the fog scattering back into the air. But gradually, the water steam grew thicker, forming droplets, until the fog became rain, falling from great thunderheads. It would be tens of millions of years more until that rain began to reach the surface.

●

After a long, long time had passed, the first droplets of water made it to the ground, only to evaporate the instant they touched the steaming crust. And yet that fleeting contact, though it lasted less than a hundredth of a second, marked the most important moment in the history of this planet. Over time, the process that it began would eventually lead to the first standing water and the wholly novel development that was to follow.

Time passed slowly on . . . one hundred years, then one thousand, then one hundred thousand, then one hundred million . . . and the rain grew stronger, more intense, becoming a sizzling torrent. Steam heated to incredible temperatures blasted up from the ground, rending the atmosphere over and over again, until enough time passed and enough water fell to begin to cool the flaming sea of lava, a single degree at a time.

For tens of thousands of years, then hundreds of thousands more, the rain fell without pause, and eventually the sea of flame became a plain of hot mud where water and fire fought ceaselessly. Black ridges of igneous rock rose slowly between the superheated clouds of swirling steam.

Grudgingly the flames undertook their long retreat.

Water began to collect in the lowest reaches, where the land lay sunken after the last gouts of lava had cooled.

Once the porous skin of the cooled cinder-stone had absorbed all the water it could, small fragments in the pores stopped the water, forming a seepage barrier.

Pools emerged where the water collected. The rain continued to beat mercilessly upon the land. Countless tiny seas gradually joined together to form a mighty ocean, while the numerous volcanoes raged on, their violence unfaltering. Brimstone still fell like rain, dark clouds of ash covered the sky, and cascades of lava rushed down the newly formed valleys of the world. Incessant earthquakes and landslides changed the face of the surface daily, all while the rain came down in such a torrent it seemed like it might wash everything back to the void from which it had come.

Then, when the great circulation of energy in the atmosphere had slowed just enough, narrow rents like arrow trails opened in the thinning clouds, and the first ray of the sun fell upon the broken land. This single beam of light, piercing the thick layer of gas that was not quite cloud and not quite smoke, lit the cracked edge of a scorched eruption crater and revealed with a glimmer the surface of the great, steaming ocean within. On every side, volcanoes spewed forth their dark effluvium while the lava streamed down their steep sides.

It was in moments like these that the first rainbows rose above the shattered plains, brightening against the veil of rain that swept between the land and the ashen clouds above.

In the nights that followed, stars appeared through new rents in the clouds, their light faint and wavering in the violent currents that flowed through the atmosphere. For the first time, the planet looked up at the great universe that had birthed it. Perhaps it then heard a voice, calling to it from a distant place. The stars cast their glorious light down upon the broken surface of the world, telling of the calm that was to come. History had just begun for this new, ageless place; there would be many long years of change ahead.

●

The warm pools of rainwater filled with a muck of minerals, developing into a thick primordial soup. Water, a potent solvent, dissolved much of what it fell on and flowed around; as more and more was added to the mix, new things appeared that had never before existed. Organic chemicals compounded together, creating the first proteins.

Still time marched on, silent and steady.

The water falling from the sky and the water pushed up from inside the ground came together in the crevices on the surface, until it covered a full third of the planet's surface. For the first time, it was possible to distinguish land from water. The water that collected in the depressions stayed there, until its sheer weight pushed against the planet's mantle, causing the ground beneath it to sink even further. Around the expanding watery regions, the volcanoes continued their furious activity, spewing forth ever more acidic and alkaline substances to dissolve in the water.

The sun reached through the clouds now, streaming a vast amount of energy into the spreading waters. It rained, hard, several times a day, filling the seas and washing the land, water mixing with inorganic material to enrich certain regions within the expanse of the ocean.

The charcoal clouds grew thinner and thinner, scattering over years, until a vivid blue sky domed the land. The towering stacks of vapor dimmed the outlines of the mountains, which rose to lofty peaks along the shores of the sea. These mountains, which formed the high spine of the land, were growing at the rate of several centimeters a day. The constant earthquakes and landslides were an ever-present indicator of growth and change.

Continents emerged, advancing and retreating through the seas that surrounded all. Simple coastlines quickly became more complex, carven with bays and inlets; shallows marked where the eroding slopes filled in the ocean near the shore.

●

Here, somewhere under the surface of the gentling waves, were formed the basic building blocks of life—sulfur, phosphorus, potassium, and calcium, as well as nitrogen and carbon dioxide and ammonia, in endless combinations. The conditions under which these substances mix to form the basic building blocks of organic material are rare in the extreme. How many times they must all have come together only to fall apart. Somehow, as this endless process of trial and error continued, the simplest form of life—a substance that could propagate itself and metabolize energy—came into being. It is difficult to say whether this was truly life as we know it.

Such primeval entities were so simple that it would be hard to define what about them was *life* and what about them was not. Gradually, however, a hierarchy emerged among them. Some became absorbers while others were absorbed—the opening act in a harsh struggle for survival. From the chaos that ensued, only the most successful entities would emerge. It was almost inevitable that this simple, primal material that sprang up from the rich soup of the ancient shallows would, one day, develop a higher intellect, as if to challenge the very natural world that gave it life.

Meanwhile, a change both gradual and violent was taking place in the sea as well. The narrow sea that had split the land mass in two gradually disappeared, until a single great peak dominated the surface of the planet. Its heights were sheathed in thick ice, hard as steel, from which glaciers flowed, bearing down time and time again upon the land far below.

Four great oceans ruled the climate of the planet and split the land into four great continents that rose above the waters, creating their own unique interior environments.

By now two billion years had already passed on the young planet; the next two billion were fast approaching.

Uncountable new organisms formed in the seas, drifting, swimming, crawling; some dividing and multiplying, some laying eggs.

Trilobites appeared and spread, dominating the shallows across the planet. With their thick carapaces and sensory organs far more advanced than those of their contemporaries, they dominated the early ecosystems; for a long time they held their watery domain against all intruders. Though the mollusks and the echinoderms had developed equivalent internal complexity, their defensive body structures made them particularly unsuited for vying with the trilobites for supremacy. Their rule unchallenged, the trilobites diversified into species ranging in size from two centimeters to a full two and a half meters, and their kind flourished.

And yet, though harried by the trilobite swarms, in the depths of the sea another variety of life was gathering the strength it would require to carry the next age.

Though these creatures too first began with the thick shells that were the fashion of the day, they gradually abandoned their unwieldy carapaces, their armor diminishing to small scales of chitinous plate. External gills folded inside, and flat bodies morphed into more aerodynamic conical shapes. Small, round eyes developed convex lenses, and a multitude of jointed swimming appendages became a smaller number of highly efficient fins.

This kind of change does not come about in a hundred years or a thousand. It was only by fierce tenacity that these new creatures persevered over tens of millions of years until the processes of mutation and selection had remade them into something wholly new. In the face of the incessant onslaught of the trilobites, they paid countless sacrifices, pushed nearly to the brink of extinction on several occasions. Yet every time the fish came back stronger, better suited to their environment. Against such highly efficient, highly energetic life-forms, the offensive weaponry and defensive structures of the past age would ultimately give way. At last the entire vastness of the ocean was a stage for life. The lords of the coastal shallows, the trilobites, could no longer stave off the invasion. There was a limit to how deep the trilobites could survive, and once the fish pushed them and their heavy carapaces down to the seafloor, there was no returning to the shallows.

When members of one species must sink to the seafloor when they stop swimming, and members of another may rest their fins in fatigue and yet remain afloat, it is clear which will win a battle for the same region of water.

To make matters worse, the fish loved to eat trilobite eggs and young above all other food. Surely the trilobites, too, ate what fish eggs and young came drifting in toward the shores. But with the fish controlling the vast reaches of the ocean, the trilobites felt ever more pressure upon their confined habitat.

Amidst the roaring spray along the rocky coast and in warm inlets surrounded by lush jungle, one by one, the trilobites slowly disappeared.

There could hardly be any more dramatic a transition in the history of life on this planet than the one that came when the mantle of dominance passed from trilobite to fish.

●

In time, the fish would expand their great realm even farther. Near the end of the age that followed, several groups among them left the receding seas, congregating where the sun shone brightest and the air was clear, braving the dangers of the land and penetrating the continental interiors. These intrepid adventurers were to mark two great achievements in the annals of life.

The first true terrestrial animals appeared. And it was inevitable that eventually, a new sort of animal would arise that could stand on its hind legs alone. Meanwhile the sea rang on, in constant motion, recording the songs of effort and of the rise and fall of the multifarious creatures living within its borders, their unfulfilled dreams and their courage.

Constellations changed their shape in silence: the Leviathan to the Dragon, the Dragon to the Amphora, the Hunter to the Necklace. Many of the twinkling stars burst, spewing immense energy during their brief death fires, and then disappeared from the sky, leaving nebulous clouds of fading light behind.

The long years passed, as they always had and as they always would.

Until the end of time, if such a thing exists.

Surging and receding . . .

Surging and receding . . .

Rolling in, rolling back out again.

Into night, then into day, then back into night.

The traveler falls to his knees and speaks: "Aah, I thirst!"

The sea is filled with sounds unnumbered. Sound travels through water more quickly than it does through air, and water makes countless noises of its own. The complex flow of the currents, the shape of the seafloor, the thick forests of kelp, all divert whatever waves of sound may reach them—gathering in, then scattering them in all directions.

There is the tiny sound of bubbles stirred by currents along the bottom, finding their way through the cracks in the rocks of the seafloor. And there is another sound: the continual plinking of small shell fragments passed along by the tide as they fall slowly into the clusters of coral. At the shoreline, air mixes with the rising waves, forming a froth that curls back down onto the surface with a roar as of distant thunder. High on a sea cliff, the rock face crumbles and falls, creating deep vibrations in the ocean trenches, ominous ripples in the pressure of the depths.

And then there are the sounds created by the myriad creatures living in the sea:

grrk . . . grrk . . . grrrrk . . .

—The somnambulant spinning-wheel sound of a bivalve sucking in water.

kak . . . krikkrik . . . kak . . .

—The faint echo of starfish bending and stretching their pallid legs for purchase on a rock.

klak . . . klak . . . klak . . .

—The jaws of crustaceans clacking in long unsated hunger.

worrr . . . wrroorrr . . . wrroorr . . .

—The threatening rumble as a school of massive cartilaginous fish courses by.

The fish sweep their fins through the water in broad, powerful movements, sending eddies to toss the smaller creatures around them. Then, as the sound of their passage recedes into the distance, small holes open in the soft mud of the seafloor, and annelids extend tassel-like gills to sway in the current. A grayish-white head emerges from a larger hole; then, startled by the sway of a nearby clump of seaweed, it retreats, drawing its gills back in behind it.

shwoo . . .

—A jet of water shoots from the hole.

zwoosh . . .

—A rushing sound like rain beating down upon the surface of the water heralds another approach. An enormous school of tiny crustaceans sweeps by in a netlike formation. The sound lingers until the school reaches a trench and disappears into the depths.

High above, the shadow of a large fish streaks in pursuit, carving an elegant curve through the water.

sha sha sha sha

—The sound of fins pushing with incredible force against the current reaches the seafloor.

When that, too, recedes, a moment of silence visits the ocean.

Only the sound of the striking of waves on a distant shore comes slowly through the channels between the reefs.

He stuck his head out of his hole again and looked around. Something was swimming deep in the kelp forest. He caught occasional glimpses of a broad tailfin, part of a dorsal fin, a scaly side. Finally, it came closer: a big, docile cartilaginous fish.

He marked its course and slid from his hole. Flitting up past the undulating kelp, he headed for the shore, choosing a path through the narrow gaps between the reefs. The big fish seemed startled to see him, and it whirred its pectoral fins to beat a swift retreat. A school of smaller fish streamed into the channel between the reefs, sweeping like leaves in the wind, filling the entire waterway. For a moment he could see nothing but their glistening scales all around him. Then he emerged into open water, a place where the seafloor dropped away at an incredible pitch. He knew that if he followed its slope down, he would reach a dangerously deep chasm where vast quantities of water came spilling from a river into the sea. He knew these depths were inhabited only by strange fish and seaweed of a variety not seen in his usual territory.

He cut straight across the underwater gully, quickly reaching the reef on the opposite side.

Something was lurking down at the bottom of that dark chasm that piqued his interest. It was half buried in the silt between the two reefs and had been there for a very long time. Even though it just lay there, covered with red rust, wrapped in blackened fronds of kelp, it made his skin tingle with warning each time he crossed over it.

Already, a long time had passed since he first noticed the strange object. Yet he had never once descended to take a closer look. Occasionally, other sea creatures would venture down into the dark depths of the trench in pursuit of prey, only to come rushing madly back to the shallows as though spurred on by some terrible fright. Perhaps others simply sank farther and farther, unseen, never returning from that dark gulf. He twisted around, heading for shallower water.

Suddenly, the surf nearby began to whirl ferociously. Glancing backward, he caught the briefest glimpse of a dark shape as it darted past like an arrow; he recognized the silhouette of a large, lethal bony fish.

He spun around, belly rubbing against the reef below, then shot upward so that when the fish made its next approach he would have the advantage of elevation. Once again it darted at him, and he dodged aside. On the fish's third pass he struck, and the battle was over.

Quickly taking only the most delicious entrails into his mouth, he thrust the still-writhing carcass away. The seawater around the two combatants was stained red, and several blood trails snaked out along the currents. A cloud of smaller fish had already gathered. He swallowed his meal quickly, ejecting the water he had taken in with it through his dorsal vent—a blast of foam that scattered the scavengers. It would not be wise to linger here much longer. Larger, more violent fish would come when they caught the scent of blood—they'd be here any moment. He shook off the school of smaller fish that were trailing him and rode the crashing waves toward the shore. One flurry of fins and he was safe on a low reef where he liked to rest. Here, the frothy waves beat upon his back as he crawled up onto an outcropping where jets of water shot from cracks in the rock.

From this vantage point, he could look out over the lead-colored sea on one side and the dry, brown flats on the other. The sea and the land were almost the same elevation here, with only the white belt of crashing surf that stretched on as far as he could see separating them. The wind blowing in from the distant deep sounded a constant whistle in his ears. He imagined that wind crossing over the sea, then over the flat plains beyond the surf. He lifted his body and stretched out his neck, staring across the reaches of the plain. Not a hint of movement anywhere. A thin, brownish haze obscured the distance. To his left, far on the horizon, something like a forest loomed, its spirelike tips emerging from the haze.

It was quiet. Truly quiet. The only sounds were the voices of the wind and of the waves against the shore.

How many days had passed since he had first seen this sight?

A familiar unease rose again in his mind—an inherent distrust of this motionless, eerily quiet world.

The wind grew steadily colder and the surface of the sea grew rough, spraying foam.

He leapt, catching the wind, then plunged back into the water with a loud splash. For a while he swam parallel to the shore. Now and then, his glistening, dark blue skin would disappear under the gray waves. Fighting his way through the reef, he made his way up a flat slab of rock protruding from the waves. There, he sprawled his exhausted body and blew out the water that had come down his alimentary tract. A hard wind caught the water he expelled, turning it into a fine plume of spray. He stuck his head underwater several times, shaking it to wash away the innumerable bits of grit and sand caught in his gills.

Ahead, the reef formed a complicated network of waterways. He had never ventured farther than this point. He had always assumed that even if he did he would just find more of the same gray ocean and hazy brown land.

And besides, he liked it here on this flat shelf. The reefs surrounding it held a plentiful number of the large-shelled crustaceans he favored, and he liked the view of the dry flats.

Supporting himself with his hind limbs, he raised his large, round eyes, searching.

The blowhole on his back sprayed a fine mist, making a dim rainbow in the air.

There it was.

A large, squarish shape far off in the middle of the plain. He had no idea what it was, only that it was wholly different from anything else in this barren land and seascape. He had no idea when it might have arrived, or who might've put or built it there. Its very existence was a deep mystery to him. The strange object projected a feeling that was unlike the deathly silence of this place—a sensation that one could never go too near it, let alone touch it. It thrilled all of his senses to terror.

And yet he found himself coming to this rocky shelf with increasing frequency.

Even though his primal fear of the object was unabated, the sight of it sitting there in the middle of the vast expanse of nothing excited him.

The wind blew harder and colder, blasting his wet body.

For a long time he sat, facing the flats.

Gradually, the sky and the land dimmed until there was no telling them apart, until the only thing he could see was the long foamy white line of the shore. Soon, that too was swallowed by the darkness, and his awareness of his surroundings extended only to the bracing wind and the thrashing waves against his back.

He looked around as though waking from a dream, then plunged back into the water.

With the coming of night, all the creatures of the ocean emerged from their holes, filling the heavy seas. Ahead of him, two large fish fought. Their bodies twisted, revolving like a wheel. He looked closer and saw that each held on to the other's tail—each had in fact swallowed the other's tail up to the rearmost fin. Swimming closer, he grabbed the two and tore off both their heads. The large skulls caught in his throat, but he swallowed them whole. He had just broken through the gathering swarm of small scavengers when he spotted something else: a bright orange spherical shape, approaching rapidly—almost on top of him already. Strong, supple limbs darted out, wrapping around his body in several places. His assailant was one of the many-legged mollusks he had seen living in these parts. He covered his head, narrowly avoiding a snap from the creature's beak, and kicked at the water. Then he thrust his right shoulder against the mollusk, trying to shake it off. This was usually effective. But this time, the move did nothing to weaken the thing's grip on his body. Changing tactics, he bit at the thick tentacle that clutched his head, trying to tear it off. This worked, and once he had the rest of the tentacles off his back and sides, he tore the baglike thing into three pieces and tossed them aside. The many-legged mollusks were not bad tasting; it would make a good meal for the tasseled annelids living along the seafloor.

He sped onward, passing through a dark channel to reach a familiar section of reef in the shadow of a kelp forest, where the beating of his gills slowed for the first time since he had been attacked. The pod that was his home lay on its side beneath the reef's overhanging edge. The pod was covered with stony shells, and its top was wrapped in broadleaf seaweed, but the round hole through which he entered and exited had been worn to a polished silvery color by his passage. If its full mass were lifted from the silt where it lay, the pod would likely be as large as the towering reef above it, but he knew nothing of this.

He went through the opening and settled himself inside a double-walled cocoon within. At once, a rush of air bubbles erupted from the base of the cocoon, surrounding his body. The air clung to his dark blue skin, forming a beaded mantle. Something flowed deep into his body then. At the same time, something that had accumulated inside his body began to dissolve and flow away. He rested on his side at the bottom of the cocoon and began to sleep. He had never looked to see exactly what made the bubbles at the bottom of the chamber, but it made this place very special to him, and he would not have left it for anything.

The seafloor at night was filled with a cacophony of noises, both far and near, mingling and echoing all around him. Nestled in his pod, he was only dimly aware of the furious activity of the sleepless annelids and echinoderms and the movements of even simpler organisms through the water. He shifted once, then fell into a deep sleep. A passing fish with glowing green points of light along its belly poked its snout momentarily into the pod, but then, startled by something, it swiftly retreated into the black depths.

●

More long years passed.

Every day, he made the trip from his lair between the two reefs to look out on the leaden sea and the brown land. Aside from that he hunted and slept, and that was all. There was plenty of food, and his occasional battles with the larger cartilaginous fish were more a source of entertainment and stimulation than any real threat. He had never thought to want a companion, nor had he ever encountered another creature like himself.

Another day came that began as usual: he left his lair, passing through the kelp forest, and slid into the narrow channel between the reefs. At some point, the echinoderms had multiplied until they covered the walls of this passage, growing more like seaweed than animals. He noticed that the usual swarms of translucent fish were nowhere to be seen. Then he saw that the other schools of small fish had also vanished, leaving the channel eerily quiet. He thrust against the water, slowing his speed, and looked around. Something was different, of that he was sure. The little annelids that dug holes in the seafloor and waved their gills in the water were all hiding, their hard heads sealing the entrances to their tubes.

What were they afraid of?

He checked the reef, his nerves tingling, yet there was no sign of danger anywhere, so he returned to his regular route.

When he passed over the dark chasm, he looked down to see a school of large cartilaginous fish swimming furtively in the murky depths.

It occurred to him that they must be down there hiding from something. But what?

Fish rarely went down there. Yet something had driven them to seek the safety of deeper water, causing them to forget their usual fear in the face of a greater danger.

He felt the first pang of unease in his heart. An instinctual sense of warning filled him, a feeling of fear such as he had never known. For a moment, he wondered if he should return to his lair or perhaps seek the shelter of the depths like the lurking fish. In the end, he chose a third option.

He advanced, body tensed, acutely aware of the water around him.

By the time he had reached the rocky shelf beyond the reef, he was convinced that this day was unlike any other day out of all the days in the long years he had known. A fear he could not place gripped his whole being. Driven by a burning desire to know what it was that seemed so threatening, he clambered up onto the flat outcropping.

Around him spread the leaden sea and the brown expanse of the flats. The wind blew in from the open sea, strong as always. He shivered in the icy cold.

Far across the plains, a thick haze rose like smoke, swaying into the sky. His body stiffened.

Farther, beyond the haze, something like a giant mountain range was *moving*. It stretched all the way up to the ashen sky, forming at least three peaks. He had never known such a thing to exist on the land, nor had he ever seen such a thing—even on the clearest of days, which this was not.

Then he saw more—another thing just like the first one, looming far behind it, and another one, so far away he could just make out a silhouette on the edge of the horizon, sliding from right to left.

There was something queer about the way those shadowy shapes moved, something that chilled his heart with terror.

What could they be?

If he had, at that point in his life, ever seen a mountain or even an undersea ridge, he would have realized how closely these things he was now watching resembled those massive rocky formations, and the fear would have driven him mad. Fortunately for him, he knew nothing about mountains or any such lofty things. That something as massive as a mountain might move struck him as no more odd than the shifting of the tides.

Then he noticed something else and stretched up to stand on the highest point of the rock that he might get a better view.

Far off to his left across the plains, the same spires he always saw deep in the mist were standing, almost floating over the ground like a mirage, and the giant peaks were heading right toward that phantasmal forest.

●

For a long time he sat there, gazing out at that strangely solid illusion. The moments stretched into long, long hours, during which he asked the sky and the sea more than once what it was that he beheld.

And another question he asked of himself: *What is this place?*

He could feel something that had been locked up within his heart begin to unfurl, sending a tingling sensation through his body.

A storm loomed over the water. For several days and nights he sat in the driving rain. The sea roared in his ears relentlessly, and the waves that beat upon the rock broke over him like a drumming waterfall, wetting his body. Purple discharges of electricity lit the wave crests bluish white; the rumbling thunder sent its own trembling waves across the breadth of the sea.

He lay flat upon the rocky shelf, ceaselessly rocked by the waves.

The crustaceans that had once swarmed around the reef and the fish that had leapt over the waves, their scales flashing silver, were nowhere to be seen. Even the forest of kelp that covered the seafloor nearby had been drained of its color—he saw it flitting in pale strips or ripped from its roots to spin amongst the restless waves. For a long while he saw it drift in translucent sheets on the surface until gradually the currents pulled it out to sea.

A howling blast of wind brought him suddenly back into the moment. The ringing, discordant whine in his ears tickled his auditory nerves, stimulating him, awakening a large part of his brain that had until now been dead to the world. He lifted his body and stared with blank eyes across the vast ocean for a long time. Then, his entire body shivering, he tossed himself forward into the waves. It took some time before he was again aware of his surroundings and again wanted to see those strange, massive shapes upon the plains.

Time and time again, he rose up to the crest of a wave, stretching out his neck, only to find that he could no longer see anything on the land. The hazy, brown flats were once again as featureless as they always had been.

Far to the left, he saw the strange forest of tall spires, dim in the distance. That was all.

Had it been a dream?

He shook his head.

Unease still smoldered in the recesses of his memory.

He swam straight through the channel between the reefs, flitting quickly over the dark chasm. He saw not a single fish, not a bit of kelp— only the reefs, lined thick with old shells, and the naked white sand. The clear water was as silent as death.

What had happened to all the kelp that once grew along the seafloor?

And what of the lively creatures that spread their gills like flowers from their muddy holes?

And all the crustaceans and the bold cartilaginous fish?

The only sounds drifting along the dark sea bottom were the low, distant crash of the waves upon the shore, and the high-pitched friction of the current against the reefs.

The roar of all those creatures of the sea was gone.

He wanted to find out why. And yet, he sensed, this was a dangerous question to investigate now. He beat with all his strength back toward his lair, plunging through the opening headfirst.

Fatigue such as he had never known assaulted him. The movement of his gills slowed abruptly and his head sank down as he fell into a deep sleep.

A minute later, the sphincter-entrance to his lair shrank, then quietly closed. The faint sound of a compressor grinding into motion drifted up from somewhere below. From the walls, manipulation arms of various shapes and sizes extended, sticking silvery needles deep into his dark blue skin. The tubes attached to those needles began to swell as liquid passed through them. More needle-tubes extended. A hemispherical cap was placed over his round head, and the bundled cables extending from it filled the inside of the pod like a spider's web. Then, two pairs of thick tubes thrust out from the layer of shells outside the pod. One pair began sucking in seawater with a loud gurgling noise, while the other, a moment later, began blowing out thousands of tiny air bubbles. Like a chain of silver the bubbles rose toward the surface, their wavering shapes bringing motion to the lifeless, barren seafloor.

Unaware, he slept.

As from dust ye came, so to dust ye do return.

It was another hot day in Sais, parching winds whirling across the white cobblestones of the street. Red pitch oozed from a structure of thick pine logs that had been set to shore up a broken arch, its scent mingling with the smell of baking salt.

A small donkey laden with a mountain of woven baskets plodded over the stones, panting and shaking its head. A horsefly with huge blue eyes perched on the beast's sweaty neck like a dangling jewel. Unguided, the ass turned at the corner and passed through another arch into an alleyway.

Now the donkey's master appeared from behind it and gave the reins in his hand a sharp crack.

It was hot. Unbearably hot. Plato clutched at the robes he wore—white ankle-length robes, in the style of the Arabs—and hiked them up to let in a breeze. "Is that priest's house far, Gladius?"

His follower, an Arab, answered through brown whiskers. "It is off to the side of the courtyard you will find at the other end of this lane, Master. Just a bit farther." Plato had hired the Arab as a servant upon his visit to the island of Rhodes four or five years earlier. He had been invited there to help the local nobility set up a *pre-academia* and had been so impressed with the breadth of the fellow's knowledge—quite uncommon for a member of the lower classes—that the man had swiftly become Plato's most trusted personal assistant.

Plato squinted in the blazing sun. "It'd best be close," he grumbled. "And this venerable priest best have the collection they say he does."

"The magistrate in Rhodes, Telypolius, said he'd seen a stack of the scrolls himself."

Plato wiped the sweat off his brow with his sleeve.

They passed through the cool shade of the arch, entering a narrow courtyard where an unusually large tamarisk grew, lending shade to the uneven cobbles beneath. The sunlight passing through the leaves made countless spots on the road, tiny versions of the round orb hanging above them in the sky.

"It will be over this way. There, see the mark of the priest upon the wall."

Beside a low doorway of white stone, a piece of wood in the shape of the sun god hung slightly askew. The baskets stacked in the entranceway were open, and one contained a mostly empty bag from which a couple grains of wheat had spilled.

"I will see if he is home," the Arab said, setting down his pack and leaving Plato by the tree. His leather sandals slapped across the cobbles toward the house. "Is the venerable Plikton within? My master, Plato of Athens, is here to see him." Gladius's voice echoed in the courtyard. Windows opened in the modest stone homes surrounding the courtyard, and people looked out to see who was speaking. Some pointed and shrieked with alarm when they saw the Arab. Standing there in his grave-colored hempen tunic, sheepskin shoes, and skirt studded with copper rivets, a silver band across his forehead, he looked far more regal than Plato, who idled in the courtyard behind him, the picture of a servant with abandoned baggage at his feet.

The curtain of plaited reeds that hung in the priest's shadowed doorway was pushed aside, and an old man stuck his head out and exchanged a few words with the Arab. Gladius turned and beckoned for Plato to follow.

The interior of the dwelling was so simple it might well have been mistaken for a storehouse or stable. The two visitors passed through the stone entrance, only wide enough for one of them at a time, into stifling darkness. It took some time for their eyes, accustomed to the blazing sun outside, to adjust. And it was frighteningly hot. Plato staggered under the assault of the scalding air and the reeking scent it carried. The Arab took his master by the hand and led him forward a few halting steps.

"Here, please sit."

Having no other choice, Plato did as he was instructed, finding a spot upon a small round stool woven from tamarisk branches. Belatedly, he realized the low muttering voice he could hear was being directed at him.

". . . distant relative to Solon the wise . . . distinguished family of Athens . . . son of Ariston . . . Master Plato . . . the scrolls I have . . ."

The words came to him in fragments. He nodded in the direction of the voice two or three times, then gave up trying to listen and instead peered around the dim room. As his eyes gradually adjusted, the details of the small residence became clear. In the middle of the stone-tiled floor a square hearth had been cut; a weak flame flickered upon it. Something bubbled thickly in a kettle above the flame, and it was from this source that the horrible stench and hot vapor came. Along the edges of the floor stood a haphazard assortment of jars and pots. In one corner, wooden boxes and baskets stained black with soot had been piled precariously atop slanted shelves.

Plato noticed that the muttering had ceased. He turned his attention back to the crouching figure that had addressed him.

"You are Plikton the Venerable, he who possesses the scrolls of Atlantis?"

The wizened man muttered something again, too low for Plato to hear.

"Gladius," Plato spoke, "our gift." He held up one finger. "No, wait." Plato held up two fingers and shook them a few times for emphasis.

"Yes, Master." The Arab produced two sacks of gold dust from his bag and offered them to Plato, bowing his head as he did so.

"Venerable one, please accept this trifling gift." Plato set the two small yet bulging sacks upon the floor before the old man's knees.

"A gift! This is most unexpected," the man said, his voice rising clearly for once. Reaching forward, he undid the strings on one of the sacks and pinched the gold dust between his fingers with obvious satisfaction.

"Venerable one, let me explain the reason for my intrusion upon your honorable solitude—" Plato began. Then his lips curled into a frown and he withdrew his hand into his tunic, reaching around to his back. Something living had crawled in there, and he could feel it unsettlingly heavy upon his skin. He plucked it off with his fingers, threw it to the ground, and crushed it beneath his heel.

"I know well the reason why you have come," the priest said.

Plato contemplated the venerable Plikton. Among priests there were officiants who played a role in governance and celebrants who served only at the temples. In the past, many celebrants had gone on to become ministers or generals, but the king had strongly discouraged this in recent years. With their prospects for advancement curtailed, both sorts of priest now tended to direct their efforts chiefly toward the accumulation of wealth. In particular, it was an open secret that regional legates often purchased a priest's august opinion to help smooth over their own mistakes, lining the pockets of the clergy in the process.

The old man crouching before him did not seem to be this kind of priest. *Perhaps he left the temple due to poor health?*

The old priest rose slowly to his feet and disappeared into a room in the back.

"Curse this heat," Plato muttered. "I won't be able to read in here either."

He pushed away the round mat and sat his naked posterior directly on the cool stones.

A moment later the old man reappeared, dragging a small bundle of slender, woven tamarisk branches behind him. Peering closely, Plato saw that the bundle contained dust-covered scrolls of parchment inside narrow tubes.

"Master Plato, the records of the Kingdom of Atlantis."

The philosopher's eyes shone. Pushing back his sleeves, he drew out one of the scrolls and spread it open on the floor, heedless of the cloud of dust and grit that rose around him. But it was too dark to see. Rising to his feet again, he snatched up the parchment and hurried nearer to the small hearth in the middle of the room. Along the way, he knocked over something with one foot, making a terrible noise and splashing liquid across the floor. But he paid it no mind. Thrusting the parchment toward the flickering light of the fire pit, he could see lines of writing in the language of Etruria.

From Atlas came many lineages of famous houses. They possessed wealth uncountable, such as no kings or nobles before them ever held and none will likely hold again. So vast was their empire that many of their possessions came from far beyond the borders of their own land. And yet to the good fortune of the people, everything that was truly necessary could be procured from their own great island.

Plato read on, forgetting to wipe the sweat from his brow, ignoring the line of insects that had begun to march along his calf.

The orichalcum mined within the kingdom's borders adorned the edifices of the city of Atlantis, making their walls more beautiful than gold and stronger than bronze—

"Orichalcum!"

Plato pulled his eyes away from the letters upon the parchment and stared at the weak, sputtering tongue of flame in the pit. The name of that legendary metal was mentioned in the few stories of Atlantis, that great continent to the west he had heard about upon his visit to Fayum the year before.

Those had been nothing more than muttered rumors, but this document in his hands right now spoke of that lost city with supreme confidence.

Countless bridges spanned the canals that ringed the metropolis in concentric circles. Spurs connected each canal to its neighbor, so that the king and queen were able to use the network to travel anywhere within the city. The canals led withal to the open seas, and even those most central were deep enough for three-decked sailing ships to navigate. The sides of the canals rose high, allowing tall masts to pass beneath the arching bridges without hindrance. Where it was not possible to build the walls so high, the bridges were devised to open that the ships might pass. The island in the center, where the palace was built, was a near-perfect circle, defended by tall towers set with mighty gates. The stones used to build these towers were taken from surrounding islands or from the subterranean recesses of the inner and outer rings of the city. One of the towers was white, another red, and yet another black. The quarry pits beneath the city were made into safehouses, armories, and wine cellars. These cavernous holds had roofs lined with stone and double walls all around. Some buildings were made a single color, while others were speckled and mottled with different hues. The walls of the outermost ring of the city where it faced the waves were made of stone with copper reinforcement, and the inside face was covered with silver and tin, while the acropolis was constructed of flamelike orichalcum.

Plato repeated the strange metal's still-unfamiliar name to himself. It stuck in his mind; the more he thought about it, the deeper seemed the mystery.

After a long moment's thought the philosopher rolled up the parchment and tied it with a leather string. He gave a deep sigh.

"Perhaps we could bring these scrolls back to our lodgings for tonight," Gladius whispered from behind him. ". . . Master?"

Plato looked up for the first time. "Yes," he said softly, as though waking from a dream. "A good idea. Gladius, send word to the legate's villa."

He stood. "Venerable sir, I would impose upon your favor and borrow these Atlantean documents. I will be staying several days at the legate's villa, and I promise they will be guarded most carefully."

The ancient priest muttered something too quietly for Plato to hear and bowed his head low.

Rising and gathering up the scrolls, the philosopher walked out through the curtain into the courtyard without so much as a glance behind. The midday light stabbed at his eyes so painfully he felt as though he were emerging from a cave.

Plato wobbled into the shade of the tamarisk like a man intoxicated. His mind was filled only with thoughts of meeting the Atlanteans who were said to be still living in villages along the western coast of Mauretania, that land facing the Isles of Hesperides. He had heard of these villages from both Phoenician and Tyrrheanian sailors. The hints of the priest he had visited the year before in Fayum returned to him now, burning like a torch within his breast.

He had first heard the word *Atlantis* from his grandfather Critias. Critias had told him, in that way the elderly have of over-explaining themselves, that he had learned about Atlantis when he was still young from Solon himself—one of the legendary Seven Sages.

Critias's description of Atlantis had taken on an incredible weight within the young Plato, sinking deep inside him. He had thought, even as a youth, that one day he must see the lost city with his own eyes and hold its artifacts in his own hands. The young Plato had been no prodigy. He had been more interested in learning how to sail a boat and experiencing the products and customs of other lands than in his formal academic studies. One day, he had decided, he must venture to the Sea of Marmara, beyond the Straits of Hellespont and to the Argo Sea beyond that, then past the Pillars of Heracles to the end of the world where the great ocean falls like a waterfall.

And the stories of the great kingdom of Atlantis that once existed far across the western sea—the realm that had sunk to the ocean floor in the space of a single day—were enough to stir excitement in his soul.

It was at the age of twenty-eight, when his name was becoming known in the larger cities such as Athens, Mycenae, and Terinth, that Plato first set foot in the town of Sais. There he learned that the stories that Solon the Wise had told were common knowledge. It was then that the name Atlantis had quite suddenly taken on a new degree of verisimilitude. He wrote of his excitement at that time to his friend Tethys of Terinth. Then, three years later, the philosopher-adventurer once again made his way to Sais. This was when he first heard the rumor that a venerable priest of that town possessed a trove of parchments in which much about Atlantis was written. Unfortunately, his official research duties interfered, and he was obliged to return to Athens empty-handed.

But his interest in Atlantis only increased.

Some who came after Plato interpreted his yearning for Atlantis as a facet of his quest for the ideal state, but this couldn't have been further from the truth. The thing that drove him westward was his passion, undiminished since youth, for adventure in unknown lands.

After the sentencing of his teacher, Socrates, Plato had gone to Megara, homeland of his elder Eukleides, and there he had first learned of other peoples—barbarians—living within the Greek world. Humanity, went the common opinion of the day, was a distinction reserved only for the Greek; to educate a barbarian was to welcome him into the fold of civilization. Yet many barbarians proved intractable, unwilling to participate in the glory that was the *polis*—the Greek city-state. Persia threatened from the east and Carthage from the west. At times, Plato felt as though the non-Greek world would overrun the world he knew. To a citizen of Greece such as himself, the downfall of Greece meant the collapse of the polis, and there was only one way to save his society from fading away altogether—to realize a strong and resilient "ideal state." Yet, rather suddenly after their inception, Plato's political dreams turned down the path of pessimism.

The age called for empire. It was already being said among a certain segment of the *cognoscenti* that the uniform rule of a single archon over all Hellas was preferable to the chaotic polis society of independent city-states.

In later years, Plato visited Archytas, who was serving as director of a Pythagorean school in southern Italy. Then he went to visit Dionysos the First in Sicilia, where he first made the acquaintance of Dionysos's brother-in-law, Dion. He made no small number of friends there and returned later, at Dion's request, during the reign of Dionysos the Second. There he was subjected to a scathing counterargument to his theory of the ideal state from actual politicians. A shadow passed over these thoughts in his mind. During this time, he also traveled to many other lands: Crete, Carthage, Algeria, and even as far as Judea and the Sinai Peninsula. It would be difficult to sum up all he saw in those travels, but it is clear that his solitary drive toward the unknown kept him far better company than the rapidly fading patina of his ideal state. For Plato, all roads led toward Atlantis.

That night, Isus, the legate of Sais, held a great banquet for the famous scholar of Athens. Isus's villa was a magnificent affair constructed of slick polished rock, white with deep brown speckles, that faced the central courtyard in town. It was decorated all about with lit sconces, and even the two hundred or so slaves who bustled about the grounds seemed an insufficient number to carry all of the wine jars up from the cellars.

Plato found himself holding a silver goblet filled with retsina as he peered at the fires that burned atop the elegantly carved pillars. Long blue flames wavered from three saucers of oil on each capital. Meanwhile, a warrior in the middle of the courtyard moved through his forms in a demonstration of skill. He was a large man with a brown beard—a foreigner from the East by his appearance—and the two swords he swung around him danced like waterwheel shadows. As the man moved, the long scar that ran from his shoulder down his back seemed to stretch and contract upon his skin like a living thing.

"Master Plato?"

Isus leaned across the table. His light blue eyes peered at Plato's face. *A good man, by his bearing and demeanor,* the philosopher thought. Plato took a sip of wine while his free hand went to a nearby saucer, plucking out an olive drenched in sheep's milk.

"I'll need Gladius and four others," he said quietly. "And donkeys."

The journey Plato was about to undertake would make any other he had experienced seem like an afternoon stroll by comparison. His sister's child Speusippus would look after the Akademia in his absence. He would have to skip the fall seminar this year, but he could always make up for it with a special session the following spring.

Plato's face tilted upward as he sank into his thoughts. For a long moment his expression was as vacant as that of a fever victim, until a slave poured fresh wine into the goblet in his hand and its weight brought him back to his senses.

"Master Plato, I have a request—a small request," Isus began, his voice hesitant and quiet, as though he had been waiting for this moment for some time.

"A request?" Plato said without turning to look at him. "How could I, your guest at this sumptuous reception, refuse you anything?"

The man's face broke into a broad smile. "Isus is honored by your words," the legate purred. He twisted around to give a hushed command to an old retainer who hovered behind him.

In the courtyard a woman was now dancing, having replaced the foreign warrior some time ago. She plucked a lyre even as she moved with windlike grace.

The old retainer led a tall, younger man up to the table.

Isus spoke. "Master Plato, this man is Eamos, head instructor at our college in Sais. He revealed to me some time ago his great desire to learn from you, the great philosopher, the true heir to Socrates. If you would be so kind as to oblige me by fulfilling this, Eamos's one wish."

The tall man bowed his head low before the seated philosopher.

Plato cursed inwardly. More than anything, he felt deceived. He knew it was popular, especially in places such as this where Eastern influences ran deep, for provincial legates to establish a so-called "college" in part of their villa where they kept pet philosophers and poets and the like in order to show off the refinement of their own noble education. This legate Isus would doubtless be thrilled to boast that his own resident scholar had studied at the foot of none other than the great philosopher Plato.

Plato turned his eyes away from the man and took a spoonful of honey-stewed lamb from a pot on the table.

"Go on, Eamos, go on." Isus gave his own fledgling philosopher a shove on the hindquarters, pushing him toward the suddenly grim Plato. The poor fellow was rigid with nerves, and his limbs trembled violently.

"Ask your question."

Plato's thick brown beard framed his face harshly; in the glow of the flickering sconces, his sunken eyes seemed to burn with an unearthly light, and the lines of a weary frown across his brow made his visage suddenly fearsome. Isus's philosopher startled at his look, staring like a hare in a trap, and he reddened with embarrassment. His eyes jumped to the courtyard beyond the table, as though trying to avoid the older man's gaze. Plato looked down at his stew and said quietly, "You do have a question, do you not?"

His voice was gentle. He saw no point in shaming the man or spurning him. *If scholarship is what this man has offered in exchange for receiving bread and board from this provincial noble, then he has done very well for himself, and who am I to judge another's livelihood? Besides, I am sure there is Truth to be found even within a man such as this.* He brought another spoonful of stew to his mouth and favored the scholar with a smile. *Whatever he's going to ask, he'd better ask it quick or his employer will fear his money wasted.*

Suddenly, Eamos lifted his head. "A-are ideas unchanging?" he asked, thrusting the words out like fists.

There, that's more like it.

Plato shifted in his chair so that his body was now facing Eamos.

38

"Ideas have an objective existence. They are not the material of thought, but the object of thought, outside the thinker. The world we experience is a phenomenal world, a reflection of the world of ideas. The vicissitudes of life merely suggest that all things are in a state of flux because of the inherently unstable manner in which this world receives the Truth of ideas. Thus it falls to us to endeavor to see through that fluctuation to perceive that which is universal—that which exists objectively," Plato explained, his voice deliberately assertive.

Eamos muttered something, but the words failed to pass his own lips. He looked up again. "And the ideal state?"

Plato noisily sipped at his stew and reflected on how this was the first time he had lectured in quite this manner. Of course, he often found himself pontificating on Truth and Beauty while drinking wine or soaking in the baths, but this game he played now followed an entirely different set of rules. In this game, not only was he expected to inform, he was furthermore obliged to award his participant a medal.

"The ideal state holds as its governing ideology a philosophy based upon the fundamental concepts of Truth, Goodness, and Beauty. In other words—" Plato took a swig of some pungent goat's milk to wash down a lump of meat from his stew. "As reason is illuminated by the lens of wisdom, so does it develop from something experiential into something universal. Only with universal reason may we perceive the fundamental Truth shared by all things." He cleared his throat. "Truth, mind you, is not some *thing* existing in a solid, unchanging state; it is universal objectivity itself. Now, while 'will' is the sum of the choices we make by virtue of our courage, the fundamental concept of Goodness is none other than the universal will. As for Beauty, that beauty which we perceive is limited, a mere projection of the phenomenon of a greater, limitless Beauty. Within men this quality manifests in the form of the passions and the moderation of arbitrariness. It is only by achieving harmony between these three fundamentals that the entire soul may take on the virtue of righteousness. This is a basic qualification for one who would rule, as it is for those who would aid him and, indeed, for all citizens of the ideal state."

Plato spoke succinctly, one word after the other, as though he were speaking to a student at his own Akademia. Eamos stood with his head hanging low. He remained quiet as Plato finished, leaving his teacher un-sure whether he had understood any of what he said. A sudden weariness came over Plato and he lifted his wine goblet. But Isus sprang to his feet, jumping like a boy at play, thanking him repeatedly. It was at that instant that Plato knew with certainty he would leave upon his journey to the west the next morning. He wanted to be alone. And he felt a longing for that great continent, touched by the wrath of the gods, alone in Poseidon's end-less sea, as though it were his own homeland.

It was a very long time before Plato forgot the events of that night. In fact, that banquet marked the last time he spoke on philosophy to an-other. Contrary to popular opinion, Plato did not write *Timaeus* or *Critias* himself. These were compiled by his followers in later years. What he be-gan writing shortly after that night in Sais was an account of his long journey from Libya to Numidia and farther west, past the Atlas Mountains into Mauretania. It was these writings he sent in a great volume to his prized disciple Aristotle—though it remains doubtful whether his able pu-pil showed much interest in them.

In the face of pressure from Persia in the east, Carthage in the west, and the newly risen Macedonia in the north, mounting strife had worn away at the freedom and independence of the Greek polis. The evening bells of Greece were ringing when Speusippus—heir to the Akademia—and others of Plato's disciples collected their master's scattered writings into new works, ten of which remain to this day. Of these, *Timaeus* and *Critias* held but fragments of the records of his travels.

In 347 BC, in a chamber within his Akademia, built within the sacred grove of Akademos, Plato passed from this world. This is true. But there are few who know the other truth about Plato's later years.

Gladius, Plato's follower upon his journey to the West, who became Plato's shadow and trusted assistant, spent his last days in solitude in Biskra near Carthage. For the most part, he avoided the company of others, yet there were times when, lips loosened by drink, he would tell stories. At these times he would claim that he had seen the hero Atlas from ancient myths with his own eyes. That Atlas was indeed a titan who held up the world from his glorious country of Atlantis. And that his master, Plato, had gone on to heaven in search of the true titans.

●

Plato's entourage left Sais and headed west beneath the blazing sun. Thanks to the enthusiastic support of Isus, legate of Sais, the philosopher had been able to acquire a total of eight slaves and four donkeys. Plato rode one of the animals, Gladius another; the third carried their food and water, while the fourth was kept in reserve. Behind them followed the slaves, laden with a variety of goods purchased in Sais. They spent just a short while on the road before turning aside to the coast, where they hired a ship. Only twelve days after leaving Sais they arrived in Carthage.

The king of Carthage was pleased to have such an esteemed guest in his domain, and he prepared extra supplies for them to take on the next phase of their journey along the main road south of the Atlas Mountains. In the town of Capsa, Plato sent back the slaves he had borrowed from Isus and took on three hardy youths the king had supplied. They headed southwest along the foothills, following a dry riverbed from Biskra to the town of M'sila. From there the road passed through a vast wasteland of desert, heading toward Iguidi. They had already reached the farthest outlands of Carthage. Now they made for Elcasia—a small oasis in a corner of the desert, and Plato's first major goal.

The journey to Elcasia was a hard one. They split their baggage between the four pack animals, and Plato, Gladius, and the youths leaned on their walking sticks as they treaded across the shifting sands. Eight days out of M'sila, Plato climbed up a tall dune from which the sand spilled in a soundless torrent and spotted the tiny village in the distance. It was little more than a few low roofs huddled beneath the meager shade of two or three barren tamarisks.

"Elcasia," the philosopher said simply.

The traveling party made its way straight down the far side of the dune toward the houses. Passing through a barren valley, they were startled by an unfamiliar bird taking wing. By the time they had climbed to the top of the next dune, the village was directly beneath them.

As they approached, several men emerged from the dwellings. They wore short tunics tied with leather belts and shallow hoods on their heads. Plato noted their clothing with interest—this was nothing like what the people of Persia or Egypt wore.

"We mean no harm," Plato called out. "I am Plato of Athens, and these are my men." It was doubtful that these people had heard of the philosopher of Athens, though it would certainly make things easier if they had.

An older man stepped out from the crowd. He said something to those around him and they formed a line with him at the head and came closer.

"Plato of Athens, long ago it was that we first heard your name. I am Seim the Elder of Elcasia. You are welcome among us." The man opened his arms wide in a gesture of greeting. "Indeed, we have been expecting you for some time now."

Plato frowned. "Expecting me? How is that possible?"

The old man paid no mind to Plato's muttered question and led them into the village. Low houses squatted in a circle around a spring where the meager tamarisks grew. Their walls were made of deftly carved limestone, with large windows and doors set at regular intervals. The philosopher spotted several people peering out from the windows, some looking and then ducking out of sight. Seim told the three from Carthage to wait outside and led Plato and Gladius toward one of the stone buildings.

"It's a temple," Plato whispered. "See how ornate its decorations are."

The door was open, revealing a few small flames lighting the dim interior. Before the open door, the old man reached out his right hand and made a gesture as though he were pushing something away from the entrance, though there was nothing there for him to push. He stood to one side and ushered the two of them in.

How curious.

Plato looked down at the old man's hand as he walked through the doorway. It appeared he was still pushing something back toward the wall with it. Plato stared at the old man and the wall, making no attempt at subtlety. The old man grinned.

"Looking for this, perhaps?"

The old man relaxed his arm and Gladius jumped back with a yelp.

A large panel of something transparent—*perfectly* transparent—had come swinging out, pivoting on an axis set flush with the stone wall. When it had swung out all the way, it closed the entrance with a perfect seal.

"*Glaes.* This is *glaes.*" The man tapped the translucent panel with one finger. It made a hard, clear sound, like metal. "Not even an arrow from the tallest bow wielded by the strongest man may pierce it."

Plato stared at the swinging door, speechless. He had never seen any-thing like it. He had heard once from a Persian trader of a material that allowed light to pass through as though it were water, but he never imag-ined it to be so wonderfully transparent. He realized that the people of Elcasia must be using the same material in the windows in their village. How else could they possibly admit light to their homes in the middle of a desert such as this? Plato recalled the many windowless houses he had seen in Egypt and Carthage.

There is knowledge here of a level not seen in Persia, Egypt, or any of the lands farther east. This is of a different nature than anything I have encountered—an en-tirely different nature.

Plato stepped silently through the entranceway. The room beyond was filled with brilliance and splendor enough to dazzle the eyes. The wall reflected a beautiful orange image of the setting sun, painting Plato's out-stretched hands and illuminating Gladius's stern features.

"Orichalcum!" Plato gasped. In one corner of the shining wall stood a large square window where scintillating waves of green light rippled. "And what is that?"

The old man glanced over at the window, then motioned for Plato to take a seat at the table. "That is the window of the suzerain."

"The suzerain?"

"You will meet him presently."

As Plato watched, the rippling of the light seemed to slow, until he could look past its brilliance to see the silhouette of a man's head. He gripped the edge of the table convulsively, with such strength that his knuckles cracked.

Now, framed by the clear green light, a large head and broad shoulders appeared. The light shone painfully bright, washing out any detail in the man's full silhouette.

"Master Plato, our suzerain." Seim the Elder made a short bow to Plato, then another to the silhouette.

"This man is the leader of your tribe?" Plato narrowed his eyes and stood, taking a step toward the figure in the light. It was quickly becom-ing unbearable to him that he could not make out the suzerain's features, though something did give him the impression that this man was slightly more advanced in years than himself.

"Master Plato of Athens, I welcome you. I have always had a great admiration for the depth and breadth of your theories. It does the people of Elcasia much honor to receive you."

Plato could not have cared less about pleasantries. One question weighed upon him—why, if the Elcasians were so truly honored to receive their guest from afar, did the suzerain choose to speak with him through a window? The philosopher turned to Seim and whispered. "Elder, why does the suzerain not leave his chamber? Will he not come out and sit across the table from me that we might talk? I do not call him impolite. If this is his custom, so be it. I would merely know his reason."

Seim the Elder did not respond, instead drawing back, away from Plato and the suzerain, as though in deference to them both.

"Master Plato," came the suzerain's low but resonant voice. "I know you have a deep interest in the kingdom of Atlantis. I am sure that your present journey is, at least in part, to ascertain the truth of that which you have read in the ancient records maintained by a certain priest of Sais."

"You are well informed."

"Master Plato. For five thousand years we have protected a past glory and a great legacy that would otherwise have been lost. We have protected it because it is worth our protection, and it teaches us the truth that man-kind must never forgot. Yet we find our own words too poor to relate the meaning of that memory, and our attempts at comprehension fall short. Nor are we even sure that men today would listen were we to relate that truth to them. That is why, Master Plato, we have chosen you to carry out part of our great and difficult work. We have placed much faith in your wisdom—the wisdom of the Greeks."

Wariness spread across Plato's face as he listened. "Faith? What do you expect of me?"

"Master Plato. You must go west. You must go to the lands where the tribes lay in hiding, the remnants who protect the fading light of Atlantis's glory. You must observe carefully the reasons for Atlantis's demise and the particulars of what followed. Then, you must tell the world what you have seen."

Plato leaned forward. "Indeed, my calling upon the venerable priest of Sais was but my first stop upon a longer journey that led me here, to Elcasia—and will lead me further beyond, past the Atlas Mountains, to the seacoast that looks out upon the Isles of Hesperides."

"And you do this without even our asking."

Seim slipped quietly from his chair and made his way to a corner of the room. He busied himself there for a moment, then returned to the table bearing two large goblets of silver atop a tray. The goblets let off a brilliant light. A serving youth who had entered the room a few moments earlier stood waiting behind the elder, the jug of wine in his hands.

"Master Plato, please drink."

Plato's and Gladius's goblets were filled to brimming with crimson wine. A rich, fruity aroma suffused the room.

Fig, perhaps? Plato flared his nostrils.

Seim tilted the jug, pouring some of the wine into his palm. He sipped it carefully. Then he bowed and returned to his seat. The youth holding the wine jug quietly left the room.

Goblet in hand, Plato stared at the dark silhouette of the suzerain.

"Well then, Suzerain. There are two or three things I would like to ask you."

"What would you know?"

"I have heard that in antiquity, when the gods divided up all lands to give to their children, the sea god Poseidon desired a great island floating upon the ocean, which he bequeathed to the descendants of his human wife. Poseidon's eldest child Atlanta, with his tribe, ruled this island that had been left to him by his father, and many dozens of islands around it besides. His realm expanded until he considered all lands from Libya to Egypt to the warmer seas, and the mountains and oceans of Tyrrenia, Syria, and Hellespont, to be his domain. Furthermore, he counted another great continent, one as yet uninhabited by man, that lay far across the western waters, to be part of his territory. Suzerain, I have long harbored a great interest in the tales of this kingdom of people with divine wills, who never warred, who loved beauty and music—their courage, their nobility, their honesty, and their hearts that shirked no labor."

Plato stared at the dark silhouette of the suzerain, who stood unmoving, as though affixed to the green light behind him. He continued. "I have heard furthermore that the kings who divided this country amongst themselves never took up arms or rose against one another, but instead followed the teachings of their forebears, and did only good for their people, while the house of Atlas, King of Kings who stood above them, worked only to realize the divine will on behalf of those kings and their people. Is this not true, Suzerain?"

"It is."

"And I understand that the edicts of Poseidon were, for the people of his kingdom, like the edicts of Heaven which none might disobey. For the rule of Heaven was the rule of the people, and the hearts of the people were the hearts of their kings, and the heart of the King of Kings as well. So closely entwined were the people and their God that to observe the sacred rites was, in fact, to practice government. Is this not true, Suzerain?"

"Indeed, it is so." The suzerain nodded deeply.

"Then let me ask you this question: if these people of Atlantis followed always the will of Heaven and received within them only that which was good and beautiful, and carried always Truth in their hearts as a guide, why then did they perish? If the laws were created to bear forth the divine will, and the people never hesitated to do their utmost in the pursuit of Goodness, what brought them to ruin? How could it not please the gods to watch over them for eternity?"

Plato stared at the suzerain floating in his window of green light with unblinking intensity. "So it should have been . . ." the philosopher continued after a moment, his voice filled with pain. "Yet it was not to be! I have heard that iron fire erupted from the earth, scorching the land, and a great stinking cloud of sulfur engulfed the sacred land entirely, dragging it down beneath the waves. They say that hardly any escaped the destruction. Why? How did such people warrant the wrath of the divine? What possible reason could the gods have for burying their own children?"

The suzerain's form was like a black shadow, unmoving. Behind him, the brilliant waves of green light had begun to swirl violently. At last he spoke, his deep voice even and low. "You have every reason to wonder at the justice of these things; yet if you would have the answers you seek, you must find them with your own eyes. Then you must tell your world what you have seen. You must tell all of your people—that is your duty. Understand that it was a destiny that brought you to this place. And as you love your world, I would have you accept my request and treat it as your obligation. Do you understand? According to your own words, a great philosopher must at the same time be the best of all politicians. It is you who must lift the shadow of misfortune that lies across your world."

"Wait. What is this shadow of misfortune of which you speak?"

"To tell you that would require explaining from the very beginning the reason why the Kingdom of Atlantis disappeared from the face of the gods' waters; why it *had* to disappear. Know that the manner of this world's creation, the manner of its maintenance, is connected to the laws and permissions we have received in the name of the gods. An *end* such as that great kingdom's end is not part of this process; it is no mere worldly *change*."

"Then you mean to say that no reason whatsoever exists for Atlantis's destruction that can be explained in terms of the apparent world?"

"It is better perhaps to say that such a reason cannot have existed."

"Wait!" Plato shouted, standing. "So the reason for Atlantis's destruction lies *outside* of this world?"

The suzerain did not speak. Instead, his black silhouette quietly dissolved into the waves of rippling green light.

"Master Plato. The audience has ended." Seim the Elder's head hung low. Plato blinked, suddenly aware that the green light had faded. The suzerain's voice still echoed in his ears, an oddly metallic sound that seemed to ring from within his own head.

Dazed, the philosopher reached out for the goblet he had unconsciously set down. Holding it in his hand, he let his eyes lose their focus as he reflected on his strange audience from its beginning.

Who was the suzerain? Why had he not revealed himself entirely? And how had he anticipated Plato's arrival? The questions left an unsettled feeling in his breast. The one thing that was clear to him was that the suzerain expected him to act. Plato had planned this trip to satisfy his own personal curiosity; now he was astonished to find that it might hold a far greater significance altogether.

"What is the meaning of this, Elder? What your suzerain said troubles me deeply—in truth I am quite confused. For it seems that your suzerain has placed upon me a very weighty mission the likes of which I never before imagined."

Seim the Elder shook his head in deference. "Master Plato. You must do only as your will bids you. If you wish, you may forget all our suzerain has said. It can be as though you never heard him speak—"

A thin smile came to the corner of Plato's mouth. "Indeed," he muttered, staring at his own reflection in the orichalcum wall. But there was no laughter in the philosopher's eyes—his smile seemed to throw his face out of balance. "Forget it all? Pretend I heard nothing?"

Those who did not like Plato—especially those who had met him in debate—privately resented his peculiar smile. He was quite aware of this, yet it was not something he chose to care about.

Plato tilted his goblet, returning it empty to his host. The wine left a bitter residue on his tongue.

"Gladius. We go west. Prepare for our departure."

Gladius lowered his head in silence. Plato rose to depart without a glance at the window behind him.

"Elder. I do not remember the words of your suzerain—in fact I did not hear them. My journey from here to the west of the Atlas Mountains was already decided upon my departure from Athens. I continue on to my original destination."

The old man lowered his head, his face expressionless. "Very well, Master Plato. Yet I insist that you spend tonight here with us. From the look of the sky, there will be a sandstorm coming. Tomorrow I will send a youth with you who knows the road west of here well. However, he is currently in a village to the south, with the merchants."

"Of course. One more night will make little difference on a long journey such as this. Then, Elder, we will presume upon your hospitality. You agree, Gladius?"

"Aye, Master," Gladius replied, his relief evident. The suzerain's words had filled even the stalwart Arab with a deep unease. He had not been eager to embark on a nighttime desert crossing, and it showed in his face.

"Come this way, please."

Plato and Gladius followed Seim from the building. Outside, twilight had already begun to spread across the vast desert beyond the village walls. Far across a sea of burnt yellow sand, the fading sun had set halfway, sending its rays upward to paint the high clouds blood red. Crimson spread out across the darkening sky even as night seeped from the eastern horizon toward the vault of heaven, reddish gray melding with crimsonblue. The wind was completely still, and the twilight pooled like heavy oil upon the sand. There was not a sound. Plato wondered what the people who lived inside the stone houses of the village must be doing for such silence to reign—not a single spoken word, no faint echo of evening song. All was filled with the barren quiet of the sand sea and the silence that comes with the death of something long forgotten, unchanged for thousands of years.

Gladius hunched his shoulders. "The sunset here chills the heart, does it not, Master?"

Plato did not answer. He turned his broad brow to the evening light in silence. He felt as though something momentous were about to begin . . . Yes, something *was* beginning. The light held a strange tension and unease—a chilling sensation the philosopher had never felt before: the sense that something unknown, something that could not *be* known or truly seen—something unspeakable—was quietly creeping closer.

"This way." Seim the Elder stood across the central courtyard, beckoning for Plato to follow.

"Let us go, Gladius." Plato began to walk across the sand.

"You may sleep in here tonight," the old man said, indicating a small stone house flanked on either side by two of the largest houses in the village. "I'm afraid I cannot offer much in the way of comforts, but please, if there is anything you need, do not hesitate to ask."

Inside, the house had but a single room. In the wall facing the courtyard was a panel made out of the rigid, translucent material Seim the Elder had called *glaes*. A square fire pit had been cut in the center of the floor, atop which had been set a metal washbasin, also square. The fire beneath it was unlit.

Seim lingered while Plato and Gladius settled in, and after a few moments several women entered with food for the visitors. The women were not young, but they wore long skirts down to their ankles fastened at the waist with belts of linked metal that shone with a golden luster. On their heads they wore the same shallow hoods as the Elcasian men. The women moved like shadows, setting up a table and laying out various dishes. Finally, one of them set down a large water jug that she had carried on her shoulder; then all vanished as silently as they had come.

"It is not much, but please eat." Seim the Elder bowed low at the waist and departed, but no sooner had he walked out than he reappeared in the doorway. "Should you require anything, press the button you see there upon the wall. I will come immediately." The door closed without a sound.

The meal consisted primarily of mutton and vegetables, and despite their host's modesty, it seemed quite a feast to Plato. Though neither of the travelers had been particularly hungry, they found the food to be the most delicious they had ever eaten, and they partook with relish. *Surely,* thought Plato, *these people possess wondrous talent in the culinary arts.* Many strong spices had been used with skill; clearly the cuisine of this village was both rich and refined. It might even surpass the food eaten by the wealthiest nobles of Egypt and lesser Asia.

As the philosopher continued to eat, a doubt grew in his mind. "Gladius. It cannot have been a simple matter to prepare such a delicious variety of victuals out here in the middle of this barren, sandy waste. Even assuming that they prepared this especially for us as their guests."

Gladius lifted a piece of food from his dish between two fingers and showed it to Plato. "Look, Master. This mutton was fried in the fat of some other animal, then wrapped in a barley mash that was dissolved in water and kneaded before being baked again. Master, the fat they used to fry this mutton is something I have never eaten before. Nor was it made by any process with which I am familiar. The taste is very unusual. Usually such a thing would taste much more sour. And they used something most unusual to heat this food. I would very much like to see their oven. Look—this morsel has clearly been cooked through, yet nowhere has the surface been burnt."

Gladius was well traveled, and his knowledge of foreign cuisines was startlingly rich and, Plato had found, largely accurate.

"Master," the Arab continued, "do you not find their cooking style and this refined flavor to be different from anything else you have ever tasted?

It is practically not of our world!" Gladius frowned even as he stuffed his mouth with food.

Plato contemplated Gladius's words. It seemed to him that the astonishment his servant felt toward this food was no less impressive than that which he himself felt toward the suzerain's window. Clearly, Gladius sensed the strangeness of the feast better than Plato, if he wanted to see the oven. Together, they ate every last bit of the meal without further conversation.

"Allow us to clear the table," a female voice said. The women who had served them before had reappeared as quietly as shadows. In a matter of moments they had taken away the empty plates and vanished once again.

The room was now so dark that Plato could no longer see Gladius's face. "Would that we had a candle," he said, peering at his friend.

That instant, his eyes filled with a brilliant light as the chamber brightened like a courtyard lit up by the noonday sun. Reflexively, he lifted his hands to cover his face. In that flood of blazing illumination, he saw Gladius draw the short sword at his waist.

"Master!" the Arab shouted, moving quickly to stand before Plato, shielding him from any danger.

But all that happened was that the room remained bright. Nothing else.

"What in Zeus's name is that?"

An impossibly bright sphere of light had appeared in the middle of the ceiling. Its light fell upon them like a shining curtain, casting wavering shadows on the wall at their backs.

"Master, outside!"

Squinting against the light, they began to move toward the doorway. Still, nothing happened. Plato paused, keeping one eye on the room around him while he focused his attention on that bright sphere of light.

It did not seem dangerous. In fact, it seemed to be nothing more than what it appeared: a light source. The fear left his face.

"Gladius, I believe that sphere is intended to light this room."

"Like . . . a torch?" Gladius hesitated, short sword gripped at the ready, and glared fiercely at the sphere on the ceiling. Plato walked over until he was directly beneath it. He had noticed the circular porcelain umbrella that hung overhead when he first entered the room, but he had not been aware of the small light-producing sphere within it. Now as he stared up at it, it seemed to him that the light was somehow trapped within a container made of *glaes*. Looking closer, he could see threads of light suspended inside the container. That was where the illumination came from.

"Look, Gladius! It is like a reservoir for storing light. Though by what means it captures the luminescence I cannot say." Until that time, the only indoor lights he had seen were saucers of fish oil and the rock water that burned in Syria. Compared to those things, this was sorcery. "It is like a tiny sun." Plato pointed at his own shadow cast upon the wall and heaved a sigh. "It is becoming increasingly clear with each new marvel that Atlantis possessed a culture of the highest order."

Gladius quietly sheathed his short sword. Then he turned and peered out the window into the darkness with eyes that seemed to gaze across a great distance. In his profile, Plato saw lines of age he had never noticed before.

"Master, I cannot help but feel that this journey is a mistake. Though I know there is no way my words could stop you once you have decided on a course."

Beneath the bright light, Plato considered the deep sadness upon Gladius's face. "Why would you have me cease this journey?"

The Arab said nothing. His fingers twisted around the decorative rope tied to the hilt of his sword.

"Why, Gladius?"

Gladius looked up. His gray eyes met Plato's, then looked away. "I can give you no reason. It is merely how I feel."

"I see. Gladius, you know how much I admire your intuition. And I think the fear that grips your heart and leads you to advise me against continuing is not misplaced. Perhaps it would be better if we heeded it. No, for certain it would be better. But, Gladius, do you really think that I, Plato, could turn away after the events of this truly extraordinary evening? No. Even should I never again take the podium at the Akademia, even should I never pass east along this road again, I must forge onward. This is what it means to seek knowledge, Gladius! No, where is the sense in posturing? I do this out of curiosity. It is a fancy, nothing more."

Plato waved his hand at the glowing sphere on the ceiling, pointing at it as if to confirm that it was still there.

"But, Master, your pupils at the Akademia await your return. You could not come back one day too soon in their eyes." Gladius's words came without conviction, as though he knew their ineffectuality before he even spoke them. "The lady Cassandra too." He shook his head—the slightest gesture.

"Cassandra . . ." Plato looked at his servant with eyes suddenly weary, as though he were just awakening from a long night of drink; and in his mind's eye he pictured that quiet girl of Lesser Asia. As always, something pricked at his heart. She lived in solitude deep in a villa covered with vines that stood facing the Square of the Warriors' Well in the northwest of Athens, where it had been his habit to visit her in the night once a week or once every ten days. That now seemed a lifetime ago.

Cassandra was the widow of Peloponteus, a general of Athens. The young, talented general had been mortally wounded in the endless war for control of the Greek peninsula and had fallen in battle, and so it was the duty of his pure, young, and beautiful widow to preserve his glory and his honor. This was a source of great unhappiness for both Plato and Cassandra.

The philosopher pushed open the door of the house and stepped outside. The moon had come out, making the sand in Elcasia's central square shine white. Beyond the houses, an endless sea of sand palely glowed. Light spilling from many windows made broad streaks of color through the pools of moonlight. Plato saw a figure walking in his direction. Presently it came close enough for him make out the features of Seim the Elder.

"If you would retire, allow me to arrange for bedding. Is the *taub* not too bright?"

"*Taub?*"

"Ah, it is the light in your room."

Another curious word. Plato whispered it to himself, trying to master the unfamiliar pronunciation.

"As it happens, tonight is the Night of Silence."

"What is that?"

"An old tradition in our village. It is . . . a night when we remember our ancestors."

"I see," Plato replied. "It is a good thing to remember one's forebears. In this village in particular, I would think. Often one can find Truth hiding in the sayings passed down to us. Yes, I find your Night of Silence most appropriate."

The silvery light upon the desert grew gradually brighter, bathing both of them so completely that it seemed to weigh upon their skin.

"Excuse me. I will prepare your beds." The elder disappeared, his feet making no sound on the sand.

Presently the serving women arrived again, carrying mats and blankets of the finest quality. Seim accompanied them, carrying a jug of water, and he inspected the beds, adjusting the lay of the sheets and the positioning of the pillows.

"If it is too bright for you to sleep, I recommend extinguishing your *taub*. Twist this knob here and it will go out." The elder indicated a black button set into the wall. When he touched it, the room fell dark in an instant. Plato could hear Gladius's quick breathing as he leapt like a bird to get his back to a wall.

"Merely turn it gently, like this," the elder said quietly, and the room returned to its former brightness. His face hard, Gladius returned his short sword loudly to its sheath. A silvery metallic echo trembled in the air.

"Now, I bid you good night."

Seim bowed low and left without looking back. Plato watched him leave, then lay down on his bedding, feeling as though he were sliding into a deep sea of fatigue.

"Gladius, put out the light."

Darkness fell upon the room again, softened by the silvery moonlight spilling in at the window; the floor of the chamber shimmered like the bottom of a shallow pool.

"You should rest, Gladius."

The Arab remained sitting, back to the wall, sandals on his feet and sword strapped to his waist.

"What is it? You should sleep in your bed."

"No. I must remain ready. Here is best." Gladius spoke as if to himself. He was particularly adept at feeling the tremors of someone approaching through floors and walls. No matter how deeply he slept, he could awaken at the slightest footfall of a burglar or assassin, springing to consciousness quickly enough to strike the first blow. When Plato was attacked the year before in Sicily by an old retainer of Dionysos the Second, it had been Gladius's sword that saved the philosopher in the nick of time.

"As you like."

Plato rolled over and shut his eyes. Though he knew Gladius remained against the wall, he heard not a sound. Plato drifted fitfully toward sleep. Each time his eyes fluttered open, the moonlight fell across the room at a different angle. He let thoughts of all that had befallen him since leaving Sais play through his mind. There was a strange momentum to the cascade of events. He was aware of his own headlong plunge into something from which there very well might be no egress. With each passing day, he could sense his own self waning, being swallowed by the specter of Atlantis. He did not require Gladius's warnings. He had already passed beyond the point of no return. Neither his seminars at the Akademia, nor any of his disciples, nor the debates with Aristotle that could move his spirit as well as his mind, nor the woman who lived by the Fountain of Warriors held any purchase on his heart. Nor did this stir the slightest sadness within him.

Before long, he was deep asleep.

●

How long have I slept?

Plato awoke to a noise that came from outside the building. For a moment, he felt as though he were on board a ship. Then he sat up, and the memory of the previous day came back to him.

A sandstorm was blowing outside the window. The little stone house trembled with each buffet of the wind. The sand on the window and door made a gritty roar as it swept from right to left, from left to right.

"The elder was right about the storm," Plato muttered as he listened to the howling wind. "This will bury the road for sure. I do not look forward to our journey tomorrow." He pulled his blankets up over his head.

When next he woke, the sandstorm still raged. Dawn would be close now. The chill air of night had begun to stir in the room. Then Plato thought he heard another sound under the roar of the storm—*a basket left outside, tossed by the wind, perhaps.*

He tried to return to sleep.

The door shook under a blast of wind. Now he was sure he heard a different noise.

"What could that be?"

He lifted his head and pricked up his ears.

Wrrrrrrr . . .

It was a low sound that cut beneath the sandstorm. It was coming from outside.

"It sounds like something spinning."

Another blast of wind shook the entire house. When it receded, he heard it again: *Wrrrrrrr . . .*

"That is no trick of the ears! There is something out there." Now the whirring noise mixed with the clamor of the sandstorm, sometimes sounding high, sometimes low, now far in the distance, now right outside the door. Plato sat up in bed. Slipping on his sandals and his sheepskin tunic, he made his way to the door and swung it open.

The storm hit him with its full force. He shrank back as the sand blasted his nose, mouth, and eyes. Clinging to the wall for support, he lowered his face and listened.

Wrrrrrrr . . .

It was coming quite clearly from the village square. Staggering into the gale, Plato took one step, then two steps into the dark, swirling cloud of sand. When he had gone a dozen or more paces, he could stand against the wind no longer, and he fell to the ground, choking on grit.

To his ears came that sound—

Wrrrrrrr . . .

He could hear it louder than ever before.

●

Plato lifted his torso off the ground, struggling for purchase in fine sand that gave way at the slightest touch. His scrabbling hands reached out until the tips of his fingers found the flat surface of a large stone. Getting both hands on the solid mass, he was finally able to push himself to his feet. No sooner was he upright, however, than a wave of dizziness swept over him.

Someone's hand on his back steadied him.

"Lord Orionae, how weary you must be. You have not had a moment's rest for two or three days."

Orionae? Who's that? The melancholy question drifted through Plato's mind, but a moment later recognition came—

Ah, of course. I am Orionae. Plato nodded inwardly. *And I am rather tired.*

He had the unsettling sensation that his feet were not his own, and it irritated him greatly. "We must hurry, Europa. The Council will begin shortly." Plato-who-was-Orionae looked back at his Minister of Finance. Europa was a trusted advisor, his chief counselor when it came to all matters of money. With the kingdom facing such danger, Europa's arm was one of the few things that Orionae could rely upon.

There were stairs ahead, stone steps leading downward. Orionae descended, entering the shadow of the high gables of the palace. The great bulk of the edifice hid the night sky. Soldiers stood guard before the giant four-paneled golden doors; they snapped to attention, then immediately bowed and moved aside.

As he stepped into the Grand Corridor, Orionae turned to look back upon the night city. From this vantage point he could take in the entire sea of lights spreading beneath the palace hill. White lights. He was able to make out the individual windows of houses all the way from the base of the hill out to the banks of the first canal. Beyond that, the lights became an indistinguishable flood of brilliance that stretched unbroken to the Sea of Atlantis beyond. In the daytime, he would be able to see the shining blue of the ocean, but now all was cloaked in darkness. The city looked as it had looked every night for the past several decades. Nothing changed, nothing out of the ordinary at all. Nowhere the slightest hint of sorrow or tragedy. Only the good life, and the elegant music, sculpture, poetry and song to which that life gave birth. The night was adorned with quickening glory. The hours just after the sunset were the city's happiest, and Atlantis was enjoying them to the fullest.

Surely it would remain this way—for one hundred, one thousand, even ten thousand years; the nighttime sea of light never faltering, never failing. Every citizen believed this, and Orionae himself had accepted it as an incontrovertible fact upon which he could rely.

"Let us go, Lord Orionae." Europa's voice sounded softly behind him.

"Europa. Have you ever imagined the moment it ends? The moment in which the city of Atlantis—Poseidon's metropolis, in all her glory and prosperity—will crumble?"

Europa made no reply, but turned to look instead at the giant mural upon the corridor wall.

Orionae shook his head. "Forgive me, Europa. It was an unfair question. I myself would never have given such terrible thoughts any consideration until three or four days ago. And yet, I feel as though this is something we should have thought about before, and deeply. I believe we have let ourselves get carried away with our rich life and its many pleasures. We have been careless." Orionae cast his eyes once more upon the sea of light below them, then turned, robes swirling, and strode into the building.

The many kings had already assembled in the great council chamber on the first level. Dozens of light projectors set along the walls cast several layers of illumination upon the floor, leaving the vast vaulted ceiling in shadow where it hung high above their brilliance.

When Orionae entered the chamber the kings turned to look at him with desperate pleading in their eyes. He moved to the table in the center of the open space, feeling the weight of their collective gaze upon him. How well he understood that he would not be able to give them what they wanted. He took his seat, feeling something leaden fill his breast, and he placed the dossier Europa offered him upon the tabletop. An oppressively heavy air hung in the council chamber. Not a word was spoken between the assembled.

For the first time since the kingdom's birth, there was no hope to be found in this meeting of the highest council.

A bell rang. The sound shook the air in the chamber; several of the kings broke out in a cold sweat.

"His Majesty King Atlas the Seventh and the king's father, Poseidonis the Fifth," the voice of Privy Counselor Ilias sounded over the loudspeaker.

Two large golden panels adorned with an engraved map of the kingdom stood at the front of the chamber. Now they opened silently, revealing a large stage beyond. In the center of the stage were two chairs, each as large as a small house. Fashioned of solid silver, the chairs seemed even larger for their simple, unadorned lines. Now another wall behind the stage slid soundlessly open and two figures appeared, swaying like tiny trees beneath headdresses so large they seemed as if they might scrape the very ceiling. Simultaneously the two figures lifted their bronzed faces to gaze across the council chamber, eyes like flame burning into the hearts of the assembled kings. With utmost serenity they took their thrones, one in the center and one slightly behind.

The king in the forward throne addressed the throng. "I would now hear your final plans. I have already revealed my thoughts to you in writing. What I consider most important is this: that we move the base of our economy and the functions of our government and citizenry to Atlanta, land of our forebears. My method of rule, though experimental, has shown tremendous success over these many years, for which I have your unfailing cooperation to thank. The success of my kingdom will serve as a very important guide for future planetary development. So, you see, remaining here is not an option. Let us hear your plans for the exodus now. Legate, speak." The king's sonorous voice betrayed no hint of hesitation. Rich and textured, it rolled across the chamber like a thick carpet unfurling.

Orionae stood, taking a deep breath to still the fluttering in his breast. "I hereby pledge anew my ever deepening fealty toward Your Majesty Atlas the Seventh, King of Kings, and to the king's father, Poseidonis the Fifth. With your leave, I would speak on Your Majesty's proposed move to the kingdom of Atlanta . . .

"Your Majesty," he continued, "we have thought deeply on this all day and all night, and though as your humble servants it pains us to say this, we feel that, given the current circumstances, the exodus you propose is not realistic."

All present in the chamber froze. So still were the gathered kings that it seemed they had ceased even to breathe. A long silence passed as they felt that stillness weigh upon them. At last, the clear tones of Atlas the Seventh rang out.

"Legate, I know well the realities of the situation. As I said the other day, I wanted you to consider my plan *despite* the circumstances. I'm not unaware of your struggle. But you must realize that this is all part of a very detailed development program laid out by the Planetary Development Committee. All we do is informed by their larger design. The proper steps must be taken at the prescribed times! Assembled members of the Council, this is Heaven's will—and when I speak of Heaven, you know I do not refer to some abstract concept, some artifact of the human psyche. That is why, Legate, I asked you to consider with all haste a means by which we can make this exodus a reality."

Tiny beads of sweat glistened in the deep wrinkles running across Orionae's brow.

"Your Majesty," he began after a moment, "we are able to live in this rare paradise solely due to your overwhelming benevolence, and for this we are immensely grateful. Yet so perfect is this paradise that I fear the people will not be able to understand why we must leave it to move to an unknown land. Our orchards are filled with bountiful fruit, our factories work tirelessly, our merchant ships, our hospitals, our schools, all bring happiness to our people. But our citizens are conservative in the extreme, Your Majesty. All the more so because their lives are so blessed. They are well satisfied with the bounty of their homeland. Were we to tell them they must leave their home for another, that we must move our kingdom entire, it would bring chaos. Please, Your Majesty. We beg your understanding in this matter. With all our hearts we beg it of you."

Orionae felt the strength in his body rush out through his pores. He had managed to fulfill at least a part of his responsibility by relating to the king what had been decided over the last two or three days in the provincial assemblies.

"Legate." Atlas the Seventh spoke again, his voice devoid of compromise. "You have not answered my question in a satisfactory manner. I asked you to describe to me your plans for the exodus of the Kingdom of Atlantis."

"Your Majesty."

King Dominica, minister of the province that lay along the western coast of the kingdom, rose to his feet. He wore an elegant linen shawl and a beautiful shell necklace. His thick brown whiskers were trembling. "The moment the people hear the extent of this plan, their shock, sadness, and rage will lead swiftly to violence. There are many examples of this to which

I might refer; suffice it to say, that even should this great plan be the direct provenance of Your Majesty's benevolent will, that is not how it will be reflected in the hearts of the people. It is a certainty that they will turn against the royal house of Atlas, saying that we have replaced the kind rule of yesterday for an outrage today."

As King Dominica once again took his seat, King Ajax of the central mountainous highlands stood.

"Your Majesty. We have moved our kingdom in the past, yet only in response to long years of drought or to escape the predations of barbarian tribes—we've moved only as a last resort, when it was the express will of the people."

"*I say this to you again!*" came the voice from the throne, and it shook the room like a crash of thunder. "I am King of Kings. I have received the will of Heaven and devote myself to its promulgation alone. You will heed my words and devote yourselves to the divine will."

Poseidonis the Fifth, silent until then, opened his mouth and spoke, the tone and character of his voice almost indistinguishable from that of Atlas the Seventh. "Legate and assembled kings. What has happened to the reverential loyalty you once showed to the Royal House of Atlas? I can still hear the oaths you swore to our House when I passed the title of High Officiant on to my son. Your words ring fresh in my ears. Take care that you do no injury to that loyalty today, for your devotion to the Royal House of Atlas reflects in turn the loyalty of the House of Atlas to the Planetary Development Committee."

The assembled kings sat still as a forest of stones.

"Legate, assembled kings. I ask you, who was it, one thousand years ago, that took his first steps upon this barren continent as it drifted in an empty sea? Who harnessed the atom's power, carved the mountains and the plains? Who planted groves of trees and taught the people how to gather their fruit and cultivate their seeds? Who built roads and towns, waterways and aqueducts? Who showed the people the art of metallurgy, the smelting of iron, and made chariots that ran on electricity? Who taught the people how to build and sail their ships? Tell me."

"The founder of our kingdom, Poseidonis the First." The voices speaking in unison echoed through the council chamber.

"Now, Legate. Tell me the founding ideological construct of our kingdom. Speak!"

Orionae stood as though possessed. *I know the ideology. I know it all too well. But what has that to do with us here, now?*

"By the reckoning of the Twin Suns, from Blue 93 to the summer of Yellow 17 in the New Galactic Age," he intoned, "the Planetary Development Committee on Astarta 50 received a directive from *Shi* to attempt a *helio-ses-beta* development on the third planet in the Ai System. This required that a religion be engineered for the indigenous peoples whereby the influence of the Planetary Development Committee could be ascribed to *divine will*—" Abruptly Orionae stopped the flow of words spilling involuntarily from his lips. Then with a wrenching act of will he shouted at the towering shapes upon the stage, his voice so loud he felt as though his mouth would split all the way back to his ears: "Why did you tell them there were gods and not tell them about the Planetary Development Committee?"

A rustle passed through the assembled kings like a breeze through rushes, and their faces went white as corpses.

"Why didn't you tell them?!"

A great dizziness came over the legate and he crumpled to the floor.

Why did you say nothing of their existence? he wanted to yell again, but he could not summon the strength. Only his lips quavered weakly.

Then the sky fell and all was lost in primal darkness.

●

He heard the occasional clink of metal objects coming from somewhere down below his feet, mixed with the voices of several people engaged in stealthy conversation. A strong, medicinal smell stung his nostrils.

What are they doing?

Where am I?

He tried to turn it over in his dark, soggy head, but the thoughts mischievously slipped away from him. In a wave of fatigue, he abandoned the attempt altogether.

Without warning, a sharp pain ran down his arm. He groaned and tried to sit up, but all he could manage was to move his shoulders slightly.

"I think he's coming to," someone said.

Coming to? What did I–? All at once the memory came back to him. *That's right. The council chamber . . .*

Orionae-who-was-Plato sat up in the bed.

"You should lie down a little longer. The neural stimulant we gave you is still working—if you stand you'll lose your balance."

Orionae frowned at the scent in his nostrils.

"What happened? I remember falling in the council chamber." As soon as he said the words, he had the strange sensation that his own memories were not to be trusted.

"Wait . . ." he muttered. "I mean, I was in the desert on a journey. There was a sandstorm at night, and stars, many stars, and a bright light spilling from the window . . . When was that again?" The legate put a hand to his forehead. He couldn't have been traveling in a desert. So what was this strange feeling in the pit of his stomach—this conviction that he was somehow in the wrong place?

A man dressed all in white stared at Orionae's face. The stranger's dark silhouette, framed by the light on the ceiling, stirred up a memory long buried in the sediments at the back of Orionae's mind. But no sooner had the recollection risen than it too drifted away. The dark silhouette disappeared without a sound, leaving the bright light to shine down on Orionae, hurting his eyes. For a short while, Orionae slept.

When he awoke again there was no one around. He sat up and slid his legs over the edge of the bed, searching with his feet for something to wear. He found nothing but stood anyhow, broad shoulders swaying, and drew his hospital robe more tightly around him.

Orionae was in a fully equipped medical chamber. A variety of surgical instruments sat on metal shelves running along the wall, and a wheeled medical cart held boxes with syringes and vials, scalpels and long needles, all giving off a cold gleam in the bright lights. He looked around, but no one was to be seen.

"Who would abandon a patient like that?"

Careless! Orionae frowned and gave the door to the room a push.

He was clearly in the palace's medical ward. It occurred to him that he had never had occasion to visit here before.

Beyond his room, the ward was in chaos. Physicians and assistants ran back and forth, all of them practically steaming with activity.

"What's going on here?" Orionae wondered aloud.

It occurred to him that the chamber he had just vacated also showed signs of disarray. There were empty spaces in the lineup of medical devices on the shelves, as if the most important items had been removed, and one of the vials from the cabinet had toppled, its powdery contents forming a small pyramid on the floor. Whoever had been in there gathering supplies had left in a hurry.

Orionae began moving quickly toward where he thought the exit must lie. There was an elevator with its door open to the corridor that appeared to have been stopped or stuck in place. It was full of wooden boxes stuffed with an incredible assortment of medical supplies. Just beyond, an electric-powered gurney lay on its side.

"What's going on? What happened?" the legate called out to a physician headed in the opposite direction.

The man saw Orionae's face and stiffened.

"Tell me what has happened." Orionae stared the physician in the eye. The man returned his stare, then lifted a hand and pointed down the corridor.

At the end of the passageway was a large sunroom with windows of *glaes* stained a beautiful crimson.

"What about the sunroom?"

Orionae's gaze shifted back to the physician, then back to the colored *glaes*. He noticed that the *glaes* was shimmering, brighter and darker, like a fluttering flag. For a moment he stood there watching, then ran toward it.

As soon as he entered the sunroom, Orionae realized that the giant windows there were not set with colored *glaes*—they were reflecting the light of a vast fire outside.

A carpet of raging flame was spread over the entire city below the hill, rolling in waves toward the heights. There was a strong wind blowing; Orionae could see shreds of flame flying up from the edges of the inferno, dancing like phoenix fledglings into the sky. Wherever they fell back to earth new fires sprang up. A dense layer of smoke roiled above the city, glowing eerily with the reflected light of the blaze beneath. He saw a huge golden column of flame burst up through the smoke and then explode in a shower of sparks, and guessed that it had risen from somewhere beyond the second ring canal. A sudden sound of gunshots came up from somewhere below the palace walls.

Orionae ran down the line of windows. The fire had spread in a semicircle along the ring canal and was pushing further inward toward the center of the city. From his current vantage point it was difficult to see the entirety of the damage.

Again, a brighter burst of flame erupted from the middle of the blaze, and this time the city around it—both the buildings and the earth itself—clearly lurched skyward. He saw people fleeing in a dark stream down the road away from the flames. They looked tiny.

Orionae ran farther. Something that he could not even begin to comprehend had pushed this great city to the brink of destruction, and he had been completely unaware.

What could possibly have happened?

Why had the city watch done nothing?

Where were the ministers and the pages?

He lurched from window to window like a wounded beast. At last, halfway around the arc of the sunroom, he saw something that gave him a sliver of hope, and he breathed a deep sigh. From this vantage point he could see the other half of the city, and it was still dark. The flames had not reached there; nor was the wind blowing smoke in that direction, for he could see stars twinkling in the sky above.

The people will have a safe haven.

There would be squads of firefighters and rescuers organizing in the dark side of the city, away from the flames. Despite the chaos, much could be salvaged. The palace medical ward alone was capable of saving many wounded. Orionae felt that he should go down, into the city aflame. He desperately wanted to know what had happened in the council chamber after he collapsed, but the fire was clearly a far more pressing matter.

The fact that the lights in half the city were out was a sure sign that the nuclear reactor had been damaged.

We will have to get that back online as quickly as possible.

In the face of such an unprecedented and unforeseen disaster, Orionae felt the urgent need to return to his duties as legate—he had never felt such distress at being away from his post as he did now. Cursing under his breath at the frozen elevator, he found a stairway and sped down it. At its bottom he found a series of hallways that twisted and turned like a labyrinth, and he raced along, looking for a way out into the undamaged part of the city. He ran fast—faster than he had ever run before.

Three hundred feet ahead, the well-lit hallway plunged into darkness.

That must be where the blackout starts.

A large section of the vast palace belonged to the side of the city that wasn't on fire, so it followed that it would suffer the same fate as the streets below.

Orionae ran, gritting his teeth in frustration at his own sluggish legs. The darkened part of the corridor opened before him like a cavern.

Wait! There's a separate nuclear reactor inside the palace. A blackout in the city shouldn't affect us—and the medical ward was well lit.

Then he saw points of light in the darkness ahead of him, so many they were uncountable, so many he could scarcely even gaze at them all. A chilling premonition rose inside him, and he forced his already faltering feet to stop.

There, not more than two or three yards ahead, the floor gave way to the void. The lights he saw in that darkness were the fires of one hundred billion stars.

The corridor opened out onto a vast, empty space that cut the city clean in half.

Putting a hand on one wall for support, he stared out at the sea of twinkling stars like a child staring at the night sky. His head hurt so fiercely he feared it might split; thick beads of sweat ran down his cheek and chin. He felt as though his brain was on fire, and the rest of his body had gone cold as ice. Unable to grasp what had happened, he knew only that everything had changed.

So what do I do now?

Could it be that I am dreaming?

He stood, swaying, repeating these questions to himself. But the sea of stars that spread out before him was not the stuff of dreams or illusions. Some of the stars seemed close enough to touch with an outstretched hand, while others were so distant they proved the vastness of the void of space.

Slowly, he made his way back along the corridor.

His vision of a safe half of the city, dark and free of flames, had just been torn from him. All that remained was a raging pyre.

Orionae descended another stair, walking mechanically like a marionette, emotionless. The corridors below were silent, save for the sound of an automatic cannon firing from somewhere in the far reaches of the palace; he saw no sign of the other palace inhabitants.

Where has everyone gone?

He passed another line of windows that looked out over balconies reflecting light from the blaze below and arrived at the steps down to the central hall on the first floor. Now he could see people—refugees—in the darkness beneath the tamarisk in the central courtyard, and he hurried outside. Making his way across the cobbles, he spotted a six-wheeled auto-carriage lying on its side beneath a marble wall. A ragtag group of soldiers, their faces drenched in the light of the fires, rounded the guardhouse and approached him through an arch in the castle wall.

"Do not leave the palace," the leader said. "The mob has broken through the outer perimeter."

"The mob?" Orionae stopped at the unfamiliar word. "You mean they're rioting?"

"Yes, sir." One of the soldiers recognized the face of his own legate. He quickly held his automatic gun at attention and bowed.

"You mean rioters are responsible for this conflagration?"

The fighting men stared at him, suspicious that the highest of all ministers in their government had no clue as to what was going on.

"Th-that is," Orionae stammered, "I've yet to receive a full report."

"The proclamation from King Atlas was met with unrest from nearly every quarter of the city. The offices of administration were attacked, and before we could properly respond, the mob had taken over half the city— and us with no way of putting out the fires."

The soldier shifted the weight of the heavy ammunition bandolier on his shoulder.

"Your name?" Orionae motioned with his jaw to the man directly in front of him.

"Heracletos, gunner with the Royal Honor Guard Light Infantry."

"How many are you?"

"Seventeen, plus one wounded, so eighteen, sir."

Orionae nodded. With every word he spoke, he could feel himself regaining his authority. "Good. Hold this position. Don't let a single one of that mob inside the palace proper."

Without waiting for a response, Orionae stepped out onto the wide thoroughfare that ran along the front wall of the palace. The fire had already engulfed the large building across the roadway, the regional ministers' quarters; now the blaze was spitting golden tongues of flame out onto the road.

A violent gust of wind crossed the city like a cresting wave, picking up a fireball of wood and debris and hurling it against the offices of the guard that stood imposingly at a corner in the road. For a moment, the city was hidden from Orionae's view behind a swirling river of flame.

Then he saw shapes, people staggering through the wall of fire like lost souls. They reached out toward the edifice of the palace behind him, hands dripping molten flesh, shouting incoherently. Their bare feet slapped down upon the smoldering bricks like swollen water skins.

"Here, quickly!" Orionae shouted, running out from the shadow of the palace walls.

He heard a long chatter of gunfire; a few of the shapes running toward him were plucked up off the road and thrown back into the flames.

"Hold your fire! Hold your fire, I said!" Orionae shouted up to the top of the high palace wall above him, but in the wind and roaring of the fire there was no way he could be heard. He ran along the bottom of the wall, no destination in mind, only a feeling that, as legate, he must do something. His feet moved of their own accord and he heard himself shout, "To the harbor! To the sea! We'll find boats!"

The people ran in a group behind him now, making their way from patch to patch of open ground beyond the reach of the flames. Orionae found himself on a narrow side street, where he could hear the weeping of women, the crying of children, and the shouting of men echoing loudly off the high brick walls to either side.

A government autocarriage, marked with the wide horizontal yellow stripe of an official vehicle, came careening at breakneck speed around a corner, then slammed directly into a wall without slowing. The body of the car split in half, its batteries erupting in a shower of blue incandescence. Several corpses—some of them children—rolled out of the shattered vehicle onto the street, the stench of their blood mingling with the ever-present choking cloud of dust and smoke.

Dozens of people were huddled or sprawled in the dark courtyard of Oriental Chariot Square. Orionae stepped over several men and women who lay on the cobblestones, making his way to the small fountain he knew stood in the middle of the open space. He knelt and drank eagerly from the basin. Though much of the cool water slipped through his cupped fingers and spilled onto the stones below, what reached his mouth was the most delicious he had ever tasted.

As he drank the legate became aware of two human shapes engaged in a hushed argument behind a rose thicket not far from the fountain.

"We must go to the harbor. The boats will leave us behind."

"What's the use of running? We should follow the king's orders. I don't care where he wants us to go. We'll go."

One of the voices sounded like that of an old man; the other, young.

"What are you saying?" the older voice demanded. "There is fertile land enough over the sea. We can go there, begin anew. My son, we are not horses or cattle. Must we follow meekly along when we are told we must leave this land our forebears cultivated to go off to some distant sun across the starry sky—some 'planet'? Are we slaves to do our master's bidding?"

"But, Father," the other voice said, "how will we get through this wall of fire to the harbor? You heard what they said—the bridges over the second ring canal have all burned and fallen. There are so many corpses floating there, one cannot even see the surface of the water. Please, Father."

The voice of the older man was hoarse and tired, yet it still had not lost its strength. "Get up. If I'm fated to serve the House of Atlas, those men who are not men, I'd rather toss myself into the boiling stewpot of the canals."

"Father!"

"Bah—a curse upon the House of Atlas! They are not humans in truth! They are avatars of evil. How long they must have waited for this day to come. Yes, they gave us treasures, priceless things beyond measure.

All to buy their absolution in advance for this day of days!" The raw pain in the old man's voice stung Orionae's ears. "Get up, my son! We must get on that boat. We must tell the people of the world what happened here this night."

Orionae crawled through the smoke, making his way toward the two debaters.

"Who's there?"

The legate could feel an icy hatred stabbing at him through the darkness.

"I am the legate Orionae."

"The legate?"

The two huddled figures craned their necks to look in his direction.

"He tells the truth."

"And what is the legate doing here?" the old man asked, his voice harsh and suspicious.

"I lost consciousness during a meeting of the council and was carried to the hospital ward. When I awoke, it was to this chaos. Tell me—what is the darkness that has swallowed half our city, and what caused these fires?"

The old man whistled in his throat. "That star-filled sky appeared at day's end, quite suddenly. One moment the western half of the capital was basking in the evening sun, the next moment it was gone. The fires came afterward."

"Do you know how they started?"

"I do not," said the old man with a shake of his head.

The youth continued where his father had left off. "Poseidonis the Fifth announced that he intended to move the kingdom. He proclaimed a great exodus. When the other kings didn't follow his command, Poseidonis borrowed the power of the gods and judged them. Legate, some of the people took up arms. Others protested with words, begging their liege to change his mind. But it was all too late. The heart of Poseidonis the Fifth no longer lies with his people, if it ever did."

The true shape of what had happened was finally becoming clear to Orionae.

The old man's wiry hand grabbed him by the arm. "Legate, we'll give back our hospitals, our schools, our autocarriages, our nuclear reactor. We'll give back everything the House of Atlas dangled before us as bait. All of it!

We can return to the primitive age of a thousand years ago for all I care. It's better that way. We never asked the royal house for their assistance! They came of their own accord from who knows where."

"But, Father," the son cut in, "can we really just return to our primitive ways? Do you even know how to make a flame? Are you going to twirl a stick or pound two pieces of flint together? Will you hunt your food with a bow and arrow? No. I want no part of a life with no food—a life spent waiting to die of some trifling illness."

Orionae put a hand on each of the men's shoulders. "Both of you, you must get to the boats. Stay here and we'll all die in flames. To the harbor!"

"Legate! Have you not heard a word I've said? We were like animals in a laboratory! Always given newer and tastier delicacies to distract us, while our reactions and changing lifestyles were monitored. To hell with this exodus! To hell with the king's orders! Can't you see? The only thing one thousand years of rule by the House of Atlas has proven is that our happiness, our bounty, everything about our lives was an illusion."

Orionae pulled the old man up off the ground. "I know. All the more reason why you should get on that boat and go to the land across the ocean and tell people what you have just told me. Tell the people the meaning of happiness and a rich life. Tell the world of the bitter defeat we of Atlantis have tasted. You must do so—or this kind of tragedy could very well occur again."

The old man shook in Orionae's arms.

"Now go!" the legate said.

"No! I'm going to the palace!" the son shouted, turning to dash across the courtyard.

"Wait, no!" The old man jumped as though he'd been electrocuted.

"I will find your son," Orionae said, giving the man a push in the direction of the quays. "You must go ahead to the harbor. Quickly!"

There was no one to be seen on the stair in front of the palace; the great edifice itself sat like an abandoned ruin, distinct in its darkness from the brilliance of the fires below. From halfway up the stair, one could look down on the raging sea of flame and the starry sky where the other half of the city had been.

The layer of smoke that rose from the fires stopped where the starry sky began, as though blocked by some invisible wall. Any flames that reached that dark divide were cut off there, their flickering tongues bending down and spiraling upward, searching for some egress.

What could have happened to an entire half of the city? Orionae wondered as he had many times already. Still no answer presented itself.

The great ringed metropolis, populated by four hundred thousand souls, and forty kilometers across until today, had been reduced to rubble. What had been home to so many was no longer a fit place for human survival.

I must meet with Poseidonis the Fifth. The need for answers threatened to burst Orionae's heart. *From whence did the House of Atlas come—and who were these people?*

Bizarrely, this was the first time he had ever thought to ask this question. The story of the founding of the Kingdom of Atlantis, told in tales by his forebears and recorded in the ancient texts, was already legend. It seemed that the people of the kingdom didn't actually wonder, even out of plain curiosity, where the House of Atlas had actually come from.

One day, they came down from the sky.

That was all they had—the beginning of everything—and that was enough.

One day, they came down from the sky.

As long as everything was going well, who needed more? But when the time of peace had passed and the people began to feel uneasy about their welfare—when tragedy struck, and they looked for the causes and origins of their unhappiness—every doubt led back to this one question: *from whence did the House of Atlas come?* A question for which it was no longer possible to claim an answer.

The corridors of the palace shone brightly with cold light. These giant passageways, built to accommodate the massive frames of Poseidonis the Fifth and Atlas the Seventh, rose almost twenty meters from floor to ceiling. But the only living being moving through all that space now was Orionae.

The legate hurried along the angled slidewalk that led up to the second floor, a vast conveyor that crept along like a giant annelid. Enormous doors stood in pairs on either side of the passageway. The doors were equipped with sensors and would slide open to admit any who stood before them. Some of the rooms were familiar to Orionae—the council chamber, the offices of the Privy Council. He passed them all by, running from the second floor on up to the third.

The third level also appeared deserted. The palace was said to have sixteen or seventeen floors in all, though even the legate Orionae had never been higher than the sixth. He had only a vague conception of the work that went on within the palace and had never really thought to find out more. He knew that Chief Secretary Iras and his dozens of aides took care of most of it, though Iras himself was rarely seen in public.

"Your Majesty!" Orionae shouted down a vacant corridor. "It is I, the legate Orionae! Where are you?"

His voice drifted down the passage, fading into the distance. After an instant's hesitation Orionae continued on, his pace wavering slightly, following the receding echoes of his own voice. He hadn't the slightest idea whether he was headed deeper into the palace, or making his way toward an exit.

"Your Majesty! Orionae has come! Your Majesty, where are you?" he shouted in both directions.

"I'm here."

A tremendous fear struck Orionae, and he braced himself so he would not collapse on the spot.

"What do you want, legate?"

He looked around but saw no sign of Poseidonis the Fifth—only his own shadow wavering in the bright, cold light that fell upon the metal of the corridor floor. And yet with his entire body Orionae could sense the presence of Poseidonis the Fifth looming powerfully above him.

"Your Majesty! You must tell me what this means. Why do you strike down your own people?"

"Legate. I will soon report on my failure to the Planetary Development Committee. Yet understand that this failure is only one of my results. Legate, you saw the fire? It was that fire that foiled my plans, the greatest barrier to the designs of the committee, and our final answer."

"Your Majesty!"

"It is likely that we shall never again appear before you or the people of this city."

"Your Majesty—wait! Where did the other half of the city go? How did it disappear? Will it come back? Please tell me, Your Majesty! What is the starry sky I see outside that has appeared in place of the lost city?"

There was no answer. Orionae felt the towering presence of Poseidonis the Fifth grow gradually weaker, fading into the distance.

He could smell smoke in the corridor now. The fires must have reached the palace walls. It was all over.

Everything was over, headed for an ending beyond the reach of his hands to save.

What would come next? A primitive society, such as the one the old man by the fountain had described? Would darkness visit the hearts of men?

Or would everything be consumed by that dark sky and those mounting flames?

Everything—

●

The storm had blown its last.

Plato lay sprawled across the stone, half buried in sand.

The quiet wind of dawn gently brushed the sand from his body.

By the time one of the village women came out to fetch water and found him there, the philosopher was already dead. The woman ran to inform Seim the Elder, and within moments a crowd of Elcasians had gathered. They carried Plato back to the small dwelling he had been given for his night's lodging. Gladius was still there, leaning up against the wall, fast asleep. He awoke with a start.

A physician of the village stuck silver needles into Plato's arms and legs. The needles were connected to tubes; into these the man poured liquids from several different bottles of *glaes*. Then many strange and curious devices, the purpose of which baffled Gladius's imagination, were carried into the house. They made whirring and burbling noises such as those heard when air and liquid mix. Gladius stood rigid in a corner of the room, watching the hurried yet precise movements of the men and women who encircled the sickbed. When the sun had risen quite high in the sky, Plato moaned suddenly, and the men and women slowed their activity.

"There. He will be able to stand in two or three days," the physician told Gladius. "We must not rush him. He was entirely dead, you see, and needs time to recover." The Elcasian busied himself picking up the various medical devices that had been placed around the bed. His assistants left the room in silence.

The physician closed the curtains on the windows, straightened the blanket over Plato, and then departed, a wooden box filled with vials of medicine and small surgical instruments tucked under his arm.

The philosopher slept with his head pressed into his pillow, barely moving. At times Gladius feared that his master might yet be dead. His eyes filled with tears as he watched over the old man.

What siren beckoned you out into that raging sandstorm, he wondered, *and what did you see there?*

The Arab was painfully aware that their great journey had now begun in earnest.

●

Plato spent the next several days drifting somewhere between wakefulness and sleep. Gladius tried speaking to him, but the old man never responded. When Seim visited, the sight of Plato lying there seemed to give him a great deal of pain.

"Elder," Gladius asked him during one of his visits, "could there be some connection between that custom of your village, the Night of Silence, and my master's sudden illness?"

Seim gave no reply but stood solemnly, gazing down at Plato. The philosopher was sitting up in bed, his back against the wall, but his eyes stared off into space, seeing nothing.

"Ahem. Master Gladius. The Night of Silence, as I have told you, is a ritual in which the people of our village receive a revelation from our suzerain. Yet not all of us receive this revelation. Only a select few glean anything from the Night when it comes—and those who do are forbidden to speak of what has been revealed to them. Thus, no one knows who in the village has received such enlightenment—not even myself."

"Hrm," Gladius muttered. "I suppose that's fitting for a Night of Silence."

"In days long past, they say, everyone in the village received revelation from our suzerain. Through the ritual they would learn firsthand about an event in our past. This knowledge brought us closer together in mind and spirit. Now, such togetherness is beyond our grasp. Master Gladius . . . in truth, I have begun to lose confidence that Atlantis, our suzerain, and the revelation ever existed at all."

"If you seek enlightenment, you're talking to the wrong man."

Seim turned to leave the room.

"Elder—" Gladius called out, and the older man hesitated at the door. "Before entering the service of Master Plato, I lived among many people in many lands. Over the course of those earlier years, I adopted the customs and ways of numerous people, different tribes . . . too many to count. I could not have survived otherwise. One thing I discovered is that in the tales and legends told by all of these peoples, there are always stories of destruction and salvation. I've wondered why this is. Why would there be so many tales about a horrific destruction and the salvation that followed when no one alive could possibly have witnessed either? The tales seemed too close to truth to be mere fancies, and too inevitable to deny."

Seim the Elder stepped out the doorway and vanished, leaving Gladius to wonder whether the Elcasian had even heard him.

●

Three days later, a rare rain fell from the muggy morning through to the night, moistening the desert sands.

"Gladius. Today we head west," Plato announced, standing suddenly.

"M-Master," Gladius stuttered. "How do you feel?"

"How do I feel? I'm fine. Should I not be?"

"I . . . when did you wake?"

"Gladius," Plato said, a bit testily. "This rain is the sort of opportunity that comes but once or twice a year. The journey to the west of the Atlas Mountains would be brutal under any other conditions. We must hurry. Prepare for our departure!"

Gladius could hear in his master's words the obstinacy and sudden passion he knew well. There was no better indicator that Plato had returned to full health. The Arab nodded. "Very well. I will get ready at once," he said, thinking that all he really needed to do was to fill their donkeys' water skins and the two would be ready to depart. "Master, do you know which route we will take?"

Plato peered out through the window at the misting rain, seeming lost in thought. "Four days to the northwest of here, west of the Sawai Valley, lies the village of Tovatsue. He awaits us there."

"Awaits us, Master?"

"Indeed."

"Ah—who awaits us? When was this appointment made?"

Plato turned to his servant, lifting an eyebrow. "How unlike you, Gladius, to forget such things."

"I beg your pardon, Master." Gladius bowed his head, desperately trying to make sense of the old man's words. Not only had he never heard of any village named Tovatsue, but the name sounded so unfamiliar as to be meaningless to him. What people speaking what language would name a village so? He also wondered who might be waiting for them there—he could recall no such arrangement.

Still milling these questions, Gladius went to call on Seim the Elder to announce their departure.

Three donkeys were laden with food and water skins, and they borrowed a fourth, upon which Plato rode. In the writings that Plato sent to his friend Tethys of Terinth, it is noted that when the philosopher made his farewells, he invited the elder to call on him, back in Greece.

Plato and Gladius left the village in the misting rain alone, Plato having refused Seim's offer of a guide. The people of the village gathered and stood watching the two travelers depart.

The dampened desert spread out, vast and barren, before Gladius's eyes. He wondered what was waiting for them on the other side. He cared not whether Tovatsue meant life or death for him; the distinction hardly seemed important.

After they had gone a short distance the two men paused and looked back. Elcasia seemed sunken and faded, far off in the sea of sand behind them.

"Master?" Gladius pointed. "What do you think that might be?" Though he had not noticed it when they entered the village, he could now see a curious structure like a large bowl set on its side, towering a short distance from the houses. It appeared to be fashioned of some kind of thin metal framework.

"That is the suzerain's tower."

"Whose tower?"

"Are you quite all right? We met him just the other day."

I fear you are the one who is not all right, Master, Gladius thought as he chuckled bitterly to himself.

Plato, his thick beard trembling in the desert breeze, stared at the strange bowl looming over the village. It was not the first time he'd seen it, of that he was sure. It was familiar to him, even—yes—surely it was something he had seen dozens upon dozens of times before.

But where?

Plato wracked his brains for some memory of the thing, but every time he felt as if he were about to succeed in dredging it out of the depths, it would slip away, back down to the bottom. With a sigh, the philosopher abandoned his fruitless mental efforts and turned to Gladius.

"Let us go."

Lost to Plato was the memory that he had seen a bowl-shaped dish tens of times the size of this one over the royal palace of Atlantis—and that he was Orionae, the Atlantean.

Prajñāpāramitā

T he weather was unbearably hot from the moment the sun rose that morning. A steamy wind blew through the vast fruit orchards down from the Buddsāli Hills to the west of the city of Kapilavastu, clinging to the skin like hot syrup. The cicadas chirped in a cacophonous drone so omnipresent it seemed as if the sky itself chirped on a regular cycle, now high, now low—a relentless background noise that usually went unnoticed but that every now and then could rise suddenly in the aware-ness and swiftly grow overwhelming, like the roar of the sea in the ears. Once this happened, it was very difficult to cease being aware of it.

That was how it was now for King Śuddhodana. He wrinkled his per-simmon-colored brow and turned to the captain of the guard, old Uddaka, standing behind him.

"What a racket those insects make!"

Old Uddaka nodded silently. Several beads of clear sweat trickled down the violet-tanned skin of his broad, bare chest. He was the most loyal, trusted captain of the king's honor guard, and it pained him that he lacked the words to soothe his monarch.

I should have cut down those Brahmin monks when I had the chance.

That was all Uddaka could think. With fingers like gnarled branches, he toyed with the tassel upon the hilt of the crescent-bladed *kora* that hung on the leather belt at his waist.

I should have cut them. All four of them.

He'd had the chance many times. Yet he knew of the king's deep-felt love for the prince, and it was this that had stayed his hand. The four Brahmin monks the prince had welcomed as teachers had given several sermons in Kapilavastu at the prince's request. Uddaka had himself sometimes gone to listen. Yet the abstruse philosophies the monks purveyed held no meaning for him. To the simple, loyal captain of the honor guard, these monks' plan to take Prince Siddhārtha—heir to the rule of Śākya—away and show him the "path to salvation" or some other fanciful thing made them the enemies of Śākya and a danger to Kapilavastu.

"Where could they be?" King Śuddhodana said, his voice betraying a mounting agitation as he gazed down on the thoroughfare that passed beneath the palace gates.

On either side of the white stone road, a great throng of onlookers had gathered to see off their young prince as he left Kapilavastu to live in the wilderness—together with the four vaunted Brahmin monks he had taken as his teachers.

"My king," whispered Kabahla, Exchequer for the south of the kingdom.

"What is it, Kabahla?"

The king frowned as the minister leaned in. Kabahla's stern features looked strained; he was wearing a cloth on his head against the heat, and his cheeks glistened with sweat.

"A Kosala elephant regiment has entered the eastern part of Bashi Valley, Your Majesty." Kabahla spoke softly so that the other ministers standing nearby would not overhear his report.

"What?" King Śuddhodana gripped the armrest of his chair and stood halfway. "Uddaka! Why have you said nothing of this?"

The captain of the honor guard made a sour face. "Perhaps the Minister of Markets would care to explain why I have not received this report and he has?"

"Indeed," the minister said with a hasty bow. "I sent an inspector to the valley not ten days ago so that he might properly estimate this year's cane harvest from Zamba Village and surrounding fields. My inspector returned this morning quite early. He rode his horse fast some eighty *li* to bring me the news."

"So their elephants are in Bashi already." Śuddhodana's face flushed, and he turned to Uddaka and whispered, "We won't be able to fight the Kosala troops there . . . How many elephants can you field?"

The captain of the honor guard shook his head. "Eight at most.—No, seven. And about forty foot soldiers."

It wasn't enough. Kosala was Śākya's neighbor to the southwest, and the skill of their elephantry and armed retinues was without equal amongst the sixteen *mahajanapadas* of the Indus Plain. The invasion was certainly more than the tiny and poorly armed Śākya could hope to face. Never had the armies of Kosala moved into their territory so boldly.

"And on this day of all days!"

Uddaka gritted his teeth and ran his large hand down his face as though weeping with regret. Something—a bead of sweat, or a tear—shone as it traveled down the ridge of his nose. Nothing troubled the old soldier more than to see his own kingdom's frailty revealed.

"If Kosala is truly invading—" Uddaka began calculating in his head the troops he could muster. Whichever way he counted, the numbers fell short. He couldn't afford to levy soldiers from the villages either. It was far too close to harvest time to empty the fields.

"My king, we should meet them near the second confluence of the Sawa River."

The king did not respond. His gaze was fixed upon the five palanquins now entering the palace gates.

Uddaka swallowed his words.

On this day of all days . . .

The old captain felt then that he had lived just a little too long.

Even though the kingdom was poor and her warriors largely untrained, Śākya's four thousand two hundred troops had a chance of driving back the armies of Kosala if a great general would lead them—and that general was none other than the young Prince Siddhārtha who was, on that very day, to leave Kapilavastu forever.

"My king!"

Uddaka would have sat down on the spot to draw up plans for attacking the armies of Kosala, but all the king's attention was taken at that moment by the imminent departure of his son. So the guard captain stood as still as stone, his hand gripping the hilt of his beloved sword.

The procession of palanquins, guarded before and behind by several dozen *śramaña*, moved slowly across the stone-tiled courtyard. On each palanquin, symbols resembling a feathered golden sun sparkled in the light, dazzling the eyes of the onlookers.

From the balcony where the king stood, it was impossible for him to see the prince standing directly below; he could only watch the palanquins approaching for him. The javelins of the honor guard in the courtyard shone like a field of tall rushes in the sun.

One by one, the palanquins stopped. Then their hanging mats of woven wisteria lifted, and the four Brahmin monks stepped out onto the courtyard, casting pools of shadow on the sun-drenched stones.

King Śuddhodana sighed deeply, struggling to maintain his royal demeanor.

From beneath the balcony, the prince appeared, clothed in simple robes. He faced the monks, bowed deeply, and then began to walk in silence toward the resting palanquins.

"My prince!" Uddaka leaned out over the balcony railing and shouted. "Do not go!"

The prince lifted his thickly bearded face to look up at the guard captain and said something. Uddaka could not hear his words, but having known the prince since he was a young boy, he could tell from his posture and the way he moved his arms that they were words of parting.

"My prince! Kosala's elephants are in Bashi! It is an invasion!" Uddaka exclaimed, though he was painfully aware that nothing he could say would stop the young warrior.

From the high balcony, Uddaka couldn't see if the prince's expression changed at all. The prince moved across the courtyard, getting into the centermost of the five waiting palanquins.

For the first time, a burning rage pierced Uddaka's chest. The kingdom faced threats from without and within, Kosala was invading this very moment, and their own prince was leaving them with no means of defense.

If he wants to save people from their unhappiness, he should start by dealing with the realities of the day! How can there be salvation otherwise? Uddaka scowled. *Damn your enlightenment!*

Then he knew with great clarity what he had to do. Bowing to King Śuddhodana, he quietly left the observation area. Walking slowly across the luxurious carpet of woven peacock tail feathers, Uddaka made his way down to the hall on the first floor. The scene outside beneath the blazing sun was painfully vivid when viewed from the shade of the dark stone hall.

Uddaka steadied his breath, then stepped out into the light-filled courtyard. A number of unfamiliar, strong-looking men were in the process of hoisting the five palanquins to their shoulders.

Uddaka thought he heard the sound of women weeping.

A strange, quiet smile came to his battle-worn face—so deeply split with scars that it was hardly a face at all—and he put his hand upon his kora.

"Hold, Brahmins!"

The naked steel of his blade cut an arc through the sunlight, leaving a rainbow trail in the air.

"What's this?"

Shouts went up from the crowd.

"Uddaka!"

Quickly, the palanquins were returned to the ground. The monks slid from their seats to stand upon the cobblestones.

"What is it, Old Uddaka?" the prince asked in a quiet voice that made the blood boil in the guard captain's ears.

"My prince. I know you may not have the ears to hear my words now—"

"Wait."

"No. You must hear me out, my prince. I do not understand the teachings of the Brahmins, and I do not understand how to save the people, but I understand all too well the plight that Śākya finds herself in this day."

"Old Uddaka, please."

"Listen. Saving the people from the hardship and pain of this world is the duty of the king, and you are the one who will become king of Śākya in time. I understand why you want to sort out your personal troubles, but what about the troubles of your own poor? It is all well and good for you to seek the path of enlightenment, but what of the many who seek safety in your strength? Your people suffer!" Uddaka said.

Siddhārtha shook his head. "That is where you and the other ministers must help them. My father the king has asked you to be his hands and feet, has he not?" The prince's eyes were like perfectly still pools of water, while Uddaka's eyes burned like flames. The old captain understood the workings of the prince's heart as though its design were inscribed upon his own. Yet now was not the time for sympathy or compassion.

"My prince, if you will not remain of your own free will, then you leave me with no choice but to end this journey with steel."

Uddaka realized then for the first time that he would, in fact, be able to cut down his own prince if it came to it. He lifted his sword, its crescent blade as slender as the branch of a willow tree. The prince smiled sadly—the smile of someone who suffers that particular kind of agonizing loneliness one feels upon losing the friend who knew them best.

Uddaka placed the point of his blade on the prince's chest.

"Now, my prince, will you leave with these Brahmins? Will you abandon us?"

Siddhārtha laughed like a summer breeze. "Old Uddaka. If cutting me down will solve your problems, then please, end this life now. I care not."

Uddaka felt the color of his face fade like a wilted leaf. "My prince. I have been appointed chief of the honor guard that serves you and your father. Though it is perhaps not my place to say this, I am the most loyal of your subjects. Do you say these words to me thinking that there is no way I could possibly bring harm to you?"

A sudden hardness came over the prince's face, and a strong light shone in his eyes. "Old Uddaka," he said, "it seems to me that life and death are as one within that kora you wield. Should you swing it down upon my body, you may end my life, but you will never cut my heart. My heart is here in this stone-tiled courtyard, and in those red flowers blossoming over there—it is everywhere within Kapilavastu, it fills this land. Tell me, Old Uddaka, how will you cut that?"

The old captain was at a loss for words, now that he was faced with the very situation he had feared might come. In silence, he steadied his grip on his sword. "My prince." Uddaka lifted his blade.

"Wait!" called a voice from where the four Brahmin monks stood, as silent as wooden statues until now. Uddaka could not tell whether one of them had spoken, or all had spoken in unison. The sun blazed on his up-raised blade, paused at its zenith, and Uddaka felt as if he himself might fade in its light.

"Great warrior," the monk farthest to the right spoke. "Your prince does not abandon Śākya."

"Explain what you mean."

"Great warrior—"

Udakka took two strides toward him. "I am Uddaka, captain of the honor guard to King Śuddhodana."

The Brahmin monk faced him directly and pressed his hands together, elbows out to the sides. "I am Maudgalyayana, Brahmin of Dowa Mintaka Temple."

The next monk spoke. "And I am Subhuti, of the same."

"Mahākāśyapa."

"Pūrna."

The four Brahmin monks looked startlingly alike. All had large an-gular heads, thrusting jaws, short necks, broad chests, wide noses, and deep-set eyes rich with shadows. Uddaka had always thought they looked rather countrified and dull, and he thought no better of them now.

"The prince goes to meet Brahmā."

"What did you say?"

"Surely you know of the God of the Brahmin?"

"I know that Brahmā is Heaven."

Subhuti stepped forward. "Warrior. Brahmā is the highest reality. Brahmā is the procession of the sun, moon, stars, and constellations; the birth, growth, destruction, and death of all things. Brahmā is the existence of all and the negation of all. Brahmā is the divine basis of everything in the universe."

"So the prince is going to meet this Brahmā? Is he even a person? I have a hard time understanding how something could be both all of exis-tence and a man of flesh and blood."

"Warrior." Pūrna made the *abhaya mudrā*, the gesture of no fear, with his hands and bowed to Uddaka. "Brahmā holds this vast universe in his hands and meditates upon it. That all things change form is Heaven's will, the will of Brahmā." A bead of sweat left a shining trail down the side of Pūrna's wide, flat nose.

Uddaka shook his head in silence, then finally spoke again. "Monks. Let me ask you this. In Śākya last year and the year before the crops withered so badly we collected hardly anything in taxes. In Kapilavastu, the mending of the waterways has failed. The farmers abandon their fields, the merchants have left the markets, and entire families line up every morning to receive alms porridge. And a terrible illness has been affecting the poorer folk, leaving many severely crippled. Monks, if this truly is the will of Brahmā, then Heaven is not here for the sake of man, and it never was!"

Uddaka glared at Maudgalyayana with the eyes of a wounded hawk. His gaze went to Pūrna, and Subhuti, and Mahākāśyapa, finally coming to rest on Prince Siddhārtha.

The prince bowed deeply to the four Brahmin monks, then stood before Uddaka.

The sun beating down upon the courtyard felt hot enough to sear the flesh of the six men standing there. Sky and earth were filled with the resounding sound of the cicadas, and yet in the space before the palace a quieter sound held sway, a low twilight hum. The crowd surrounding the courtyard waited like a shadow.

"Old Uddaka."

"My prince."

Such tension ran across the three paces of air between the two men that they might have been joined by ribbons of steel.

"The will of Heaven does not serve man. All laws flow and change by the workings of mutual dependence, relationships, and karma. Man is the same. The changing of relationships determines the form of existence. Reality is not a fixed entity within the cycle of life and death, reality is *change*. Existence is impermanent, form is empty, emptiness is form."

"My prince, tell me. Is the suffering of your people the will of Heaven?"

A look of deep pain came over Siddhārtha's thickly bearded face. "I believe this is but another face of the world. Heaven includes all things. That is why it is called Brahmā. However, Old Uddaka, I cannot say this with utmost heartfelt conviction, for there are many questions to which I have not yet found answers.

"Hear me, Old Uddaka. The continuation and sustenance of an individual's life is a temporary manifestation, subject to the strict laws of constant change. There can be no rigid, unchanging self. We find that if all men cling to the self and do not allow themselves and others to change, it leads to the great misfortunes of unhappiness and interminable social evils. Yet if we accept this basic truth that all is in motion, what of Heaven? Must we deny the existence of Heaven? The existence of the gods? The existence of the self? And what of love? These are the matters I wish to contemplate. No, I *must* contemplate."

He spoke softly, yet long years of anguish showed in his voice.

"If that is so, my prince," said Uddaka, "if there is no unchanging self in this cosmos and the body must perish . . . then I will be the agent of that change!"

Uddaka's kora swept from the brilliant sun down onto the prince's head.

For a moment, the stone-tiled courtyard, shimmering in the heat, flattened like a painting. Nothing moved across the sun-baked stones save the hot wind that blew oily thick through the railings on the serpentine stone stair, stifling the onlookers.

Old Uddaka was frozen, every muscle rigid, as if he had turned to hard clay; the naked blade in his hand was stopped a hair's breadth from the prince's forehead. Only his keen eyes looked as though they might erupt with flame.

"We should be going, Prince Siddhārtha," Maudgalyayana said with a wave of his hand. One by one, Mahākāśyapa, Pūrna, and Subhuti turned and walked toward their palanquins.

Yet still the prince could not depart, for a beautiful woman was now clinging to his leg. Her abundant black hair tumbled in disarray, and from between its flowing strands, two eyes like deep lakes stared up into his face. This was the prince's wife—the Princess Yaśodharā. The golden beaded necklace that hung upon her breast sparkled by the prince's feet.

"My prince! Why must you leave us? Why must you leave me?"

It was often said that the Princess Yaśodharā most resembled Siddhārtha's birthmother, the king's first wife, Māyā. Māyā had been a princess of Koliya, Śākya's neighbor to the east, and a famed beauty. During her pregnancy, following the custom of the day, she had left Śākya to return to her home village for the birth. Yet the prince had come early, in a place called Lumbinī halfway between the two kingdoms, and seven days later, the mother had died.

A carven stone monument marking the spot—one that stands to this day—was erected in later years by King Aśoka. Bereft of his birth mother, the prince had been raised by the king's second wife, the princess Maha Pajapati, who was Māyā's sister. Though both father and mother showered the prince with their affection and spared nothing in his education, he had not grown up to become the *cakravarti-rājan*—the universal sage-monarch to unify and rule the world—his father had wished he would become. Had the prince wanted such a role for himself, he might very well have succeeded in becoming that great ruler. Yet his grief over the loss of his mother Māyā and his understanding of the unhappiness and destruction fated for all men had led him ever further from the expectations and the passions of those around him and toward a life of solitary thought.

Even though there were times that the prince looked upon Yaśodharā and saw in her face the image of the late Māyā and felt himself saved not once but twice, the love of the princess was not enough to keep the prince from leaving.

●

Siddhārtha was twenty-nine years old. He already had a child with the princess, a boy named Rahula. As it was the primary obligation of the head of the household in ancient India to ensure that the bloodline was continued, one could say that the prince had already fulfilled the most essential part of that duty. In truth, there was nothing in his heart that held him back from leaving the palace. He had been waiting for this day for a very long time.

"Be well, my princess. And take good care of Rahula. And my father, as well—he is nearing the age when his legs and back will pain him. He will need your help."

Siddhārtha leaned over and gently pried Yaśodharā's fingers from his foot. The princess's hand was as soft as an infant's to the touch. Then he lifted her up and hugged her close. She wore a thin, silken gown and her breasts were warm against his chest.

"I will always be beside you." He gazed down at the clinging princess and, suffering a pang of worry, he caught his breath and looked up to the sky.

Subhuti called out to the prince, asking him to make haste, and joined Pūrna in making a *vajra mudrā*, the *mudrā* of thunder, with his hands.

Then the sharp voice of a woman rang out behind them, and to Siddhārtha, it felt like a blow to his back. "My prince! Wait!"

The prince stopped and turned around to see the wet nurse Vamsa running toward him, her footfalls upon the stones breaking the hush in the courtyard. She was dressed in finery but her hair was disheveled, and the jeweled crown she wore as a sign of her nobility was hanging from one ear. She carried an infant in her arms, and she laid it at the prince's feet.

"Why, this is Rahula!" Siddhārtha exclaimed.

"My prince, you must tell me why you would abandon your only child in this way!"

Siddhārtha sighed. "The time for such explanations has passed, wet nurse. I entrust his care to you."

Vamsa bit her lip. Below them on the stones, the young Rahula was now sitting up, crying.

"My prince! If you will insist on leaving us, then tread upon your own son as you leave."

Vamsa stared directly into Siddhārtha's eyes. A stillness sharp as glass filled the courtyard. Uddaka still stood, his kora frozen in the air just above where the prince's head had been, while Maudgalyayana and the other Brahmins did not move so much as an eyebrow as they watched beneath the blazing sun. The only noise came from the surging sea of cicadas.

Without a word the prince strode forward. In his heart he felt only the vastness of the void. When his foot touched Rahula, the child screamed as though burned.

●

The five palanquins passed through the ornate gates of the palace like a shadow before the throngs of onlookers.

The prince, gazing out through the wisteria hangings, saw a flower growing off to the side of the road, its large yellow bloom swaying wildly despite the lack of a breeze.

"To Tuṣita," he heard Maudgalyayana say from one of the palanquins ahead of him. The bearers quickened their pace and turned at the next corner.

●

"To Tuṣita."

The voice reached Siddhārtha deep in his clouded consciousness.

At this very moment, he was on his way to meet the world's ultimate being, and the thought made him shake like a child with anticipation.

Could this be the fear that comes before attaining enlightenment?

Gingerly, the prince put his hands together.

Snow was falling all around.

It fell endlessly whirling, soundlessly filling the land around them with pure white. With every breath of wind, he caught a glimpse of vast plains, visible only as a dim, bluish shadow beyond the thick white curtain of snow. The sun was out somewhere between the snow and the ice that seemed to cover both heaven and earth—he could see its brilliant light reflected in one part of the storm.

"The Eight Cold Hells!" Siddhārtha muttered, and he moved to draw his robes more tightly together at the neck. This was when he noticed that he seemed to have no arms. And not only did his arms appear to have vanished, but he also lacked a chest to cover with robes, a waist to tie with a sash, and legs below . . . in fact, his entire body seemed to be missing.

Perhaps I am meant to face the world without form?

Lose the self, and you destroy suffering. All that is left is the barren snow and ice. Strangely, he felt no pain. Though there was thought, there was no sensation—even though he had always assumed there could be no consciousness without the five senses.

"What I don't understand is, how can I see all of these inanimate things around me without having returned to my body?"

Next to him, Maudgalyayana nodded. "We are in the Trayastriṃśa, my prince. Already we are 320,000 *yojana* distant from Jambudvīpa, the island of man." Maudgalyayana said the numbers as though he were reading them aloud.

"Jambudvīpa, as I understand it, floats in the seas to the east of Mt. Sumeru," said Siddhārtha, his voice echoing too loudly. "This is the world where men live. I did not expect the heights above that, the Heaven upon Heaven—this Trayastrimśa—to be such a desolate place."

"My prince, we are currently on the second level of the Six Heavens of the Realm of Desire, those being Cāturmahārājika of the Four Heavenly Kings, Trayastrimśa through which we currently pass, Yāma, Tuṣita, Nirmāñarati, and Paranirmita-vasavartin. Here we find our paradise. Alas, in no more than eighty thousand years, it will perish."

"But why is this, Maudgalyayana? Where in this second of the Six Heavens, this celestial world beyond the realm of man, do you find this shadow of destruction?"

The four Brahmin monks were standing in a circle now with Prince Siddhārtha at its center in the ice and snow. The wildly sweeping flakes passed both within and without their bodies.

"We believe the origin of the problem lies in a warping of the space between imaginary coordinates two and three in the Delta quadrant, just above the Cāturmahārājika."

●

Two suns burned in a copper sky overhead. One was large and somewhat oblong and gave off a dull orange light. The other was small and possessed a brilliant white incandescence at its core, ringed farther out by a silver corona. Large eruptions of reddish gas flowed from the surface of the orange sun, swirling through the void at a frightening pace, extending toward the smaller, bluish white sun. The flowing gases painted land and sky in startling colors, and whenever the gases wrapped entirely around the smaller sun, the void between them filled with an incandescent brilliance. The light cut the long flatness of space in half, sweeping aside all other illumination and shadow. Then the crimson gas flow would spiral inward and vanish in the blink of an eye, leaving the two suns to shine in the copper sky once more.

A silence, like death, came next, followed a short while later by another plume of gas that rose from the waves of flame rimming the dusky orange sun, then extended into space. So the two suns traveled through the black sky, alternately emitting flaming gases and brilliant flashes of light, a symphony of brilliance that washed away all the other stars in the sky. When the two finally passed out of sight, another pair came racing up from the opposite horizon, one of them a giant fireball, ringed with silver, with a long tail of burning gas that stretched far off into the void.

Two pair of suns made four suns in total that burned in the vast solar region of Trayastriṃśa.

The blizzard had disappeared, as though a blanket had been removed from the world. Now everywhere Siddhārtha looked was a barren icy plain. Not even the four suns burning in the void seemed to have any warming effect on the frozen ground. Nothing moved in that bluish expanse, nor was there any sign of life; everything was frozen hard as steel. Even a portion of the atmosphere had crystallized into a translucent remnant scattered across the surface.

The temperature was minus 272.8 degrees Celsius. If any civilization had once existed here, there was no trace of it now.

●

"Even with all the energy to be had, there is hardly any heat movement on this world. The level of heat entropy is extremely low. My prince, it is only a matter of time before Trayastriṃśa is lost."

"Why can you not warm it? Or prevent the loss of what warmth it has? I am sure it would require an enormous amount of energy, but surely that is preferable to losing a world entirely," Prince Siddhārtha said, struggling to understand.

"It is an insulation phenomenon," Mahākāśyapa explained, a pained expression on his face. "With the expansion of Trayastriṃśa's space, we are witnessing a rapid dispersal of its heat energy."

"But why?"

"My prince, this region has been cut off from the rest of space by a fluctuation in its gravitational field. Through our efforts, we have been able to free a small portion of it, but it is not enough."

"What did you mean by . . . Trayastriṃśa's space expanding?"

"Even as Trayastriṃśa is sequestered by the local gravitational field, it grows larger."

"But why here? Why only Trayastriṃśa?"

"Sadly, it is not only Trayastriṃśa's space that is affected. All of the Six Heavens of the Realm of Desire are showing similar, fatal changes. We cannot afford to be optimistic about this. It may come to pass that we are forced to stage a mass exodus from this space altogether." Maudgalyayana's words were heavy with the weight of his sorrow.

"We had hoped for a solution in the past, but nothing has improved in the slightest," Mahākāśyapa added.

The five now rode in a large translucent sphere that contained them and them alone. Beyond its confines, uncountable twinkling stars formed a sea of light all around them. Siddhārtha saw the monks only as vague shadows against that starry backdrop.

Gazing out into the vast expanse of star-studded darkness, he could see a giant torrent of light filling a third of all that was visible. It cut across the darkness, and the colors spilled from it like a waterfall: navy blue, deep green, indigo, and all the way across the spectrum to a brownish red. Bands of color split the darkness in half, seemingly in mid-explosion—yet no matter how long Siddhārtha watched, the light stayed perfectly still, neither blinking nor ebbing. That great field of light seemed stuck against the dark sky, frozen still as death. Which, he realized, was exactly what it was.

"My prince, there are over a hundred billion spiral galaxies here in Yāma, yet the warping of space has begun dispersing them, or collapsing them, or eliminating them entirely. Look—" he pointed—"that spiral galaxy has been gravitationally sequestered. See how its nucleus contracts and releases its energy. We call this a *quasar*, but it is only a name. We do not understand what is actually happening."

Pūrṇa pointed with a finger toward the unmoving light. "That spiral galaxy is roughly 3,800,000 light-years distant from us. It was once comprised of one hundred billion stable stars—but I fear that most have already been lost. Here in Yāma, we have already lost ten billion such galaxies."

Prince Siddhārtha stood in silence, looking out on that glorious light of death.

"Maudgalyayana, we should transport the prince to Tuṣita as quickly as possible," Pūrna said quietly.

"Yes. I'm sure that Brahmā awaits his arrival." Maudgalyayana turned to Mahākāśyapa beside him. "Make for Tuṣita with all haste. We'll be traveling from coordinates 713.081 to 429.993 . . . through imaginary space, but I don't think that can be avoided."

"Is there a particular danger in keeping to normal space?" Mahākāśyapa inquired.

"Yes. I've received word that slight warping has been detected in the vicinity of coordinates 799.341. If this should happen to be a typical relativity-theory gravitational field I see no problem, but if it is an engineered field, going there would be tantamount to plunging headfirst into the abyss."

Mahākāśyapa raised an eyebrow. "Does their reach already extend so far?"

"One can never be sure with that phantasmagoric lot," Maudgalyayana spat in a tone most unbecoming an enlightened holy man.

The bubble that held them passed through the blackness of space like a shooting star.

Maudgalyayana and the three other monks stood still, hardly seeming even to breathe. Alone, Prince Siddhārtha turned to watch the brilliant veil of light recede behind them into the distance.

Three million eight hundred thousand light-years.

Whatever he was seeing there at this moment was probably already long gone at its point of origin. The brightness that reached him now was nothing but an avatar—the temporary likeness of what was in reality, nothing. Powerful radiation would soon reach the nearer regions of space, bringing true death to the darkness around them.

●

An edge of crimson crept along the border of the indigo sky. The blending of colors cast a deeply unsettling glow upon the vast sea of sand that spread in all directions. The landscape was so flat that the rising and falling of the dunes was almost imperceptible—and yet, incongruously long shadows stretched out, as though drawn by an unseen hand into long tracks across the plain.

Here and there, brown objects thrust from the dune sea like fallen branches. Their surfaces had been polished to a shiny luster by the moving sand, yet it was impossible to tell of what substance they were made. Siddhārtha judged that they had been lying here buried for a good hundred thousand years.

"My prince, here is where Tovatsue, capital of Tuṣita, once stood. Now it is nothing but desert. The only signs that anything was here at all are the remnants of the buildings that emerge like fossils from the sand."

Maudgalyayana and the other monks pressed their hands together in silence. Siddhārtha followed suit.

The translucent sphere in which they traveled floated over the dunes at a height of several centimeters. Suddenly, a blindingly brilliant light cut across the indigo sky above. It was made by a giant object, and for a while fragmented streaks of incandescent ions glowed in the wake of its passage. Some amount of time later, a blast wave of immense heat swept across the desert.

The faint crimson light at the edge of the indigo sky grew brighter and dimmer, a fluctuation that inspired an irrational fear in Siddhārtha.

"The proximity warning system has indicated our arrival path," Pūrna declared, looking back over his shoulder.

Without a sound, the vast sea of sand split in half, revealing a giant city in the depths below.

Siddhārtha struggled to move his legs, but found the effort baffling. A feeling of resistance troubled every motion, as though his entire body were submerged in water. Each time he tried to step forward, his foot would shift in a different direction of its own accord.

Tuṣita's capital, Tovatsue, was enormous, full of complicated devices and structures with functions that staggered the prince's imagination. He grasped that the vast city was in fact a single edifice, its countless parts interconnecting in an immense cylindrical shape. The walls and ceilings of the giant corridors that served as the primary streets glowed with a beautiful aquamarine light, giving a sheen of vitality to the faces and bodies of the five travelers. An incredible number of side streets connected at right angles to the corridors; down these, Siddhārtha could see the edges of living quarters and manufacturing districts. There was a faint floral scent to the air, which was pleasantly dry and a comfortable temperature against his skin.

Siddhārtha blushed when he reflected back on the gloomy, unhealthy design of Kapilavastu, and its sad lack of facilities—the city's water supply and sewage system were barely sufficient at best. The situation cast shame on both his kingdom's way of life and its leadership.

And yet, the prince thought, *perhaps I am wrong even to compare the two. Is not this Tuṣita, the Pure Land? Am I not the first man to visit this place while still alive? It profanes the sanctity of the divine to compare this hallowed land above Heaven with the refuse-strewn streets of man below!*

Prince Siddhārtha hung his head low.

They moved through several levels of the city. Along the corridor, he saw large vertical cylinders at intervals on either side, fashioned from some transparent material that transported crowds of people upward and downward. Of course, the prince realized that the figures he saw were *devas*, not people. And yet some among the *devas* wore clothes of silver, with hard-looking helmets, and carried what seemed to be strangely fashioned weapons in their hands.

After a time the five travelers boarded one of the transparent cylinders, and it carried them down into the ground at an alarming speed. The prince's eyesight dimmed and he found himself suddenly confused as the blood drained from his head.

"Is something wrong?"

"Just . . . a spell of dizziness."

"Ah, I apologize. Pūrna, a bit slower, if you would."

The voices of the monks sounded unnervingly distant.

Then a howling wind sounded in the prince's ears—a wind that bore a great deal of sand. The flying grains blasted his cheek.

Why would there be sand flying through the air down here? the prince asked his wavering heart.

"Prince Siddhārtha, you are in the presence of Brahmā," Maudgalyayana whispered by the prince's ear.

Siddhārtha stood upon the sand, supported on either side by Pūrna and Subhuti.

It was hard to say from the ink blue sky—there was a sky here, the prince suddenly realized—whether it was night or day, but when he stared upward, he saw an incredible number of stars hanging there.

"Is it nighttime?" the prince asked, looking up into the thin light.

"Prince Siddhārtha of Śākya?"

The ancient, quiet voice seemed to seep into his heart.

Lord Brahmā!

The prince fell to his knees upon the sand.

"You have journeyed a long way to come here."

"You must tell me the way to enlightenment. That is my only request!"

In the deep indigo sky, several hundred billion stars suddenly glared more brightly.

"Brahmā is deeply impressed by your dedication to the path of salvation, Siddhārtha." Brahmā's voice was deep and grand, and it filled the prince's chest with its energy as it erupted from the very axis of the world—and yet it contained within it a subtle hint of sorrow. "These Heavens, however, now stand in terrible peril. We are pooling all our strength in an attempt to save them, yet the solution is still far from our grasp. It is difficult even to predict what will be required of us. Thus, though I welcome your visit, I cannot guarantee you will be satisfied with what we have to offer you at this moment."

The prince peered upward, trying to see Brahmā's glory; yet though he felt that the god must be near, he saw nothing but the deep spreading indigo of the sky.

Siddhārtha's head fell as though he had been struck by lightning.

Of course—Brahmā has no form. Brahmā is the universal principle, the will of Heaven! Siddhārtha found that he, too, had lost his physical form, becoming part of the vast indigo void.

"Listen, my prince. Do you know that this place, Tuṣita, is a full sixty thousand *yojana* above Yāma? By another way of reckoning, that is roughly 160 billion light-years. Up here, we have created clouds of interstellar material by stacking layer upon layer of near-vacuum. And so have we created this great world, an experimental model, here in Tuṣita, which is itself eighty billion light-years across.

"Listen, my prince.

"In the center of the universe, Mt. Sumeru extends above the Golden Ring. Its four sides are bounded by seas of fragrant waters, and beyond that, the Seven Golden Mountains and the Seven Seas. Beyond that is an ocean of the kind you are accustomed to, with salt in its water. The outermost perimeter is the great iron ring of the Cakravāda mountains—think of them as the rim of the great saucer that holds these many seas and peaks. The Cakravāda are made of iron, copper, and steel, and nothing—neither *deva* nor demon—may ascend their walls. We might interpret this as the limit of the universe as defined by the speed of light.

"Now, my prince, in the outer ocean float four continents, one in each of the cardinal directions. The continent to the south is Jambudvīpa, where man dwells—your world.

"The summit of Mt. Sumeru is the place called Trayastrimśa, where Śakra, lord of the *devas*, maintains his Seeing-Joy Palace. Looking from the palace, down the slopes of the mountain, one can see three terraces below—Sadāmada, Mālādhara, and Karoṭapāni. Gazing farther to the south one sees Jambudvīpa; to the east is Pūrvavideha, to the north is Uttarakuru, and to the west is Aparagodānīya, all great continents, each with seasons of warmth and icy cold. Just below Tuṣita is Cāturmahārājika, where reside the Four Heavenly Kings: Dhṛtarāṣṭra in the east, Virūḍhaka in the south, Virūpākṣa in the west, and Vaiśravaṇa in the north, all serving Śakra and each commanding a retinue of elites—though not the Eight Generals, who fall directly under Śakra's command. In particular, Virūpākṣa—who is called 'he who sees all'—is in charge of the advance warning system. It is he who monitors all surrounding space for shifts in the gravitational field.

"The warning system is part of a defense network split between the two heavens upon Mt. Sumeru and coordinated through the four heavens above that, all of which are called together the Six Heavens of the Realm of Desire. Some distance above Tuṣita are the three Heavens of the First Meditation, which include the Mahā Brahmā, ruled by Brahmā himself. Above that are the Three Heavens of the Second Meditation, and above that the Three Heavens of the Third Meditation and the Nine Heavens of the Fourth Meditation, with Akaniṣṭha at the very top. This world is thought to lie beyond the light-speed barrier—and thus its existence has not yet been confirmed, my prince."

Siddhārtha's mind strained to comprehend this model of the universe. He felt overwhelmed.

"In Tuṣita there are forty-nine satellite cities surrounding this city of the Pearl Palace. The Pearl Palace is the last line of defense, responsible for protecting all the Heavens. It is our last hope," said Brahmā.

Finally Siddhārtha found the courage to speak. "Allow me to ask you, Brahmā . . . Why do these vaulted heavens harbor such catastrophe? On my way here, the monks led me through countless places where I saw nothing but waste and destruction. I thought in my journey I would witness the truth behind those dark principles that bring ruin to the world of men—yet what I find here is more of the same: devastation and death. Lord Brahmā, what is the cause of this heavenly catastrophe that affects Tuṣita?"

Brahmā answered in a voice filled with bitter grief.

"My Prince, it is the invasion of these heavens by the *asura* that has brought us to these desperate straits, where we struggle even to defend Tuṣita."

"The *asura?*"

"Yes. Misshapen creatures—beings with three faces and six arms. Whence they come we do not know. But their leader, whom we call "Asura," is full of cunning and violence. His warriors are many and deadly; even our powerful yakṣa cannot defend against them without great casualties. Asura has warred with Lord Śakra, defender of Tuṣita, for some four hundred million years and shows no sign of ever abandoning the assault. Asura is the very essence of evil in the universe. Be warned, my prince, and be wary."

Siddhārtha felt Brahmā's mind focus intently upon him, and with a start he realized that all of their discussion had taken place without a single word being uttered. As he lacked form, so too did he lack words.—No, he thought, *it is not a lack or loss.* For where one must rely upon words to convey meaning, one can never have a true dialogue.

In gratitude Prince Siddhārtha turned to the vast space above and pressed his hands together, formless though he was.

"My prince, the first thing you must learn is the nature and appearance of the destruction that assails this world. How might we save Tuṣita from its fate? The many sorrows of the human world originate here, you understand. Where will you find the source of this destruction, this unhappiness? That is the question to which you must find an answer."

A long silence passed. Siddhārtha could not say how long he had sat hunched upon the dry, drifting sands.

"My prince, let us be off," Maudgalyayana said, and he and Subhuti helped the prince to his feet.

The immense sea of sand had disappeared before the prince's eyes, replaced by a long corridor of scintillating light. They were just outside the boundaries of the city.

Which is the real Kabahla, Siddhārtha wondered, *the barren desert where the wind whips the sand through the air, or the shining city I see now before me? In what world did I meet with Brahmā?* He could not say with certainty which it had been. And it didn't really matter. He would have been equally pleased by a sand-strewn wasteland or a perfectly constructed city of ideal beauty. No matter where he was, he knew that his body was void, already a part of the cosmos. And he would be taking that void-body to confront the very substance of evil.

●

"Maudgalyayana. I wish to meet Asura. I would encounter this most evil of all evil kings and ask the true meaning of his actions."

The four Brahmin monks exchanged glances, seeming impressed at Prince Siddhārtha's willingness to face the ultimate evil and his desire to find the path to enlightenment.

"Very good, my prince," said Maudgalyayana. "You would do well to meet Asura and ascertain for yourself the true nature of that being. However—"

"Yes?"

"We are students of the Way of the Heavens under Brahmā, and as such, are unable to escort you to such a one as Asura."

"I understand. You need only tell me the way to Asura's camp and how to contact him."

Subhuti nodded thoughtfully. "There is a single subspace communication circuit established between Asura and Śakra. You may use that."

"Yes," Mahākāśyapa said, "though it has lain dormant for many tens of millions of years, ever since Śakra and Asura abandoned the way of peace. Now—" the monk's voice took on a new urgency—" we must relocate to an expansion of refracted subspace at once, before Asura's attack begins."

The thin crimson curtain of light near the horizon had begun to flicker intensely.

"What's that?" the prince asked, casting an unsettled look at the sky.

"The aurora. Asura is beneath that changing light."

It occurred to the prince that the shifting colors in that arc of brightness revealed minute changes in the heart of the enemy.

"Here," said Maudgalyayana, "I will instruct you in the operation of the gravity bubble." Guiding the prince with a hand on his back, the monk directed their progress into the walled city of Tovatsue.

From the moment they entered the giant cylinder it was clear that the city was well defended against all manner of attacks. And yet the place had a smell of tragedy, as though it had already lost something it would never be able to reclaim. It was alone, resigned to await its fate.

How odd to think that Tuṣita was a city of future glory—for as Siddhārtha's studies had taught him, 5,670,000,000 years from now this place was to be the city of Maitreya, the being who would save humanity by opening the way to a perfect world.

But 5,670,000,000 years was such a long time that it was effectively an eternity for Tuṣita and the distant world of men to wait. And yet waiting—that simple act—was all they could do in the face of Asura's promised destruction. Unlike the city, holding on for a distant salvation, Asura was acting in the now. Asura had no tomorrow.

"Perhaps," Siddhārtha muttered, "Asura has nothing to lose."

●

Gradually, the silent, barren sea of sand took on the same deep indigo color as the sky. Occasionally, a stiff wind would pass across the dunes, lifting up a dust cloud that raced along as though some invisible creature were galloping across the landscape, kicking up a long trail in its wake.

The gravity bubble carrying the prince moved slowly across the sand toward the burning crimson aurora on the horizon.

Siddhārtha was uncertain whether the passage of time continued or whether it had stopped. *Surely, if it continues, it is not proceeding in the normal fashion*, he thought, resigned to wait. The nature of time in these heavenly realms seemed bizarrely different from that in the world of men. Much to his own surprise, the prince was stricken by a sudden feeling of longing for his own distant kingdom.

The fragments of once-great buildings dotted the dry desert around him. Mighty edifices lay stricken and crumbled into ruins on the ground. Sections of walls, huge pillars, and leaning towers loomed like phantasms in the indigo light. Some were made of metal, others of beautiful translucent crystal, and still others of some rare and precious wood.

A large dome stood cracked and partly fallen. Through the rifts in its beautifully patterned surface he saw the light of the aurora shining.

Occasionally on the sand he saw what appeared to be parts of living things. Shriveled bits of living tissue, they seemed wracked with raw emotion—choked with sand, panicked at their own rapid loss of moisture. Their voiceless screams stabbed at the prince's heart. Far beyond the horizon, he saw an incredible number of lighted spheres flying wildly across the sky. The spheres seemed to form a line, moving from right to left as though joined by a single thread. He watched them waver upward and then plunge abruptly below the curve of the land. Where they landed, violent gouts of light and flame burst up and whirled heavenward.

This, Siddhārtha was sure, was nothing other than a horrific battle being waged far, far away. And yet he could sense none of the fear or disturbance that comes with such bloodshed. It was like viewing a strategist's painting of a war upon a scroll—he saw in it the cold calculation and heartless direction of killers who seek to take the maximum amount of life with a minimum of effort.

"Prince Siddhārtha?"

A young girl stood, her back to the flickering light of the aurora.

"Asura?"

The girl's skin was the color of barley, and her brown hair, tinged with purple, was bound into a knot atop her head, fixed with a tiny hairpin.

"Yes."

The prince quickly found his imagination captured by her boyish, muscular frame and clear, piercing black eyes. Siddhārtha leaned forward. "Asura, I would ask you a question."

The girl frowned, and in her innocent expression, Siddhārtha saw a single-mindedness of purpose and a passion burning hot enough to kill.

"The Brahmins tell me that, driven by former karma, you have invaded Tuṣita and fought with Śakra's armies for some four hundred million long years."

"This is true," the girl said in a voice like a song.

"Asura—"

The girl frowned again slightly. It seemed to be a habit of hers whenever she looked at something intently—and the effect was not unattractive. Quietly, she began to toy with the necklace she wore. It seemed to be made of fragments of bone strung on a silver thread. Their dry clacking sounded like the ringing of tiny bells to the prince's ears.

"Can you tell me why you have invaded Brahmā's heavens?" he asked her. "What is it that you desire? And where have you come from? Where is the world in which you dwell?"

The prince sat down on the sand, straightening his back and staring at the girl. A smile played around one corner of her mouth; her lips parted to reveal a startlingly white canine tooth.

"Asura?"

"Siddhārtha!"

Suddenly, the girl's voice was the voice of all creation. The wind began to blow with fury, and her long hair fluttered like flames. Her anger and sorrow were transformed into a blinding shower of fiery sparks.

"Siddhārtha! Go to see Maitreya! Go to see this Maitreya who is destined to save you 5,670,000,000 years from now!"

Not thinking, the prince threw himself bodily upon the sand. His hands shook with embarrassment as he clasped them together.

Asura vanished in the wind. But her voice seemed to continue on, from somewhere far off toward the distant horizon.

See Maitreya—those words pierced the prince's chest through to his back and burned the bottom of his heart to a cinder.

"Siddhārtha! I have heard the Brahmin talk of a *śramaña* called Maitreya in the Pure Land of Tuṣita who will come at the end of this world and save us all. But tell me, my prince—"

Asura was there again before him. She put her hands behind her and gracefully knelt down, her large eyes glimmering with sardonic mirth.

"Tell me, what will be here 5,670,000,000 years from now? What sort of destruction will visit us then? Can you even imagine such a thing?"

Prince Siddhārtha shook his head sadly, remaining silent as a stone.

"Did you ever think, my prince," Asura continued, "that perhaps it is because Maitreya knows what form this destruction will take that he chooses to wait such a very, very long time? Perhaps he would claim that he is only able to save humanity because he can predict the nature of the destruction so precisely. I wonder then why he does not describe it to us. Should he not describe it? And should he not explain how he intends to save us? If he truly were a savior, shouldn't we expect him to prevent the destruction from coming in the first place?"

Asura leaned forward, as though to peer directly inside the prince's heart.

"Well, it seems to me—" Siddhārtha began, seeking some counterargument, but no more words came to him.

"Do you have the answer, my prince?" Asura asked, fixing him with an icy stare.

"It seems to me that he does not save us because the destruction has yet to come."

She laughed without a sound, one edge of her mouth drawing back into a lopsided smile. "*The destruction has yet to come?!* My prince, have you not seen the devastation all around you? Examine any of these worlds stacked upon worlds and you will find them filled with ruin and despair so deep they appear beyond recovery. Is this not destruction? The very destruction for which Maitreya waits and waits?"

The prince's arms shook; his hands clenched into fists on his lap. Swallowing his fear, he looked up at Asura.

"But who brought this ruin here? Who brought the calm of death, the peace of destruction? Was it not you, Asura, and your minions who visited devastation upon this place?"

Asura ignored the prince's words, letting them pass by her as though she had no ears with which to hear him. "Do not forget, my prince, that I am a part of this world too. My existence is but one aspect of its reality. Listen well, my prince." Asura's cheeks were red in the light of the aurora. With each passing moment, another part of the sky was burning.

"The cause of this world's devastation does not originate within this world. Destruction and growth are merely two aspects of change. Even the death of a man is not a true destruction—it is one step in the cycle of re-incarnation. However, the destruction that threatens this world now is the true destruction; it will leave this place unchanging, forever stilled. All the energy of this world will be converted in the end to heat energy, and that will spill out into the universe until perfect equilibrium is reached and heat death arrives."

Asura averted her eyes, as though she were seeing her prediction play out before her. "Brahmā does not heed my warnings. He would claim that the source of this devastation is my army of minions and the violence they represent. And he is welcome to his theories. And yet . . ."

The eerie light of the aurora sent flames up the side of Asura's face. The light seemed to pierce her robes, painting the thin muscles at her shoulders the color of the sky. "He must know of the cakravarti-rājan."

"And what is this cakravarti-rājan of which you speak?"

"The Brahmins can tell you as well as I. He is the King of Kings, the master of karma. He stands without this world, and has viewed its life and growth for more than one trillion years."

"Have you ever met the cakravarti-rājan?"

Asura glanced at the prince, a surprised look on her face. Then she slowly shook her head. "My prince. No one has seen the cakravarti-rājan. Nor do we know where he might be. Yet all who know his name know that, not long from now, the cakravarti-rājan will appear in this world. And when he does he will rule over all as the one great God, the Creator, he who transcends karma."

"But is it not Maitreya who is destined to save humanity in the time of the last dharma?"

The dim flames lighting the distant horizon seemed to spread nearer now, scorching the sky, surging forward like a giant wave. Bands of deeper crimson appeared; then blue rings of light rose again into the sky. The brilliant colors were reflected in Asura's clear eyes.

"My prince, no one knows what Maitreya is in truth. They say that he waits in the Tuṣita Pure Land for the age of the last dharma, yet it is unclear whether he awaits the end of days itself or the salvation of humanity. Which is it? Is Maitreya truly worthy of the hopeful worship that is showered upon him? That is the question that none will answer—that *must* be answered. That is why I raised an army and moved against Brahmā. It is because I believed the fate of our world had been left to hang solely on the existence of Maitreya."

"I had heard it was because of past karma, but I see you had other aims. Why did Brahmā not listen to your words?"

"I do not know, though I suspect—"

"Thought control?"

"Precisely. It seems we agree on one thing at least." Asura crossed her arms and grinned, her white teeth stark against her dark skin.

"I would like to see for myself what Maitreya is," Siddhārtha muttered, his eyes watching the kaleidoscopic sky.

"You would do well to do so, my prince. Even the Brahmin monks have not met Maitreya. Yes . . . find him, and see the truth for yourself."

Siddhārtha stood unsteadily. He detected the faint smell of oil and decay on the icy cold wind that blew across the plain. Turning his back on Asura, he strode away in silence. He hadn't the faintest idea in which direction Tovatsue lay, yet he knew with conviction that so long as he moved forward, his feet would unerringly lead him there.

The icy wind blew at his back, a reminder of the distant montage of battle. Something far away was burning. The curtain of flame in the sky was spreading wider in pulses, its brightness increasing and then retreating, sending new jets of flame in all directions.

"My prince," said Asura, who seemed to be walking alongside him, though he had not seen her approach, "Maitreya is in the center of Tuṣita, in the Pearl Palace. I will lead you there."

"Lead me? Can you even enter Tovatsue?"

"Though the Brahmin may not enter my camp, I can enter all Six Heavens of the Realm of Desire, and all the other heavens besides. They will not see me. And even if they could, they cannot harm me. This is why even Śakra with his Four Heavenly Kings and Eight Generals has been fighting me for four hundred million years and has not won a single victory."

"Why can they not see you? They are no primitives to be so easily deceived."

"They cannot see me because they do not try. It's a form of self-hypnosis—an information processing error. Recognition is merely the re-sult of information processing, you know."

Asura extended her right hand toward the prince's face. A fearsome light blazed in her eyes.

"For example—"

●

The walls of the honeycomb-shaped compartment were slightly warped, as though they had been crushed from above. A forced-air device attached to some kind of humidity controller was malfunctioning, and it gave off a rattling, threatening sound. The muggy air blowing in through the duct carried sand inside, creating a brownish yellow pattern on the walls of the corridor. Metal containers had been stacked along all the walls—most of them were corroded, their doors hanging open, the equip-ment inside covered with thick red rust. Dozens of pipes and electrical lines ran along the high ceiling, and all were coated in a thick layer of dust.

"There is an express lift up ahead. The one with the lit orange sign goes to the control area."

They moved into the corridor. Its floor was layered with a thin car-pet of grayish sand, or perhaps dust, and it sucked at Siddhārtha's feet as he walked. Several lifts were visible, but only two appeared to be opera-tional. The shutter door covering one of them had buckled and ripped like old paper, parts of it falling away to reveal the cavernous depths beyond. Siddhārtha heard the echoing sound of a compressor working somewhere off in the distance.

"Why is no one here?" he asked, peering up and down the long corridor.

"Once, this place and every level above it was filled with citizens. It was a lively city. Clothing, food, shelter—everything was meticulously managed and planned. People here lived to be five hundred years of age on average, and they lived rich lives."

"What happened?"

"I do not know. When we first came to this land, Tovatsue, at least, showed no signs of decay. This was truly the kingdom of the gods that the Brahmin said it was—and many were the men who saw the city in her glory."

"Men? Humans?"

Like a shadow, Asura glided down the corridor. Perhaps she was weightless, for where she stepped she left no marks in the dust.

"In those days, there was a close connection between this place and the world of men. Some of those who came here built the city-states of Sumer and Mohenjo-Daro. The aqueducts and sewers, the paved roads, the centrally controlled lighting, the moving stairs . . . all were built with knowledge obtained here."

"I did not know that any men had traveled to places such as this."

"Have you ever heard of the towers in Egypt they call the pyramids?"

"The *stupas*?"

"You could call them that."

"I heard stories of them from merchants who came from the west. They said they were as large as the hills and mountains."

"The technology used to construct the pyramids was obtained here," Asura said. "They were built using a variety of gravity field generation."

The prince continued on down the corridor, his mind empty, his gaze drifting aimlessly ahead. He could not begin to imagine how Tuṣita was connected to the world of men, but he could understand how, if men came here, it would have a profound influence on their world.

"Get in."

Asura had paused before a lift. Siddhārtha turned and stepped inside the square metal box that served to carry its passengers.

There was a slight vibration and the lift began to move, yet though he knew they were in motion, the prince had no idea whether they were going up or down.

A sudden fear struck his chest, becoming a physical constriction in his throat.

Perhaps I will be stuck in this tiny space for an eternity?

"Asura!" he cried, half choking. His own voice in his ears sounded deadened, like a voice at the bottom of the ocean. "Asura!"

"Yes, my prince?"

Siddhārtha heard a soft, familiar voice behind him.

"You are here!"

Asura stood, back to the metal wall, legs slightly crossed. Her large eyes glimmered mischievously.

"Might we say that man prefers the company of evil to the ache of loneliness?"

The prince hung his head. Sweat mingled with the chagrined tears that ran down his cheeks.

Asura laughed gently. "No worries, my prince. I do not judge you. That is just what Maudgalyayana and that lot would say; pay it no mind."

The lift continued its downward progress. As the two descended through the many levels of Tovatsue, the signs of devastation grew steadily worse. Abandoned compartments stood like dark caves behind countless rusting doors. Though parts of some walls still emitted a greenish luminescence, many sections had gone dark entirely. Others were split by enormous cracks, their tiles askew, fallen to the floor or smashed to dust. Sections of the corridor walls were severely warped and discolored to a sickly yellow hue by what appeared to be fire damage; in some places the damaged walls bulged out into the middle of the passageways, nearly cutting off all travel. Clearly some form of intense heat had hit the corridors from the outside. *Perhaps Asura's attacks penetrated this far.*

Only one section of the ruined city still bustled with activity—a corridor that ran alongside the power lines that stretched up from the nuclear reactor at the bottom of the city, crossing the metropolis at its center. The prince could see a well-illuminated area where it seemed workers had once been housed. He could also hear sounds from within the undamaged corridor—people talking, some kind of work going on. Whoever they were, they seemed strangely separated from the rest of the city down here, like miners stranded deep in a mine.

Siddhārtha wondered if they even knew what was going on outside their walls. And he wondered if human misery was an eternal constant. *Were men fated to live their lives knowing nothing, understanding nothing?*

"Just how large are your armies, Asura?"

Asura lifted an eyebrow at Siddhārtha. "Some say they number sixty million, some say six hundred billion. Whenever one falls it will rise again as two. When two fall, they rise again as four—and we have been fighting Śakra's troops for a very long time, so I've completely lost track of their numbers. Śakra's troops are well trained, well equipped, and eager to provide me with reinforcements in this manner."

The prince thought gloomily about the soldiers' future, wondering how many of them knew their own origin or the meaning or purpose for which they fought, or how long the war would last.

"We are here," Asura announced a moment later. She stopped the lift and pointed toward a large set of doors. There were cracks in the luminescent material that covered the doors, and a pale, silvery metal was visible beneath.

"Here?"

"This leads to the level where Maitreya may be found."

Gingerly, the prince put his hand upon the doors and pushed. They opened inward without a sound. A waterfall of pale blue light spilled down from the high ceiling above. Siddhārtha's shadow stretched across the room. He looked down at the floor and his eyes widened. "Asura! You have no shadow."

"Shadow?"

"Look upon the floor! Only my shadow can be seen."

"My prince, this is because I'm not actually here. I remain upon the battlefield where we first met. From where I stand, I can see the sky above Tovatsue and the blue-ringed explosions of the lithium bombs. The sky-shell over Tovatsue is such that even with the incredible heat generated by the bombs and the radiation, we're having trouble breaking through. It'll take another several thousand, perhaps a million, years before we see real progress. If this is what those monks meant by 'former karma,' they may have been more accurate than I thought." Asura's voice came drifting into the prince's mind like a gentle breeze over a great distance.

He glared at her. "Asura!"

"We'd best continue on, my prince," she said, pointing down the corridor with her chin. "Go see what Maitreya is, and then return to your world at once. You must not forget what you find here—what the faith of your world rests upon."

Then the prince walked for what seemed to be an impossibly long time—hours, days. He grew greatly fatigued.

At last he heard Asura's voice again. "There, through those doors. Maitreya is there."

The corridor ended at a giant pair of doors. They were flat, made of silvery metal without ornamentation, and were several dozen meters in height and width. They closed off the entire end of the enormous corridor.

"How can I possibly open such large doors?" The prince craned his neck to look up at them.

"Do not stop, my prince. Keep walking," Asura said from behind him. His legs carried him forward of their own volition. A numbness crept over his mind, dulling all thought and emotion except the nightmarish fear that began to rise within him.

"Straight ahead! Go!"

The doors were directly in front of him now, filling his sight. He walked steadily, propelled by a mysterious strength, striding directly into the flat metal surface.

For a moment he lost all sensation. For the first time, the prince felt that his own death was near.

●

Is this . . . an ocean?

All around the prince clear, blue light stretched as far as he could see. The light seemed to flow into his body like air into his lungs, swirling inside him.

He heard not a sound. The prince's heart beat faster than he thought possible, and the fear made his breath as ragged and wild as a storm, yet he could not hear the hammering of his heart nor feel the rasping of his breath. He felt nothing.

Everything was wrapped in an eternal silence, as though he'd stepped into the land of the dead.

He moved out into the thin light. It shone through him from the right and left, the front and back, until he became transparent, shadowless.

What is that?

Far off, deep within the pale blue light, he saw a giant shadow.

"Maitreya . . ."

Now he could see the form of a single śramaña far off in the pale sea of light: the future savior, deep in eternal contemplation.

The prince ran without blinking, eyes fixed on that dark shape looming in the void.

So this is Maitreya! At last!

Abruptly Siddhārtha stopped, standing as though turned to stone. Errant thoughts boiled upward in his mind, somehow bursting with a roar in this soundless place.

Maitreya—

The being called Maitreya was seated right there in front of him. His right leg was tucked in above his left knee; he had put his right elbow on it and had leaned forward to rest his cheek upon his upturned hand. His eyes, half lidded, stared out at something beyond space and time. Insurmountable pain played across his brow. He wore a crown shaped like an upturned boat, its top so tall it seemed it could touch the glowing blue of the ceiling.

"Maitreya!"

The prince's voice wavered wildly through the blue expanse. All that he knew of the being before him came flooding into his consciousness.

Maitreya. A Brahmin from the Deccan Plateau in southern India. Through his devotion, he had been reborn in Tuṣita, where he would remain in the Inner Court until the age of the last dharma, 5,670,000,000 years from now, when he would once again be sent to the world of Jambudvīpa, there to be born to a father, Subrahmana, and mother, Brahmavati, and attain Buddhahood in an orchard beneath a Dragon Flower Tree.

The world Maitreya would descend upon would be very different from the world of today. There would be no mountains or valleys, only a flat plain like a mirror. All land would be fertile, and there would be no want of food, nor any need for storage of grains. All men would enjoy a perfect balance of labor and rest. The cities would be lively; there would be no change in the seasons, no harsh summers nor any cold winters. As long life would be assured, all men's thoughts would grow similar—there would be one language and no borders to restrain people from going wherever they wished. In that far-off time, men would live two hundred years, three hundred years, or longer, and be able to travel to the moon and among the stars as they wished.

This was the true promised land, the land of the gods for which mankind had been searching for an eternity. In time, they would call this Heaven. They would call it Paradise.

When Maitreya came down to the world of men, he would save the world by changing its very construction, its nature, so that it was in essence no different from the world of the gods. This was why people looked forward to Maitreya's coming with such eagerness, even across such a long span of time—Maitreya was the promise of the Kingdom of Heaven. It was this one person who inspired the fervent belief that gave the Brahmin monks the power to capture people's hearts. And yet the darker side of that faith, the fact that mankind would have to wait such an impossibly long time for its salvation, was also a reflection of the despair that lurked in the hearts of men.

All of that—the hope and despair, the yearning for a new world—was right here.

"Maitreya!" the prince shouted toward the massive form. "Maitreya!"

There was no answer.

Suddenly, the prince heard laughter in his ears. The sound made his chest quiver as though he were a bow of silver and an archer had drawn him to full; his mind echoed with the noise.

"What are you laughing about, Maitreya? I am Siddhārtha, Prince of the Kingdom of Śākya. I came here to see you, our future savior. I've come all the way to the very root of Tuṣita."

Instantly, the laughter stopped. All was enveloped in deep silence again, a silence more frightening than death.

"Look upon Maitreya, my prince," Asura's voice whispered by his ear. The prince started but stood his ground, staring upward from Maitreya's massive foot.

Suddenly, he felt as though he had made some terrible mistake, though what it was he could not be sure. He peered around him like a frightened child. Something was wrong. He looked back up at Maitreya, the hope gone from his eyes.

It was not a man, but a statue—a giant, silvery statue, marred here and there by ugly gouts of rust. The statue sat silent as a mountain by the edge of the sea of pale blue light.

"Well, my prince? This is a statue of Maitreya. A statue of the great being who will come down to the world of men in 5,670,000,000 years to save us all." Asura spoke in a singsong voice, mocking the prince's faith.

The prince turned, slowly, as though he had suddenly aged another twenty or thirty years, and looked at her. "Where did Maitreya go?"

Asura shook her head. Her necklace gave a little death rattle across the slender, girlish lines of her neck.

"Where did Maitreya go?" the prince muttered, pressing his hand to his head. He had a splitting headache; cold sweat dripped down his back and chest.

"To tell the truth," Asura said suddenly, "no one knows what the statue represents. The Brahmins gave it the name Maitreya. My prince, it was the men who came to play here in Tuṣita who made up that story about a god who would come to save them in the far future."

"That is too cruel. Everyone believes in the coming of Maitreya. It cannot be a lie . . ." he said, his voice trailing off into a hoarse whisper.

"My prince, look again upon the statue. This giant statue was built to an exact likeness."

"An exact likeness? So there truly is a Maitreya, then?"

Asura shrugged her shoulders and stepped in front of the prince, staring deep into his eyes. The breath that passed her ruby lips carried with it a fragrance of flowers, and it brought him back to his senses. "Asura! Which is it?"

"Have you understood, my prince? Do you know whose statue that is? Not even Brahmā, ruler of this world, does. The great god after whom that statue was modeled was a resident from another world who visited this region and claimed it for his own. This world is to be ruled from without, you see. Five billion six hundred seventy million years from now, he will once again appear in this world and determine the fate of all who remain here. *That* is what they call Maitreya."

"What of salvation? What of salvation in the time of the last dharma?" The prince shook with rage. It was too cruel. The truth was the exact opposite of everything for which mankind was waiting.

"Let us go, my prince. We can stare at the statue all we like, but no salvation will come of it. Do not worry. You can be like Brahmā and still believe if you want to. It's all right. This god will visit Jambudvīpa, your world, at the appointed hour. He will be born to a mother, Brahmavati, and a father, Subrahmana. That is all true. But what will Maitreya do in your world when he comes?

"Brahmā did not listen to my warnings. I doubt you will accept the reality of the situation either. The sutra that the Brahmin like to read about Maitreya and Tuṣita tells a compelling story. One always likes to hear about paradise. What would you give to secure that paradise, I wonder? Your wisdom? Your life? Your heart? There is still time. Plenty of time to think, my prince."

Asura's voice grew increasingly distant and faint.

The dry, barren sea of sand spread beneath a dark sky. The scattered remnants of life and the fragmented ruins of buildings visible in all directions were ample proof that nothing lived here anymore.

●

"Prince Siddhārtha?"

Asura stood, the flickering aurora at her back.

"There's one more thing I wish to ask you."

Asura stared intently into the night. "I think I can guess."

The prince looked around and saw a giant, fiery orange sphere rising massively toward the top of the sky. Its brilliance scorched the night, vaporizing a vast expanse of sand below. A wave of heat and radiation moved across the plain like a tsunami, leaving nothing in its wake.

"You want to ask why I still fight with Brahmā, my prince?"

Strangely shaped ships cut silently across the arc of night, appearing from the darkness of one horizon, vanishing into the darkness of the other.

"My prince, as the Brahmin tell it, I was spurred to invade this Tuṣita by past karma and have been fighting Śakra's armies for some four hundred million years. Past karma, my prince. Have you thought about what that might mean? How did this past karma come about in the first place?"

Brilliant flashes of light erupted from the horizon where the strange ships had disappeared. Siddhārtha had no idea what form Asura's armies might take, but he imagined that the armada of ships in the sky might well be part of them.

"We will meet another day, my prince. You should go. The Brahmins will be worried."

Siddhārtha thought he should say some word of farewell to the beautiful girl, but no words came to mind. And he felt certain that Asura was right—they *would* meet again, some day far in the future.

The prince put his hands together and bowed to Asura, then silently turned and began to walk away. After he had gone a short distance, he turned to look back and found that she, the flickering aurora, and the brilliant lights that cut across the sky were all gone without a trace.

An icy wind blew from the empty dark.

Was it all an illusion?

The prince stared long into the darkness, trying to see beyond it. The image of that girl who could not possibly be Asura, and yet who was Asura beyond a shadow of a doubt, was forever burned like a brand into his heart.

In the beginning was the Word.
And the Word was with God.
And the Word was God.

T he large scallop shells hanging in the corner of the room rattled like dry bones as the air stirred.

"Come in," Pontius Pilate called out as he tossed his writing quill down on the desk.

What a grating racket those shells make, he thought. *I'll have to have them replaced.* They had hung from his ceiling ever since a merchant from the East had given them to him as a gift many years before—and Pilate had hated them for almost as long.

A hand brushed aside the curtain in the doorway and his advisor, Ceint, entered, catching his breath. "Prefect!" he huffed.

"What is it, Ceint? I don't think I've seen you looking so agitated in my life."

"Well, it was *most* unexpected," the advisor grumbled, brushing back his cape and folding his thick arms across his chest.

"What was?" Pilate leaned forward.

"That carpenter fellow, Jesus of Nazareth—Yeshua, the locals call him. He's come to Jerusalem."

"Made his move at last, has he? That complicates matters." The wrinkles deepened on Pilate's brow. The carpenter from Nazareth had already been giving him headaches for the past four or five days; he could only imagine what it would be like now that the man was sharing the same city.

"What about the Jewish priests—what do the *kohanim* have to say about all this?"

If there was anything that gave Pilate bigger headaches than prophet carpenters, it was the kohanim.

"Plenty. They've been gathering in the courtyard in front of the hall since a short while ago."

Pilate cursed under his breath and looked in the direction of the courtyard—though several walls stood between it and his quarters. The white petals of a large dragon-tongue orchid that sat in the window swayed in the breeze.

"Well? Drive them off, Ceint!"

His advisor frowned uneasily. "Er . . . I'm afraid that if we ignore the kohanim's feelings on this matter we'll pay dearly for it later." Ceint knew as well as Pilate that governing Israel without the support of the priesthood would be an exercise in futility. It was his acceptance of this fact that made him such a valuable advisor. "Which is to say," he continued, "it's almost tax collection time, and their requests for exemption grow louder with each year."

This Pilate knew without being told. The Jewish clergy's tax payments accounted for a good four tenths of his entire income from the Roman territories of Israel. It was one of his most important duties as Prefect of Jerusalem and representative of Rome in Israel to badger the kohanim into coughing up a portion of the coin they received from their congregations.

Ceint was warming to his topic. "Prefect, the missteps of the Roman empire in recent years have made it very difficult to administer these provincial territories. Even the proud Roman army is mostly made up of foreign mercenaries these days. Should the unthinkable happen and an uprising against the Empire take place here in Israel, I do not think we can expect much support from the homeland. We must keep that in mind when dealing with the locals."

This too, Pilate knew, and the knowledge gnawed at him. Just as the midday sun begins to descend toward the western horizon the moment it reaches its zenith, the Roman Empire had begun to weaken year by year, almost imperceptibly, yet with undeniable certainty. The word had passed from mouth to mouth in the markets, dispersing in every direction on the lips of Jewish pilgrims, until every scruffy-headed street urchin in the province knew it for a fact. This knowlege gave the kohanim more influence and made it easier for them to be openly defiant of Rome and her representative.

"Prefect!" someone shouted from outside the room.

"What's that now?"

Ceint went out to check.

Pilate heard his advisor and another man speaking intently outside. His head felt heavy. They had thrown a banquet the night before for Tethias, the head of the Roman garrison in Jerusalem, and it had left him exhausted. Tethias was a famous lover of alcohol, and the wine they had served, made from some grain grown in lands to the east, was heady stuff. The morning light had already begun painting stripes of light across the dusty cobblestones of Jerusalem's inner streets when Tethias's men had helped the inebriated prefect back to his quarters.

"Macillus!" he called. "Where's Macillus?"

The door in the rear opened and the prefect's servant came sidling out. "Yes, Master?"

"There you are, Macillus. I require a bath."

"Very good, Prefect."

Macillus shuffled from the room, his belt of silver chains clinking across his wine-colored sheepskin tunic.

Ceint came hurrying back in. "Prefect?"

"What is it now?"

"Simon has come with a request from the kohanim."

"So? What do they want this time?"

Ceint leaned in closer. Pilate caught a whiff of scented oil.

"They want you to arrest Jesus and hand him over to the Sanhedrin . . . or execute him yourself."

"What? Since when do the kohanim give orders to the representative of Rome?" He spat. "Fine. If it's blood they want, then it's blood they'll get!"

Pontius Pilate picked up the longsword that rested behind his chair and strode out of the room, his face flushed with anger.

Ceint yelped. "Wait, Prefect, wait!" He scurried to stand in front of his chief, holding out both hands in desperation. "You must wait!"

Pilate paused, his jaw twitching with the embarrassment of being manipulated by the kohanim. How could one rule a people if you were forever frightened of angering them?

"Prefect! Er, I was thinking—what if we gave this Jesus a summons instead? It would look better than arresting him. After all, he has committed no crime.

"If necessary," Ceint continued in that way he had of stating things so evenly that one might take them to mean whatever one wished, "I could do the questioning myself."

Pilate considered. If they served this "prophet" with a summons now, they would always be able to jail him afterward under the pretext of incivility toward a Roman agent.

"Not a terrible idea," the prefect admitted with a sigh. In truth, it was a great annoyance to him to have to question and try heretics. Prolocutors of faith had a way with words, but they always seemed to lack a basic grasp on logic—and yet pointing out their errors never seemed to have any effect, much to Pilate's consternation.

"Perhaps, Prefect," Ceint continued, sensing his master's hesitation, "we should have a look at this Jesus fellow first. I will be happy to join you. We can watch him anonymously, then decide his fate."

If they did so, Pilate knew, Ceint would be sure to slowly win him over to his way of thinking. But the realization did not upset him. It was often the case that Ceint's stated plans were what the prefect had been unconsciously planning anyway—another reason that he was such a good and loyal advisor.

"Right. Let's go see for ourselves what all the fuss is about."

Pilate returned his longsword to its customary place behind the chair and stuck his head into the gallery behind the office.

"We're going out."

Pontius Pilate mounted his horse and Ceint walked beside him. Several guardsmen completed the entourage, one holding the horse's bridle, the others bearing spears.

"Where do you think he is?"

"Preaching in the Plaza of the Dead, most likely."

"He's popular?"

Ceint looked up at Pilate with a frown. "Quite popular, strangely enough."

"He'd have to be to get the kohanim so riled up."

Ceint pulled his long robes more tightly around his body. "He came into Jerusalem last night. I hear he was proselytizing out to the west, saying something about receiving a revelation from God."

Pilate squinted—a habit of his whenever he was particularly wary about something. "How have people been responding?"

"Apparently, many in the city knew of his imminent arrival half a month ago. Some disciples of his, a group of twelve or so from what I hear, came to the city ahead of time to do some publicity."

"Aggressive, aren't they?"

"He's calling his arrival 'The Entry into Jerusalem,'" Ceint said with evident derision.

"Fancies himself some sort of great religious leader, then?"

Ceint nodded. "This is what has gotten the Jewish priesthood so, as you say, *riled up*."

If the man was as big a braggart as it sounded, Pilate thought the kohanim probably had the right of it. This carpenter turned preacher was a fool, and worse, a popular fool.

The entourage made its way down the cobblestone streets, turning into the arcade that led toward the Plaza of the Dead. The merchants there, who had spread their wares so thickly upon the street as to block all but a narrow stream of foot traffic, panicked at the sudden arrival of the Romans and hurriedly gathered their wares and took shelter beneath the eaves of the houses. One who was late in pulling up his blanket received a whack on the back from the haft of one of the guards' spears.

It was then that a bundle of greens tied with a hempen cord flew out of the crowd and struck Pontius Pilate directly in the chest. Pilate's face went red, but before he could react further, Ceint stepped to the leader of the guards and whispered an order in his ear. The guard captain took three of his men and plunged into the milling crowd. The two remaining pointed the tips of their long spears toward the throng that had gathered around the horse.

"Prefect, they have caught the man responsible."

Pilate looked to see his guardsmen dragging a young man out of the crowd by both arms. The man was wailing something, a look of torrid fear upon his face. An old woman clung to his shirttail and howled. It was hard to see her clearly in the dim light of the stone arcade, but her despairing cries were clearly audible above the noise of the onlookers.

Ceint strode over to the captive. He said something to the guard captain, who pointed the gleaming tip of his spear at the young man's chest. The unexpected silence that came over the crowd in that instant planted a sudden black fear in Pilate's heart.

The guard captain tensed his muscular arms. In a moment, the spear would surely pierce the captive's chest.

"Wait!"

A sharp and yet oddly calm voice sounded from amidst the crowd behind Pilate's horse.

"What?"

The Roman prefect turned his horse around to look.

A lone man stood in the middle of the street.

His face was gaunt, framed by a long beard and long hair that was gray with ash. His eyes gave off a piercing light. He held a gnarled stick of wood in his right hand as a walking staff.

"Will you not spare the life of this young man? Lord Pontius Pilate, great emissary of Rome, humbly, I beg your pity," the man said with a reverent bow. His face and body were soiled and his bearing no better than a slave's, yet something in his manner struck Pilate as earnestly noble.

"And who might you be?"

The man lifted his face. The clear look in his eyes made Pilate swallow despite himself.

"I am Peter, one of the twelve apostles of Jesus Christ, son of the

Almighty . . . He whom you call 'Zeus,' our Father and Lord in Heaven."

Pilate gritted his teeth. He couldn't have met a worse person at a worse time. "Are you aware that this young man threw a bundle of filthy leaves at my person?"

"Lord Prefect, are these green leaves that were thrown to you not a token of God's blessing upon this very land of Israel which you govern? It is God, after all, who has given us these life-sustaining grains and vegetables. God's love be praised!"

Peter intertwined the fingers of his hands and knelt upon the cobblestones in supplication. The members of the crowd mimicked his actions, falling to their knees and bowing to Pilate atop his horse.

"May God grant his blessings to this young man, and may He grant His love which is higher than the blue sky above us and deeper than the sea to Lord Pontius Pilate, representative of Rome. Amen." Peter's resonant voice lifted above the heads of the crowd.

Pilate despaired. The bowing, praying throng completely outdid any display of authority he might have hoped to make. As it stood in that crowded street, Rome was losing much, while the poor people of Jerusalem had lost nothing—even when many of them would have been better off dead than live the way they did.

"Release him, Ceint."

A look of defeat came over the advisor's face.

"I *said* release him."

Ceint whispered to the guard captain. Abruptly the burly soldier let go of the young man's arm and thrust him away. The freed man stumbled backward into the crowd of bowing onlookers, where the sobbing old woman, near-delusional with relief, embraced and clung to him.

A moment later a cry went up from the crowd—a victory cheer.

"Let's go."

Pilate took his whip to his horse, flying over the stones of the arcade. All he could see around him were omens of Rome's decline.

●

They did not speak of the incident until after they had stopped to calm their nerves with some refreshment. Then, as Pilate was climbing back onto his steed, Ceint drew close. "Prefect," he said. "I am increasingly of the opinion that we should arrest this carpenter when we find him."

Pilate frowned. "As representative of Rome, I really don't want to get involved in local troubles. The Jews can do whatever they want—they can even start a new religion. It makes no difference to the Empire."

Ceint shook his head.

"Ceint, as you know, it is the foremost duty of the prefect in Jerusalem to collect taxes from the land and send them back home. Next, I am to protect those Romans who work here from banditry and ensure a modicum of peace and order. Lastly, I am to ensure that the roads leading from Rome to this province are always kept in proper condition so as not to hinder the movement of our armies. These three things are expected of me. Beyond this, the representative of Rome has no business interfering in local affairs."

The administration of Rome's colonies had always hung on these three requirements. The Romans had never considered the vast territories that they held to be part of their own native soil—they thought of the provinces as barbarous lands belonging to uncivilized peoples. They had no desire to claim them as second homelands, nor did they invest much capital into developing the regions. Such was the Roman way of thinking, and it had succeeded in making a giant orphan out of Rome.

"*Pax Romana!*" the people shouted, yet in the echo of their voices, Pilate could hear the sound of an empire crumbling.

"Lord Prefect. Will you be returning to your quarters?" Ceint asked, his voice betraying a hint of mockery.

"Not yet. Let's have a look at this man they call Jesus. Show me the way."

Ceint prodded the shoulder of the servant who held the reins of Pilate's horse.

The entourage proceeded down a crooked backstreet paved with bricks of fired clay. Tiny rooms were packed like crates along both sides of the narrow way, each providing living quarters for an entire family. In these cramped stone spaces, the inhabitants had laid out rugs of woven hemp and hung curtains to shelter themselves from the street. The rugs and curtains were so dirty and tattered that it was impossible to tell their weaves or patterns, and they spilled out over the bricks, occasionally catching the feet of people as they passed.

The air smelled like stewing vegetables and sweat. The clouds of flies were inescapable, and the swarms of children seemed equally numerous. Such were the backstreets of Jerusalem.

It was no wonder that the perfumes favored by the nobles of Rome had always been greatly coveted in the provinces. In the beginning, all Roman emissaries were members of the military, and they had spent their days eating the same food and breathing the same air as the dusty, sweaty locals. Their wives and daughters likewise spent their hours in the grime and sweat. Fresh water was a valuable commodity in the provincial cities; bathing was a rare luxury. Later emissaries had established a greater distance between themselves and the local populace, but there was nothing they could do about the living conditions—thus the high level of interest in perfumes. For those who live a wholesome life in a clean environment there is little need for masking fragrances.

The great baths of Rome and the fine quality of its perfumes might be a testament to the unsanitary conditions of Roman life—but they were also a sophisticated comfort unavailable to the provincial servants of the Empire.

"Two more years," Pilate muttered. That was all he had left in his term as Prefect of Israel. He had been living here for three years already.

"Yes?" Ceint looked up from beside his horse, lifting an eyebrow.

"Never mind."

Pilate wanted nothing more than to serve his last two years without incident.

After they passed through the brick arcade with its dust and its flies and its cacophony of voices, they emerged quite abruptly into a large circular plaza that seemed comparatively empty—though there were still a large number of citizens bustling about in the course of their daily activities. In the very middle of the open space stood an ancient royal poinciana with bright crimson flowers, looking like a pillar of flame. Pilate held up a hand to shade his eyes from the sun.

Ceint stopped in his tracks. "There. Over there."

"Where?" Pilate followed his advisor's gaze.

Ceint was staring with great intensity into a corner of the plaza. There, beyond the giant tree with its fiery petals, a dozen or so people were gathered near a wall of stone. Some members of the small crowd stood, some sat, others lay sprawled upon the ground, but all were looking upward at a lone figure standing atop the wall.

Pilate advanced his horse slowly. No fewer than twenty different streets opened into this plaza; it was a central meeting place and crossroads for this part of the city. Now the movements of the merchants going to and fro, the beggars along the edges of the streets, and the town officials surrounded by weary travelers struck Pilate with a strange sort of uniformity, like the movements of actors upon a stage. It seemed that the Romans' sudden arrival at the plaza was spreading a very tangible ripple through the crowd. In the middle of the hubbub, the group standing beyond the poinciana seemed eerily quiet.

Fragments of garbled speech, thick with the accent of Galilee, reached the prefect's ears.

"No matter how much man possesses, no Kingdom of God will he build . . ."

". . . makes this . . ."

". . . man must look back upon the deeds of the day . . ."

". . . that is our Lord in Heaven, Jehovah . . ."

". . . Jehovah will judge . . ."

". . . and when He decides that yes, it is good, only then will . . ."

The man atop the wall looked like a farmer. He wore a grimy hempen robe sewn together at the sides like a monk's—probably a gift from some Roman—and garlands on his feet in place of sandals.

"Jesus, carpenter of Nazareth," Ceint whispered.

Drops of sweat gathered in the man's sunken cheeks while his small eyes darted around, taking in the citizens gathered before him.

"It will come. Don't forget it. That is—ah, that is to say . . ."

An old man hunched over at the foot of the wall lifted his face and said in a clear voice, "The Final Judgment, my lord."

"That's it! That's right! The Final Judgment is what it is! Oh, and it is a truly frightening thing! Jehovah, our Lord in Heaven, will look at every one of our sins . . ."

Pilate strained to hear the words over the bustle of the plaza.

". . . to the Kingdom of God. Those who are left will be burned in Jehovah's fire, charred . . ."

". . . which is why we must all make haste to . . ."

A breathy collective sigh emerged from the small crowd of listeners. Pilate frowned. To these poor, simple people of Jerusalem, the image of a final judgment at the hands of God should have been a nightmare vision of their own deaths. *Why are they so enthralled?*

"That's why everyone has to pray to God. You get it? And praying isn't about saying you want God to do this or do that. You have to make yourself ready! If you're a drunk, stop drinking. If you are a gambler, stop gambling. Just for one day. And on that day . . ."

There was something about the man's crude Galilean accent that perfectly matched the tone of his words. Pilate had to admit that the man's voice was imbued with a certain unique passion, a strange intensity that was altogether unfamiliar to him.

Pilate urged his horse forward until he had reached the edge of the carpenter's audience. He gazed over the heads of the listeners at the man who addressed them.

"Are you Jesus of Nazareth?" he asked, deliberately keeping his voice as low as it could be and still be heard. As one the crowd turned. Several grew pale and began edging their way toward the nearest alley.

"There is no need for flight," Pilate urged. "I'm merely asking a question."

Yet as the silence lengthened the audience gradually dispersed until only the man on the wall and the older man hunched before him remained.

"Are you Jesus of Nazareth?" Pilate asked again.

"The prefect asks a question. You should answer," Ceint declared loudly, hand on the hilt of his short sword.

"Yes. I am Jesus Christ, son of Jehovah our Lord in Heaven."

"Hmph." Pilate raised an eyebrow. "Okay. What about you, old man? We've met before."

The old man got to his feet and bowed curtly. "I am Peter, one of the twelve apostles of Jesus Christ, son of Jehovah, our Lord in Heaven."

"I see."

Pontius Pilate sat atop his horse, wondering how this "apostle" had gotten here so fast, and wondering what he should say next. There was nothing in what the man was saying about God that should concern an emissary of Rome or require his intervention. He had seen several Jewish sects of this kind spring up lately. That is, they purported to be sects, even though they rarely displayed any original thought or had anything new to say. Most were led by provincial priests who had been barred from joining the kohanim and so sought another way to make a name for themselves by proselytizing on their own.

So why are the kohanim so upset about this man? He barely seems capable of drawing a crowd, even here in Jerusalem. Not to mention that from the look of the rags he's wearing, he doesn't have many supporters. Is that blood on his feet?

Ceint moved closer to the wall. "Carpenter of Nazareth who calls himself Jesus! What is your true name? There are plenty of Christs around, but few Jesuses. I've heard the people here call you Yeshua?"

"That is my name. I am Yeshua of Nazareth."

"Good official," spoke Peter, "it is in truth his name. In the land of Nazareth, there are many with the name of Yeshua."

"Are there now?"

"What's troubling you, Ceint?" Pilate asked quietly, knowing full well what his advisor was about. He was seeking to turn this chance encounter with Jesus of Nazareth into a pretext for taking the man into custody.

"Ceint?"

"Prefect—the people of the town are watching. The supporters of the kohanim are among them. We must be wary."

Pilate glanced at the plaza behind them. Where it had appeared only sparsely populated before, it now seemed unexpectedly crowded—as if every citizen who lived off every side street that opened into the plaza had suddenly decided to put in an appearance. Fully half of the broad space was packed with people, all standing in utter silence, intently watching the discussion between Pilate and the shoddy-looking preacher.

"Jesus of Nazareth. Tell me, this 'final judgment' of which you were speaking—"

"Is something the matter?"

"Yes, something is the matter! Where did you hear such nonsense?"

"It is not nonsense. Good official, are you a follower of the Jewish faith?"

Ceint smiled a cool smile. "The Romans have no religion. At least nothing like the kind of 'faith' your lot goes on about."

"That is because your spirit has withered."

"Excuse me?"

"The Romans pilfer the gods of the Greeks and call themselves pious!" The preacher's voice grew suddenly louder. "There is only one true God. No 'god of the sun,' or 'goddess of the moon,' or 'god of lightning,' or 'god of the sea.' So many gods and they all mean nothing!"

The outburst left the loquacious Ceint tongue-tied. While most Romans understood that the gods were to be feared, they were also inclined to treat them as a kind of game, often evoked for little more than entertainment. Romans knew little of hardship; they had managed to cope rather well with the challenges and sorrows of their world, and they saw very little need for a savior in the true sense of the word. The gods of the Romans cast light shadows on the empire. In truth, for most they were little more than seasoning to add a touch of gravitas to the citizens' daily lives.

This conversation had been doomed from the start. The carpenter-turned-preacher spoke from a spiritual height that the pragmatic Ceint could not fathom.

Pilate leaned forward on his horse. "I'll admit that the concept of a final judgment is an interesting one," he said, his tone that of an instructor reprimanding an impertinent pupil. "Yet will the ignorant people not fear you for your dire predictions? It does not seem the best way to gain followers. There are a lot of men popping up these days saying very similar things, you know. They talk about how the gods will judge us, and how those with evil hearts will be burned with fire."

"But it's true. I saw it," Jesus said.

"That's what they all say," Ceint spat, unable to restrain himself any longer. "Every one of them. *I* saw it. It was *me*. Me me me. The sun lost its light, the moon and stars fled, and in the eternal darkness that followed the great God in Heaven appeared, ripping the void in two, and cast a shining spear down upon the sullied land. And where the spear falls it rends the land, molten rock spews forth like a fountain, the seas rise up and sweep the land clean, all life perishes . . . blah, blah, blah."

"Ceint," Pilate interjected, a sadness in his voice, "there's no need to take this man back to the guardhouse. Tell the kohanim they have nothing to fear."

"But, Prefect!" Ceint whispered urgently. "Should we not first take him back with us? We can release him later if we feel it is the right thing to do. If we simply let him go now, it will seem to the crowd that the representative of Rome challenged him and lost."

Pilate sighed. *At least I tried.* "All right, do it."

Ceint motioned with his eyes to the captain of the guards. Within moments the prefect's bodyguard pulled the man from Nazareth down from the wall. They held him roughly, pinioned by both arms.

"Ow! That hurts!" the carpenter yelped. "There's no need for such violence. I'll go peacefully."

"What about the old one?" Ceint demanded.

"I don't care about him. Let him go."

After a moment's hesitation, Pilate's advisor thrust the apostle Peter aside with a sour look.

"Time to leave."

With Pontius Pilate at its head, the Roman entourage led Jesus from the plaza. The prefect hurried them along, eager to get away from the growing throng.

The crowd that gathered now around the fiery poinciana watched the Romans' departure in silence, faces dark with betrayal, brows creased with a nameless yearning.

What the prophet says is true.

Surely the Kingdom of God will appear before us, a beautiful, ideal land. What need have we of harsh rules and privations, and petitioning our masters for forgiveness?

God forgives. Jehovah takes pity on mankind and forgives us all our sins. We must pray to Him.

Only those who truly let God into their hearts may reach the kingdom of Heaven. God is absolutely fair. God's heart is big enough to hold our entire world many times over . . .

Such was the God that the people wanted. They dreamed of the glory and the blessing of the Kingdom of God that would come one day to relieve them of their endless toil, their sickness and their poverty.

And yet, the carpenter of Nazareth had miscalculated.

"You know, I'd rather drink then get picked up by some God when the Final Judgment comes."

"When is this final day coming anyway?"

"Sometime, according to what he says."

"So when is sometime?"

"How should I know? Probably not while we're still alive."

"Then what's the point?"

"Maybe if we live our lives right and pray to God, our children or their children will be saved at the time of the judgment?"

"Well, I don't have any kids, so who cares?"

The crowd muttered and began to disperse, flowing back into the alleyways and arcades like a receding tide, leaving the flowers of the poinciana to flutter by themselves like lonely flames. Peter, the wizened disciple, had also vanished. Most of the citizens of Jerusalem had already forgotten about the man who was taken away—most would never again think on what had happened in the plaza that day or remember the man who called himself a carpenter of Nazareth.

When the kohanim heard that Pontius Pilate had taken Jesus of Nazareth into custody they were greatly pleased. This representative of Rome had never shown much promise before, but the latest turn of events was worthy of attention. With time, the kohanim decided, they might even be moved to reassess their views on the prefect. Future potential aside, it was an excellent sign that this man of Rome could be dealt with.

The next morning, before the sun had risen, a crowd of men in long black clerical robes had gathered in the stone-tiled courtyard of Pontius Pilate's villa. The harsh criticisms they had muttered on the day before were gone, replaced by an intense interest in the sentencing of Jesus.

The sun was already well into the sky when Pilate left his bedroom. He spent a long time straightening his hair, clipping the nails on his hands and feet, and arranging his new toga, before he finally made his way toward the annex where his official offices were located. A band of merchants from the

East had collected on the cobblestones beneath the hall that connected the main villa to the annex. Pontius Pilate recalled the amount of gold he had received from them the night before as a fee for permission to set up their markets here in Jerusalem. A great deal of that gold was destined for his own personal coffers. With that in mind, the prospect of Jesus's trial—which would probably take up most of his afternoon—didn't seem quite so onerous.

●

In the court adjacent to Pilate's offices, six judges under the direct employ of Rome sat in tall chairs along the wall. Across from the judges sat four priests, representatives of the kohanim who were there both as observers and as the plaintiffs. When the prefect arrived, the kohanim were huddled together as they discussed something in low voices.

Pilate sat languidly upon his sofa, which was covered with the thick mane of a mountain lion.

Immediately High Judge Achaioi stood beside him and proclaimed, "Hereby begins the trial of Jesus of Nazareth in the name of Pontius Pilate, Prefect of Jerusalem and representative of Rome in Israel."

"All right, let's begin," Pilate said, nodding to Achaioi. He accepted a cup of milk tea from a servant who stood in attendance behind the sofa.

"Bring Jesus forth." Achaioi signaled to a guard standing in one corner of the room. The guard went outside, his chain-mail hauberk rattling, and returned immediately with the man they had taken into custody in the Plaza of the Dead the day before. Silently the guard brought the prisoner into the center of the chamber and then held him steady there with the butt of his short spear on the man's shoulder.

"Back to your place."

The guard nodded and returned to his corner.

Jesus blinked several times and looked around the chamber nervously with bloodshot eyes. He looked as if he hadn't slept the night before.

Achaioi began to read the allegations, the grim words persisting in the heavy air until their weight seemed tangibly to press against the captive's back, pushing him toward his fate.

Pilate sipped his milk tea—it was pleasantly, mildly bitter—and withstood the long boredom. Occasional sharp calls could be heard through the open window from the street outside—the shouts of the Roman guards stationed at the prefect's villa, practicing their formations for battle. The cries seemed oddly erratic, continuing, fading, then erupting again as soon as he thought they had finally ceased. "My officers have been lacking in spirit lately," Pilate muttered from behind his bowl.

"Prefect?"

Achaioi was leaning over Pilate. He had apparently been addressing the prefect for some time. Pilate snapped back into the present and quickly handed his bowl off to his servant. He did not need to hear the judge again. Achaioi was asking him whether he, as representative of Rome, had any questions for the accused. What that meant was that the long explanation of charges was finished, and the trial was finally moving to its conclusion.

Pilate had been gradually sinking into his sofa until he was half buried in furs. Now he sat up and addressed the prisoner.

"I have but one question."

The man from Nazareth stood in the center of the courtyard, staring in Pilate's direction. His face betrayed no emotion.

"Jesus. This 'end of the world' of which you speak—exactly when will it occur?"

The carpenter leaned forward, a sudden passion kindled inside him. "You mean the Final Judgment?"

There is a certain imbecility behind his earnestness, thought Pilate.

"Yes. This judgment of God you like to talk about."

Jesus nodded several times, his face flushed, like a young boy who is asked a question regarding his favorite subject.

"Ah yes, that!"

"Yes, that. What else could I be asking about?"

"It is not clear exactly when it will come, but it will come soon."

"Soon?"

"Yes, that's right."

The accused shut his mouth with finality, as though he had said all that needed to be said on the subject. He was the star student again, eagerly awaiting the next question.

"And?" Pilate asked with the faintest of sighs. "What do you think we should do to get ready for this end of days?"

"Well, I think everyone, including me of course, should prepare their hearts to be judged by God."

"How exactly should we prepare?"

"Prepare for what?"

"Prepare to be judged by God!"

"Well, pray to Him with a pure heart. Pray and follow Him." Then he added in a deeper voice, half as though he were admonishing himself, "And we must repent, yes. That is the way to true prayer."

"What am I supposed to make of that? It's too vague, what you're saying. That's why people accuse you of things, you know."

Ceint, on Pilate's left, discreetly nudged the prefect's arm. One of the judges stood from his tall chair, faced Pilate, and bowed.

"Proceed." Pilate yielded the floor and sank back into his sofa.

"Jesus of Nazareth!" Jesus turned to face the judge. "I've heard that you call yourself the Messiah."

"I am the Messiah. People call me a prophet, but they're wrong. I'm no prophet. Prophets speak of life and death and destinies that stretch into an unseen tomorrow, but I do not do these things. I save people. I free them from their sins."

Another of the judges stood. "And you claim you will atone for the sins of all people before God in Heaven?"

"Indeed I will. I am the Messiah. I am the Son of God. That is why I will atone in anticipation of the Final Judgment that will come before long. In your stead, I will do penance for all your sins."

The carpenter's thick, pallid lips moved quickly, as though he were discussing a glorious plan for future entertainment. Spittle flew from the corner of his mouth.

"I have no desire for you to take on my sins, Jesus of Nazareth. I just want to know whence comes your confidence in claiming that you are the Messiah. I've heard you can perform miracles?"

There was a titter of laughter among the kohanim.

"The Messiah will appear as a servant to all men," Jesus said, his eyes now fixed on a point in space somewhere above the judges, as though he were reciting from memory. "He will bear mankind's sins and suffer upon the cross, offering himself up to appease God's anger. Thus will my soul act as a guide, leading all men to the Kingdom of Heaven."

"Jesus!" Ceint spoke suddenly. "Who told you that?"

Jesus blanched. "Who told me?"

"Yes, who told you? Don't tell me you heard it directly from God himself?"

"The prophet John."

Ceint lifted an eyebrow. "John? The one King Herod Antipas executed in Balqa?"

The man shook his head. "No, he's not dead. John cannot die."

Ceint smirked. "Why ever not?"

"Because he's friends with the Archangel Michael. He even introduced me. Though I only offered my greetings from a distance." The prisoner's voice was soft with chagrin.

The poor fellow wanted a closer look at the angel, Pilate thought, before realizing how ridiculous the story was, and how foolhardy.

Ceint tensed for a moment. "Are you saying you met the Archangel Michael?"

"Yes."

The kohanim stood one after the other, black rage mounting in their faces. Their murmurs of fury were audible across the chamber.

"Silence!" Ceint's voice cut through the air like a blade. He fixed the prisoner with a piercing stare. "Where? Where did you meet Michael?"

Jesus cast his eyes over toward the kohanim, then back to Ceint. "In the Jordan Valley. He came down from Heaven." He lifted a finger on his right hand, pointing upward. For a moment, the face of the Nazarene was transformed entirely, filled with an unshakeable, ironclad confidence. His profile was as rough as if it had been hastily carven with a chisel, his eyes intoxicated and wild as briars. "Yes, I saw him," he said. "I saw him!" He began to pace before the representatives of Rome, muttering loudly.

"There's not much time left," he continued. "It's just a feeling I have. The Kingdom of God may well be at hand! The Kingdom of God, the Kingdom of God, the Kingdom of God—"

He put his hands to his head as though he were searching through murky memories for some clue.

"Only those who have received the permission of God may enter God's kingdom. Heaven's gates are very wide, but how many will be able to enter? His judgment is harsh—so harsh." Jesus spoke in a monotone, as though relaying someone else's words.

"What was that?"

"Stake him to the cross!" the kohanim shouted, their whiskers bristling with outrage.

"Death to the fool who does not fear God!"

"Death, death!"

"Prefect. Order this man to his death. The worst death possible!"

Pilate grabbed the glorious silk cape that hung over his shoulders and used it to wipe the sweat from his forehead.

"Your orders, Prefect?" Ceint asked, kneeling beside the sofa. Pilate crossed his arms and frowned.

"Death to him!" The echoing voices of the kohanim hit Pilate's chest like a physical blow.

He stared at the man from Nazareth.

It would be so easy to give the kohanim what they wanted. He could think up any reason he required. This man might in fact be blameless, yet what did it matter? This was nothing more than a provincial squabble.

"Shall we return Jesus to his cell, Prefect?" Ceint asked softly, trying to read his master's mind. They had resolved several similar incidents in the past by returning the accused to his cell and there ending his life by poison or assassination. Death by "illness" in prison had a way of stifling trouble before it started.

"Do you think that will satisfy the kohanim?" Pilate had already accepted the fact that the carpenter-turned-preacher would not be returning to the streets of Jerusalem alive. He scowled bitterly. "We could have let him go if he hadn't gone on about meeting Michael like that. The fool!" A sudden anger rose inside him toward the man who had put the simple carpenter on the spot in the first place.

"Achaioi!"

He beckoned the High Judge to him. "What do you think of what this man has said here?"

Achaioi responded with his eyes downcast, one hand stroking his snow-white beard. "I believe he has a sickness of the mind. However, there is a certain percentage of the folk in the poorer parts of town who actually believe him—they think he is their savior—and the number grows. In order to avoid needless entanglements between the representative of Rome and the—the unique religious issues in this province—it falls to us to be very wary of this sort of disturbance, and careful of how we handle the present matter."

Pilate nodded and waved Achaioi back to his original position.

"Ceint. I propose we call a hiatus."

Ceint shouted a few orders and the judges and the kohanim shuffled out of the courtyard, followed by the prisoner and his escort. When the last spear-toting guard had disappeared from sight, the heat of the day seemed to rush in suddenly to fill the empty space between the walls. There was silence outside; training was over at the garrison.

"Well, Ceint. What do you think of what he had to say?"

"You mean the bit about him meeting the Archangel Michael?"

"That too."

Pontius Pilate and his advisor looked at each other for a long moment, neither saying a word. There was confusion in the eyes of both men.

"I don't think much of it at all. But the town officials say that he's been healing people—sick people waiting to die and those who cannot stand. He brings them back to health in an instant, and former cripples run like the wind. There are even some town officials who say they have seen these things for themselves."

"Some kind of sorcery, then?"

"That is what the kohanim call it, for certain. They're quite incensed. They see it as blasphemous."

"What I want to know is how you see it, Ceint. Do you think the stories are genuine?"

Ceint put a hand to his head. He always did this when he lacked a response.

"Prefect," he said after a long pause. "I wonder if some of these accounts might not actually be true." Ceint spoke slowly, carefully selecting his words.

"*Some* of them?" Pilate leaned forward. "If even *one* of these stories is the truth, we have a serious situation on our hands."

"Which is why, Prefect, I feel it is highly dangerous to allow this Jesus any more free rein."

"Why, Ceint . . . it sounds as though you actually believe this man possesses some sort of mighty Heaven-sent power."

Pilate's adviser did not answer, but instead turned his face toward the sunlight that poured in through the windows. There was a sudden pallor in his visage. "If he—" Ceint began at last, then swallowed his words. Pilate saw his throat move with the effort. "If he has truly caused cripples to run and lifted those waiting to die from their sick beds, then I would have to say that he may truly be a—well, a god."

"And someone says they've seen him do this?"

Ceint turned slowly back toward Pontius Pilate. "Prefect, if you saw him hand out a single piece of bread to a throng of the poor who came to hear his sermons, and you saw those who took the tiniest crumb and put it to their lips filled with joy and sustenance—if you saw this, what would you think?"

Tiny beads of sweat had appeared on Ceint's face. Several of them joined together and ran down his cheek, forming a glistening droplet at the tip of his chin.

Pilate stared at his advisor. He didn't move a muscle. He hardly even breathed. "You saw this, didn't you?" he said finally.

Ceint gave no reply, but his silence was testament enough to the conflict in his heart.

"Miracles." Pilate moaned. "Splendid. Who else but a god possesses such power?"

A spear that a soldier had left leaning in one corner of the chamber slid and fell to the floor with a loud echoing clang, but neither of the two men so much as glanced in its direction.

"But, Ceint. Can gods really appear just like that in our world?"

Pontius Pilate found himself struggling to grasp the situation. His Roman upbringing and secular spirit left him ill equipped to grapple with the improbable, radical gods that seemed to persist behind every shadow in this land of the Jews—and in every word and deed of the poor carpenter from Nazareth.

"Ceint. I'm afraid I don't understand how feeding a crowd of the poor with a piece of bread necessarily makes one a god."

"The gods control man's destiny, and through natural phenomena they let their existence and their will be known. Usually, they are far removed from men, but when they do appear to us . . . that's when we say a miracle has occurred."

"A miracle did occur. Does that make Jesus of Nazareth the Messiah?"

"Prefect. We must not allow Jesus to live because—"

"Yes?" Pilate said.

The light reflected from the leaves outside the window gave a greenish cast to the tense features of the two men. Or perhaps it was the unease they felt in their hearts showing on their faces.

"You know why."

Pontius Pilate uncrossed and recrossed his legs and rearranged his cape across his shoulder.

"It is time to finish this trial."

Once again the judges and the kohanim were called back into the chamber. Behind them came the guard, dragging Jesus of Nazareth by a rope that was tied around his waist. High Judge Achaioi declared the court back in session.

With the silver rod of office in his hand, Pontius Pilate pointed toward the priests.

"Kohanim. Before I pronounce my judgment upon this man, I have a question to ask of you."

As one, the kohanim inclined their heads.

"Kohanim. I would like to know what you think about the Day of Judgment this man of Nazareth predicts. Tell me."

An old man, the eldest of the kohanim, stepped forward. The depth of his anger was clear upon his face.

"Prefect, God is not some—some *thing* which comes after some final day of judgment, such as this man claims. What, I ask you, is this judgment at the end of days—this Final Judgment? Does God judge men? God gave birth to men. Men are an expression of God's will. Perhaps, after we were created, our thoughts and our actions were somewhat different than what God had hoped for." The old man had a far-off look in his eyes as he spoke. "Thus there might be a time when God reviews mankind and decides to create men anew . . ."

"And isn't that the Final Judgment?" Pilate asked.

The *kohen* waved his hands in a grand gesture. "Absolutely not. Prefect, this review will not take the form of a judgment. God speaks through his prophets to communicate his desires. Men follow these prophecies to plan their lives."

Another of the old kohen stood. "Prefect. What troubles me is what this man says about the need for us to purify our hearts and rectify our actions in anticipation of God's judgment. There is a terrible threat veiled within these words. The dread of a Final Judgment is a terrifying thing for this man to lay upon our unknowing, piteous people."

The third kohen stood. "Even if peace should come to our land as a result of the people's fear, it would be a distant thing indeed from true happiness. God is not some kind of side effect, Prefect."

Then the final kohen, unable to restrain himself any longer, threw up his hands and shouted, "Nail him to the cross!"

"Yes, Prefect," the first kohen declared, "what more questioning could you possibly require? His guilt is clear and apparent. Give him a swift death!"

Pilate waved down the kohanim with one hand and turned to the accused. "Jesus of Nazareth. I have a question for you. You must've known when you came into Jerusalem that this would happen. I cannot believe you imagined you would leave the city alive. So why did you come? What was it about coming to this place that made it worth risking your life? Did someone tell you to do this? If so, then who? Well?" Pilate's eyes flashed.

The man of Nazareth was gazing off into a corner of the courtyard, perhaps listening to Pilate's words, perhaps not. When the prefect had finished talking, Jesus turned bodily to face him. His eyes glimmered like flames. "It was not suggested to me that I come to Jerusalem, nor was I so commanded. I came because I had to."

"You *had* to come?"

"Prefect, do you believe in miracles?"

Pilate fell silent. His previous discussion with Ceint drifted up unwelcome in his mind. "What about miracles?"

"If I am to show the people that I am truly the Son of God, then I must show them miracles."

"And exactly what sort of miracle will you perform to prove that you are the Son of God?"

The Nazarene's face twisted into a smile, revealing filthy teeth that stuck out from between his scabbed lips.

"That's the thing, isn't it?" Jesus nodded, pleased that they were finally getting to this part of the conversation.

"What's the thing, now?"

The man of Nazareth extended his arms out straight to either side. "One of you wanted to put me death? Then do it. I don't care. I've come to Jerusalem to reveal my greatest miracle. I will show you. No, I will show all of Jerusalem—everyone throughout the entire Roman Empire—that I am truly the Son of the one true God."

"You mean to say that you came to Jerusalem knowing full well that you would be put to death?" Pilate shook his head. Leaning back in his seat, he tapped the silver rod in his hand upon the arm of the sofa.

"Prefect, I will be nailed to the cross. And upon that cross I will die. At that time, there will be a great miracle, and men will tremble in fright, and they will fall to the ground and beg forgiveness before God for all the sins they have committed."

Pilate took another cup of milk tea from his servant, downed most of it in one gulp, then threw the bowl at the captive's feet. It broke into shards and the remaining tea splashed across the stone tiles like a scattering of white petals.

Jesus spoke on. "For those who doubt that I am the Son of God and the Messiah, I must give them proof. The time is nigh. Put me up on the cross! It is all I wish."

From his position behind Pilate, Ceint called out. "Jesus of Nazareth. Do you understand what it means to be crucified? Have you ever seen a man die upon the cross?"

Ceint's irritation was clear in his voice. He clearly still found it frustrating that he'd been unable to win a battle of words with this man who was so poor and simple—practically a refugee. "No, let me say instead that I believe it is a terribly noble thing to follow one's beliefs even to the point of self-destruction. But, Jesus, tell us about this miracle you have planned. Is it truly so great that you are willing to trade your life for it, with no regrets?"

"Don't you want to see a miracle? You do, I know. I will show it to you—for I do believe that I'm truly the Son of God. In fact, I don't even know why I'm wasting my breath telling you this. I will show you my miracle and you will believe whether you want to or not."

Jesus's face dripped with sweat, and he thrust his arms out forcefully as he spoke. He shook at the knees like a man suffering from heat stroke. Even looking as he did—his shoulders thin and pointed, his body covered in dirt and grime—he was a living example of confidence so complete and unshakeable that it could overcome even the fear of death.

A cold and unfamiliar sensation raced through Pilate's breast. It froze his heart like ice and split it like a naked blade. The prefect exchanged a quick glance with Ceint.

"So we are supposed to love Jehovah, not fear him?" Pilate muttered.

"And when the Day of Judgment comes, God will judge all mankind and make Heaven here on Earth," Ceint intoned.

For a moment, despair flickered in their eyes.

"And we're supposed to believe this day will come and so give ourselves to God, I suppose?"

"The Messiah has come—really!"

Then the two men softly laughed. It was a laugh drier than cobblestones left all summer in the sun—for at that moment the two Roman nobles felt an insurmountable finality seep into their hearts. Perhaps the feeling was brought on by the palpable tenacity emanating from the upstart Nazarene—or perhaps his terrifying vision of the Final Judgment had grown within them until it cast its shadow wholly through them.

Pilate stood, his lip curling. There was only one thing he need say now. One wager he need make.

He was aware of the possibility that his words might draw a terrible truth out into the light—that all of Rome was lending a hand right now to the scheme of this man from Nazareth.

There was only one thing he could say. "I, Pontius Pilate, representative of Rome and Prefect of Jerusalem, have tried and judged Yeshua, carpenter of Nazareth, here before this court. He is hereby found guilty of two crimes. Firstly, he has troubled the ignorant yet good people of this land by summoning images of a dreadful 'Final Judgment,' stirring within them unfounded fears and disrupting their daily lives.

"Secondly, he has profaned the teachings of the ancient deity of the Jewish faith, slandering their sects with baseless claims and committing numerous attacks upon the faith of the kohanim.

"For these two crimes, I, Pontius Pilate, Prefect of Jerusalem and representative of Rome, sentence Jesus, carpenter of Nazareth, to death."

At once, the kohanim burst into cheers.

"Long live Rome! Long live the emperor! Pax Romana!" they shouted.

"Fools!" Pilate found he could remain in the chamber no longer. He turned and departed, his cape whipping behind him.

"Lord Prefect!" the High Judge followed behind him, calling out. "Upon what day shall the execution take place?"

Pilate stopped. "A good question. What do you think?" he called out over the judge's shoulder to Ceint, who had appeared in the hall behind.

"Today's the twenty-fourth of March. How about tomorrow, in the morning, with the rising of the sun?"

Pilate turned again and did not look back. It was only when he had reached the walk leading to his residential chambers that it occurred to him that he hadn't seen the expression on Jesus's face when the sentence was pronounced. He couldn't even clearly remember whether or not the carpenter had still been standing there. But of course—he had to have been there. Where else could he have gone?

He regretted that he had not watched the man's face more closely as he spoke the words of the sentence. Not that there was any chance Jesus would have been appropriately crestfallen. Perhaps, then, it was best that he hadn't looked at him at all. He would not have wished to carry around the memory of the man's smiling face as his death was declared.

Pontius Pilate slept fitfully that night.

◖

Jesus of Nazareth is to be crucified—

The word spread quickly through Jerusalem, and all who heard it had their own response. Some knelt and prayed to God, others nodded and said it was his just reward, while still others frowned and muttered quietly their hopes that nothing unwelcome would result.

•

Late that night, a strange light was seen far off in the sky to the north. It shimmered like a multicolored curtain, rippling in waves, flowing through the middle of the sky in great promontories of light. People ran from their houses, summoned by the cries of those who had gathered to stare.

"What could it be?" one whispered.

"An omen of bad things to come," another replied.

"It's the Devil's fire," said another.

Some called out the name of God and pressed their eyes shut, as though they had seen something they were not meant to see.

In order to quell the spreading unrest, Pilate was forced to send his company of guardsmen to walk the streets. The soldiers went from alleyway to alleyway, chasing people back inside their homes.

"In you go now!"

"Prefect's orders. Everyone inside, shut your doors, and latch your windows."

The soldiers stood out as dark silhouettes against the backdrop of the strangely shimmering light.

"Look at that, Ceint. Do you see that? It does not fade! It's growing even brighter, and redder now. It's as if the sky itself were burning."

Pilate turned to his assistant, who stood behind him on the balcony. The white night robes of both men faintly reflected the glimmering in the northern sky.

"I would guess it comes from somewhere up in Syria, north of the Tigris, perhaps? Either there is a wildfire large enough to cover every mountainside up there, or a great city is burning." Ceint's broad forehead was colored with atypical unease. "I think we can expect considerable unrest tomorrow."

"Summon a scholar!"

"At once." Ceint turned and headed inside.

"Judas Iscariot should do," Pilate called out to his back. "The man is well versed in both astronomy and geography."

The summoned man arrived a few minutes later, led by two of Pilate's men. Judas Iscariot was sixty years of age, the top astronomer in Jerusalem, and a well-known prophet among the people.

He wore hempen robes dyed deep green and a wide oxhide belt of the same color. His uneven gray hair was bound into a small knot at the back of his head and wrapped with a black cloth. His feet were large and sturdy, and he wore heavy-looking sandals of thick woven leather.

"Over here, Judas," Pilate called from the balcony.

"When I first saw that marvelous cloud of light in the northern sky this late at night, I prepared myself for your call, Lord Prefect." Judas swept aside the hanging curtain and stepped out onto the balcony.

"Well? What do you think it is? Tell me plain."

Pilate crossed his arms and turned to face the brilliance in the north.

Judas held his peace. Hands clasped behind his back, he strolled along the edge of the balcony.

After a moment Pilate spoke again. "I'm sure you know that Jesus of Nazareth is to be executed on the morn."

Judas nodded, his face dark.

"There are people who believe he is the Son of God, that he is the Messiah—they believe that his execution will be the end of our world, and they're frightened because they think this light and his execution are connected. Well, Judas? Tell me what you think it is."

The prophet put both hands upon the white marble balustrade and leaned out, his eyes searching far off into the night sky. A long silence passed.

"Judas. I must confide in you that the more I saw of this Jesus of Nazareth, the more I found it hard to believe that everything he said was a fiction."

Judas seemed to smile then, faintly. "Lord Prefect. I'm surprised to hear you admitting such things. This man must be persuasive indeed. No wonder the people take him for the Messiah."

Pilate scowled.

"Lord Prefect. Two years ago, when the carpenter of Nazareth was still proselytizing on his own up near Samaria and Arbela I requested that he be apprehended. Do you recall this?"

"I do," Pilate replied, a bitterness in his voice.

"Lord Prefect, it is true that of the many acts that he calls miracles, some do not follow the course of logic or any natural scheme. They are wondrous, to be sure. He calls them miracles of God. And he foretells that these miracles will one day govern our world. Lord Prefect, you should have sentenced him two years ago. I'm afraid that now you may have waited too long," Judas said.

The prophet had indeed recommended this course of action to Pilate several times before. *And perhaps he was right*, Pilate thought, though the realization didn't make him any more pleased to be reminded of it now. He felt a chill sting, as though he'd been struck upon the cheek by a thin razor. He wanted very much to say something piercing, something that would stab into the heart of the wise man, but as always before Judas, he found himself unable to summon the perfect retort.

"True," he said eventually, "but back then I never expected him to gain so many fervent followers in the city."

"I would not say they are that many."

"Yes, but still—"

If you do not think them too many, then why accuse me of staying my hand overlong in his execution?

"They are merely frightened, Prefect. Fear and faith are two different things . . . though tomorrow their fear will become faith in truth."

"How can you say that?" asked Pilate sharply. He was sure that Iscariot had some specific knowledge of Jesus, something about the carpenter of Nazareth he was unwilling to share, that had disposed him against the man. It was almost as if he bore him ill will.

"Do you know what his apostles do now?" Judas changed the topic, leaving Pilate's unanswered question to drift away with the night breeze.

"I've heard that they dispersed after he was taken into custody and went into hiding. Apparently, the profound guidance of their God was not enough to eliminate their fear of death altogether. They probably were worried they might pass on before their paradise came to Earth."

Judas shook his head. "I wonder how much his apostles really understood of Jesus. The love and the God he spoke of are little more than a kind of code. In fact, everything he says comes from a very different place than human thought and desire."

"So whose God *is* Jesus of Nazareth talking about? Who is it that he's preaching for?"

"I do not know, though I will admit I had expected much of him."

This time, Pilate's question seemed to have struck a chord in Judas's heart.

"When first I saw him giving a sermon, in a small village in Galilee, I knew he was different from the many other prophets I had seen—those false prophets who are so numerous that on a given day, a man might throw his sandal in any direction and be sure to hit one. Why?" Judas said. "Because he does not speak in prophecies. The things he says may indeed cause unhappiness, but they will never bring joy."

"Why not?"

"Because if a final judgment by God is truly necessary, would that not suggest that our world was on a path to ruin?"

Pilate stood still and silent as a stone. A hot wind blew up from the Jordan River Valley and swept between the two men.

Together they stood listening to the sound of the wind in their ears.

At last Judas lifted his right hand and pointed toward the far-off brilliance of the night sky. "That light? To be quite frank, this is the first time I have ever seen anything of the kind. An elder sailor of Phoenicia once told me that there is a frozen sea at the northern end of the world and a land of ice at the far southern end, and in those places, sometimes, one can see strange, beautiful lights in the skies. Yet I cannot help but think that this is something altogether different."

"Then you think it has something to do with Jesus's execution."

"No. I think it has nothing to do with that man's faith. That this spectacle should appear on the night before his execution is merely a coincidence. I believe this is a simple yet exceedingly rare natural phenomenon, nothing more. You have nothing to fear from that light, at least. You should tell this to the people and see them safely to their beds."

"Judas," Pilate said, "that still won't stop them from saying that a terrible miracle was witnessed on the night before the Nazarene's death."

Something pale and without form, invisible to the eye, emerged from Judas's body and blew directly over Pilate.

Pilate thought he heard Judas say, "It is a terrifying thing."

"Terrifying? What's terrifying?"

"I fear . . ."

"Yes?"

Judas turned away from the burning in the northern sky, as though his back might bear the brunt of the tragedy and destruction it would bring.

"Yes. The people will connect the execution of the man from Nazareth with something truly terrible, and they will tell their children." With that, like a shadow, Judas drifted across the marble balcony and returned to the chamber within.

A short while later, Ceint came hurrying out. "Prefect, Judas Iscariot gave instructions as he left."

"What did he have to say?"

"He said we should place soldiers at every crossroad in the city from the very early morning and prepare for the worst. He said we should also check our stores of food and watch the roads closely."

Pilate let his shoulders drop. "Very well, Ceint. Do it, and do it quickly."

Ceint cast a wondering glance at his master's face. "Have you received word of some rebellion? I did not get that impression from Judas."

"I expect no rebellion."

"Does this have something to do with the execution of the man from Nazareth?"

Pilate put a hand to his forehead, a pained look on his face. "Ceint, in truth I have no idea. But Judas may be right about the need for caution. Do as he says."

"Prefect, if it is a matter of such gravity, shall I not summon Iscariot once again and have him explain himself?"

Pilate pressed his fingers against his temples and shook his head. "No, Judas will tell us nothing. It is likely he himself does not know exactly what will transpire. All will be revealed on the morrow. Go now, Ceint. Go."

Ceint lingered for a moment longer, but when he saw that Pilate intended no further words, he departed.

Clouds of multicolored light continued to shimmer in the north, but when Pilate looked to the east, he saw there the watery light of approaching dawn. The stars in the north and east were already dim, filled with the premonition of a terrible ending to come, yet the strong winds that whipped past the vast star field directly overhead promised that the day would dawn hot, without a single cloud in the sky.

High in the sky over Mount Zion and the ridges of *Har Hatzofim* across the wide Jordan River Valley, gigantic thunderheads had been gathering since morning. But the sun still shone on the near side of the river, suffusing the region's famous cliffs of white granite with blinding light.

A right turn off the road that leads to the Shushan Gate brings the traveler to a barren, rocky hillside called Golgotha. Judas was standing where the two ways met, looking down at the Jordan Valley below. Several steep, jagged paths were cut into the stepped faces of the cliffs, looking like scars left by lightning bolts. The small collection of dingy dwellings near the center of the valley was the village of Jericho. Beyond that, the Jordan River curved like a silvery snake beneath a shimmering mirage.

Following the bends of the river with his eyes, Judas gazed across the vista to his right to where the Jordan swelled suddenly to become the Dead Sea. Half of that body of water glimmered a rich, brilliant blue, while the other half sat in the shadow cast by the protruding cliff of Tel Bet Yerah.

Once, when Judas was a boy, he had seen something sunken in the depths of the deep water beneath the cliffs—an ancient, empty city. There were buildings of stone there, with square windows cut in their walls; an arcade leading to a wide plaza; even trees turned to stone. All of it seemed close enough to touch were he to reach over the side of the boat. He'd asked many people why there was a city at the bottom of the Dead Sea but had never received a satisfactory answer. Some merely shook their heads fearfully and declined to speak of it, while others had made the Jewish hand gesture for warding off demons and had either promptly departed or driven him away. It was only much later that he had learned of a legend, passed down by the prophets, that identified the city under the waves as part of Sodom or Gomorrah, sunk by no lesser power than the wrathful God Himself.

When Judas was around thirty years of age, a powerful earthquake had struck the region, destroying many buildings in Jerusalem and in other towns and villages on either side of the Jordan. After that, the city at the bottom of the sea could no longer be seen. Where it had been, a large pile of boulders covered the seafloor. Judas harbored doubts about whether the lost ruin really was the remnant of Sodom and Gomorrah. All the legends were in agreement that God in His wrath had rained fire and sulfur down from Heaven, and the two towns had been swallowed by the earth. Judas took this to be a clear indication that, at some point far in the past, a severe earthquake had shaken the Jordan River Valley, causing a volcano to erupt and fissures to open in the ground. Yet the underwater city in Judas's memory had appeared whole and unblemished. How could this be, if it had suffered such a calamity? It was an unfathomable mystery, and now unanswerable for all time. As such it had joined the set of suspicions that had lingered and grown in Judas's mind for some time now.

He had always found it odd that the legends of the region pertaining to things divine were so startlingly real. It was almost as if a mere two or three generations before, it had been a regular occurrence for the people of the Jordan River Valley to encounter gods. They spoke with them, fought with them, and sometimes collaborated with them . . .

And whence the abundance of self-proclaimed prophets? Many of them did it for money, of course—prophecy was an occupation, nothing more. Yet still the people of the Jordan hungered for word from the gods as those living elsewhere did not, and they accepted uncritically the revelations of the many prophets. It was possible, Judas had to admit, that since ancient times, there truly had been people living here who had some privileged knowledge of the divine. Moses had been one of them, and Jesus of Nazareth another.

"There you are, Judas. What are you doing here? Time to head up to Golgotha. I expect the crucifixion of the Nazarene to begin shortly."

Judas turned to see Pilate astride a white horse—the Prefect of Jerusalem must have ridden up the switchbacks to the crossroads. He had several soldiers in attendance. Each of them was fully armed with javelin and shield and wore a heavy metal breastplate of a sort rarely seen outside of times of war.

Judas nodded and followed Pilate's entourage from the crossroads up the path to Golgotha.

In the center of the rocky slope stood a large wooden cross atop a platform. It appeared to have been quickly assembled, and the naked white wood shone in the morning light where axes had hastily hewn its shape. Several soldiers stood underneath it. As Pilate and Judas made their way up the slope, the soldiers turned in unison to face them, the silver tips on their long spears glinting. Though it was difficult to see from the road, it appeared that a man had already been hung upon the cross's other side.

Pilate frowned and urged his horse onward to get a better view. From high on the hill, he could see that a large number of people had come to observe; they were gathered in a semicircle further down the slope.

"Be wary," he shouted to the soldiers at the platform. "His believers might attempt a rescue."

"Prefect, those are not his believers," Ceint called out, appearing astride a horse of his own. He gave his mount's neck a blow with the flat of his hand to urge it on. "They are people from town come to see the crucifixion—that is all. I spotted several of the kohanim among them."

Pilate rode up to the cross with Ceint and Judas following close behind.

Jesus had been writhing in agony up there for nearly four hours by now, having been crucified with the first light of dawn. His arms were spread wide along the horizontal beam of the cross and tied at the wrists with crude twine, and a long nail had been driven through the palm of his left hand. The rust-covered heads of two other nails could be seen protruding from his ankles at the bottom of his limply hanging legs. A line of blood trickling from the wound on his right leg made a path across the top of his soiled foot and ran down to collect and harden at the tip of his toenail. Ash-colored hair caked with grime and sweat was plastered to his forehead, making his face difficult to see, though Pilate could clearly hear his occasional moaning and muttering.

"Any idea what he's saying?" Pilate asked Ceint.

"Something about wondering where God in Heaven has gotten to, I hear."

Just then, a stone came flying up from the crowd on the hillside and struck Pilate's horse on the rump. Startled, the prefect's mount whirled in a circle, rearing and stamping its hooves as he struggled to calm it. The exposed layers of the rocky slope were slippery, and the horse's sliding hooves made a dry sound like a clattering of bones that echoed off the boulders around them.

"Lord Prefect! I've caught the culprit—this is the man who threw that stone!"

A soldier came from the crowd, dragging a young man behind him. The captive opened his sunken blue eyes wide and glared at Pilate with all the malice of a viper.

"You there," Ceint asked the man, "are you a follower of Jesus of Nazareth?"

The man did not so much as glance at Ceint, but instead leaned toward Pilate sitting atop his horse and spat ferociously. He was too far away to actually hit the prefect, and the spittle fell short, becoming a tiny dark spot on the hot, dry ground between them.

"Insolence!"

Pilate urged his horse nearer and, lifting the rod in his hand, struck the man across the face. The prisoner lurched backward, held up by the soldiers who clutched his arms on either side.

"Forgive him. He understands nothing," said a clear voice from above their heads. All of them looked up to see Jesus gazing down on them from the cross, his head bowed as though in supplication. "Forgive that man. He is just a fool."

The blood had long since drained from the dying man's face, leaving his skin the color of clay. A brilliant green horsefly was perched below one of his ears.

"You call me a fool?" The young captive was the first to speak. "I threw that stone because I pitied you—I wanted you to see me get back at Rome for you! And you call me a fool?"

The prisoner writhed, fighting to free himself, his face filled with terrific rage. The soldiers yanked hard on his arms, pulling him back farther from the base of the cross.

"Who are you to call me a fool? If you really are the Son of God, then step down off that cross yourself!" The man's shouting echoed down the slope.

"Jesus of Nazareth. I am Judas Iscariot. Do you know me?"

At the sound of Judas's voice, Jesus again opened his eyes with great effort. His gaze wandered until he found the speaker.

"I do not recall it well . . . but I believe we met once . . . in Galilee," he gasped between breaths.

"That's right. I spoke with you about the Final Judgment you preach. At that time you told me you were the Son of God—that you were a true prophet."

"Yes, that's right, I am a prophet. I am the mouthpiece for God's will . . ." Jesus's voice trailed off into a low moan.

"Jesus of Nazareth!" Ceint called out, his voice heavy with loathing. "Will you not take back your words? Say only that you are not the Son of God, that you are not a prophet, and I will release you from your pain."

Jesus made no reply but, with head hanging low, began to softly mutter the words of a prayer.

"Father in Heaven, please forgive these poor men, my brothers. They do not know you, they do not know that you truly exist. Father in Heaven, please . . ."

"Do it!" Ceint commanded, as though he could drive Jesus's prayer back into the man's mouth with the force of his own voice.

Two soldiers advanced, brandishing long spears held at an angle. A clamor rose up from the spectators around the hill, though it was impossible to say whether they were lamenting or cheering.

"Well, liar of Nazareth? Shouldn't your God be coming to save you about now?"

The rod in Ceint's hand made a whistling sound as he swung it through the air, a final signal.

One of the spear-wielding soldiers reached upward, thrusting the silvery tip of his weapon deep into the side of Jesus. When he stepped back, blood flowed from the fresh wound, staining the soiled hempen ropes of the wounded man.

Jesus's face twisted in agony, his features changing until he looked like another person altogether. "Father!" he cried, lifting his begrimed, contorted face to the sky. "Why do you abandon me?"

The ragged cry reached the ears of all who stood around that hill, the soldiers and the people from Jerusalem and the valley towns, with startling clarity.

Then all was silent. The sound of the wind was gone, leaving only the brilliant sunlight to shine burningly upon the bare rocks. So quiet it was that Judas half expected to hear the sound of the water lapping against the banks of the distant Jordan.

The vivid blue sky over the river suddenly dimmed. Pilate, searching with narrowed eyes, could see no difference in the sunlight where it struck the land, nor in the contrast between light and shadow, and yet the change was there. A bird began to cry raucously in the distance; shouts went up from the crowd on the slope. Something was approaching swiftly from the far banks of the Jordan, spreading as it came.

Pilate gripped his horse's reins tightly and galloped down the hill.

A wind, chill as ice, enveloped Golgotha. Now the dimming was clearly noticeable. The brilliant sun faded, and darkness wrapped around the sky. The soldiers standing guard at the base of the cross began to run in a pack uphill. Quickly it became so dark that Pilate thought he had gone blind—he could see nothing, not even the tip of his own nose. Soldiers and spectators alike staggered unseeing, thrusting their arms out in front of them, or crouched and felt their way along the uneven ground.

Startled by the darkness, Pilate's horse reared high on its hind legs. The prefect had entirely lost track of where he was on the slope.

He heard a scream of terror cut through the darkness with the speed of a shooting star. Loud at first, the scream grew fainter and then stopped abruptly. He heard another. *That must be the direction of the cliffs,* Pilate thought. *Some people must've lost their way and wandered too close.*

"Miracle! It's a miracle!" shouted a man through the darkness. "The Nazarene was the Son of God in truth!"

"God judges us!" another voice cried out. "We tried to kill his son! The prefect! The prefect has brought this evil to pass!"

Then the words were lost in a chorus of insane screams and women's weeping.

Judas stood a short distance from Pilate, though neither man could see the other. The old scholar leaned upon his staff, considering the phenomenon. *I wonder what Jesus of Nazareth is doing at this moment,* he thought—and with the thought a burning need to know overcame him. Dropping to one knee, he carefully felt the ground around his feet to determine which direction was uphill, then slowly he began to climb.

Bits of dislodged earth and small rocks had begun to roll down the slope. They stung his face, getting in his eyes and nostrils. He covered his face with his hands. Then something else came flying down and struck him hard—a human body. Their arms and legs tangled, and together they rolled down the hill.

Even as he fell, Judas wondered about Jesus. *Has he undone his ropes?* He tried to grab the other man, but when he reached out, his hands closed on nothing but air. Then he noticed that his rate of descent had accelerated, and despite himself he screamed with fear. Flailing wildly, he scrabbled at the increasingly steep slope, finally clawing his way to a stop. He could hear falling earth and stones and endless screams disappearing below the shelf to which he clung. In the darkness, Judas wiped cold sweat from his brow. Though it seemed his tumble had lasted a very long time, he realized that during the entire ordeal he had only had space for two or three breaths.

All at once Judas was bathed in light. A sudden blue incandescence from somewhere high above his head illuminated the hilltop and cast the land below in shadow, giving the Jordan River Valley the appearance of a vast dark ocean.

Looking upward, Judas saw a swirling column of light atop the hill, like a pillar extending from the layered rock of Golgotha into the sky. Everything, both heaven and earth, was wrapped in a blue, icy light. All things trembled before the wrath of God.

He heard a scream and then another in the distance, sounding horribly far away.

Judas was out of breath, but he forced himself not to gasp, afraid that he might pass out. Stumbling to his feet, he began to make his way up the steep slope again. His entire being was screaming *Run! You must run! Get away!* And yet another part of him was certain this was not the wrath of God after all—no miracle come down from the heavens. Whatever he was witnessing, it was something of a completely different, if still terrifying, nature.

Now he could see the barren slopes of the distant rocky hills lit by the bluish glow, each individual blade of withered grass standing out with vivid clarity. The light had increased so greatly that it even illuminated the wide flow of the Jordan River below, making it shimmer like a mirage.

Then the cloud of light atop the hill swirled violently and took on the form of a giant figure of a man, nearly half as big as the hill itself. The giant wore a helmet low over the top part of what Judas took to be his head—a helmet not so dissimilar from those worn by the Roman legionnaires. His chest and waist formed one enormous pillar. There were two clearly defined arms and two long legs, the latter planted firmly upon the hill of Golgotha. The giant's body, wrapped in pale bluish light, was half transparent, like a glowing mist; an unending darkness was revealed beyond.

Within the borders of the brightness, the body of Jesus of Nazareth was floating upward. He was already some distance from the ground.

Then the bluish white light flared in the darkness, forming a ring in the air. Within that ring, Judas saw the giant figure carrying Jesus in his hands.

A sharp tearing sound rent the air, like the tearing of a silk curtain. The earth shook with thunder, a vibration that passed from the top of the hill down to the river valley. Several of the steep cliffs crumbled, their remains tumbling downhill in a landslide. Quakes rocked the darkened land, and the land shuddered and fell.

And yet, despite the apocalyptic noise, all who were there could hear the quiet words of Jesus as he drifted up into the sky:

> The land of Zebulun and the land of Naphtali,
> By the way of the sea, beyond the Jordan, Galilee of the Gentiles,
> The people who were sitting in darkness saw a great light,
> And those who were sitting in the land and shadow of death, upon them
> a light dawned . . .

Soldiers and citizens clung to the shaking slope, their imminent deaths assured, and they cried out the name of God.

Judas Iscariot picked himself up. He could hear another voice speaking to him from somewhere in the rolling earth below his feet.

> "Your Majesty! You must tell me what this means. Why do you strike down your own people?"
>
> "Legate. I will soon report on my failure to the Planetary Development Committee. Yet understand that this failure is only one of my results. Legate, you saw the fire? It was that fire that foiled my plans! It was the greatest barrier to the designs of the committee, and the final reward for our efforts."
>
> "Your Majesty–!"

Judas stood, flustered, and looked around. *Majesty? Was that the emperor in Rome? Surely not! And who is this "legate"?*

By now, the blue brilliance was nothing more than a dot of light among the stars that shone in the vault of the sky.

"Have you understood, my prince? Do you know whose statue that is? Not even Brahmā, ruler of this world, does. The great god after whom that statue was modeled was a resident from another world who visited this region and claimed it for his own. This world is to be ruled from without, you see. Five billion six hundred seventy million years from now, he will once again appear in this world and determine the fate of all who remain here. That is what they call Maitreya."

"What of salvation? What of salvation in the time of the last dharma?"

Judas's mind raced, his thoughts wild. *Who is this prince? And who is Brahmā? Five billion years seems an impossibly long amount of time. And Maitreya . . . Maitreya?*

Judas cocked an ear in hopes of hearing more of the strange conversation that seemed to be coming to him from some impossible distance. Yet there was nothing. He ran up the slope of the hill, stopping occasionally to listen, ears pricking like a wild beast's. The voices were nowhere to be heard.

Who was that talking? And why did it feel as though the weight of the world hung in their words?

Judas crawled up a steep ridge, then ran again. True darkness had returned to the hill around him. The memory of the distant voices filled his mind, feeling far more important than the miracle Jesus had wrought.

He had no way of knowing how long the darkness would continue—indeed, it might never end. It might actually have been a punishment from Heaven. The conversation he'd overheard, on the other hand, was certainly not divine. Judas felt himself standing at the juncture of two worlds.

He saw a line of torches, wavering in the distance.

Before he had time to catch his breath, Judas found himself thrown from the rocky ledge on which he stood, hurled out into empty space. A vast amount of dirt and rock crumbled behind him, following him into the void. The thought came to him that he should reach out to grasp

something—anything—but quicker than he could act, his consciousness
was lost to the depths of darkness.

●

The darkness that fell upon the hill of Golgotha that day began around
eleven o'clock in the morning and continued until about two o'clock in the
afternoon. According to ancient records from the region, this day fell on
the third month of the nineteenth year of the reign of the Emperor Tiberius.
It was the seventh day before the first of the fourth month, fourteen nights
after the new moon. It was also noted that this was the seventy-ninth year
by Antiochus's reckoning, since Sulpicius and Sulla tangled in Rome, and
Casius, Prefect of Syria, was designated the new commander of the region
of Jerusalem by the emperor.

Though the veracity of this report is a matter of debate, it has often
been quoted as fact. It is important to note, however, that there was no
Prefect of Syria named Casius. It is also true that there are no other examples
of the emissary of Rome to Jerusalem simultaneously holding office as Prefect
of Syria. This was primarily for military reasons—the road that led from the
port of Acre on the Mediterranean overland through Nazareth and on into
the Jordan River Valley, which then passed through Ha-arava, through Petra
and Al Lejjun and on to Aqaba on the Red Sea, was a trading route far too
important to be left in the hands of a single official. It was common practice
for three commanders, one in Jerusalem, one in Syria, and one in Aqaba, to
divide administration of the road between them. This fact alone is sufficient
to cast considerable doubt on the reliability of these records.

There is, however, reason to believe that the Roman Empire willfully
removed all mention of the darkness at Golgotha from the public record,
claiming that the occurrence was no more than a legend and therefore un-
worthy of official recognition—motivated, perhaps, by a wish to eliminate
any suggestion of misgovernment in Jerusalem.

●

On the third day of the fourth month in the thirty-third year of the
Julian Calendar, the entire region around Jerusalem experienced three
hours of darkness in the middle of the day, centered on Golgotha. Historical

astronomical analysis shows that at no time in the weeks around that date did the Middle East experience even a partial solar eclipse.

Years later, a historical theologian would claim that the stories of that day were, in fact, accounts of a lunar eclipse that occurred on the fifteenth of *Nisan,* tales that had become twisted over time. However, the darkness upon Golgotha is said to have occurred while Jesus still writhed in pain upon the cross—early in the day, not during the night.

There is more.

In Revelation 4:6–7, it is written:

And before the throne there was a sea of glass like unto crystal: and in the midst of the throne, and round about the throne, were four beasts full of eyes before and behind. And the first beast was like a lion, and the second beast like a calf, and the third beast had a face as a man, and the fourth beast was like a flying eagle.

It is thought that these hallucinations symbolizing the four apostles came as a vision, yet who can say what Saint John, Saint Mark, Saint Luke, and Saint Matthew truly saw that day?

According to the accounts of one Roman centurion, from that day forth, there were none in Jerusalem who laid eyes upon the man Judas Iscariot. Nor was Judas's body found among the dozens who fell from the cliffs that day in the darkness.

❦

Thus did Jerusalem's most devastating day come to an end.

Standing at the shores of the dead, I ask:
To where does one return?

Zaaa . . . *Zaaaaaa . . .*
Zaaa . . . Zaaaaaa . . .
He focused his gradually expanding awareness on the noise—a simple two-phrase structure, regularly repeated. Already it echoed within him, filling him, pleasantly stimulating the nerve endings of his as-yet unhardened form. Something inside him was changing dramatically, something new becoming something even newer. The rich ripple of sound raised all of his metabolic functions to their limits. As he gave himself over to the experience, something deep within him ruptured with an audible *pop.*

At the same moment, the lid of the pod flew outward. A massive rush of air bubbles erupted from the circular porthole. The tiny spheres glowed with a silver sheen in the deep indigo of the water, rising steadily toward the surface. The pod was firmly wedged between two shelves of rock, yet it shook so violently that it seemed for a moment as if it might break free.

When the shuddering subsided he considered his surroundings. All of the machinery inside the pod that had supported his life until now had ceased to function, its work complete. The silvery needles, the air pumps, the circulators, were all unneeded now. They hung limply from the interior walls.

He slid out from beneath the framework of metal pipes where his body had been held like an astronaut in a G-seat. A single, dim orange lamp lit the pod's interior, revealing features that would not have seemed out of place in a sophisticated spacecraft.

A dull pain throbbed deep inside his head, keeping time with the beating of waves against a distant shore. He flailed with ungainly limbs and made his way out of the structure that had sheltered him for so long. The water was surprisingly cold, and he struggled against the temptation to retreat back inside the pod. With every breath he took, a swarm of air bubbles escaped from beneath his jaw, racing upward and obscuring his vision. Far above, slanted light that was neither blue nor gray penetrated the veil of the water. It occurred to him that such dim light wouldn't be able to warm this ocean.

The water was ice cold, as heavy and hard as steel, and filled with an inorganic cruelty that seemed to abhor life. It took him an incredible amount of energy and willpower just to move forward.

Suddenly, something pierced his mind like a fiery hot needle. The force of the psychic impact made his body go as rigid as stone.

To the land! Out of the water, onto the land!

The voice tore through his mind, reverberating under his skin, echoing back down into his core.

Onto the land? Whatever for? What is "the land," anyway?

Words crisscrossed through his mind, illuminating the web of his memory from the inside, flashing like half-seen lightning. Within the folds of his brain, complex signals and combinations of meaning became apparent—yet he was not given the time to confirm each one, to explore or compare.

He raised his roundish head, pushing against the weight of the water, blind to and yet still aware of the unknown territories that existed beyond the unreal blue that surrounded him. And still he heard the ceaseless echoes of the waves surging and receding.

Now go! Onto the land! Go forth, and quickly!

The voice again, goading him on from behind. Ahead of him stretched a blue crevasse. He paddled through the water unconsciously, slowly drifting out over the depths. He found that his body did not move as reliably as he wanted. A place in his head was hurting—deep in his inner ears. The pain made him realize that he was swimming downward now; he had already sunk halfway down the crevasse. The pain increased, bringing him fully to his senses. Every nerve in his body screeched with alarm, and the muscles in his four limbs spasmed like springs.

Facing upward now, he pushed with all his strength to regain the altitude he'd lost. Gradually he advanced at a rising pitch, seeing the vast underwater valley recede far below.

At last the surface became visible above. He rose until his head broke through the water, and he took his first, deep breath, his lungs expanding like parachutes. The ionized air had a strong, sharp smell. Its acidity burned his nostrils and his throat and made his eyelids swell nearly shut. His eyes, narrowed to thin slivers, gave off a blue luminescence.

He made his way through a shoal where waves broke against the rocks, spray misting around his head. His round face bobbed along on the surface of the dark water, unable to leave it very easily, or for very long.

❯

The land was low and flat, barely higher than the ocean's surface. The wind wailed incessantly around him. The sky was painted a solid gray, varying only in degrees of gloom. Beneath its canopy, it was impossible to see where the sun might be, whether it was noon, or evening.

Feet still soaking in the water, he looked out over vast, barren flats. He saw no signs of life. He left the water then, stepped across the wet sand, and headed for the plains that stretched beyond the beach. The wind blew from behind him, whipping past, racing ahead of him far off across the flats. The line of white that stretched between the gray sea and the light brown of the flats, jagged as a broken potsherd, stretched off into nothingness like the line separating life from death. The land beyond seemed strangely featureless, its slight slope almost imperceptible.

Then something caught his eye far off to his left, floating like a mirage. He moved toward it, peering through the stinging air.

Slowly it came into view: a giant walled city, with pointed spires that rose thick as a forest, their tips lost in the low hanging sky. The gray curtain walls that surrounded it, rising from massive foundations, formed a distinctly geometrical pattern, contrasting starkly with the entirely alien sensibility of the complex vertical lines traced by the spires above them.

The city was very far away. For a while, he stood motionless, gazing at it. Gradually, cold fear grew within him. He looked around several times, hoping to find a different goal or direction for which to aim. Primal fear was robbing him of his basic intellectual capacity. Yet in the end, he could find nowhere else to go but toward the city. That, it seemed, was to be his destination.

❯

The sand grew drier the farther he went from the water, until it rose in fine particles like smoke from beneath his feet. Flowing traces had been left on the surface of the land where the waves had once pushed the sand, the spray from long-dried crests frozen into beautiful shapes and curves.

He was surprised when he came to a place where the sand sloped gently upward into a low hill. At the top of this rise, he could see far across the flats in every direction. As he gazed ahead, a violent expression spread across his face and the light of his eyes grew dimmer.

Midway down the other side of the hill, a wide belt of dirty white-colored material covered the ground, extending for a considerable distance before disappearing again into the sea of sand. Beyond, it appeared again, weaving in and out of the sand over and over before reaching the walled city.

He quickened his pace, going down the hill to where the pale swath began. Beneath his feet, the crumbling sand transitioned into a firm, rock-like surface.

He was standing on an immensely wide concrete road. With every gust of wind, thin sheets of sand swept across its flat surface. He wondered where the road came from and where it led. He imagined land vehicles traveling along it and people walking to and fro. Now it lay forgotten, the wind its only traveler, none but the quiet sand seeking passage. Everything else around him—the land and the sky, and even the leaden sea he had left behind—was barren, the kind of barrenness from which no life could ever hope to revive.

Why?

How did this happen?

How did I come to be in this place?

The doubt and confusion that had receded from his newly wakened mind a short while ago now returned with increased urgency, and he had to fight to pull himself back from the abyss of fear.

At last he pressed on down the slope and entered a wide, shallow valley that ran parallel to the shore, forming a broad band of lowland between the ocean and the strange walled city.

He had never seen a valley like it before. He walked along the bottom for some time, moving slowly. The blowing sand had filled the depression of the valley to half of its original depth. Before him and behind him, sand trickled soundlessly down the sloping sides.

Suddenly, a sensation spread like lightning through his chest—a signal warning of approaching danger. For a moment he stopped, taking stock of his situation. It was clear that somewhere in this valley, somewhere in this wasteland, an enemy was lurking. It was also suddenly clear, as he watched the sand sift into the valley, that it would not be long before the lowland was completely filled, which meant that it had not existed for very long.

He paused again, still as a stone. Ahead of him, the valley ended at a tall mound of sand. The wind that blew down the valley collided with the mound, whirling up its slope, whistling as it rose. In silhouette the mound formed a mighty arc, and from its very center a complicated framework of some kind extended upward a considerable distance.

Slowly, he approached the base of the mound.

Two large cylinders emerged at an angle from the sand, extending down into the ground as though supporting the sandy mass above them.

It was now apparent that what he had at first thought was a mound of sand was instead a domed object nearly one hundred meters in height. He guessed that it was actually a sphere, half of which was buried beneath the drifts. Though it might have once been burnished to a mirrored finish, it was now scorched and pitted like a sand-scoured boulder.

He stared at it for a long time, understanding intuitively what this looming object was: a massive spacecraft.

The long, shallow valley through which he had just walked was the path the huge craft had left in the earth as it slid to a fiery stop upon landing.

He approached until he was standing in the shadow of the spacecraft's hull, the gray curve hanging over him like a part of the sky.

An icy chill came over him—*my enemy is here!*

His enemy had known he would be coming and had sent searchers all the way here to find him. The immediacy of the threat only proved his enemy's power.

So where is my enemy now?

He steadied his breathing, trying to hold back the chill that spread through his heart.

My enemy—

My enemy—

Then, suddenly, he shook his head and let his shoulders drop. The breath left his chest and he looked around furtively, like a timid beast.

What is an enemy?

Why do I fear this?

He worried that he might be going mad. Everything he had experienced since awakening ran together, blurring incomprehensibly. He sensed that he had been asleep for a very long time, yet he remembered nothing of the time before he slept. Yet something was now pushing him toward the walled city that sat like a shadow at the edge of the vast flats. This he knew with a disturbing clarity at the core of his being. He turned dark eyes out across the spreading sea of sand, yet found nothing there to console him.

What did I expect? he asked himself.

If I want to go to the city it must be because I am meant to go there. And if I sense an enemy it must mean my enemy is near.

Something was telling him these things, giving him information—controlling him with suggestions that were difficult to resist. He searched the gray lands and sky, his heart closed tightly as rock.

Where is this place? When is this place?

There was so much he wanted to know, yet nothing offered any answers. Again, an icy chill spread from his spine through his chest. It was soundless, painless, and faded in an instant, leaving only an awareness of impending peril in its wake.

He began to move again, slowly, staggering.

First, he would find his enemy's whereabouts. His sense of danger had grown considerably. He looked around for something that might reveal to him his enemy's form.

He moved along the perimeter of the giant spacecraft, crawling up the sandy incline. It was difficult going, and he did not learn much. The damage to the ship was more widespread than he had first thought, and in places the hull had collapsed entirely. He found nothing resembling symbols or numbers upon its surface.

He returned again to the flats. Far back along the way he'd come, he saw the thin white line of the waves crashing against the rocky shore. Beyond that, the gray of the sea seemed fused with the sky, making it difficult for him to distinguish one from the other. In the other direction the horizon faded in the distance, with nothing to draw his attention but the city whose walls hovered like a mirage over the sand. Still nothing moved, and there was no sound but the wind.

He wondered if his enemy was hiding inside the spacecraft, or was watching him, lurking somewhere out across the flats. He strained his senses, focusing them until they were needle-sharp, trying to draw something out from beneath the discordant whine of the wind.

His eyes flashed with a blue light.

Keeping close to the massive hull, he made another circuit of the spacecraft. At the tip of its egg-shaped form, just above where it emerged from the sand at the top of the slope, he saw an oval hatch. It was open. The hatch lid had been folded to one side by a mechanism he did not understand; it hung from the hull like a dislodged fragment of eggshell.

The hatch hadn't been open when he circled the spacecraft before, which meant that either something inside was trying to get out, or it had already managed to escape while he wasn't watching.

It is neither of these things!

He ignored the voice in his head as he carefully edged up the slope, nearer to the hatch. It didn't make sense that something would have lingered inside the weathered spacecraft, waiting for him to arrive. Who could have known that he would be passing by here at this very moment?

Though he sensed that the danger facing him had grown even more urgent, he did not interpret the sudden opening of the hatch as the commencement of an attack.

By now he was just below the opening, near enough to reach the hatch that hung above him. There was a green dusting of something like rust where the hatch was attached to the edge of the portal. The hull of the ship around it seemed as thin as paper. He looked at the back surface of the door and saw that it was made of some silvery-white material, metallic and luminescent.

He put his hand on the edge of the opening and took a look inside. The interior of the craft was too dark for him to make out anything. Silence.

Gingerly, he reached into that dark orifice and felt around. He traced a small circle with his hand, then a wider one, yet touched nothing. He swung his arm around, high and low. Nothing.

Stepping back, he continued on to the far side of the spacecraft. From there he could gaze out over the entirety of the gray flats. The shallow valley dug out by the spacecraft began directly beneath his feet. He saw nothing resembling an enemy, neither in the valley nor on the flats all the way out to the horizon.

He wondered if he should leave the spacecraft where it was and continue toward the city. The enemy-presence he felt in his mind had spread across the flats, leaving danger for him in all directions. Could he simply ignore it and continue along his way? Would his enemy allow that? What was his enemy, anyway? It irritated him that he could not recall who or what it was that threatened him now.

He turned to look at the distant silhouette of the walled city. He knew he had to get there as soon as he could, yet he thought it folly to abandon this confrontation altogether.

He turned and made his way back to the hatch. The portal lay open like a dark window. Once again, he gripped the edge of the hatch and stuck his round head through into the interior.

The air inside the spacecraft was as still as it had been before. He flexed his arms, lifting his body up to the opening. Ice-cold air enveloped him. He paused, hanging there for a moment in alarm, then decided it was more dangerous to stay where he was with his arms occupied and pulled himself the rest of the way through the portal.

It was so dark inside that he could see no more than a meter ahead.

Dropping down to his knees, he advanced slowly, exhaling as quietly as possible. His chest tightened with fear. He could feel all the nerves in his body extending like feelers, groping through the darkness.

Nothing! There's nothing here!

There was no sign of an enemy—in fact the darkness seemed to hold absolutely nothing at all. Like an insect confronted with danger, he stopped, frozen. His breathing and even his pulse slowed until he became like a stone, one with the darkness and stillness around him—and yet his awareness blazed through his nerves.

Though there was no enemy here, there was something far more frightening.

What is going on here?

The oddness of his situation staggered him. Cautiously, he advanced several meters, straining his senses.

Suddenly a brilliant light flashed before his eyes. The beam extended like a bolt of lightning, emerging from a point in the darkness to his right and striking left and downward at an angle through the space inside the craft.

The light burned his eyelids, passing through their membrane to sear his visual cortex. A moment after, another light erupted, crossing the first at an angle. Then the two crossed bars of light began to revolve, hot and brilliant through the darkness. They lit the space around him, first crimson, then orange, then clear green, transforming finally to an incandescent white. Countless particles of light swirled like sparks around him.

In the center of the brilliance, a cloud of light formed into an enormous swirling spiral. As he watched, it extended fingers of light in all directions, mingling with and impeding the movement of another spiral that appeared beside it. The spirals pulsed like living things, revolving slowly, trailing shining clouds of gas.

He stepped back, marveling at the light storm before him, feeling that he had seen it all somewhere before.

The two clouds of light cutting through the darkness were each comprised of billions of tiny particles, and where the two spirals touched, floating bands of deep crimson were overlaid with a silvery radiance.

The light wavered and flickered without a sound, exploding and imploding before him, and the dark void beyond told of the passage of infinite time.

That's it!

For the first time, he understood the source of his fear. *These are two spiral galaxies. They're colliding.*

One is the Milky Way, the other . . . Andromeda!

In his heart, he screamed. Each was comprised of one hundred billion stars, with diameters one hundred thousand light-years across and thicknesses of roughly fifteen thousand light-years. They were massive, and they should have been more than two million light-years distant from each other, but here before him the Milky Way and Andromeda were colliding.

A wave of fear crashed into him, and he reacted. His energy-flooded visual cortex was already overcapacity, but he left it that way, connecting it to a circuit breaker. He withdrew his limbs and hugged his knees to his chest, placing his head atop them; then he ceased to move, as if he were some inorganic object floating in space. His breathing and pulse stopped, his metabolism went into lockdown, and his mind became a void.

The lights burned more intensely, reflecting against the surface of his mind. He activated a tri-D sensor cell antenna array, silently racing to the far edges of the two galaxies—which by now had transformed into surging currents of pure energy. Still, he detected no presence there. Nothing existed in this void of energy and light. He compelled himself to keep looking, searching in between the stars, and still he found nothing.

Suddenly the great whorls of light began to melt, their cores becoming violent blazes that rapidly spread. Their energies formed concentric rings, extending in waves out into the darkness. The deep blue of those waves was so bright it hurt his eyes and made his heart grow cold. Over and over again they swept through the dark reaches of space. Finally, one of the waves broke into several pieces, each piece becoming a giant orb of light. Then the cluster of orbs shifted directions—and stopped, silent.

He wondered for a moment if he was dreaming. It would not have surprised him to learn that he still lay on his side in that pod in the frigid water, asleep. Vague memories of himself before he entered the pod swam beneath his consciousness, yet he had no idea what he might have been, or what he might have done. He could feel his confidence in his own identity slipping away. For the first time, a powerful feeling of loneliness gripped him.

What am I looking at? What does it mean? Am I dreaming?

Have I been flung to the end of worlds, where no other life remains? Is there no one here to fight by my side and no weapons with which to do battle?

What am I supposed to do?

He replayed the movements of the swirling lights in his mind, feeling cold sweat trickle down his skin. The orbs of light did not move; but they began to grow even brighter.

Get out!

Something screamed inside him, the sound echoing through his chest.

You are in danger there. Get out now!

Out? But that didn't make sense. How would he get out of this confinement?

He felt something, somewhere inside him, despairing.

You are in danger. Get out now, the voice said with rising urgency. *Your time is short.* He felt his mind dry up like a pool in the desert, a surface crazed with sudden cracks. Death in the form of brilliant spirals of light swelled up from those cracks with frightening speed. The blazing orbs had grown to twice their original size.

It was at that moment that a memory came to him, an instant of clarity that had been lost to him until then. With a dark heart, he stared at the silent orbs of light, understanding that his own destruction was swiftly approaching.

By now, the whirling lights filled most of his vision, spreading ever more rapidly.

I can't see them moving because they're coming straight at me.

He was a target. The voice sounded once again in his mind.

Get out now!

The danger was now only an instant away. He turned and saw the hatchway behind him, a white window of light floating in the darkness. He ran toward it, fear swelling up behind him like a great wave. He ran with all his strength, leaping toward the portal.

An unknown force of incredible strength twisted and warped the dark space around him. Lines of light, like a web of occult electricity, pushed against his body. In the fraction of time that remained before the orbs overtook him he closed the impossible distance to the hatch.

He shot through the portal like a bullet, plunging down onto the sand.

Then he rolled down the slope, dust rising in a cloud behind him. When he finally came to a stop, he lay there at the bottom of the valley, awaiting the next calamity.

Nothing happened. He extended his tri-D sensor cell antennae as far as he could but detected nothing approaching.

For a long while he lay as though dead, unable even to grasp his own situation. All he knew was that he was driven by an urgent need to reach the walled mirage on the horizon, and that on his way there he had encountered a strange enemy and only barely escaped its trap. That and one other thing. There was a strange voice inside his head that projected warnings into his mind and directed the actions of his body. All of these things were shrouded in mystery.

He picked himself up from the ground. Lifting his sand-covered head, he peered back at the silvery spacecraft. The hatch was still open, small and dark. He could not decide whether this was truly some trap of his enemy . . . or was in fact a vessel that somehow contained two entire spiral galaxies. He wondered if he should investigate its interior again or abandon it as the voice had directed him to do. Either way, he understood that the actions he took henceforth would be largely determined by the strange events he had experienced inside the spacecraft. The flickering presence of the enemy he felt within his mind frightened him almost beyond bearing.

He decided to leave the valley. Cautiously he moved up the slope opposite the spacecraft, irritated that his path had been determined by a mere inanimate object.

He stood for a while when he reached the top, sweeping his surroundings with his alerted senses. He detected nothing new . . . except, just once, somewhere far across the flats, he thought he noticed something moving. Immediately he focused all of his attention in that direction, but by then whatever it was had already disappeared. It did not surprise him that he was being monitored.

He pressed onward then, leaving a long trail of footprints across the faded brown sea of sand, remnants for the wind to scatter and the sliding sand to fill.

He followed the line of the half-buried highway. It did not seem like very long before the spires of the city were towering above his head. The walled city—the mirage he had seen from a distance—was now very real and spread out before him. A collection of yurtlike buildings extended out from the shield wall, and the wall was half covered by a translucent dome that seemed to be half melted, its edge a waterfall of drooping threads and beads of water frozen in place. The yurts spilled out from the walled city in a tangle that showed no order or planning, like intestines from a ruptured stomach. The shield wall above them rose to a height of roughly five hundred meters, he guessed, without a single window or visible seam. It appeared to have been carved from a single piece of some unknown substance nearly ten kilometers in circumference. Above it the spires rose like a tangled forest impossibly high, seven to eight thousand meters above the plain. The spires' bases were thick enough to form buildings many stories high. Their tips were sharp and narrow, like spears piercing the sky. From their tips and edges bristled antennae and other objects—he guessed them to be radar dishes and laser cannons—in a pattern like some ancient arabesque, their structures seeming to defy the laws of gravity.

He stood and stared.

Though he had not noticed it until now, behind the forest of spires the quarter shell of a translucent dome arced across the sky. And there were other shattered domes beyond it, beyond the city, standing empty upon the sand, some like giant inverted bowls, others with flat mesalike tops. He guessed that the dome had once covered the city in its entirety.

He took in the sight of the great city, storing it in his neural memory web.

At last he moved in for a closer look. The yurts were half buried in sand, making it hard for him to see inside them. On further inspection he found that the buildings were arranged around a long corridor, roughly one hundred meters wide, in which nothing had been built. Both the buildings' walls and the roads between them seemed to have been made from an incredibly thin, specialized silicon. One part of the yurt closest to him was scorched where some weapon had opened a hole in its side. He approached and looked in, only to find it filled to its ceiling with sand. Then he walked on down the empty corridor, making for the main wall of the city. He guessed that he was walking along an ancient thoroughfare, perhaps the main entrance to the city in the past. If that was true, there was a good chance it would take him to a gate or some other entrance through the wall and into the city.

The forest of spires threw a jumbled shadow across the sand around him. He wondered what had inspired the city's architects to construct such high towers with such sharp points to scrape against the sky. He wondered if the people who lived here had borne the heavens some great hatred that led them to direct even their buildings upward as weapons, protected though they were by a wall and dome. He belatedly realized that he had been thinking about the city only in the past tense. This was very dangerous. Had he not just entered a derelict spacecraft only to find it functioning perfectly enough to unleash a terrifying attack?

For all he knew, something might be waiting for him in there, buried beneath the rubble and the sand. As long as that was a possibility, there was nothing past tense about this city and the danger it posed.

A giant door opened in the high shield wall. He crouched in its shadow, peering through the gate. The blowing sand had settled in beautiful windblown curves along the edges of the wall. Other than the drifts that gave way beneath his feet, nothing moved in all that space. Through the city's entry gate a dark tunnel led toward the other, deeper levels. He peered into its darkness, tense. The danger he'd faced inside the spacecraft again came to mind—clearly this was no place to linger. He went through the gate, the sand rising up to his knees.

Though the tunnel way had seemed inky black from the outside, once inside it he saw that it was dimly illuminated, its walls the same gray ash color as the world beyond the wall. He looked for the source of the illumination but was unable to find it. He decided that it must come from the high ceiling or the walls or the floor itself.

The sand stirred like a mist around his feet as he walked. The tunnel was short, opening into a large circular hall with several short radio-tower-like structures at its center, the openings at their tops shaped like the mouths of trumpets. The towers' circular bases were covered in drifting sand, and though it was apparent these were devices for absorbing radioactivity, it was obvious that they no longer functioned. He imagined the citizens of the city coming in from the outside world, always passing through this hall for decontamination, after which they would enter the city proper through one of several doorways set around the hall. He picked one of them and went through into the ruins of the ancient city.

>

He walked among fallen, shattered ceilings, cracked walls and floors, twisted electrical conduits and clogged water pipes, and vast quantities of preserved goods that had been stored for so long they were now nothing but mountains of dust and sand. The destruction Fate had decreed for this place had been so thorough that over the long quiet years, the city had marched to its ruination with an impossibly ponderous certainty.

Again, he sensed the presence of some enemy—closer this time. Perhaps his foe had come behind him and was even now standing at the city gates beneath the towering walls.

For a brief moment he hesitated, casting his senses in all directions, and then he continued his advance. He came across a line of large buildings, each about a hundred meters long. Peering into them through the openings at their sides, he saw that they were crossed with metal pipes like those in a rotary kiln, all red with rust. Many cranes and beltways hung from the ceiling of each chamber, their workings covered with thick layers of dust. A *manufacturing sector, perhaps*, he thought.

He climbed to the upper levels of one building along a beltway that hung loosely, its belt dangling in places like shredded paper. From there he passed through countless rooms and halls of many sizes, including a communications hub filled with electronics and a manufacturing facility that seemed outfitted to produce large quantities of synthesized foods. Everything was rusting, half buried in sand, enveloped in silence.

What am I supposed to do here?

Fierce doubts churned in his chest. He wasn't sure what he was supposed to be looking for, why he was driven to search.

Feeling empty and alone, he stepped into a small room with a floor buried in sand. There was a large window in one wall, and through its empty frame he could look out on the foundations of the towering spires. He stuck his head out through the window and stared up at the gray sky, then let his gaze fall back down to the dune-crowded streets of the ancient metropolis. There were symbols engraved on the foundation of one of the nearest spires—something commemorating the tower's construction, possibly. He opened his two foremost eyes wide, trying to read the symbols.

Two nine zero . . .

He directed all the energy in his body toward his visual cortex. The circuit breaker that supplied his scorched optic nerves trembled with the load.

2902 TOKYO

TOKYO . . . Did that mean this city was "Tokyo"?

Though the name did not exist anywhere in his memory, it seemed a suitable enough appellation for a place that had prospered in this sector at some point during the thirtieth century.

But why would Tokyo be in ruins? And what year is it now?

Hoping to find an answer in the rubble, he moved on, following an enormous corridor between massive structures.

Suddenly he spotted a shadow flitting at the edge of his field of vision. An instant after he saw it, it disappeared behind a dark wall. His metabolizer was running at full speed now, ready for the lethal attack that was sure to come. His tri-D sensor cells extended an umbrella antenna, seeking to detect the metabolic energy of his enemy, its strength and direction. *Nothing . . .*

Fear chilled him to the bone. He dropped to the floor, listening for sounds in the levels below while his antenna extended upward toward the high ceiling to listen for the movement of enemies above.

Still nothing.

What could be here, if not my enemy?

Though the movement he'd detected in the desert outside the city gates had surely been hostile, he had as yet found no sign of any enemy within the city's bounds.

Perhaps they have not invaded this far . . . yet?

He considered the possibility that he had fallen into yet another of his enemy's traps.

On a world like this, where energy use was at an absolute minimum, it would be impossible to camouflage any large amount of radiation. Even the hydrogen fusion reaction within the sun that lit the sky had dwindled to only a third of its former strength. The natural world had atrophied, its moisture gone, leaving the surface of Earth a cold and barren desert. Animal life had long since vanished, and even the withered remains of forests had disappeared without a trace. Only the wind moved now, occasionally trailing sand in gray clouds. The cycle of energy had been broken, and the planet lacked the strength to nurture anything new.

He was certain that the lurking enemy had by now detected his body's energy profile. An energy detector could be used to determine a quarry's whereabouts with greater accuracy than even a wireless directional finder. He would be defenseless if his hidden foe had managed to conceal its own energy emissions and approached undetected.

Moving quickly, he ran to the corner of the wall behind which the dark figure had disappeared. He found a tiny footprint where sand had been kicked up.

This is not my enemy!

Keeping his breath level, he tiptoed toward a crack between two structures behind the wall. It led into a hole of some sort; there the footprints disappeared.

A trap?

He returned again to the corridor, searching for any signs of approach. He sensed that his enemy was already inside the city, moving steadily through the corridors on the bottommost level, heading toward a broken lift. Whoever or whatever it was probably intended to climb up the shaft.

Which meant that at least he still had the advantage of higher ground.

Quietly, he slipped through a hole in the wall. Beyond it he found a spiral passageway that sloped gently upward.

An old beltway.

The small footprints continued up the passage. He followed, coming to a place where a giant shutter—long ago ruined—had been lowered to block the corridor. Electrical conduits and communications lines were tangled along the ceiling, and air-conditioning pipes hung down like strands of hair. He brushed them aside with one hand, leaning to duck beneath them;

the pipes clanged into one another with a dry metallic sound. A moment later, they crumbled as though made of nothing more than clay. The sound of their falling made a quiet echo down the corridor.

Ahead of him, the footprints disappeared into a power plant. Other footprints joined them near the entrance, also going in. He entered the plant.

The only illumination within came from clouded orange panels that looked like indicators of some kind. Beneath the dim circle of light they cast huddled several human figures.

He stood still as stone. "Who are you?" he called out after a long hesitation.

One of those in the group gave a quick, sharp cry he could not understand.

The person shouted again, the sound of it hitting him like a physical blow.

Then he felt something switch inside himself—an automatic voice translation system turning on.

"Who are you? Where did you come from?" the person was asking him.

He peered further into the plant but saw no other figures lurking.

"Who are you?" he responded. "Why are you hiding here?"

Even as he spoke, he marveled at his own ability to converse. He had no memory of any time in which he'd exchanged words with another person. Yet his current situation provided no time to consider this mystery.

"We are residents. We live here," the people said.

"Here? This is your home?" He looked around again at the ruined plant. It seemed highly unlikely that anyone could live here amongst this wreckage and death.

"You live here?" he asked again, worried that they might think him slow for repeating himself.

"Yes. We are residents of this place. Where did you come from?"

He thought it best not to tell the truth in this instance. Nor did he want to waste time explaining anything.

"This is Tokyo, right?" he asked.

"Yes. This is Tokyo. Capital of the Inner Planetary Alliance."

Something about those words bore the echo of a former glory, long since faded.

"I see," he said. "So tell me, what is the solar year now?"

As soon as he asked, he feared that it might not have been a wise question.

"The solar year? I believe, yes, it is 3905."

Inwardly, he breathed a sigh of relief—it seemed that his question hadn't raised any suspicions.

"Which would mean," he said half to himself, "that over a thousand years has passed since that engraving was made on the tower."

"Of what do you speak?" the person asked.

"What caused the city to fall into ruin?" he quickly replied. "Please understand that I mean you no harm. Come here."

In response, the group huddled even more tightly together.

"There's nothing to be afraid of. I am—" he was about to tell them that he came from another place, another celestial body, but then he thought better of it. People living in these conditions would only fear him more if they learned he came from another star. "I came from another city to establish communications."

Eventually, one of the people stepped out from the huddle, wariness burning in his eyes.

"Another city? There is still another city on Earth?" Hope mingled with a deep sadness in his voice.

"There is," he said, then stopped, fumbling for his next words until he remembered the lead-colored sea. "It lies across the sea."

"Across the sea!"

With those words, the group split into fourteen individuals. In the dim orange light, they looked dangerously thin and frail. Their height was, on average, roughly a meter and a half. Their arms and legs were thin and long, their shoulders rounded and slumping, their foreheads protruding. They held their hair with thin metal circlets, just above the ears, and they wore light brown skinlike cloth that covered their entire bodies.

Their expressions were unreadable as they gathered to get a closer look at their visitor.

"What is your name?" one asked.

He would have to answer this one. "S-S-Siddhārtha," he said, dredging the word up from some back corner of his mind.

"See-darth-a?"

"Siddhārtha."

"Siddhārtha!"

"You know this name?" he asked, worried that he had made a mistake.

"No, not well. Though perhaps I have heard it once . . . somewhere."

"Are you the leader of these people?"

The man standing closest to him nodded. "I am. We are all that re-main of the city. I am Orionae the Elder, formerly of Atlantis," he added, lifting his tanned, weathered, and wrinkled face to meet Siddhārtha's eyes. "Siddhārtha, you are."

"And you are Orionae."

The two repeated the names, each certain they had heard the other's before, that they were joined by some painful memory that neither was able to recall.

Perhaps, he thought, *this man had simply done as I had*—reaching into the back corners of his mind and picking the first word he found. Not that it mattered.

"Tell me, Orionae. How did this great city become ruins?"

Orionae came solemnly to stand before Siddhārtha.

"I will tell you," he said. "Strangely enough, the very reason I am here in this abandoned city of Tokyo is because it is my duty to explain to an-other person the reason and the manner of the city's fall into decline. You may very well be that other person."

"You were . . . placed here to do this?"

"Tragedy visited this place in the year 2900. The dimming of the sun in the sky above was the first sign of our impending doom. The average temperature of this city, and across the surface of the earth, fell to minus sixty-eight degrees Celsius."

"Minus sixty-eight degrees!"

"Indeed. After this, the earth began to dry. All the lands were trans-formed into deserts; shallow straits and inlets evaporated, leaving nothing but sand and salt flats behind."

This explained the condition of the world outside—though it was still surprising that all of this could have happened in a mere one thousand years.

"This was planned, clearly," Siddhārtha said, raising his head. "Orionae. Have you lived here then for these past one thousand years?"

Orionae nodded. "I have. For 1,180 years. I am a cyborg. As I said, I was placed here for the very purpose of recording this information and transmitting it to another."

"Yes, your story. Might I hear it?"

Orionae's companions, flitting like ghosts, had formed a circle around Siddhārtha and their leader while they talked. Siddhārtha wondered whether they were listening. Whenever they moved, their thin clothing gave off a faded luster that seemed to fit their ruined surroundings.

"Listen," Orionae said. "The Inner Planetary Alliance—"

Suddenly, an alert system embedded in the artificial ear shells at either side of Siddhārtha's head began to sound. Automatically, his metabolizer went into overdrive, preparing to pump oxygen and enzymes through his body. The supplementary processors embedded in each of his shoulders began scanning his surroundings. Finally, his tri-D sensor cell antenna indicated the presence of a dangerous enemy beyond the shattered wall directly behind him.

For a second, he regretted letting his guard down. It had been a mistake to divert his attention from his persistent follower, if only for a moment.

Orionae was a decoy!

In one bound, Siddhārtha leapt to the corner of the huge room to await the enemy's arrival, taking cover beneath a giant metallic cylinder, red with rust, that resembled some sort of electrical rectifier. A moment later, silent beams of deep crimson light struck the wall on either side of him. Where they hit, the shattered wall was reduced to incandescent steam, leaving nothing but scorched holes behind. Siddhārtha narrowly dodged the attack, leaping up to hide himself in a large crevice between the wall and the ceiling. The room was filled with swirling flames and rising dust, reducing visibility to less than a meter. Out of the dust and confusion came fragments of the screams of Orionae's people.

Siddhārtha gingerly extended his tri-D antenna from the crack in the wall, searching for his foe. He found him standing near a protrusion in the wall on the opposite side of the room. Orionae and the others were rapidly moving away, running down the corridor in a group. Though it would be a loss to let Orionae escape now, he could not risk exposing himself to his enemy in order to follow.

After what seemed like an interminable amount of time, the standoff ended when his enemy became tired of waiting and began to move.

Siddhārtha connected his tri-D antenna to his visual cortex.

A man was standing by the protrusion in the far wall. He wore dirty white cloth loosely wrapped around a thin, suntanned frame, and in his right hand he carried a short, strangely shaped weapon. It seemed odd to Siddhārtha that this man should be his enemy, in possession of such fearful technology. And yet he sensed a burning hatred directed toward himself.

His enemy moved suddenly, and another beam of crimson light erupted from the weapon in his hand, illuminating the corridor down which Orionae and his people were escaping. Siddhārtha sensed the group divide, separating into its individual members. Some of them vanished entirely.

Before the beam of light had ceased its cutting blast, Siddhārtha launched into motion. Energizing the micro-reactor embedded in his waist, he activated the discharge panel on his left wrist, propelling a large ball of yellow flame toward his enemy's position. The fireball struck the wall behind the man, exploding into hundreds of thousands of sparks that scattered in all directions.

As his enemy ran silently beneath the spreading blaze, Siddhārtha let fly a second fireball. The room was suffused with pale light and the air trembled as though electrified. Even as the flames surrounded the stranger, he ducked into a side corridor through an opening in the wall. A smile appeared on the man's chiseled brown face the moment before he disappeared, his eyes darting in Siddhārtha's direction.

Twice crimson beams blasted holes in the corridor ceiling. Then there was silence.

Siddhārtha extended his antenna to find that his enemy had retreated to the lower levels of the city. He had not abandoned his attack entirely . . . but it would be some time before he found his next opportunity to strike.

Siddhārtha went down into the corridor to look for Orionae. He found three bodies beneath fallen sections of ceiling, as well as several large holes with singed edges, which he took to indicate people who had been evaporated along with the floor and walls around them.

Orionae was lying on the floor some thirty meters down the corridor.

Siddhārtha hurried to him, picking him up in his arms. "Orionae! Awaken!"

The cyborg's eyelids fluttered open. Siddhārtha saw his own round head reflected in Orionae's brown eyes.

"Ah yes, Siddhārtha. I had not finished my story. In the year 2902, the Solar Alliance determined that the energy loss within our solar region was part of a greater energy loss affecting the entire Milky Way galaxy."

"You mean the entire galaxy was deteriorating?"

"Yes. Then, in 2905, at a summit of astrophysicists called by the Solar Alliance, an emergency committee formed to investigate the matter announced that a reduction in potential energy, its cause unknown, was affecting the entire known universe."

"Orionae, stay with me," Siddhārtha said, lifting the slumping cyborg off the ground. "You must tell me what happened next."

"I'm all right . . . They soon discovered that every spiral galaxy in the visible universe was showing a rapid red shift."

"Which would either mean the Doppler effect or a rapid reduction in potential energy."

"It is as you say. However, we knew it was not the Doppler effect, for indeed all the energy in the universe was beginning to fade measurably." A ragged cough sent spasms through Orionae's body.

"But couldn't it have been a diffusion of energy caused by rapid expansion?"

Orionae shook his head. "No. If that were the case then the Doppler effect would be sufficient to explain the red shift. But observe these drastically cold temperatures. Water and air are both rarefied, and nothing but a cyborg can even hope to survive on the planet's surface. I wonder how they fare on other planets . . . whether any humans remain."

The strength left Orionae's body. Panicking, Siddhārtha shook him. "Don't let go! You have not yet fulfilled your duty!"

Orionae barely managed to open his lightless eyes. "Siddhārtha. I have seen this with my own eyes: strange life-forms came from beyond our universe to develop this world—this was seven thousand years ago already."

"From beyond our universe, you say?"

"They said this: 'By the reckoning of the Twin Suns, from Blue 93 to the summer of Yellow 17 in the New Galactic Age . . .'"

"'. . . the Planetary Development Committee on Astarta 50 received a directive from *Shi* to attempt a *helio-ses-beta* development on the third planet in the Ai System,'" Siddhārtha said, continuing the words that Orionae had started. "Orionae. Did you see these life-forms yourself?"

Orionae nodded slightly. It would have been dangerous to force him to speak any further, so Siddhārtha used his supplementary processors to extract the memories from him. The platinum electrodes implanted in Orionae's skull activated his cerebrum with a shower of ultrashort waves. Then the extraction stimulation circuit from Siddhārtha's supplementary processor fused with the remaining gray matter in the cyborg, converting his distant memories into faint electrical patterns, which it then transmitted into Siddhārtha's neural web. Siddhārtha continued to walk quietly down the corridor, holding Orionae's body in his arms.

〉

His enemy was on the move again. Siddhārtha knew that if he were attacked now, both he and Orionae would be killed. He had to stall for time. With Orionae in his arms, he moved as quietly as possible along the corridor, following its sand-strewn slope downward. Fortunately, it seemed that his enemy had not reacquired their position.

"Yellow 17 in the New Galactic Age, the Planetary Development Committee on Astarta 50 received a directive from *Shi* to attempt a *helio-ses-beta* development on the third planet in the Ai System . . ."

The words left a strange echo in Siddhārtha's ears.

"What does '*Shi*' mean, I wonder?" he asked out loud.

In his arms, Orionae suddenly whispered, "*Shi* is the absolute being. *Shi* exists outside this universe, causing this universe to be. All things and people in this universe, and the way and direction of all things, are according to *Shi*'s will."

Siddhārtha listened with part of his mind while another part thought furiously.

"Siddhārtha. If it is *Shi*'s will that the energy in our universe fade, what will you do?"

"Orionae. Might I assume that this absolute being of which you speak is what the ancients called 'God'?"

Orionae raised his eyebrows. "I was placed here merely with the purpose of transmitting what I had seen with my own eyes to future generations. That is all."

For a long while, Siddhārtha carried his burden in silence. At last he reached the long hall that led to the city gates. Through the dark arch of the gates he could see the vast desert beyond. The air was as cold as ice and bore the faint metallic smell of ions.

Just a little farther and we'll be free.

At that moment, Siddhārtha spotted a single figure standing as still as a statue in the darkness beneath the arch of the gates. The dirty white cloth in which the figure was wrapped made an audible sound as it slapped against his bare legs in the wind.

❭

Siddhārtha's enemy had known he would have to pass through the gateway. Already the man was taking aim.

In an instant Siddhārtha thought of a plan—but it had one drawback. He could do little holding Orionae, and abandoning him here would be tantamount to murder. Quickly he shuffled backward, burying his heels in the sand. He was left with no choice. Placing Orionae in the shade of the wall, he prepared to make a decisive counterattack.

"Siddhārtha," Orionae whispered. "Be careful. Your enemy is a very dangerous man. He has already waited here five hundred years for your arrival. He is the very hand of *Shi*."

"Wait, Orionae. Don't tell me that he is what you saw—was *he* the destruction of the city?"

"Siddhārtha. What I saw was a great host of angelic beings—but now I wonder if they were not merely a phantasm."

"A phantasm?"

His enemy slid forward across the sand.

With sudden clarity, Siddhārtha understood that his foe was not merely trying to kill him, but Orionae as well. Of course—clearly the man had known well ahead of time that Siddhārtha would attempt to escape with Orionae. He had left Orionae alive so that he might catch them together.

My enemy is not this man before me.

"My enemy is *Shi!*"

Siddhārtha looked around in desperation. It seemed that the world around him had grown dim, and within that gloom a certain death was waiting. He had no time! No time to remove the electrodes from Orionae's head and switch his supplementary processors to full battle mode. Nonetheless he began to do what he could, slowly removing the electrodes, adjusting the circuits connecting his processors.

His enemy was taking his time, observing Siddhārtha's every movement, waiting for the right opportunity to let that crimson flame burst from the maser in his hand. He grinned as he drew nearer, revealing yellowed, rotting teeth; Siddhārtha heard him muttering, but all he could make out was the sound ". . . zareth."

At exactly the same moment, Siddhārtha and his enemy sprang into action, each taking a sudden leap to reach a better position. An instant later Siddhārtha noticed a girl with clear eyes standing directly between them. Her body was lean and supple, like a young boy's, and a glow like that of the evening sun suffused her face and form.

His enemy shouted something. A crimson beam of fire from his right hand pierced the girl's body. She laughed soundlessly.

"You have heard the name of Asura?" the girl asked. "She stands before you. Now tell me: where is *Shi?*"

Again, the beam of fire sliced toward the girl. She extended her hand, and the beam veered off sharply, vaporizing a section of wall behind her.

Siddhārtha's enemy shouted something and retreated several paces as swiftly as a shadow retreats before the sun. All expression faded from his chiseled, bearded face. His eyes, blue as shallow water, gazed without emotion at Siddhārtha, then shifted back to rest upon the girl.

"So it is true after all," the man said, nodding. His dirty rags slapped noisily against the bare skin of his thighs.

A gust of wind rose and the girl leaned into it, letting it support her. "What do you mean?" she asked as the wind dropped again.

The question seemed to shift the balance of their enemy's mind back toward aggression, and he began sliding to one side, moving into position for another attack.

"I recently received word that in addition to my primary target, I might find two other enemy elements waiting for me. Until this moment, I had no idea who those two might be. But now I see it is you and the cyborg."

Hatred darkened the man's sunken eyes. His toes flexed, and he moved forward. Then he stopped, raising one finger to point at the girl.

"A-A-Asura. Why have you come here?"

She fixed him with a glare. "Jesus of Nazareth," she addressed him, ignoring his question. "How long have you been waiting for us?"

"Ah . . ." He nodded slightly, considering. "Since I began my vigil for you in this barren desert already eight hundred years have passed. Yet I have been waiting for my moment since three thousand years before that. It has been a very long time."

His words rang with expectation—clearly he foresaw a swift end to his long, arduous duty. There was confidence in his look even as the dark shadows deepened over the man's small eyes.

"You—" Jesus jerked his jaw toward Siddhārtha. "Siddhārtha, you called yourself? It seems that you've unconsciously chosen your old name again. Fascinating, that."

"My old name? What are you talking about?" Siddhārtha asked, rashly turning to face his foe full on.

"Look out!"

The air split in two, and a deep red luminance painted ground and sky. Dust burst up in lines across the sand. Then the sand itself became steam, and the ground began to shimmer like a mirage. Asura flitted into the air like a feather, but the crimson beam followed her in a boiling column of fire that pierced the sky. A blast wave erupted, striking the desert like a giant hammer.

Several of the lofty spires above them broke and fell down into the city below. Where they landed, new plumes of sand rose in mushroom clouds. The faded red sky shifted to lurid orange, clogged with numberless whipping particles carrying death and destruction. The chances of escape from that apocalypse dwindled rapidly to almost nil. Their enemy's assault was as perfect as it was complete.

)

Siddhārtha lay half buried in sand, still as a lump of stone. His tri-D antenna opened slightly, shedding a tiny stream of dust.

He could sense his enemy nearby—everywhere, it seemed.

No—there he was, not more than a hundred meters away, moving from left to right across Siddhārtha's field of vision.

I wonder what he's up to?

He resisted the temptation to fully extend his antenna. In the quiet that now reigned, even the slightest movement could draw attention from a considerable distance. The release of kinetic energy was one of the easiest to detect. It would be far too dangerous to reveal himself; the last attack had proved beyond the shadow of a doubt his enemy's hideous strength.

So what is he doing?

Unable to restrain his desire to know, he let his antenna push another ten centimeters above the top of the sand.

Unthinkingly, Siddhārtha tensed every muscle in his body.

A thousand meters ahead of where his enemy slowly made his way across the flats was his destination—a small black shadow atop a dune. Asura.

Jesus of Nazareth was moving slowly, leaving footprints in the sand. The flames and explosions had singed his already tan skin to such a brownness that he threatened to disappear into the desert landscape altogether.

Jesus was almost out of Siddhārtha's range when his path began to curve as he headed directly toward the top of the dune where Asura was standing.

The sky and land were lit with scarlet for a moment. Then as Jesus began to climb the dune, the world faded again to its former monotone, and an icy wind blew in between the swirling flames. The brightness of the flames waxed and ebbed. Even the rapid energy shifts and massive discharges generated by the Nazarene's weapon lost much of their power in this world near death.

Siddhārtha searched around for any sign of Orionae, but could not detect him anywhere. Finally, he fully extended his antennae, reasoning that his enemy's attention would be fixed on the far-off dune where Asura was standing.

As he did so, he felt a terrible and urgent need to act. *I have to distract him!*

Siddhārtha struggled out of the sand to stand. "Hold! Jesus of Nazareth!" he cried, yet his voice only traveled from the top of his throat back down his neck into his own body, reverberating up into his ears, but never reaching the outside air. Siddhārtha panicked, realizing that if he did not draw at least half of his enemy's firepower in his own direction, Asura would not be able to withstand another of Jesus's attacks.

Jesus of Nazareth stopped abruptly, then slowly lifted his right hand.

Suddenly, the far edges of the flats erupted toward the sky without a sound. Higher and higher they rose into the gray atmosphere, creating a valley with impossibly steep sides, while at the same time the edges of the sky plunged toward the ground. At the limits of Siddhārtha's field of vision, sky and land joined together, fusing into a single curved wall. Lighter than shadow, more indefinite even than the void, the flats and the gray sky formed a giant cylinder, as if the very laws of geometry had broken. Far out in that vertiginous space, like a fragile image in a kaleidoscope, he could see Asura looking very small.

The howling of the wind had ceased entirely, leaving a sickening emptiness in its place.

"Stop! Do not do this!"

Siddhārtha sprinted through the deathlike silence, lacking the time to consider why Jesus of Nazareth grew no nearer no matter how much he ran.

As Siddhārtha sped across the sand, the battle structures in his body prepared for combat. Palisade tissues—resembling those in a plant, but more closely akin to the electroplaques of an eel—linked his processors and his core reactor to his weapons units; discharge panels on his shoulders opened like unfolding leaves. Automatically, his metabolizer revved up to maximum capacity as the circuit from the reactor connected to the roots of the panels. In an instant the leaves were ready to unleash their deadly stores.

Siddhārtha did not hesitate. Still sprinting, he released the high voltage inside his condensers in a single blast.

With a flash sky and land turned ghostly pale. The electromagnetic waves pulsed toward their target, tracing a circle of pure blue ions around Jesus of Nazareth.

Less than a breath later, Siddhārtha struck again. This time, the gray sky turned a dark leaden color. Seen from within, all the objects inside the great cylinder lost their individual colors, becoming translucent. Then, a circle of ultramarine light began to spread, enveloping all.

Siddhārtha watched as his attack ran its course.

The shining ring of the electromagnetic wave was rapidly spreading in all directions, losing its coloration as it went. It dispersed like a broken circlet of chain links, some sections clinging together, others severing completely until all had disappeared. Siddhārtha spotted Jesus's emaciated back standing just beyond the fading circle of light.

He shook his head and resumed his mad dash across the sand.

While he ran, the gray sky and the vast desert ground into motion, moving with increasing speed until all was rotating around him. Gaping vortices formed in the sky, while the flats transformed into a faded spiral that spun at a frightening velocity. The only things not carried by their motion were Siddhārtha and the man from Nazareth.

Siddhārtha's thoughts raced. *Why, when everything around us is spinning at such a furious rate, am I and Jesus alone still able to stand?* He felt cold sweat trickling down his back as understanding slipped from his grasp.

Then suddenly he understood: he had been pushed into a separate space from the one where Jesus and Asura stood—a fold in space-time, or a separate plane entirely.

"Let me out!" he shouted with all his strength. "Let me out of here!" But all his voice accomplished was to vibrate the air that closed around him.

❭

Yet Siddhārtha's shout reached across the swirling tumult like a single ray of light, piercing Asura's ears.

WHEEEEEEEEN

A high-pitched vibration, too high for even Asura's sensitive eardrums to detect, caused a slight stirring in the air. It pressed in on Asura's body, shimmering like a mirage, assaulting the cellular structure of her body via the sensory cells at her nerve endings, causing her nucleic acids to begin to ionize. Now the space around her began to revolve at a frightening speed. Outside that whorl, Jesus shone like a primary star with a comet tail of streaming light.

Gradually Asura's form grew more transparent. The spinning sky and land and the brilliantly shining form of her enemy were as light that coursed through her body, spreading beyond her as she dissolved.

Stretches of the rapidly spinning flats erupted in incandescent fire; fragments of molten magma rained down, trailing tails of white smoke.

Satisfied with his attack, Jesus flicked a switch on the ultrahigh frequency generator in his hand.

Deep silence returned. Several meters ahead of where Jesus stood, a number of wide, shallow trenches radiated out through the dunes toward the horizon, scars where the sand had been evaporated by the high temperatures of the ultrahigh frequency vibrations. Wisps of white smoke still rose from the trenches in places.

Ultrahigh frequency vibrations had the power to neutralize cellular activity, scramble nerves, and destroy cellular structure altogether. It seemed highly unlikely that Asura had been able to escape the attack.

Jesus of Nazareth strode across the flats, crossing a kilometer of scorched sand. When he reached the top of the dune where Asura had been standing moments before, the ashen dust lifted around his feet like smoke into the wind. No trace of Asura's presence remained. Along the horizon beyond the dunes, the lead-colored sea spread out flat and fallen. Behind him, the ruined city stood like a giant gravestone over the flats.

An ice cold wind cut through the man's heart. Of his appointed tasks, he had completed the first, which was also the most difficult. Yet he was left feeling a slight dissatisfaction that it had ended so easily. His dissatisfaction mingled with an uncomfortable awareness in his mind that his enemy was hiding out there, somewhere. Doubts assailed him. Surely such a long wait could not be rewarded with such a short battle. And it had been such a one-sided fight, besides. He wondered whether this was really the end of it, whether his victory was truly complete. With some effort, he restrained himself from plummeting into despair and made for his second target, heading toward the place where the waves broke against the shore.

Sand drifted like smoke, and the wind whistled like a flute around him. The sea was pressing toward him—baring its white fangs at him. The spray wet the long shore, turning it black, and drifted in a fine mist onto his tattered garments.

His enemy had hidden here, beneath these waters. He had known for a very long time that his enemy would likely come from here.

And yet, contrary to his expectations, his enemy had come all the way out of the sea and into the dying city.

Far-off to his left, he spotted a massive, angular object resting atop the sand.

"There you are."

He quickened his pace as he approached. The object was at least fifty meters to a side. It appeared wider than it was tall, though that was likely because its base was buried under the sand. Long years of erosion had left countless fine cracks and pockmarks on its surface. It looked entirely out of place on the vast, unbroken land beneath the flat gray of the sky.

An oval hatch was open at its upper end. From this orifice a cocoonlike cylinder of silver extended to the ground, supported on two metallic rails.

Jesus took one look at the silver tube and realized it was a free-form lift. Whatever had been contained within this giant structure had passed outside via this lift.

"So for five thousand years, you waited here. Perhaps this was once a mountain or an island. The sand covering your incubation tank was washed away, blown aside, until nothing remained but this flat land, and your vessel was revealed." Jesus of Nazareth shook his head. "We both waited for so long."

He was overcome by a strong desire to look inside the strange vessel.

He wanted to see what sort of technology, what sort of devices had kept the life-form that called itself Asura alive and growing for five thousand years—the processors and power sources, the memory inserters, the oxygen generators, and all other such devices. He thought briefly on the vast amount of oxygen and nutrients a life-form would need to consume over such a long period of time. Of course, none of these necessities could be gathered along the way during a journey through the void, and attempting to store and transport that much material would be an inelegant solution, to say the least. Which left only one option: the designers of the vessel had used some sort of atomic compositing device to manipulate matter and create the needed stores from the air. The devices that controlled that process would be extremely delicate, allowing for no margin of error whatsoever;

managing them would require a processor's judgment, guided by a powerful neural memory web. Which was how his enemy, the destroyer, had managed to wait here for so long.

His second task was to ensure that this incubation tank was never used again. He turned the beam filament of the ultrahigh frequency generator toward the towering object in front of him. When he squeezed the trigger, the atmosphere around him twanged like a slender piano wire. Ripples spread on the surface of the object, quickly becoming rapid waves. Moments later the giant object vanished altogether. A faint mirage shimmered in its place for a moment until that, too, disappeared. It all happened without the slightest sound.

Another incubation tank was surely out there, somewhere beneath the waves, but he had no way of finding that.

The sea stirred, pushing toward Jesus's feet. It drenched the edges of his tattered robe, and he disliked the feel of the cloth clinging to his legs. But for a long time Jesus stood unmoving, looking out at the sea.

He had done all that *Shi* wanted. The realization of God's will must always be done to the fullest, and it gave him great honor to have played even a small part in bringing God's designs to fruition. It was, in fact, the entire source of his own volition to live.

Jesus of Nazareth knelt in the driving wind.

"Great *Shi*. My Father who art Heaven. I have done as you commanded. Please, forgive the sinning Samarians. Summon them to you. *Shi*, the world is tired, blind, already moving toward a funeral procession of its gods. *Shi*, Father who art in Heaven. Already there are none who live upon the land, none left to worship you. *Shi*, will this world never again know her former days of glory?"

The words of his prayer were lost in the wind. Gradually, shadows deepened across the sky and land, while the wild white waves danced and sprayed.

"*Shi*! How can it be that man never earned your forgiveness? I know we are sullied by evil and sin, that our hands are stained with blood, and yet . . ."

The direction of the wind shifted, and an icy cold breeze struck the back of Jesus's neck.

"Shi . . ."

All that was left to him was prayer now. Yet he swallowed his words as he felt the presence of something behind him in this wasted world of wind and surf and sand.

Who's there?

The presence was almost inorganic in its absolute stillness. Whoever it was was not even breathing.

Who are you?

Drops of cold sweat trickled down the Nazarene's back like tiny insects made of ice. He could feel his mouth grow as dry as the sand beneath his feet.

He realized he was in a place of absolute death. Were he to stand, his life would surely end.

So what do I do?

His metabolizer was running at maximum capacity. He felt the tingle of the insulin as it spread through him, thinning as it reached his hands and feet. Each passing second brought him closer to death.

The wind ceased. All sound vanished. In that instant, he ran, swift as a shadow. Something in Jesus's chest felt hot, as though he had been burned. He still had two small cylinders in his pocket; he fished them out and tossed them over his shoulder. Then he pulled off the magnetic field generator wrapped around his left arm, pressed the switch, and threw it on the ground beneath his feet.

Can I escape this?

He was not entirely without hope.

The ultramarine light of a lithium nuke suffused the flats. A massive white ball of flame expanded with hideous speed, boiling the sea and fusing the sand beneath it. Nearly five hundred meters in diameter, the fireball suddenly inverted behind Jesus as he ran, becoming a crater in the ground, swirling with energy. Like a giant wave crashing against an iron seawall, the fireball surged and swelled, trying to break through an unseen barrier.

Glumly, Jesus admitted to himself that his attack had probably failed to destroy his enemy. His opponent was clearly as well protected as he was. Ensconced within his own barrier, he would make his way through the sea of flame created by the nuclear explosion and launch an assault on the barrier that Jesus had erected on the flats. Still, even if his enemy had not been defeated, his assault would surely be slowed by the blast.

It was only another five hundred meters to his own pod—suddenly a despairingly long distance.

A small black object slid through the sky, white flame ejecting from its anterior: a hand-fired missile. He waved toward it with the laser gun attached to his wrist, and a brilliant arc of light split the sky, swallowing the missile entirely.

My enemy lives!

The black hatch of his pod was open before him. Something exploded behind his back, sending crimson flames streaming over his head. Stinging particles of sand followed, searing the air like glowing embers, but even as they began to strike around him he made it through the hatchway.

The hatch slammed shut automatically behind him. As his eyes adjusted to the dim interior light, he saw two silhouettes in front of the pod's luminescent xenon wall.

"Now, you will take us to *Shi*."

The figures' cruel smiles turned Jesus's despair to loathing. Trying to keep his spirit from crumbling altogether, he peered furtively around the inside of the pod. His two enemies slid forward from either side, their expressionless eyes glittering like stars.

They have me, Jesus thought, and his confidence guttered like a candle flame. Then, in his moment of greatest terror, he spotted something—there was still a way for him to escape! Leaping several meters in one bound, he reached out to the subspace positional circuit on the far wall.

❯

In an instant, Jesus of Nazareth had vanished.

"Where'd he go?"

"He's escaped!"

Siddhārtha and Asura exchanged bitter glances. A moment's hesitation had cost them their advantage. There was only one thing left for them to do. It would be highly dangerous to pursue their enemy now, yet with every second they delayed, their ultimate victory became increasingly distant and less likely.

Siddhārtha reached out through the hatch to pick up Orionae and drag him inside. The cyborg's protruding forehead cast a deep shadow across his largely featureless face.

Asura was focusing, expanding to her full height, as though listening for some far-off sound.

There was a panel near the ceiling on one of the side walls from which a transparent case extended, housing three multifaceted electrodes. On the floor below it sat a turntable platform large enough to support several humans. The cylindrical space above the turntable glowed with a faint reddish light. The rhythmic sound of a rotating scanner emerged from the structure nearby.

Asura nodded to Siddhārtha, who thrust Orionae's body into the reddish light upon the platform, then jumped onto it himself. A fraction of a second later, Asura joined them. The sound of the revolving scanner increased in speed until it sounded like a storm.

Immediately before Siddhārtha lost consciousness, the image of a great galactic spiral burned with incredible brilliance inside his mind. The swirling light was made up of two distinct parts, one horizontal, the other vertical, and the waves of fusion energy erupting where they met soundlessly swallowed the darkness.

Unthinkingly, Siddhārtha screamed, and the sound of his voice held his consciousness for the briefest of moments. He remembered having seen this sight before.

One of the spirals is the Milky Way, the other is Andromeda.

He wondered briefly how he knew those names, yet decided almost as quickly that it did not matter. All he understood was that something terribly destructive was happening to these two galaxies, and that this destruction was not a natural phenomenon, but something caused by an external power.

. . . Yellow 17 in the New Galactic Age, the Planetary Development Committee on Astarta 50 received a directive from Shi–

Siddhārtha's waking mind melded with the void around him, and he was lost.

Night gathers at the base of the torch.
Darkness seeps into the traveler's chest,
And raises there a flag of fear and shame.

"Emergency Sirocco from Ai System Planet 3-3-3," a neutral voice by Siddhārtha's ear whispered. "Leave the spaceway immediately. Emergency Sirocco from Ai System Planet 3-3-3. Leave the spaceway immediately. Too many unknown quantities. Repeat, there are too many unknown quantities."

Complex symbols flashed on the metallic panel before him, signaling some sort of emergency. A large part of his head still felt frozen, hard as a wall of ice, but his consciousness was rapidly recovering.

"Let's get out of here."

The three travelers slipped out from between the multifaceted electrodes. They were standing by a long tube that stretched off into infinity. A short distance to one side was another tube—one of the spaceways the voice was talking about, Siddhārtha presumed.

He looked around at the space around them. "What a long narrow room," he began, then he shook his head. "No, this is a very large room. As large as a spacecraft's storage hold."

The wall running beside the spaceway was little more than a partition. Above it, there was a considerable amount of empty space between the top of the partition and the ceiling high overhead, from which white light fell, the color of the noonday sun.

Siddhārtha extended his tri-D sensor cell antenna as far as it would go, observing what lay beyond the partition.

"Well, there are thousands of these spaceways here. I can see several people moving in the distance."

"Travelers from the Ai System, please report to survey department nine in sector four. Travelers from the Ai System, please report to survey department nine in sector four. There are too many unknown quantities. Repeat, there are too many unknown quantities."

Asura's eyes darted around.

"Asura," Siddhārtha said, "I daresay that announcement is meant for us."

"I would imagine so. This business about 'too many unknown quanti-ties' sounds extremely dangerous."

"Ai System Planet 3-3-3 likely indicates the third planet from the sun. But what is an 'emergency sirocco'?"

Asura frowned. "Perhaps these are the closest words for whatever it is they mean. Or perhaps the pronunciation is merely similar."

Siddhārtha shook his head. It seemed that the autotranslator in his outer ears was terribly confused. It was having difficulty transposing what-ever language they were hearing into standard solar speech. The language was so unusual that he lacked samples of it in the neural memory webs in-side his supplementary processors. The two exchanged glances again.

"Let's get out of here."

There was a small door on the side of the hall. No one was in sight.

The soft yellow light outside hit the ground at a slanting angle, re-minding Siddhārtha of the light in the evening when a rainstorm is close.

"What is this place?"

The surface of the space into which they had emerged was covered with needlelike plants standing about thirty centimeters high and deep indigo in color that painted the faces of the three travelers with reflected light.

On the other side of the open space stood a line of windowless, boxlike buildings. Giant spires, about five hundred meters tall and covered with strange, winding patterns rose from the rooftops.

"Let's cross and go inside one of those."

The needlelike plants were remarkably brittle. Merely stepping through them caused them to snap, and something like crystalline powder fell from where they broke. They reached the far buildings and looked back to see that the building they had left was massive, at least a kilometer to each side.

"What *is* this place?" Siddhārtha muttered again to no one in particular.

"A good question," Asura said. Even she had no idea where they were.

"Do you think Jesus of Nazareth is here somewhere?"

Sunlight spilled from around the edges of the large building they had left, casting long shadows across the bristling tops of the indigo plants. Siddhārtha looked between two of the closer buildings, spying a wide flat surface beyond that sparkled with a silvery light.

"Is that an ocean?"

The three hurried between the buildings up to the lip of what appeared to be a vast crater. Down the slope from where they stood stretched a smooth, silvery plain apparently made of some hard material that was neither metal nor glass.

"What is it?"

"No natural formation, though I see no seams, nor any openings for ventilation. Perhaps something spilled out of the ground here and hardened?"

"Like magma?"

The three looked around again. Behind them, their view was cut short by the row of buildings.

To the front, the curious flat surface stretched at least one hundred kilometers toward the base of a ring of towering mountains that cast a dark silhouette against the light yellow sky.

"It's as though they took a valley one hundred kilometers across and put a lid on it. Perhaps to build a city below?"

"There are easier ways to fashion an underground city," Siddhārtha said.

"Perhaps the city was here first, and they constructed the barrier over it."

To defend against an attack. Siddhārtha and Asura understood the value of defense with painful clarity.

Orionae, however, stood saying nothing, his round head reflecting the yellowish light of the sun. He appeared to have no interest in the strange scenery.

"Let's see if we can't examine the inside," Siddhārtha proposed. "Perhaps we will be able to figure out where we are."

The edge of the silver plain was about fifty meters below them. Siddhārtha began to make his way slowly down the slope. The ground of the slope was firmer than expected, being comprised mostly of large rocky chunks.

"This looks igneous."

Asura picked up one of the chunks and held it before her eyes. "Not igneous. These are granules of metamorphic rock created by applying intense amounts of heat to a sedimentary rock with a high calcium content."

"What does that tell you, Asura?"

Asura narrowed her eyes, her thoughts ranging far off into the distance. After a while she shook her head. "Nothing yet. But I may remember something before long."

The three stood on the silvery surface, the glacial hardness of it strange beneath their feet. It was as flat as a mirror, but upon closer inspection, there was a faint weblike pattern with crosshatching lines just beneath the top surface.

They advanced for a while until they could look back and see a small sun hanging low above the cluster of massive buildings that housed the spaceways. Its soft yellow light cast long shadows behind the three of them atop the featureless flat plain.

Suddenly, Orionae stood, a violent expression spasming across his usually blank face as he began to speak. "Yellow 17 in the New Galactic Age, the Planetary Development Committee on Astarta 50 received a directive . . ." His voice was jagged, sounding like a recording played backward, and the words struck the other two like hot irons upon their chest.

"Orionae! Is this Astarta 50?"

Orionae craned his head to look again at the pale yellow sun, then returned his gaze to the silvery expanse around them. "Yes. This is Astarta. I would presume that now we are in the age of the Yellow Sun—an age that is near its end. Next we will enter the age of the Blue Sun, which will last for many hundreds of years. This time of transition is called the New Galactic Age."

Orionae's already small body seemed to shrink further as he began to walk around on the hard surface.

"Which means that the Planetary Development Committee is somewhere here on this planet."

"And so is *Shi*."

Orionae looked up. "The Ai System is none other than our solar system. Which would make the third planet Earth," he said, his words a stream of rote information. "Though I cannot tell you exactly what the *helio-ses-beta* development that took place on our planet entailed, I can assure you that it was a very elaborate process that brought life from simple single-celled organisms all the way to humanity."

Siddhārtha and Asura stared unblinking at the diminutive cyborg.

"A *helio-ses-beta* development uses a great deal of energy. Because of this, it cannot be attempted very often—even within our solar system, it was only performed on Earth."

"Interesting," Siddhārtha said. "There are those who once postulated that life developed on Earth alone because only Earth was capable of supporting it—but perhaps it had nothing to do with the conditions on the planet at all."

"Exactly what kind of organization is the Planetary Development Committee?" Asura asked.

"And what is *Shi*?" Siddhārtha added.

Orionae pointed down toward the surface beneath his feet in silence.

"All our answers lie below, is that it? Then let us go."

The three widened their search across the plain, but they could find nothing resembling an entrance.

"Asura," Siddhārtha called out, touching his antenna to the surface at his feet. "Let us try to open a hole in this strange material."

"I can judge the ionization potential; I'll just run a high current through the material and see what happens." Asura directed the energy from her miniaturized reactor pile to the sapphire laser in her finger. That energy was condensed into a gravitationally directed beam with a diameter of a hundredth of a millimeter, which she pointed toward a spot on the ground several meters away. A section of the hard silvery surface roughly one centimeter in diameter where the beam hit transformed to a faded gray, then the dirty brown of singed paper.

"There."

She stopped the laser, and the discolored section returned to its former silvery hue.

Siddhārtha spoke. "The ionization potential is roughly 207,000 volts. S.H.00913. When reactance is zero, 4.462. Asura, the surface is neither metal nor silicon. This is gravitationally sealed space."

"Which reflects light, making it look opaque."

Which meant that the diamond-hard surface supporting them, the material that formed the buildings and the spaceways, and everything else in this place were not physical objects at all, but barriers of gravitational energy.

"But why create such a barrier?" Siddhārtha wondered. "Was some sort of assault launched upon this planet? I'd like to know."

"Siddhārtha, let us open a way through here." Asura steadied her aim carefully, firing her laser for about thirty seconds to open a fifty-centimeter-diameter hole in the hard silvery surface.

The three took turns looking down through the hole. An icy cold wind erupted up from the darkness within. There was no sound.

They exchanged glances. The darkness inside spoke only of destruction and death. Asura produced a bundle of wire from somewhere among the folds of her clothes. Sitting down at the edge of the hole, she carefully wove three rough mesh nets, large enough to hold a man. She handed one to Siddhārtha and one to Orionae. Then, gripping the third, she leaned out over the hole and was sucked into the darkness, electricity playing across the metallic webbing beneath her.

Siddhārtha jumped in after her, his head reflexively shrinking back at the icy cold, as he sent a large current through his hastily constructed ionocraft. Below him was a bottomless sea of darkness. He saw Asura's ionocraft moving through it, trailing a long tail of emerald light. Siddhārtha summoned all his strength to follow her. Rather a long while after, Orionae too came down through the hole. In a group, the three of them rapidly descended. After a long while in darkness, they saw the city below them.

)

In the center of a plaza, three obelisks stood pointing toward the dark night sky. The obelisks were made of a material that glimmered like gemstone beneath the light of countless spotlights. Several dozen ropes extended from the obelisks out through the crowd toward the edges of the circular plaza, making the whole thing look like a giant wheel, with the obelisks for an axle and the ropes for spokes. The crowd shouted in unison as they pulled on the ropes. With each coordinated pull, the three obelisks wobbled. Flares went up, one after the other, creating tiny stars of light above the surging throng. From somewhere rumbled the sound of explosions.

Suddenly, a swarm of rotodynes descended from the sky onto the tops of the tall buildings around the plaza, from where they unleashed aqua laser rays upon the crowd below. Flames rose up in every direction—people swarmed away from one blaze only to be engulfed by another. Their shouts and cries gradually became one unified scream, like the roaring of the sea. The obelisks toppled, then fell—slowly at first, then quickly, until they lay flat on the ground, pointing toward one edge of the plaza. The impact when the obelisks struck the ground sent up great plumes of dust, and one of the buildings standing at the edge of the plaza collapsed from the power of the shock waves.

The rotodynes began tossing small explosives down into the plaza. The charges were small, yet they exploded with such ferocity that even from a distance they echoed in Siddhārtha's gut. Flares of light shot into the sky from where the explosives landed, sending up a spray of severed hands and feet. The remaining crowd flowed into a single line like a river and made for the far side of the plaza.

Another explosion rang out, not loud enough to drown out the cries and screams of terror.

The three travelers pressed themselves against the cavity high up on the wall of one of the towering buildings, looking down at the chaos far below them.

"This is more than just a demonstration. This is rebellion," Siddhārtha observed.

"Look," Asura pointed out across the city. "Another fire over there."

An eerie crimson light soaked the sky behind a tall cluster of buildings. More explosions echoed from that direction, accompanied by distant columns of flame.

"We must find the Planetary Development Committee," Orionae said, his eyes filled with the sort of abject terror that comes from deep experience. "This city will soon cease to function."

The three went in through an open window in the side of the building and found themselves in a wide corridor. Several rooms lined the sides, but the walls had been stripped and the doors blown off their hinges into the rooms. All had been abandoned for a very long time. They found the doors that had once opened to a lift, long since blown in, the metal remnants hanging like scraps of torn paper.

"Guess we'll take the stairs," Siddhārtha said dryly.

The paneling of the stairs and parts of the walls had been stripped, exposing the skeletal framework beneath and making the footing treacherous. They descended cautiously. Halfway down the building, they found more chaos—a wide corridor filled to bursting with people chanting "Death to the leader! Kill the leader!" As one, the crowd lifted their arms and opened their mouths wide, shouting for blood.

"You!" Siddhārtha shouted, grabbing the shoulder of a man passing by them. "Where is this leader of whom you speak?"

The man turned eyes like lenses toward Siddhārtha.

"Where is your leader, the one who governs you?"

The man paused, considering the meaning of the words. "Our leader, yes, our leader . . ." he mumbled.

"Yes, your leader, where is he?"

The man grabbed Siddhārtha's wrist. His grip was incredibly strong.

"What are you doing?"

"I will take you to him. I will take you to our leader," the man said.

"I only require you to tell—" but before Siddhārtha had finished speaking, the man broke into a run.

"Wait, hold up! Let go of me!"

The man dragged Siddhārtha along as though he weighed no more than a burlap sack. Though it should have been an easy thing for Siddhārtha to wrest his arm free, the man moved with superhuman speed, not giving

Siddhārtha time to think. The crowd turned at the sound of the shouting, dark suspicion in their eyes. Abruptly, those around them stopped moving and surrounded Siddhārtha and the man. With eyes devoid of emotion they reached out to grab him. He felt a grip like iron close around the antenna on his shoulder, and left with no other recourse, Siddhārtha diverted power to his discharge panels and generated a fireball. A ball of flame swelled to an enormous size, rolling through the crowd around him, the smell of ions mingling with the stench of scorched flesh. One of the walls burst into flames. The rage of the crowd quickly transformed into terror. Siddhārtha took advantage of the confusion to slip from the main corridor into a side passageway, leaving both the crowd and his companions behind.

"You have come from another star, haven't you," said a voice.

He whirled around and saw a man standing in a brown and yellow jumpsuit. The man's porcelain-smooth forehead gave off a cool gleam in the glow from the luminescent walls.

"Another star? I suppose so, yes."

"You wish to meet the leader?"

"That was my intention in coming here, but I'm afraid I got caught up in the crowd—"

"Come with me," the man said, turning and walking away.

Hoping that Asura and Orionae would be able to determine his location, Siddhārtha followed after the man.

The man passed from corridor to corridor, increasing the distance between them and the confusion back in the hallway. From windows opening in the corridor wall, Siddhārtha occasionally caught glimpses of red blazes in the city.

They crossed through a high overpass and entered a grand building that was surely the seat of the government.

"The leader's chambers are at the end of this hallway." The man stood by one wall, lifting a hand to indicate the direction.

Siddhārtha walked on alone, acutely aware that so long as Jesus of Nazareth was at large, he could be walking into a trap.

A door at the end of the hallway opened automatically at Siddhārtha's approach.

A single tall man was standing in the middle of the large room beyond, wearing yellow-brown robes that cast a long shadow in the dim illumination.

"You are the leader here?" Siddhārtha called out from the door.

"I am. And you are a traveler from another star. You have come here to meet me," the leader replied in a low voice that nonetheless was clearly audible in the spacious chamber.

"My name is Siddhārtha. I came from Earth, in the Sol System," Siddhārtha said, sensing a sudden increase in the leader's interest.

"The *Sol* System?"

"Is this surprising to you?"

"No, it is just that, as you can see, we are in the middle of a great rebellion here, and it is very dangerous for travelers from abroad. You should remain here within the government complex for your own safety."

Siddhārtha nodded noncommittally and walked closer.

Observed from less than two meters away, the leader's cheeks were shiny, with the same porcelain smoothness he had seen in the face of the man who led him here. He had a smooth head and silent eyes with a cruel gleam to them.

"If I may ask, what is the cause of your rebellion?"

The leader nodded. "Our citizens are of two minds, and these two schools of thought have developed into armed conflict. That is to say, an armed conflict though one side has yet to even show itself."

"I believe I heard them shouting they were going to kill the leader, which I assume to be you."

The man averted his eyes, anguish rising in the lines on his forehead.

"Unfortunately, I cannot acquiesce to the rebels' demands. That is why they protest."

Siddhārtha tried piecing together all he had seen in his mind. Still, he was unable to reach anything like a satisfying conclusion.

"Soon, the rebels will come here," Siddhārtha said. If it came to it, he and his companions could protect this leader while developing a strategy.

"No, do not worry. The only way into these offices is by the suspended corridor you came through, and it is already sealed by a barrier. Nothing may pass through."

"Why do you not try to appease the two factions? Is that not a leader's role?" Siddhārtha asked, an edge to his words.

"Already I have tried reconciliation dozens of times, not entirely without success. But it is a lost cause now. I'm tired. But enough of that. Tell me, why have you come here?"

Siddhārtha paused, unsure of what to say. In truth, he had no real purpose in coming here. He had jumped onto the spaceway in pursuit of Jesus of Nazareth. Yet he still didn't know why he even had to fight Jesus. The only thing he knew were those words: "Yellow 17 in the New Galactic Age, the Planetary Development Committee on Astarta 50 received a directive . . ." and a vague sense that this curious, shielded city was somehow connected to the Kingdom of Atlantis where Orionae claimed to hail from, and to the barren flats and ruined city that Siddhārtha had found upon emerging from the sea. There was an overall trend toward destruction and ruin in all that he had seen, and lately Siddhārtha had begun to think that some power had placed him here for the sole purpose of investigating that trend and possibly divining its cause and origin.

"I'd like to meet with the other faction of your citizens," Siddhārtha announced, dodging the leader's question.

The leader considered this for a moment, then waved his hand off toward his left in a silent gesture. The entrance door slid open and a man stepped inside. This man, too, was wearing a jumpsuit with bands of yellow and brown.

"Take this man to the A-Class Citizens' compartments," the leader instructed the new arrival.

"A-Class Citizens?" Siddhārtha echoed out loud, lifting an eyebrow.

"At once," said the man behind him, and he led Siddhārtha out of the leader's chamber.

"So your citizens are divided into two classes in this place?" If that were the case, a rebellion made a certain kind of sense, he thought to himself.

Outside of the leader's room, the corridor began a gentle downward slope, suggesting that wheeled vehicles had been used both inside and outside the building when it was first constructed, making the age of the building at least two thousand years old, judging by the level of the technology he saw.

Together with his guide, Siddhārtha went farther into the depths of the government complex, following the gradually sloping corridor downward. From the length of the descent and the lack of windows, he guessed that they were probably underground by now. At last they came to a giant door at the end of the corridor. Siddhārtha's guide spoke several times into an intercom on the wall before a red light lit above them and the door slid upward into the ceiling.

The man motioned for Siddhārtha to go through, explaining that he was unable to accompany him any farther.

Steeling himself against the chill that ran through his heart, cold as a polar wind, Siddhārtha strode through the doorway. He glanced up at the bottom of the door as he walked beneath it, noticing that sandwiched among its many layers was a composite silicon layer for filtering radiation. The heavy door shut behind him.

)

The corridor continued on straight for a very long time. The luminium coating the ceiling and both walls provided dim light, though it had peeled off in places, and a thin layer of dust upon the floor rose in small clouds around Siddhārtha's feet as he walked. The dust was finer and lighter than volcanic ash, and the clouds that rose from it thinner than a northern sea fog.

"No one has passed this way for over a thousand years," Siddhārtha muttered to himself. He approached one of the doors along the side of the corridor and pressed gently on it. It opened without a sound. What luminium remained on the walls of the room beyond lit the space with a lonely light. A storage shelf built into one wall was half open, and a mountain of dust spilled out of it, covering whatever contents it had once held. Along the far wall, he saw three chairs fashioned of metal tubing, the rust making the metal look like fossilized bone. A single pilot lamp on the back wall cast a small circle of orange light that made the abandoned room seem unreal, like a place from a dream.

Siddhārtha turned and was about to leave when he sensed a presence behind him. He looked around to see a large gray creature emerging from one of the walls. It had a large head, sturdy limbs, and thick scales like tree bark covering a cylindrical torso. Siddhārtha retreated to the entrance as the creature's hind legs emerged, followed by a long serpentine tail. The end of the tail was pointed, and it lashed violently against the walls and the floor. Moving as quickly as he could, Siddhārtha slid out into the corridor and shut the door behind him. A moment before the door slid completely closed, he spotted another of the strange creatures emerging from one of the walls.

Siddhārtha leaned against the door, catching his breath. Then, stepping quietly, he walked farther down the corridor and pressed on the next door. The room behind this one was exactly the same construction as the previous room, and likewise abandoned. Instead of chairs, this room had a single bed that seemed to have been made of some kind of reinforced glass. It was remarkably transparent once he blew the dust off of it. Siddhārtha sat down on the bed, suddenly feeling very weary. Emotions rose inside him, tugging at the corners of his memory, binding together snippets of something that had been familiar to him once, yet now felt very distant. He could feel his subconscious trying to piece together the self he had been from the parts of the self he was now. Threads of memory slowly wound together in his mind, creating a picture. But when he tried to look at it, opening his mind's eye wide, he felt it recede into the distance, his memories like strangers standing on the opposite shore of a wide river. He could see them with his eyes, but never know or touch them.

He looked up to see a vast blue sea stretching out before him. The sun cast vibrant rays across the water. As he watched, amazed, the surface of the sea split in two, and a single enormous fish swam out of the depths. In the blink of an eye, the fish transformed into two spacecraft, their photonic engines displacing the water beneath into the shape of an inverted umbrella.

Siddhārtha assumed, without explicitly thinking it, that this was some kind of dream, or perhaps a phantasm. He tried to shake it out of his head when he realized that what he was seeing was no phantasm at all, but an actual scene existing in reality. With a start, he leapt back out into the corridor in a single bound, his inertia causing him to trip and roll across the floor in an ungainly ball. He stood, but found he lacked the courage to look back into the room behind him. He ran.

The corridor seemed as endless as it was empty. Siddhārtha could sense no people anywhere along its length, nor did he detect any presence in any of the rooms to either side. Only one of the rooms he found with its door half open. He peeked in to see strange forms rising underneath the dim illumination, rising and falling in the center of the room, spewing flame and smoke.

"What is this place?" Siddhārtha wondered out loud. "Are these the A-Class Citizens?"

He reflected back on what he had seen thus far in the rooms along the corridor—scaled monsters, creatures of fire and smoke, photonic spacecraft—and did not think that any of these could be what one called "citizens."

He was contemplating returning and speaking to the Leader once again, when at last he came to the place where the corridor ended in a wide, hard panel made of a light green metallic substance. Glowing letters across the panel read A-CLASS CITIZEN AREA.

The panel slid into one wall at the slightest touch, revealing darkness ahead through which long rows of lamps along the floor and ceiling lit and faded, making it look as though the lights were jumping up and down in time to an unheard rhythm.

Siddhārtha lit the light projector fastened to the end of the leather cord wrapped around his waist. It cast an intense white circle of light, revealing an enormous complex structure ahead of him. The structure looked like some kind of shelving system for storing files or physical media, save for the vast number of pipes that ran horizontally and vertically in front of the metal panels providing access to each compartment in the system. Most of the pipes seemed to contain wiring of one kind or another, while others were clearly designed to carry liquids as they were fitted with automatic adjustment knobs at regular intervals. High above, a hoisting mechanism like a giant, flattened crab slid quietly along a silvery rail near the ceiling.

"Are you the otherworlder who seeks an audience with an A-Class Citizen?" came a strangely undulating voice from the direction of the crab.

"Yes. I would know the truth behind the rebellion outside these walls."

"Very well," the voice continued after several seconds of silence. "I will bring one out to you. You may ask it any questions you like."

Two arms extended from the sides of the crab. One of them shot downward, pausing in front of one of the many small panels where it split into four manipulators that deftly opened the container. From inside, one of the manipulators withdrew a thin, silvery dish. Another arm picked a single square tab of metal off of the dish, which it brought back up to the crab and slid into a slot in its side.

Some sort of identification card? Siddhārtha mused, wondering at the high level of security here.

He looked up at the metal crab hanging high over his head to see a green light flicker on just as a bubble emerged from the crab's underbelly and ran along one of the vertical pipes, descending toward Siddhārtha like a translucent gondola.

A single human shape was crouched inside the gondola. Siddhārtha narrowed his eyes to scrutinize the crab and found it far too compact and flat for a person to fit inside. The gondola landed on the floor directly in front of Siddhārtha. Its canopy opened to either side, and the man inside stood and stepped out. For clothing he wore a simple piece of cloth, hardly more than a bed sheet, and silvery circlets on his wrists. His eyes seemed strangely far apart and filled with suspicion as they looked at Siddhārtha. His thin lips parted halfway, exhaling a surprisingly warm breath.

Siddhārtha observed the man closely. Though he stood only a meter tall, the man's eyes, nose, and ears were fully formed. Those expressionless features, like something molded out of clay, his round head, and slender arms were elegant in their shape.

"Are you an A-Class Citizen?"

The man looked up at Siddhārtha, his face a mask, leaving Siddhārtha with the nagging feeling that there was something lacking in the man's expression.

Something is very amiss here, Siddhārtha thought, trying in vain to discern exactly what it was about the man standing in front of him that bothered him so much. "Tell me," he said at last, "what is different between you and those who are in revolt in the streets outside?"

The man stood, listening intently to Siddhārtha's words before he spoke. "They are B-Class," he spat. "Robots, nothing more."

"Roh-bots?" Siddhārtha echoed. The word was unfamiliar to him.

"Yes," the man replied impatiently, "that's how they are different from us. They're robots." He seemed to have already grown disinterested in the topic of conversation.

"And what are robots?"

The man looked around uneasily and said nothing. The light Siddhārtha's projector cast on the man's expressionless face contrasted starkly with the gloom of the stacked compartments behind him.

"What are robots?" Siddhārtha asked again, feeling that he had heard this word before, but a very long time ago. He tried to force himself to recall its meaning, when he felt part of his mind grow suddenly tense. There was something in that word that he found desperately tragic, a tragedy that seemed out of place here in this quiet, cool underground world. Seeds of memory drifted up from the outer darkness that was his distant past, striking the surface of his mind where they bloomed into dark premonitions. He tried to read the message they contained, yet frustratingly found that his memories remained incomplete. It would take a considerable amount of time before they were ready for him to access.

"I ask again, what are robots?"

The man turned suddenly to look at Siddhārtha, a look of blatant surprise on his face. "Who are you?" he asked, wide eyes taking in his visitor from the top of his head down to the tips of his toes. It seemed that Siddhārtha's presence had finally become real in the man's mind.

"Before I tell you this," Siddhārtha said, speaking slowly while keeping eye contact, "you must answer my one question."

"Who are you and where did you come from?" the man asked again as Siddhārtha asked, "Why do the B-Class Citizens rebel?"

The two questions crossed in midair, like salvos from two ships. The two stood, glaring at each other.

"Why do they rebel?" Siddhārtha asked again before the man could say anything more.

"There is a rebellion?" the man asked, his face softening once more.

"Yes. One that threatens to destroy the city."

"I know nothing of this."

"How could you not know? Do you not live here?"

The man swayed slowly back and forth, showing no interest whatsoever in Siddhārtha's words.

Siddhārtha frowned. "Do you even understand me?"

"Where is this place?" the man suddenly asked.

"What do you mean? This is your city."

The man laughed out loud, a sound like a discordant harmony in the key of A. "No," he said, "this is not our city."

Siddhārtha looked around, agog. "But—"

"Listen," the man said. "I know not how this place appears to your eyes, but I know that it is empty. Not a single one of those people outside may enter this place. Not a one."

"The people outside?"

"You call them B-Class Citizens, but no one has called them that for centuries. Their very existence is immaterial to us now."

"And you are no longer called A-Class Citizens, I suppose?"

"Those words are meaningless," the man said simply.

Siddhārtha pondered the situation, trying to make something out of the confusion and disorder. "Then perhaps you can tell me something else," he said after a pause. "What is the name of this place?"

"You are in ZEN-ZEN."

"Zen . . . zen?"

"No, ZEN-ZEN," the man repeated, accenting both words equally.

Despite the lacunae in his memory, Siddhārtha was fairly sure there was no city with such a name in the solar system he knew. Not just in the solar system—in any of the twenty-four inhabited star systems in the Milky Way. At any rate, certainly not in any of the thirteen systems on the side of the galaxy closest to his own. He wondered about the other eleven, his eyes going blank as he reached back into the depths of his memory, finding nothing.

Suddenly, a great fear washed over the man's face, and he clung to Siddhārtha's arm.

"What's wrong?" Siddhārtha said, almost shouting.

The man's ears perked up, listening for a far-off sound.

"What is it? Can you hear something?"

Siddhārtha trained his ears on the darkness beyond the light of his projector, but he heard nothing. All was unmoving light and shadow, a stillness more quiet than death.

"Did you see God?" the man asked, his grip on Siddhārtha's arm tightening.

Siddhārtha reflexively pulled away, feeling only the slightest amount of resistance. It was as though the man were practically weightless.

"I have seen no god," Siddhārtha replied, wondering what sort of deity would be worshipped by the strange people of this strange city, and at the same time feeling a strong desire to meet one. "Although," he continued, "I was under the impression that it was a god who led me to your world."

The man blinked as though waking from a dream. "God brought you here?"

Siddhārtha looked up at the countless small lockers covering the vast wall while the man continued talking, his tone pious. "When the signs of our world's demise became clear, we abandoned the city. Our God protected us, preventing all fear and destruction from reaching this sanctum. Here, we know eternal serenity."

Siddhārtha gaped, finally understanding what it was he thought was missing from the man's face. What he noticed wasn't a lack, but the presence of a complete emptiness, the sort possessed only by those who have obtained absolute tranquility. Those who are connected to an existence greater than their own.

I must see this god of whom he speaks. Siddhārtha strode forward.

"The audience is over," the voice from the ceiling announced abruptly. "The subject will return to his sleeping nest."

Siddhārtha had forgotten about the crab. The silvery hoist was stopped on the rail above him. It must have been listening to them the whole time.

The crab moved its multi-jointed limbs, forming them into four individual small diamonds that whirled above the man's head. What remaining expression lingered on his face disappeared. His widely separated eyes completely lost their focus and his already small ears lost their lobes, leaving the sides of his head perfectly smooth as a veil of weariness wrapped around his body like a thin cloud. The man turned his back to Siddhārtha, then moving like a shadow, he lay down in the gondola in which he had arrived.

"What is a sleeping nest?" Siddhārtha shouted.

The gondola glided soundlessly up a vertical lift rail until it was drawn back inside the hoist.

"The sleeping nest protects its occupant from all physical and chemical change, preserving and recording their biological characteristics in their original form, so that they may be reconstituted perfectly whenever the need arises."

Siddhārtha quickly worked his supplementary processors, trying to chase down the connotations of the crab's words. To his disappointment, he found no mistranslations nor any marked untranslatables in its statement. "What does that mean?"

One of the crab's arms rotated in a large arc, extracting the single square piece of metal from the hatch in its side, then it swung its arm around again, replacing the card on the dish inside the compartment. The hatch closed. There was nothing organic about the crab's movements. Everything was smooth, mechanical.

"You may leave," the crab said from above.

"What is that card inside the locker?" Siddhārtha shouted out to the crab as it began to drift away along the rail. "Wait! That thing I just met here was not human!" His voice echoed hollowly off the high ceiling. Siddhārtha ran. "Answer me! Do any living people remain here at all?"

The crab continued to recede into the distance, moving faster though making no sound. Siddhārtha chased along beneath it until his way was blocked by another row of metal lockers extending as far as he could see.

"Answer me!"

The crab twinkled with a silvery light before it disappeared. There would be no more answers here. Siddhārtha stopped running. There was nothing left for him to do but extract his information in a more direct fashion. He ran up to the bottommost row of lockers and placed his hand on the metal door of one. It didn't budge. Siddhārtha curled the panels on his shoulders, narrowing their discharge surface, and directed them toward the door. A brilliant blue light erupted, dissolving the door into a rain of silvery metal. The silicon fiber door beyond the outer door burned easily. The flames extinguished themselves in a moment, revealing an additional lead-colored metal barrier. Siddhārtha punched the paper-thin barrier with his fist, and it shattered into several pieces on the floor.

He reached in and plucked out the square metal card on the tray inside. The card was covered with indecipherable symbols. The back was scorched brown. Siddhārtha slid it into his pocket, when a high-pitched whine tore at his eardrums. He felt a wave of dizziness wash over him.

Crouching low, he clapped his hands over his ears. All the blood in his body rushed upward into his head. Siddhārtha looked up, seeing the crab return, quick as lightning at the edge of his vision. Fighting to retain a hold on his fading consciousness, Siddhārtha prepared for the crab's assault. But try as he might, all he could do was sway back and forth as wave after wave of dizziness swept over him.

His vision dimmed. A faint feeling of regret gnawed at his heart. *I should never have trespassed here. What if this is Jesus of Nazareth's trap?*

The image of his enemy's face, covered in hair and grime, flickered like distant lightning in a corner of Siddhārtha's mind.

❯

Several dozen beltways extended from the terminal in every direction like the spokes of a wheel. Some immediately began a gentle upward curve, while others disappeared sharply downward, while still others went upward in a slow spiral, like a tangle of ribbons that could never be undone. Each beltway carried an immense number of people and goods, looking like dark spots scattered across the glowing luminium of the belts. Another terminal hung in space several hundred meters up. All beyond that was lost in a thin mist. Far below, a third wheel-like terminal floated in the depths like an aquamarine star.

A single rotodyne descended through the foggy night air. As Siddhārtha watched, its wings morphed into different shapes to navigate traffic. The rotodyne left a trembling wake in the mist above it.

Immense walls rose all around this vast space, suffused with darkness. The walls were made of translucent glass, inside of which could be seen sparkling colors like the broken fragments of gemstones. There seemed to be many layers of glass, more than a thousand, through which cavities and passages housed the daily lives of all the people in the city. A thick outer wall, built to withstand all climate change and drastic weather, separated them completely from the world beyond. A nuclear reactor on the bottom-most level of the city powered a vast electrical network. The citizens of this place had no need to work at manufacturing or production of any kind. They were—

What is this place?

Siddhārtha stood, blinking. The city vanished from before his eyes. He stood, and a powerful dizziness struck him. What he had seen was no vision or dream. The giant metropolis had been there, right before his eyes, a classic tower city capable of supporting a vast population and completely shielded from the outside world.

With dark eyes, Siddhārtha looked over the row of lockers in front of him.

"We abandoned our city . . ." Siddhārtha said, repeating the citizen's words. Siddhārtha looked up and saw the crab hanging in space over his head. He tensed, readying himself for another psychic attack.

When nothing came, he waited awhile, then spoke. "There is something I want to ask you. Why did you have to abandon your city?"

Deep silence swallowed Siddhārtha's words.

"Also, has a man calling himself Jesus of Nazareth come here?" There was no answer, but Siddhārtha continued on regardless. "Just now with my own eyes, I saw a massive city stretching into the sky. I believe that this is a virtual city, its citizens the memory cards found inside each of these lockers. You are keeping them there, protecting them from the world outside, watching over them—you are their god."

"This is so," said the crab from high above. "The great city you have just seen was revealed to you because you interfered with one of the circuits." The city, the crab explained, was generated using perfect hypnosis that allowed people to walk through its streets, to live their lives in the company of others. Yet it was all a phantasm, taking place in the span of a few minutes during which time the person might still be sitting or lying on the floor.

"But the people in these lockers—only their biological patterns have been encoded. You might inject one into an artificial body as you have just done, but that does not make it human—it does not even make it alive!" Siddhārtha said, choking back rust-colored nausea.

"Are you any different?" the crab asked. "Can you say with absolute certainty that the planet upon which you were born, the objects in your life, and all of the events you have witnessed are not aspects of some grand phantasm?"

Siddhārtha shook his head. "I can make observations that are shared universally between people—"

"And what if all these people are in the same virtual world, experiencing a shared phantasm?"

"What?!"

"Physical phenomena are not an emergent property of reality. No technology or means of observation can prove that they are."

"Strange to hear an agnostic argument from a god," Siddhārtha said.

"To call something unknowable is to assume that anything can be known," the crab replied.

Siddhārtha smiled. "What happens to the self when you're on one of those cards?"

"What happens to the self when you are asleep?" the crab rejoined.

When you're asleep, or when you're dead . . . Siddhārtha shook his head. "Why did you abandon your city?"

)

It would've taken a bit of courage to call the line of silver compartments Siddhārtha could see in the light from his projector "rooms." Each compartment sported a circular silvery hatch of an unknown alloy, and their contents were a mystery. The compartments lined both sides of a dark hallway that continued on for what seemed like an eternity in both directions. Electroluminescent material on the ceiling sagged and faded like old paper. He wondered how much time would have to pass for material like this to cease bearing its own weight. He guessed it would have to be counted not in thousands, but in tens of thousands of years.

He walked down the hallway, eventually coming to a place where it split in two, then again into three. No matter which way he turned, the same silvery hatches lined the walls on both sides.

It's like a mass grave.

Siddhārtha considered the mindset of the people living here in the stagnant air and desiccated darkness, never showing their forms. To them, Siddhārtha must have been an unwanted interloper, a terrifying enemy from the outside. Yet he encountered no signs of resistance, nor any obvious security. Either the city was defenseless, or its architects were confident that no one would ever be able to remove those silvery hatches that doubtlessly held their citizens.

As he walked, he wondered how many levels there were in this place and how far it stretched in every direction. He had been walking now for what seemed like days, at first looking for information, but now looking for a way out.

It's a trap!

He had suffered the same worry since the moment he set foot inside the "city."

Siddhārtha walked up to one of the hatches, illuminating it with the beam of his projector. Set in the middle of its compartment, the hatch had a slight outward bulge, like a convex lens. Siddhārtha connected the output from his micro-reactor to the maser on his arm.

A brilliant red beam of light struck one of the hatches, continuing its assault for ten, twenty, then thirty seconds. The hatch glowed like a gemstone with reflected crimson light.

No good!

The light of the maser faded, and darkness massive as a mountain settled over Siddhārtha. The faint reddish glow of the hatch quickly faded. The citizens of this city were well protected in their castle. No wonder they required no alert system or defenses. Siddhārtha had been able to infiltrate all the way to this corridor, what should have been the heart of their fortress, only to find his way blocked—and no exit in sight.

Removing one of his discharge panels from his shoulder, he connected it to his high-frequency agitator and pressed it to one of the circular hatches. Faint, high-pitched vibrations began, softly at first, then increasing in strength. The silver hatch began to audibly whine as the frequency climbed. Siddhārtha lifted his maser again, directing a beam of light toward the center of the vibrations. The ghostlike report of a brittle fracture echoed down the hallway. He turned his maser off at the very instant that the hatch ruptured and fell to the ground.

Beyond, he found a translucent portal made of high-density crystalline silicon. He melted the hinges with his maser and gave it a push. The light metallic screen he found beyond was easily removed.

Inside he discovered a narrow space that was less like a room and more like the engine access bay of a small spacecraft. The room was filled with countless pipes and electrical lines large and small running this way and that, burying the walls and covering the ceiling. A cylindrical console protruded from the center of the floor. The console was connected to several dozen electrical filaments that stretched out to where an atmospheric adjustment unit was spinning its emergency self-cooling fan at full speed. It seemed that by opening a hole in the door, Siddhārtha had dealt a fatal blow to the ecology of the compartment.

A large, organic lump sat in the light from Siddhārtha's projector, giving off a smell like warm, raw meat. Siddhārtha trained his projector on it, hunching over to get a better look. He could make out a round head on the lump, connected directly to swollen shoulders, and incongruously short arms and legs protruding from a thick torso. In the brilliant light, the thing's exposed skin was light brown in color.

"Are you the occupant of this compartment?" Siddhārtha asked, leaning forward, not really expecting an answer. The organism was quivering irregularly, its breath growing thinner and quicker. Apparently, even the desperate countermeasures taken by its life support system were not enough to prevent the compartment's occupant from heading toward a swift death.

Siddhārtha straightened up and was about to leave when he noticed a pipe roughly five centimeters in diameter extending from either side of the organism to small holes in the sidewalls of the compartment. The pipe was not attached, but rather was an extension of the organism's body itself.

He touched one, detecting a slight pulse and the trickling of liquid inside.

Siddhārtha removed the tantalum steel cover from another of his discharge panels and pressed its sharp edge to one side of the pipe until it broke. The organism began to spasm wildly, flopping around inside the confines of the compartment. Siddhārtha looked closer to see that the pipe's interior was divided into three compartments. Out of one sprayed a translucent liquid that wet Siddhārtha from his elbow to his chest. Another of the compartments held what were clearly nerve bundles, sheathed in a soft, gelatinous protein that was now being pushed out to drip onto the floor by the organism's internal pressure. The final compartment seemed to be a blood vessel. Deep green liquid oozed from the crushed opening where Siddhārtha had cut the pipe in two.

Out of curiosity, he slashed through the other half of the pipe, finding it identical to the first.

The organism shook two or three more times before it stopped moving altogether.

"Perhaps it's dead."

Siddhārtha exited through the destroyed hatch back out into the hallway. Outside, he peered in both directions through the darkness, hearing nothing. He flipped the switch on his light projector, sweeping away the gloom around him, finding nothing but the same deathlike stillness he had found upon his first arrival to this place.

No, wait, I can hear something!

Siddhārtha directed all of his nerves to his ears, listening through the silence around him. Something like a breeze was coming from the depths of the darkness on one side. He raised the power going to his supplementary processors, broadening his range of hearing. The sound rose high, then went low, swirling around Siddhārtha like the crashing of waves.

What is that?

Siddhārtha began to advance quietly down the corridor, looking for the source of the sound. Yet the faint trembling in the air seemed to come from above him at one moment, only to sound as though it was emanating from below a moment later. He went right down the corridor and felt the trembling come from the left. Continually, the noise shifted so that he could not determine its source. With a sudden clarity, Siddhārtha realized he was the target of a powerful enmity. He extinguished his projector, put his back to the wall, and attempted to conceal his own presence.

Rage made tangible and viscous as tar crept closer, an unseen wrinkle in the fabric of space around him. He could feel the rage emanating from a vast number of points surrounding him in every direction—at least one hundred million, he guessed. It was coming from the compartments—the agony and death suffered by one rapidly spreading to all, becoming a virulent wrath.

Here, suffering and death are shared equally!

He ran down the dark hallway.

This was no city.

It was a hive.

)

Outside, cold rain fell without ceasing. The sky seemed close enough to touch, and gray clouds hung low, no more than one hundred meters off the ground. With each gust of wind, the rain fell harder.

The light metal roof was brown in places and spotted, and the rain leaked through. Fragments of reinforced glass covered the floor, where the rainwater formed rivulets soaking down into the ground. Not a single spot remained dry. The cold rain penetrated through Siddhārtha's clothes to his body.

Beneath the slanted roof, several figures huddled beneath carbonic-vinyl tarps. The frigid rain splashed, rattling as it sprinkled onto the spread vinyl. Empty, desperate eyes looked out from underneath, following Siddhārtha.

As far as he could see, there was not a single home here worthy of the name. The rooms were warped, the walls half fallen, the streets were rivers that lacked even proper drainage ditches. *What's going on here?*

Siddhārtha stopped, feeling six pairs of eyes from six round heads staring at him.

"I would not imagine this city to be so poor that its residents could not afford to build homes for themselves," Siddhārtha muttered to himself.

He looked back toward the giant cylindrical obelisk that towered behind him. This was the center of the city, this was everything.

"Do you know what that is?" asked a voice from the shelter, and a thin arm extended from beneath the vinyl sheet to point toward the giant cylinder.

"I do indeed."

"More than three thousand years it's been since they locked themselves up in there. What were we who were left behind supposed to do? We would rebuild our city, if anyone knew how."

Siddhārtha wondered what use a people unable to build with their own hands would have of a city in the first place, but he kept his thoughts to himself.

"Why did only *they* move into the cylinder?" he asked at length.

Another of the round heads answered him. "They say that was the n-n-nah er . . . natural progression of development."

"Natural progression?"

Do they mean to suggest that turning their society into a giant hive was a natural, necessary progression for a city?

"Why did you not follow them in?"

Beneath the vinyl sheets, the people exchanged glances before one of them responded, "Because they are human."

As one, the round heads nodded in agreement.

The rain blew sideways between the posts holding up their ramshackle roof. An orphaned panel of lightweight siding came tumbling along, driven by the wind. It fell into a puddle and sent up a fine spray of water like smoke. Beyond the falling rain, the giant cylinder stood like a cutout silhouette against a screen in a shadow play.

)

"As our natural environment worsened, humanity adapted by developing into a new communal body, with individual compartments for shells to house each individual. The simple act of forming the communal body was an excellent strategy for ensuring our survival. However, an environment that necessitates such an act will ultimately fall to ruin. In order to stay that destruction, a more high-level strategy becomes necessary. Thus were all citizens reduced to simple code, protected from all change."

"But that is neither evolution nor development."

"Where do these things lead? Only to destruction."

Siddhārtha nodded. "Who are you, really?"

The hoist above his head was quiet for a time, then it spoke, spitting out the words.

"I am God. More precisely, I am what the inhabitants of the city used to call God."

Siddhārtha thought he detected a hint of lament in the crab's voice.

"I see. For a god, you have a very peculiar shape."

The god on the sliding rail seemed to laugh at that. "Is there a pre-ordained shape or role for a god? No, for it is a fact that depending on the world in which they manifest, gods take on many forms. They may be benevolent beings, made of kindness and mercy, or a high-tech machine or an incubator. They can even take the form of a financial organization."

"Are all *ses-beta* developments performed by gods, or indirectly via their influence?"

"Pardon?"

"Did a man named Jesus of Nazareth come here?"

"Beats me. What is this 'Jesus of Nazareth' of whom you speak?"

Siddhārtha shrugged. "He was the coordinator of the *ses-beta* development on Earth. I want to know who put him in that position, who gives him his orders," Siddhārtha said, feeling with some certainty that this director was none other than the god hanging over his head. "What is your name?"

"ZEN-ZEN."

Siddhārtha muttered the word to himself, feeling its shape in his mouth. "I believe that Jesus of Nazareth is hiding somewhere on Astarta 50," he said, realizing that he had yet to find a single trace of his enemy here.

"Could it be that this man whom you seek belongs to the Planetary Development Committee? If that is the case, then leave the city and go north. I have heard that the building of the Planetary Development Committee lies upon a small plain surrounded by hills."

Siddhārtha turned and walked back down the long dark hallway, hearing the words at his back. All ways in this city were barred to him, but one of them must lead to *Shi*.

）

The three obelisks had broken just above their bases and lay flat across the stones. Several of the buildings around the plaza joined them on the ground amid piles of rubble. Fragments of shattered concrete and dust rose in a giant umbrella cloud over the city. Aquamarine laser light still coursed across the top of the crowd that ran like fleeting shadows toward safety. Incredible explosions and gouts of flame rose upward, the sparks flowing like a river into the sky.

Siddhārtha had found his way back to the chamber of the leader. The leader stood like a statue, trailing a long shadow in the dim light. Siddhārtha wondered if he had even moved since his last visit.

"Leader. I believe I now understand the rebellion. And the cause of this city's downfall."

The leader slowly turned to face him. "You must have met God."

"Yes. He said his name was ZEN-ZEN."

"A great God, yes. Yet not even he could save this city from destruction."

"Oh? As I see it, ZEN-ZEN has abandoned you."

The leader chuckled, dark shadows playing across his face. "It is only natural. God was not ours to begin with." With a sudden surge of emotion playing across his features, the leader advanced to stand in front of Siddhārtha. "Yet is it not we who support the city now? Are we not the engine of this city's economy? Are we not her true citizens?"

That may be, Siddhārtha admitted to himself, *but it would have little meaning to* Shi. *Shi* was not interested in the people who felled the obelisks in the plaza, but only in the people who slept eternally, reduced to single data cards deep within the city.

"I'm afraid you have been abandoned, just like those who squat out in the rain."

The Leader looked toward him, his eyes focusing on a great distance. "It seems that our time in history will not come for a long while yet."

Siddhārtha left in silence.

❩

Red flames reflected across the skin of the ionocraft where it sat abandoned beside the building. Two figures stood in the shadow of a protruding section of wall.

"So you met the god in the deep." Asura smiled, flames near her feet casting a flickering light on the lower half of her face.

"How did you know?"

"I can know things through your mind and through your eyes," Asura said with a laugh, though it was unclear whether she spoke truth or not. "Which is how I have learned that the Planetary Development Committee is to the north, on a small plain surrounded by mountains."

With the three aboard, the ionocraft slid above the smoke from the blazes in the city, heading toward the dark canopy above.

Outside, the vast silvery surface reflected the outline of the small pale yellow sun like a halo.

"Think those are the mountains?" Siddhārtha asked, pointing toward the ring of mountains on the horizon.

Ahead of them and on the horizon to either side rose dark mountains.

"What will we find on the other side?" Orionae wondered out loud.

"The Planetary Development Committee."

"Those who act upon *Shi's* directive?"

"The very same."

"So is this thing called *Shi* also upon that plain?"

"Who knows?" Siddhārtha muttered.

"Both Atlas the Seventh and the Poseidonis the Fifth were as large as small mountains," Orionae said.

"You've met them?"

"They said they came from the land of our ancestors, Atlanta. They tried experimental methods for forming their kingdom and were quite successful. The success of their experiments in Atlantis were to inform other planetary developmental efforts."

"Atlanta, land of ancestors . . ." Asura muttered.

"Where is this place?" Siddhārtha asked.

"Siddhārtha, it's—" Asura paused, crinkling her nose and looking up at the tiny sun. "It's clear that the *helio-ses-beta* development attempted on the third planet of the Ai System was a failure."

"As it was here on Astarta 50."

Siddhārtha and Asura exchanged glances.

"So the Planetary Development Committee was unable to carry out *Shi's* directive."

"Humanity advanced into the stars, taking their wars and their incessant economic crises and their population problem, yet they could not dominate the Milky Way. They couldn't even revive a once green land that had fallen to desert."

Siddhārtha felt his chest tighten as though he were about to weep. "It seems to me," he said after a moment, "that since the very beginning, humanity has been walking upon a path toward destruction. Everywhere is disease and disaster, death and conflict. These things have always been part of civilization, right by man's side. I wonder if any human, anywhere, has truly been at peace from the bottom of their heart."

Asura looked up at the rapidly approaching black shadow of the mountains and said nothing.

The small, pale yellow sun was about to slip closer toward the distant horizon, its weak rays striking out horizontally in bands of light across the land below them. They were passing over another flat surface, apparently an ancient seabed that was now completely dry. They had left the silver shield covering the valley far behind to glitter in the distance like a glacier. Beneath that, organisms that had long since given up being organisms continued their frail attempts to stave off their own doom. A civilization whose story of destruction had begun after history had already ended.

To the north, there is a fence.
A sign upon it reads:
"When the star crosses, the sky will burn.
And there will be great sorrow."

The bottom third of the pale yellow sun had already slipped below the horizon when they crossed the high ridgeline and gazed down on a flat, smooth, steep-sided plateau. The plateau was nearly perfectly square, roughly two kilometers to a side; it had the appearance of an island that had once risen from the foaming waves of an ancient sea that had long ago dried up. The side that faced the setting sun sparkled reddish brown, while the far side cast a long shadow across the basin beyond. A flat, semitranslucent structure sat near the center of the plateau, its appearance suggesting that it had been built by stacking enormous calcite crystals.

The three flew across the basin, descending onto a rocky shelf within sight of the building. The sun had now set halfway, and deep indigo crept across the sky from the opposite direction. It was extremely cold—so cold that the three feared their hearts would freeze. All was silent; the dim sun glittered in the chill.

"Do you think this is the Planetary Development Committee's head-quarters?" Siddhārtha asked.

If it is, then why is it so quiet?

Even from a distance, they could look through the semitranslucent material of the structure to see many rooms dividing it into compartments of indeterminate use. A row of six columns stood in a large hall toward the middle of the structure, and another hall that held a large flat table appeared to be some kind of conference room. There was also a wide staircase, its edges tracing complicated lines as it rose through the structure.

"Doesn't look like anyone's inside."

The weak rays of the setting sun passed directly through the vast, empty building's interior. Nothing moved.

One of the large doors at the main entrance had been pulled off its hinges; it lay just inside the wide, slanting entry hall. Cold air ripped through the opening, scattering thick brown dust in a fan pattern beyond the doorway.

The three entered in single file, stepping over the fallen door. Their feet sent up plumes of fine dust with every step.

"It's been a terribly long time since anyone used this place," Siddhārtha said.

Several thousand years, he judged from the appearance of everything on the ground floor. Hallways extended from either side of the entry hall. These connected in turn to the many smaller rooms the companions had seen from the outside. In each of the small rooms, they discovered powerful gravitational barrier generators, now inactive and quietly decaying.

"Sandstorms must have damaged the place," Asura said, her eyes taking in the signs of severe abrasion on the exterior wall. The whole structure had probably once been perfectly transparent. "What's that?" she added, pointing toward a large metal bowl-shaped object lying at an angle just outside the far end of the building. Metallic panels and tangled wires were scattered over the ground beside it. "Looks like a parabolic antenna."

The antenna had been attached to a rotating platform that had, over the course of thousands of years, decayed to the point where it could no longer support the weight of the dish.

Orionae placed his forehead against a wall, staring through it at the fallen dish. "I have seen something like this before. Twice." He wore a vague, clouded expression as he turned to face the others.

"A parabolic antenna?" Siddhārtha asked. "Where?"

Orionae craned his neck to look up at the thin yellow sky. "The first time was by that village in the desert, Elcasia. The second was on the roof of the royal palace in Atlantis."

"Interesting," Siddhārtha said. "Could it mean that the Planetary Development Committee here on Astarta 50, and the village of Elcasia, and Atlantis, were all connected?" He imagined an invasion coordinated along a single line of communication. *Could the fall of Atlantis have been dictated remotely from across the galaxy?*

"Yes," Orionae nodded. "That might explain the window of the suzerain. And the mystery of the orichalcum. Now that I think about it, I wonder why I didn't look into things more closely back when I was there. It is most vexing."

"Orichalcum, you say?"

"Yes—a strange material that was used everywhere in the construction of Atlantis . . . yet there were no records at all concerning its composition or means of fabrication."

The last pale rays of the setting sun painted the large hall on the upper floor. The walls sparkled as the light passed through the dancing dust that marked their progress through the lesser rooms. Other than the dust, there was nothing at all in any of the small rooms that added to their information.

The upper hall had an arched ceiling over fifty meters in height. It had clearly lain abandoned for a very long time. The only sound there was the sough and echo of the wind as it swept down the corridors. Toward one edge of the building was a section that looked as if it had been struck by some kind of meteor; a large hole had been opened in the exterior wall, facing out toward the basin beyond.

In the center of the upper hall stood a large spherical object constructed of thin translucent pipes interconnected in a complicated weave. The sphere was about ten meters across.

"I wonder what that could be?" Asura asked.

It looked out of place, a memory stripped of its context—perhaps the last remaining vestige of whatever civilization had once thrived here. A thick layer of dust had settled on the thin pipes and the short metal bars that supported the sphere at its base.

Twilight had fallen outside, casting the world into depths of indigo. As one, the three travelers were stricken with homesickness for their own planet, and in that mood they contemplated the staggering length of time in which this place had sat as a ruin.

Asura had seen tragic devastation many times in her long life, but she had never seen anything quite so barren as this. The sort of devastation from which there can never be a recovery comes quietly and over many years.

"Well," Siddhārtha said simply. "Even if this were once the Planetary Development Committee's headquarters, that was long ago."

"So our hunt ends here," Asura said, perching on a fragment of fallen wall.

"But this cannot possibly be the end of the trail. This must be Astarta 50. We will find something. Let's look again."

"I am not so sure," Orionae said, his voice solemn. "Those words we all know mentioning the Planetary Development Committee on Astarta 50 are from five or six thousand years ago. It is rather unlikely, in fact, that anything remains here at all."

"I suppose they could have moved someplace else," Siddhārtha admitted. "But since we're here anyway, let's take a better look around. The enemy we seek is not human. Just because this place is a ruin does not mean they aren't using it. It would be dangerous to assume anything."

"True," Asura said. "And if there is no way to influence one's destination on that spaceway we traveled, then we can say with some certainty that Jesus of Nazareth did come here before us." Abruptly, her eyes focused on the darkness overhead. "Look!"

The ceiling above them had begun to emit a pale aquamarine light. The light grew steadily brighter until the hall was suffused in a beautiful brilliance. Quickly the three retreated to a corner hallway from which they could see through the walls back into the main hall—see, and also be seen.

The sphere in the hall began to emit light in many colors. Bright crimson orbs appeared, traveling along the pipes, and from these emerged minute particles of illumination that scattered like dust. Soon, the entire hall was scintillating with projected color. The light breathed, growing in intensity and then fading in pulses. It must have seemed fantastically and eerily beautiful from outside the translucent building.

Siddhārtha and Asura could feel their spines growing cold. Whatever was happening, it seemed likely that this was the trap they had long expected.

"Someone's there!"

The light wavered like a mirage as it passed through the translucent wall, suddenly revealing a figure on the other side. Siddhārtha engaged the polarized filters on his light-condensing contact lenses, while Asura extended infrared night vision sensors from a bracelet on her wrist to scan the hall.

The figure—a human man, apparently—was walking around inside the hall, wearing something like a monk's robe that fell halfway down his legs and was sewn beneath his arms on both sides. On his feet he wore leather sandals. His eyes sparkled and darted with an eerie quickness that left a glowing trail across the imaging readout on Asura's screen, making it easy to see where he was looking. His eyes seemed to shift regularly toward the sphere, then back to the walls of the hall.

"I wonder what he's doing?"

The figure walked slowly in a wide circle, then paused as though listening. He raised the small object he held in one hand.

Part of the corridor that led from the great hall vanished. The destruction had happened without a sound; not even the chilly night air moved. The man continued walking, moving slowly as though he examined something as he went. Once again, he lifted the object in his hand. This time a section of wall next to where the meteorite had hit vanished, along with part of the rocky shelf beneath it. Where the crumbled wall had stood there was now just a gaping hole, like an empty pool. The figure returned to the sphere, staring deep into its intricate structure. His silhouette was clearly discernible against the light from the sphere.

"It is Jesus!" Siddhārtha gasped. "Perhaps this is one of his bases of operation?"

"But why destroy his own facility?" Asura asked.

Jesus lifted his gaze from the sphere to look out at the dark night sky.

"Perhaps he is removing traces of his organization's presence here?"

Siddhārtha said. Even as he spoke he became certain that this was what they were witnessing. Jesus's organization had accomplished all of its objectives, so its members were now removing their strongholds, eliminating proof of their own activities. They had reached the end of their plans—now they were starting to worry about cleanup and the possibility of pursuit. "Let's grab him, then, and find out what that sphere is!" Siddhārtha moved quietly from column to column like a shadow gliding along the corridor.

Asura slipped outside through a crack in the wall. A scant number of stars glittered in the dark sky. She strode toward the front entrance to the building, making no attempt to soften her footfalls. Stepping over the fallen door, she headed directly into the large hall.

"Man of Nazareth!" she shouted. "It seems you have finished what you came to do!"

Jesus glanced over at Asura as she walked in, showing just the slightest bit of interest.

"So," she continued, "is your Final Judgment done, or are we still waiting? Either way, no one remains to be judged."

Jesus waved away her words with one hand. "You did well to follow me this far," he muttered, "but now it is over."

Asura switched off the infrared device on her wrist, returning it to a regular bracelet. "Yes, and I lost. When I realized that a transcendent being was responsible for the destruction and decline that began on Earth five thousand years ago, I made all efforts to determine the nature of that entity's existence and stop it. Yes, I was too late. Their plans have come to fruition. As you say, it is over."

Jesus looked away, snorting with derision.

"Man of Nazareth, allow me to ask a question."

A look of alarm spread across Jesus's face.

"Don't look so frightened," Asura said. "I merely want to know what that sphere is."

Jesus stared up at the large object looming above him. "This thing?"

"Yes. Its meaning has eluded me."

The Nazarene peered at the sphere with weary eyes, then returned his gaze to Asura's face. "These paths of light here are galactic longitudes, and the green paths there are galactic latitudes." He trailed one sick finger along the surface of the sphere where the brightness rippled in waves. "This is the galactic equator. An entropy D index is overlaid on this curve, indicating that an entirely different spatial dimension will be generated in this area." Slowly he moved his right hand, and the aquamarine glow within the sphere slid diagonally to follow. "See, it will be like this. You understand?"

Jesus pointed toward the sphere with his chin. He scratched the back of his left leg with the tip of his right sandal.

Choosing her moment, Asura launched into the air. Her right hand extended in a flash, striking him squarely in the chest. He staggered, and when he regained his footing, Asura was standing between him and the sphere.

"What are you doing?" Jesus shouted, his whiskers bristling.

Asura fixed him with an icy glare. "Finally, I understand!"

Jesus clenched his hands into fists and stepped forward. "What do you understand?"

"The Archangel Michael—the being you claim to have seen coming down from Heaven by the Jordan River? I know who that was. As I know the identity of the great god who plunged Jordan into darkness the day you were executed upon the hill at Golgotha, and spirited you away into the sky—"

"You know nothing!"

"I'm not finished. I know now the provenance of the two giant kings—Atlas the Seventh and Poseidonis the Fifth—whom Orionae served in Atlantis, and I understand the statue of Maitreya in the Pearl Palace. I know now of Tuṣita, that land I desired so greatly to see. I have thought long and carefully about these things—where they could possibly have come from and what their intentions might be. Though the latter are still clouded to me, man of Nazareth, I now know the path by which they entered our world!"

Jesus peered at Asura through the hair that hung loosely down over his eyes. "Gods sometimes do violent things," he said, his voice soothing, "but it is a mistake to want to exact revenge upon them." He held up one hand, as though offering salvation.

"Say what you wish," Asura spat. "Yet to revere a herald of destruction as some sort of heavenly father figure is surely a sin—"

"Herald of destruction?"

"Perhaps you do not understand. In this Milky Way, there are many planets upon which higher intellects have thrived. Imagine, if you will, that these beings you look up to as gods did not approve of these emerging sentient life-forms and decided to remove them. How would you go about doing this, if you were them?"

"What do you mean, 'how'?"

"I will give you one possibility," Asura said. "You could visit the life-forms at every stage in their development, sowing seeds that would, over the course of millennia, result in inevitable destruction."

Jesus's face twisted.

"You could build in economic dead ends, military strife, population problems, declining health, psychological and physical atrophy, and much more. Take any one of these calamities that plague humankind, and you can see that its true cause lies far in the past. Some hail from as far back as the ancient age when humanity's forerunners existed only as single-celled organisms living in a warm, shallow ocean."

"Blasphemy! You have it wrong—"

"Not that they had to predetermine everything. Some of the conditions could have been arranged later on, when there were more variables to work with."

Jesus fixed Asura with two eyes blazing like fire. "O, dear God who is in Heaven—"

Asura laughed merrily. "Jesus! There is a legend which says that when you were born into our world, the King of the Jews was terrified by news of the Savior's birth, and so he took every male child from his mother's arms and killed them."

"A terrible thing, yes."

Asura clapped her hands with mirth, laughing again, though in her eyes there swelled a hatred strong enough to make a strong man quail with fear. "Terrible, you say? That, I suppose, would depend on your point of view."

Jesus looked away.

"It was I who whispered murder into the mind of the king," Asura said. "Would that he had been more thorough in carrying it out, for in the end, the massacre was for naught. You escaped, and in later years, you joined forces with the giant beings you call gods and angels. If you had died along with all those other children, how then would things have been different? . . . Well, *Jesus of Nazareth*? Speaking of which—your Final Judgment never came, did it?"

Jesus looked out toward the dark horizon as though searching for an escape route.

"When the four wise men appeared to Siddhārtha, they came as Brahmin monks. Yet in his case they made a terrible error of judgment. The prince never would have met me at all without their intervention, man of Nazareth. And the knowledge they gave to him! Their teachings speak of the cakravarti-rājan, and Maitreya who is to descend to Earth in 5,670,000,000 years as the Savior, and all the cosmology—why did they carelessly leave so many words suggesting the truth? I believe they underestimated the human capacity for understanding."

Jesus staggered, his face pale.

Asura raised a hand, pointing toward the dark horizon. "Go, Jesus of Nazareth! Go into that barren, shadowed plain, and do not return. It is a most fitting place for you."

Jesus cursed softly under his breath. Cold sweat trickled down from his ashen forehead, collecting on his chin to drip between his feet.

"Well?" Asura's glare grew darker.

Jesus's eyes suddenly widened and the sweat on his brow visibly retreated. An instant later, all noise ceased.

)

Finally, Asura thought, *some results.*

"Asura!"

By the sound of his voice, Siddhārtha was moving rapidly from right to left behind her. Asura didn't need to turn—she knew what was happening. They had reached the moment of maximum peril. Springing into action, she ran from the hall on silent feet. The moment she was through the outer door she crouched and rolled across the cold, dry ground. She could feel Siddhārtha and Orionae moving off to her right. Inside the translucent building, Jesus had become a receding silhouette.

Something like a dark tide had begun to spread from inside the great hall. It expanded in all directions as it came, pushing back the vast night before Asura's eyes. As it grew it transformed in shape until it had become a gigantic figure looming over the plateau like a towering peak. There were arms and shoulders like mountain ridges, a chest like a sheer cliff face, immense pillared legs. Strangely molded armor wrapped around the chest and shoulders.

The giant silhouette looked out over the barren stillness of the basin, seeming to envelop all the endless spread of night. Something like a crown grew from its head, concealing the few stars in the sky.

You appear at last. Asura's terror at facing the most dangerous of enemies mingled with her elation at the realization that they had at last found the entrance to their enemies' world. Her enemies' achievement had been near perfect, yet Asura and her companions represented a final remaining threat, a pinprick that had turned into a wound their foes could no longer afford to ignore.

The giant figure stepped slowly out onto the basin. Beneath the shadow of its headdress, the features of its face were impossible to make out. Shrouded in darkness, it took another step.

"I saw your statue," Asura said, her voice traveling low through the frozen darkness. "When was it you were supposed to appear and save the masses? Five billion six hundred seventy million years from now? As I expected, you are big enough to reach the heavens, yet in places your statue rusted—"

For the first time in her existence, Asura understood that there was a kind of fear in this world impossible to overcome. It began deep inside her and came with a terrible dizziness and nausea that swiftly developed into a bottomless whirlpool of madness she was unable to contain. She realized she had only one or two seconds remaining in which to escape this place of death. She took a step.

"You did well to come this far," a voice echoed down from the darkened sky. The force of the giant god's words was almost enough to stop Asura's heart on the spot. She had no time to think.

"We did not expect anyone to reach this gateway to eternity. Yet this is the end of your road. The path beyond here is not one you may travel."

The great being's denial scattered the shadows of Asura's reality in every direction. Mountain ranges and giant oceans lost their shape. Before her loomed an unfathomable emptiness, a barrier which nothing in her world could hope to overcome. It seemed to block even the flow of time. *No wonder he called it the gateway to eternity.* This was the end of the world, of all worlds—the bridge to the true void.

A wind blew across the dark basin, its passage through that unsympathetic darkness reminding Asura's crumbling mind of where she stood. Slowly, she felt her former self returning from someplace deep within her shattered heart.

"Where did you come from?" she demanded, thinking the question more than speaking it, unsure of whether her words would even reach the god before her.

"You may decide that for yourself. The place you choose is my origin." Her enemy's response bored through Asura's mind, scattering sparks in its wake. She wondered where exactly in the space-time continuum that enveloped her home world a presence like this had found entry. These beings had revealed themselves several times on Earth in the past, and doubtless had done the same on other planets and in other galaxies. *Where did they come from, and why?*

"It appears you have questions concerning my existence, yet you know that I exist to the same degree that you exist. You seem secure in your knowledge that your solar system and the spiral galaxy you call the Milky Way, and all the hundred billion other galaxies in this universe, occupy the same space-time continuum on the same time axis. Asura, it appears you think of your universe as being on the inside of the sphere which extends to infinity, and that is well. But have you considered what lies beyond the borders of that sphere? What lies beyond the limits of your universe?"

"It is meaningless to consider that which lies beyond infinity," Asura responded.

The god looked down with pity. "You understand that infinity is nothing more than an abstract concept, do you not? Or do you believe that there exists true infinity in this universe?"

The being's words sent a shadowy coil across Asura's mind that threatened to paralyze all thought. Yet she understood instinctively that now was no time to consider the structure of the universe—not with her own destruction looming.

"Maitreya!"

A shooting star streaked above the shadow in the darkness, leaving a long fiery tail between the scant stars.

"What possible purpose could you have to make a wasteland of this world? What reason could you have for doing everything in your power to drive humanity to extinction?"

An aurora the color of blood flickered on the distant horizon, spreading like a thin curtain as it shifted from red to blue, then back to red, its light ebbing. The dark sky was visible behind its thin red veil, looking deeper and vaster than ever she had seen it.

Asura's mind went blank as she faced its light. Then she noticed the giant Maitreya moving soundlessly, the distant aurora reflected in his face and across his chest. His face was visible now beneath his boat-shaped crown. She saw long slitted eyes, set deep under long eyebrows, that held the calm glimmer of a bottomless lake. The giant's chest was full and rolling beneath the lines of the garment he wore, and she noticed a necklace around his neck that radiated an unusual energy; its emanations struck the sensor on Asura's chest, causing it to glow a bright orange.

"Asura. There is something I would ask you."

Asura smiled, revealing a glimmer of white teeth. "You have quite the nerve to say that when it is I who have come such a great distance with so many questions."

"Answer me, and I will have no reason to destroy you. I will send you wherever you wish." There was a tone of peaceful kindness in Maitreya's voice that might have been interpreted as curiosity.

"But not before reducing me to a husk of my former self, devoid of memory." Asura laughed as though she were talking about someone else's fate entirely.

"Don't be greedy."

Asura felt the tension between her and Maitreya quietly increase. "Fine," she said, breathing out a long sigh. "What's your question?"

"You are here with two others. Who is it that gave you your mission?

What organization maintained your sleeping webs for some five thousand years?"

The instant Maitreya's words rang in Asura's mind, she switched off the circuit that connected her brain to her supplementary processor's neural memory web. Asura became empty, filled only with the darkness of night. A feeling of release spread from her emergency circuitry, making her feel lighter than the wind itself.

"Speak, Asura! Who gave you your mission? What is the name of your organization?" Maitreya's voice grew increasingly irritated.

By the time the first blast hit, Asura had already become one with the night around her. The fear in her heart fled into the darkness, leaving nothing in its place but an empty hollow.

"Well? Asura? You cannot escape. I will give you another ten seconds."

In the unmoving silence that followed, even the wind died. It lasted for exactly ten seconds, during which Asura stood, quiet, her mind frozen and unchanging.

The second blast hit.

Asura felt herself plummeting at a terrifying speed through endless space in which there was no up or down, left or right. No stars shone in the monotone darkness around her.

Somewhere off in the distance, the aurora flickered a lonely red. She tried to focus on the color but it slipped away, and her consciousness followed.

Neural memory web still off-line, Asura's supplementary processor activated a secondary metabolizer, designed to handle massive expenditures of energy. Her processor began to rapidly analyze her situation. Once all internal systems had been checked and no abnormalities were found, the processor turned its attention outside. With the neural memory net inaccessible, this was an extremely difficult procedure. The processor was forced to pick targets for analysis based on an endless reiteration of basic logic patterns.

One of her eyes saw only the darkness of a deep night sky with a scattering of stars. No cause for her current state could be found there. The other eye looked out over the cold basin. The faint sound of wind stimulated her auditory nerves, then both of her eyes moved together, focusing on the giant shape that loomed ahead of her. Her processor noted the animosity radiating from that figure like a tidal wave, and all became clear. Only a sliver of time remained.

Her supplementary processor connected directly to her cerebellum. In a flash, Asura sprang to her feet. Her right hand reached up to pull out the hairpin from the back of her head and fling it forward. The hairpin left a faint trail of light, golden ions scattering into the night behind it. At almost exactly the same time, the god-figure towering in the darkness began to waver like a mirage. The hairpin burst into flame and fell to the ground.

Asura regained consciousness. She welcomed the ache in her head—though it felt as though her skull had cracked wide open, it was the surest sign yet that at last the advantage had passed to her side. This was a chance she could not afford to waste.

Bands of pale blue light swept between Maitreya's form and her own. She could feel her body shivering under the terrifying brunt of her enemy's psychic attack. If her supplementary processor hadn't been engaged to run her systems automatically, she would have died without ever waking again. Quickly she cranked her micro-reactor to full and extended the agitator from the magnetic field generator on her bracelet. Its tip touched the next band of blue light as it approached. There was an incredible flash.

The high-voltage stream generated by her agitator arced between the two gravitationally sealed spaces between her and Maitreya, and both barriers collapsed. Before the sparks had even faded, Asura dived into the remains of the crystal building. The floor was now a sea of flame, but she felt no pain or discomfort. She stood with the sphere of translucent pipes at her back. Supported on short metallic bars, the sphere appeared to be floating over the intense flames that licked along the floor.

"Maitreya! How can you possibly destroy me, you who have come from another world? To me you are void, like the sea of darkness from which you emerged."

There came no answer.

Moving swiftly, Asura wrapped the sphere inside a dimensional barrier. There it flickered faintly like a failing neon sign. She could sense a violent struggle taking place somewhere nearby in the remains of the building—but though she knew this was likely Siddhārtha and Orionae engaged in a battle to the death against Jesus of Nazareth, it was far too dangerous for her to pay any attention to their combat. If she lost her own engagement, she would have no way of ever knowing the true nature of the being that had turned this world into a wasteland.

Outside the translucent walls, the sky began to lighten until it was as bright as day. Its color shifted from yellow to green, from green to blue; then the basin and the sky arcing above it were filled with a shimmering purple radiance. That too faded and was replaced by a faint, pale light suffusing sky and land.

)

A grayish curtain of snow hung down from the clouds to touch the ground to the north. Gusts of wind blew flakes down to swirl and sweep across the icy slope. The snow increased in intensity, quickly reducing Asura's visibility to zero.

A ceaseless wind screamed in Asura's ears. In the few moments when the snow let up for a moment, she spotted a vast number of shadows moving across the white glacier in the distance. In between gusts, she saw the shadows multiplying, approaching. Then she spotted an object in the distance, a strange shape like a flattened disk with a complicated protrusion on its top. From its tip a blinding light erupted. The light formed a revolving beam that swept across the snowy plain, transforming snow and ice to scalding steam that drifted up toward the gathered clouds. Off to her left, a cannon mounted atop an igloo-shaped base began to fire. Plumes of snow shot up into the air like trees in a forest, incandescent light flaring between them—cannons on the hills engaging each other across the glacier.

Off on the distant horizon to the west, a river with a name Asura didn't know undulated slowly, the color of lead. If only she could reach the river, she might awaken from this nightmare.

She took stock of her surroundings. Her enemy had already advanced onto the icy plains beneath the rise on which she stood. Thin wisps of smoke rose from impact points halfway up the low ridgeline to her right, spreading until the entire side of the mountain was veiled. Her enemy's armored vehicles were already advancing onto the plains. The dozen or so vehicle-mounted heat-ray cannons that formed Asura's final line of defense at the base of the rise were already engaged in combat. Pale arrows of light crisscrossed in the sky, and tanks and armored vehicles spit sparks like crucibles between the billowing clouds of steaming snow and ice.

Asura gathered her infantry amidst the flames and the steam and sounded the retreat. They went around the foot of the ridgeline, making for a snowy valley between two ridges to the west. Missiles skimmed across the tops of the high cliffs, making the air shake around them. An incredible explosion sounded from the entrance to the valley ahead. The blast wave hit the walls of snow and ice like a hammer, echoing like thunder in the distance. The enemy was asserting his control of her escape route.

Another missile exploded ahead of the infantry, sending shattered chunks of ice and rock up to ricochet off the cliff walls; fragments continued to fall back down into the valley for what seemed like several minutes. Columns of flame rose around her line, blocking their advance.

Their route into the valley was now piled high with shattered ice and rock. Asura turned the column and led her men up the cliffs on her right, climbing until she reached the top of the ridge where she could look down across the entire battlefield. It appeared that now their only possible route for retreat was via the great river to the west.

With a start, Asura realized she had no idea where she was, nor how great her own forces were. Was this a small section of a vast battlefront, or was this the only engagement, the struggle on which victory or defeat would hang? The only thing that was clear to her was that the enemy army covering the snowy plains behind them was led by none other than Maitreya.

There was not much hope to be found here. Surely she would never reach the river with the dozen or so foot soldiers remaining to her now. They stumbled along, ice forming like cold flowers on their chests and limbs. She called for them to move faster, directing them along the ridge toward the west. Yet it was not long before she noticed that her troop was no longer visible—though she guessed that the burning pyres that dotted the ridgeline behind her were their remains.

"Well, Asura? You know you will never make the river. Join my forces, Asura. It is the only future remaining to you in which you survive."

The familiar voice echoed in Asura's chest. She raised her snow-encrusted face toward the western sky. Not a single living shape moved in that uninterrupted vista of snow and ice. Suddenly, she was reminded of another battlefield from another time, beneath a dark night sky.

An aurora had rippled in the distance on that battlefield, colors of light crossing through the frozen air. In that bleak place only death had thrived.

Where was that again?

When was that again?

Here, there was only the white landscape as far as she could see in every direction. No night. No aurora.

What was that?

What?

What?

The image she held in her mind's eye burst abruptly into flames—this was a nightmare battle from which there was no escape. Everything had begun here. Everything returned here again.

Memories of bitter fighting for long, long years against the forces of Śakra crawled across her vision, intermingling with the white wasteland before her. The giant statue of the god hidden in the depths of the Pearl Palace was nothing more than a promise of destruction, and yet those she fought believed it to be a symbol of their salvation. The distant memories burned in Asura's breast. She was trapped in a phantasm of struggles past. *Trapped!*

Asura stood.

)

Wrapped in its protective barrier, the strange sphere loomed above the sea of flame. Hatred and enmity swirled through the tongues of fire, burning Asura more than the heat that flooded over her.

This is all part of Maitreya's psychic assault! I must be strong!

She held a hand to her forehead and shut her eyes tight. She felt the inside of her skull grow suddenly cool as her supplementary processor employed a secondary circuit to transmit high-frequency waves into the gray matter of her cerebrum. Filters activated, absorbing the hypnotic electrical emissions that were targeting her, reflecting them back at their source.

Even under the brunt of the psychic assault, she retained her control over the barrier around the sphere.

Using the brainwave detector attached to her tertiary semicircular canal, she searched for Maitreya. Unable to pinpoint him, Asura measured the hypnotic wave patterns and fired a hand missile back along their trajectory. She lamented the lack of any form of psychic attack in her own personal arsenal. Compared to Maitreya's mental assault, even an antimatter proton bomb and an antigravitational barrier were sticks and stones.

Asura's missile flew, trailing a long tail of fire behind it, the power of a splitting lithium atom turning one of Maitreya's radiation shutters into scalding steam. Before the light from the blast had faded, Asura fired another. But the jet of super-hot gas following the second missile struck the metallic fastenings of another shutter and reflected back, sending a wave of molten metal splashing toward Asura's face fast enough to cross the distance in a few hundredths of a second.

Asura twisted her body. No time to raise a barrier—her processor went into hyperspeed, rerouting her reflex pulses from her cerebrum down toward her spinal column, shaving milliseconds off her reaction time.

Danger!

)

If only dawn would break. The thought was on the mind of every soldier and general on the field. Their enemy's attack had begun halfway through the night, growing in intensity as the crescent moon dipped down toward the west. Anticipating the night attack, Asura had placed skirmishers in black camouflage at intervals along the battle lines, but she had not expected an assault of such intensity. Apparently, the enemy was hoping that this battle would be the turning point in the long and grinding war. By the time the reports of failure from the front lines reached her headquarters and Asura was able to send out reserve forces, the enemy had already penetrated deep within her lines.

Great blades and halberds shimmered in the dark, sending up warm sprays of blood into the wind. Screams of terror and roars of rage over-lapped with the shouting of men on both sides, and the soldiers mingled like fighting ants, slashing and grappling, rolling on the ground. In the dark, the psychological pressure on the defenders heightened to a fever pitch. For those who tried to flee, the darkness itself became an enemy.

If only dawn would break. Asura bit her lip and gazed toward the crescent moon, now low in the western sky. It would still be a long while before daybreak, and the tide of battle was rapidly shifting against her. The enemy had already reached the basin in front of the high ground where she now stood. A storm of arrows fell around her headquarters, sounding like a monstrous bird flapping its wings through the trembling night air.

"General Vajra, go!"

Vajra, one of her finest generals, defender of the northern banks of the Jinsha, descended from the high ground with his troops, his leather armor creaking. The soldiers moved silently, their footfalls as soft as those of nocturnal beasts drifting through the woods, until there came the sounds of violent hand-to-hand combat from midway down the slope.

Fire rose up in the deep forest to the north of the high ground, quickly engulfing the trees in a sea of crimson flame. The incessant reports of splintering trunks sounded across the intervening distance; every leaf became an arrowhead of fire, whirling up in the sky only to rain down around Asura's camp. Soon the grass and the shrubs along the plateau began to burn. The dark silhouettes of Asura's soldiers as they stomped the fires out looked almost beautiful, as though they had spontaneously abandoned war to engage in a great and graceful dance.

The fire wrapped around the rise, reaching the plains to the west. Their enemy was cutting off their route of escape.

Two or three of General Vajra's men came staggering back, accompanied by a terrible smell of blood. One of them fell like a stone amongst the burning grasses. The stench of scorched flesh stung Asura's nostrils. Now the enemy's advance guard came dancing in among the wounded. Their silvery helmets reflected the flames, shining like red jewels. Asura cut down three of them personally with her greatsword while her guard rallied, managing at last to push the enemy back down the slope.

The white blush of dawn began to creep into the sky in the east and a chill morning wind blew across the battlefield. By now, the front lines were firmly engaged on the slopes. During the time between midnight and early morning, Asura's ten thousand troops had been reduced to a tenth of that number, the rest killed, captured, or wounded so badly they could no longer fight.

A moist wind blew low over the field and rain began to fall. Gray clouds hung low like shredded flags, drawing a watery veil of light over the upland fields. Black smoke continued to rise through the rain, and the burning ground spat hot steam.

Now, a barrage of fiery cylinders arced through the sky, each trailing golden flame as they plunged into the high ground. Where they hit, huge gouts of flame burst up, dancing over the grasses, becoming a sea of flames too intense to face. The shock wave swept everything before it. Men ran wild like dancing matchsticks soon to be ash.

"Asura!" Another of her officers, General Tāshkand, raised a gauntleted hand and pointed. Explosives had already melted off the man's ears, nose, and lips. "Their launchers are positioned over there!" At the base of a hill off to the right, Asura spotted a six-wheeled vehicle sporting a launching platform on its upper surface. A new salvo of twelve fire tubes had already been set on the metal wires that guided them. They were pointed straight at Asura's position.

"General! Do we have any long-range crossbows remaining?"

Tāshkand darted out into the sea of flame and returned, carrying a crossbow in his hand. A small incendiary bomb had been fixed to the tip of the bolt. Asura raised the weapon and fired toward the launching platform. The bolt traced a line like a single silken thread through the rain, crippling its target on impact.

It would have been meaningless to remain there any longer. Asura's front lines were collapsing; enemy forces drew closer with every passing moment. She gathered her remaining troops and began a retreat. The rain increased in intensity, turning the battlefield into a churning sea of mud. Enemies rose on all sides, and Asura's foot soldiers fell one by one, but they left ten times their number in enemy corpses behind them.

A great rumbling sounded through the earth ahead of the retreating column. Asura wiped the rain from her face with one hand and stared. A line of shadows like small mountains were advancing through the white veil of water. This was their enemy's main force, an armored elephant brigade. They swiped at her men with their long trunks and beat the ground with their massive feet, rumbling toward Asura like an avalanche. Crouching low, she rolled like a ball through the mud. A giant foot stomped down, barely missing her shoulder, and the shock threw her up into the air. She got to her feet, only just making it between the legs of the next elephant. One after the other the giant beasts stampeded over her. She lifted a hand to protect her eyes against the flying mud, dodging between thick pillars of gray flesh that shot past her with the speed of the wind. She twisted and spun like an acrobat, running till she was out of breath.

"Asura!" A voice sounded from far above her head. "There is no longer any escape. Abandon your cause and join me . . . or I'll stomp you to a pulp right here in the mud."

She looked up and spied a stern man seated in the gondola atop the clifflike flank of the nearest elephant.

Asura smiled, the line of her white teeth showing brilliantly against her mud-streaked face. "Śakra, you coward! Why don't you come down from there and fight me, sword to sword!"

Śakra put a hand on the edge of the gondola and looked down. His silvery armor shone in a stray ray of sunlight. "Asura! Look around you."

She didn't have to look. She was standing in a sea of mud, a circle roughly fifty meters in diameter defined by nearly two hundred elephants standing side by side. Soldiers perched in the gondolas on the elephants' backs leveled several hundred crossbows directly at her.

"You may possess miraculous talent in battle, but there is no way for you to escape this encirclement. You should know that better than anyone else. Well? Join my forces. It's about time." Śakra looked down at Asura as she stood in the muck at his elephant's feet. "Who sent you to wage this endless war and plunge Brahmā's world into chaos?" he demanded. "For how many years have you fought against my celestial army, never realizing the sin you wrought, not once suing for peace? Whence this ceaseless animosity you bear for me? Why continue this profitless struggle?"

Asura raised her sword, pointing it straight at Śakra's face. "I will tell you this! I know your objectives already, you who call yourself Śakra, and even those of Brahmā who rules this world. Already you have destroyed too many civilizations. Mohenjo-daro, Sumer . . . all have disappeared into the flow of time by your design. Why? Was it because you saw in them the potential to become aware of your existence and thereby endanger your own world? Is that why you doomed their civilizations to eventual destruction? Is that why you seeded their hearts and their beliefs with pathways to ruin? Ever since you placed that statue of Maitreya deep in the Pearl Palace, you have been working to fulfill that singular purpose. And to this you added the great insult: the lie of promised salvation! Tell me, how long is 5,670,000,000 years in your reckoning? One year? One day? The merest blink of an eye? I would drive you from this world! I would destroy *your* world! Those were my—"

My orders. Asura snapped her mouth shut.

"What's that?" came the voice from above. "Everything is as you say, but what were you about to say next? Having second thoughts, perhaps?" Śakra tilted his head toward her, urging her to continue.

"I . . . I . . ."

"Yes, you. What about you?"

A look of despair crossed Asura's face as her eyes went from Śakra above her to the elephantry all around her. She was trapped, a tiny squirrel among wolves. The great sword fell from her hand.

"Cakravar . . ."

)

A powerful shock wave fragmented Asura's thoughts. Her enemy's psychic assault was incredibly powerful—more powerful than any she had before experienced. She felt cold sweat running in torrents down her body. Her enemy had brought all of his power to bear in an attempt to destroy her, here in this corner of this cold basin—and not just to destroy her, but to expose her to a higher existence than her own, exalted and unbearable.

Searing pain ran across her shoulder. Without thinking, she probed with her hand and found a fragment of metal panel buried deep in her shoulder. She yanked it out. Fortuitously, the tip of the metal had damaged part of her secondary circuitry, sapping the effectiveness of the hypnotic waves directed toward her cerebral matter. *This will be my last chance.* Asura brought her gravitation-generation device to full power and closed the dimensional space where Maitreya was hiding. Negative heat entropy resulting from the adiabatic change shrank the closed space to a singularity in an instant—an infinitely dense, infinitely negative space, awash in a Dirac sea.

)

The darkness thickened; only the lingering hot breath in the air told of the flames that had raged there moments before.

"Asura! Are you okay?" Siddhārtha and Orionae came running out of the corridor. Orionae had his emergency respiratory system cranked to maximum—he was breathing with his entire body.

"Our enemy is very powerful," Siddhārtha gasped. "We were almost destroyed ourselves."

For the first time in a very long while, Asura let herself relax.

"Jesus escaped west across the basin," Siddhārtha told her. "We were going to give chase but were concerned about you."

Asura smiled bitterly at Siddhārtha's words. They were right to be worried for her. She had been on the defensive from start to finish and had only narrowly escaped destruction. Maitreya's next assault would surely not be long in coming.

"Siddhārtha," Asura said quietly. "Have you ever wondered . . . ?"

"Wondered what?"

"Wondered if, perhaps, we are working under someone or something's orders?"

Siddhārtha raised an eyebrow.

"How about you, Orionae?"

Orionae shook his head in silence.

"As it so happens," Asura told them, "just now in my fight with Maitreya I was held captive by a psychic attack and surrounded by a phantasmal army led by Śakra himself. He spoke to me from atop an elephant. He wanted to know who had ordered me into battle—who launched the assault on his world. He wanted a name."

The three exchanged glances. It was as though the veil that covered their hearts, unnoticed until now, had peeled back, revealing something they had never glimpsed before: the idea of an entity supporting their minds and bodies from time immemorial—a power in opposition to the endless war that threatened to demolish their universe, a transcendental being that actually wanted to save their world from destruction.

"Have you ever thought about it before now?"

"At times, yes," Siddhārtha admitted. "I wondered what power had fashioned us into cyborgs and placed me near the shore in that barren, life-less land—and buried you in the sands. There had to be some design behind it all, or at least I thought there was. But whenever I tried to recall what it was, I found a complete blank in my neural memory web. The circuit had been cut, you might say. Perhaps as a defensive measure. And, seeing that Śakra had to resort to ordinary words in order to try to badger information from you, I would say that our designer's plans met with perfect success."

Siddhārtha turned to face the vast basin of the night, as though he might find the truth of the world buried within that darkness. "Do you have any idea who it might be, Asura?"

She shook her head. "I feel like I should, and yet—"

"Orionae?"

The cyborg philosopher tilted his head, frowning, then began hesitantly. "A long time ago, I heard of a civilization that believed in an evil supreme being who existed in opposition to their good god. I have visited the village where they believed in a god of night in opposition to the god of day. The good god is the sun god, and the sun itself, and eventually the god who is heaven—the heavenly father. I always thought that the evil god, the night god, was a purely allegorical being."

Asura and Siddhārtha stared intently at Orionae.

"So the people who believed in an evil god believed in something other than, or perhaps even directly opposed to, the ancient god of the sun?"

"Yes," Orionae said. "Or perhaps they realized that God was only a pathway to destruction and saw in the god of night the means to save their world."

"Is this, then, the nature of the transcendent being who designed us, Asura?" Siddhārtha asked.

"I do not know," she said. "Gods who administer death, sin, disease, and poverty have featured in the folk beliefs of many cultures. What do these gods mean? And to what end were they eventually abandoned and forgotten?"

"You are one of them, Asura," Siddhārtha said.

"All right," she said, "then it could be possible that my very existence is part of the effort against those beings that want to destroy our world. If that's the case, then who sent me here? And sent me here to coincide with our enemies' arrival?"

Orionae strode across the stones, hands clasped behind his back. "Your existence, Asura, was hidden from the people's eyes by the religion started by Siddhārtha. I believe it was this transcendent being who opposed the destruction of our world that inserted concepts into that religion such as the idea that 'all is void,' and the story of how souls cross a river to reach the afterlife. Such details suggest the true nature of our struggle to the minds of humankind.

"Siddhārtha—" Orionae turned. "You believed your teachings could lead to an escape from the misery of life, a path toward enlightenment and freedom from the endless cycle of reincarnation. Yet you erred. Why should existence be a void? Is the void not a denial of consciousness itself? Your words were twisted and used against you by those desiring our destruction. I presume that the transcendental being, as a final measure, sent both of you into the far future, and that is how you came to be standing here, at the very entrance to our enemies' realm."

"Yes." Siddhārtha nodded gravely. "There's even a sutra claiming that Asura became a believer in the Buddha . . . Their ploy met with smashing success."

Dark orange clouds stretched out across the sky. The air grew gradually colder as an ancient stillness wrapped around the ruins.

"When I looked out upon the distant gray land from those barren reefs, I saw shapes like mountains sliding toward the city ruins on the horizon. Many of them. That was the moment when I first realized how odd my situation was. Asura, do you have any idea what those mountainous shapes were? And there was another mystery—a large, black shadow that lay deep in the sea trench near the reef where I had been hidden. The fish, when there were still fish in the sea, were too frightened to approach. Yet I couldn't help but feel that it bore some deep meaning for me."

Asura turned her eyes to the distant clouds. "It is dawn. Another day begins—I do not know whether I will live to see night. We must leave here at once. But before that—Siddhārtha, those shapes you saw, could they not have existed in an alternate dimension? A warping of space beneath that troubled sky could have created a mirage, amplifying whatever was passing across the flats."

"Perhaps," Orionae said. "Whatever they were, they were looking for us—me buried beneath the dust of Tokyo, Asura ensconced in the desert sand, and Siddhārtha under the surging waves, all back when we knew nothing of our future selves. Though their repeated search attempts did not meet with success, it is likely that this was the time they first learned of our existence."

"Then what was that thing sunk at the bottom of the sea trench?" Siddhārtha asked. "It bothers me. All the more so because we lack the means to go back and find out."

Asura took a deep breath. "Okay, let's go. We need to take that sphere someplace safe."

The three tugged on the glowing construct, enveloped in its gravitational barrier. They brought it out in front of the ruins of the crystalline building. "I see no point in returning to that city beneath the shield. Let's go to the foot of that mountain range to the south. There we can examine how this sphere works."

By now the orange light reached halfway across the plains. The sun still hung below the horizon, as yet unrevealed. In those fleeting moments between day and night, the three hurried southward, carrying the sphere between them.

)

"Well, can you fix it?" Siddhārtha asked, peering down at Orionae's hands as he worked. He had been asking the same question every minute or so, and each time, Orionae had answered "I think so," though it was doubtful whether he was listening at all.

Siddhārtha shrugged and turned around to Asura. "Do you think he can fix it? Shouldn't we consider other options?"

Asura was lying down on the cold earth of the basin, gazing up at the indigo sky. Her eyes betrayed no emotion. She seemed indifferent to the icy ground, her arms and legs sprawled out unfeeling.

Looking at her, Siddhārtha ruminated on how different he was from his strange companions.

"Give him a chance," she said at length. "We'll consider other options if he fails."

Orionae was struggling to reconnect a pair of broken supports beneath the sphere. If these could not be fixed, the secondary coils that slid along the outermost surface would remain stuck in place.

"Well? Can you fix it?" Siddhārtha asked again.

Orionae used his maser to separate the broken pieces into three sections. "I think so."

Siddhārtha extended a hand. "What if we melted some metal and fashioned a pipe the same length? We could probably find some in the city."

Orionae pushed Siddhārtha's hand away. "We won't need to do that."

Orionae cut another section, fusing it to part of the sphere.

"If you break it, it's all over." Siddhārtha frowned over Orionae's shoulder.

"I know."

Carefully Orionae measured out a second, equal length of pipe, cutting off the excess from the part he had fused. Then he took the remaining fragments and fused them together to make a small orb that he then passed through the polls of a gravitational generator, reshaping it into a length of wire. Siddhārtha walked away, shaking his head.

The whole time, Asura laid splayed out on the ground, as unmoving as a stone.

Siddhārtha looked up at the sky. Through the barrier dome they had erected over themselves, the edges of the small, yellowish sun appeared to stretch to either side, like a strange mouth opening in the sky.

In Orionae's hands, the sphere had lost half of its size. A considerable bundle of tubes, twisted into all manner of shapes, were stacked at his feet. It appeared as though he was in the process of constructing something entirely different.

"What's that?"

"Please don't touch. It will destroy your processors."

Siddhārtha withdrew his hand at the last moment.

)

Again, night visited the plains. The thin atmosphere rapidly lost its heat. A dry, cold wind blew from one edge of the basin to the other. The scattered stars winked in the sky above the ancient stillness.

"It's done." Orionae sat up.

"You finished it?" Siddhārtha leapt to his feet, then gaped. "What is it?"

The sphere they had taken from the ruins was completely gone. In its place rested a pair of coils, one inside the other. Lying on their sides, their height was roughly the same as Orionae's.

Siddhārtha's gaze shifted suspiciously back and forth between the coils and Orionae's face. "You've rebuilt it?"

Orionae turned slowly toward Siddhārtha. "No. I did not rebuild it. I've made an entirely different thing. Though I did use two or three of the basic principles that were fundamental to the original sphere."

Asura slowly rose to her feet behind them.

Orionae lifted the coils and placed them in front of her. He touched a part of the device, and the coils and the cylindrical space inside them shimmered a beautiful aquamarine. Fine bands of light formed on the surface of the cylinders, moving from one end of the coils to the other at an incredible speed.

"This flow of light reveals an extraordinary transfer of energy from the exterior of the coils to the inside."

"Where does the energy come from? I don't see any kind of generator attached."

"Asura, look here. See the part that looks like a diffraction grating woven of wire? I made this wire out of the supports from the original device—though one of these also existed in the sphere. If you induct this with a secondary coil, an incredible amount of power will flow through it. I believe the source of its power to be the Dirac sea."

"The Dirac sea?"

Asura and Siddhārtha stepped forward.

"Yes, the birthplace of all protons."

The two others scanned their own neural memory webs, discovering recollections of this strange term from ancient atomic physics.

"And so?"

"I aim this secondary coil's deflector toward an unlimited function index. This is the same as orienting it toward the entropy D index that was in the sphere. Then, observe—another space is generated on the inside of the larger coil."

The primary coil's diameter was about a meter and a half; Orionae reached over it and held down the deflector on top of a rail fastened to the secondary coil. The deflector slid down the rail.

ZZZZING

They heard a faint sound like a metallic wire trembling, a vibration that echoed at the bottom of their ears.

Suddenly, the space within the coil grew dark: a true darkness, permitting absolutely no light to escape. The blue brilliance of the coil wrapped around it grew in intensity until it was blinding.

"What is the inside of this coil connected to?"

Orionae returned the deflector to its original position. The darkness inside the coil gradually brightened into the original blue bands of shimmering light.

"The thing that was hardest to understand at first was the coordinate system of the grid. I had no idea what the numbers represented. However, while I was analyzing the Milky Way's galactic latitude, longitude, and the equator baseline range, I figured it out. According to my results, the darkness we just saw here originated from the following coordinates: $Y=88.5711$; $X=43.026$; $Z=19.3920$; $T=n^{-n} \Delta t$."

Asura's eyes grew as narrow as needles. "Those coordinates sound like they're inside the Andromeda galaxy."

Orionae nodded quietly. "Indeed. They lie within the second arm in the eighth quadrant of Andromeda."

A deep silence followed. No one said a word; even their breaths were drawn lightly. Starlight twisted by the polarizing effect of the gravitational barrier played across Asura's still features.

The path toward destruction that had begun far in their past had taken a new turn here, heading off into the night sky. Destruction had come to their galaxy, their solar system, their Earth along that path several times— the result of some transcendent being's displeasure with human progress. The seeds that being had planted had grown into inescapable tethers, and the once great civilizations of humanity were now reduced to ruin and dust and sand. It was already too late to try and stop it. The damage was done. Their enemy's work was complete, leaving no tomorrow for the three cyborgs.

"Let's go."

The necklace around Asura's neck sparkled in the blue light, reflecting in the eyes of her companions.

His face expressionless, Orionae once again reached out to the deflector. The coil emitted a bright blue light.

"I will go in last. It would not do to leave this here behind us."

Asura crouched down, stared at the darkness inside the coil, then slid inside.

Ziiiiiiiiiiiiin.

The strange vibration struck her skin like countless needles. She thought she heard Siddhārtha shout something, but in an instant, everything was swallowed in darkness.

The traveler left behind a pot.
The villager hung it on a tree.
The traveler returned and said:
"This pot is your home."

The sky was a single band of light, sending vast waves of brilliance like nuclear flames to beat down upon the ground. To one who gazed through a polarized screen, however, the blazing torrent was distinguishable as a rush of countless particles. Some of these light fragments were enormous—bright enough that had they been placed in a starry night sky, they would have drowned out stars of the first magnitude, or even negative first.

For a while, Asura stood staring vacantly at the falling light, forgetting her purpose entirely.

"What do you think it is?" Siddhārtha whispered at her ear, bringing her back to the present. A vast glacier spread out before them, its ice harder than steel, its polished surface reflecting the forms of the three travelers where they stood.

Not far off to the right, cliffs of ice formed a continuous wall that stretched into the distance. The cliffs were steep and perfectly vertical, as though cut deliberately from the glacial ice. Their upper rims melted into the sea of light extending from the sky.

"What a sight!" Siddhārtha said. It seemed impossible for even a cloudless, star-filled sky to give off so much light. "It's as though someone covered the sky with some stupendous sheet of electroluminescent material."

Though the idea was outrageous, there were no better words to describe it.

"Where are we?"

"Where we intended to be," Asura said, checking her readings. "$Y=88.5711$; $X=43.026$; $Z=19.3920$; $T=n^{-n} \Delta t$—the eighth quadrant of the Andromeda galaxy, in other words. Roughly 130,000 light-years from the center of the galaxy, just outside the two spiral arms that pass near these coordinates."

"Doesn't seem to be much life here," Siddhārtha noted. "Or perhaps it has all withered away, as it did on Earth and Mars and Astarta 50."

Orionae looked around, taking in their surroundings. "Together with seven other planets, this planet we're on orbits a single star. Judging from the deviations I'm reading in our coil, the star radiates sufficient energy to support life. It is about twice as massive as our own sun. And yet, we're standing on a glacier—"

"Orionae. We have already seen another planet brought to ruin for reasons we do not understand, have we not?"

Orionae shook his head firmly. "That is not so. There have been reasons for all the devastation we have seen thus far. For example: our failure to take appropriate measures when the earth began to dry out or to revitalize the failing production in our cities. But there is nothing here, nothing at all. The sun gives off sufficient warmth, and it's shining directly on this location."

"Let's climb those cliffs and see what we can see," Asura suggested.

Orionae hefted the coil on his back, and the three set off single file across the glacier.

"I do not understand why our observations do not match the numbers," Orionae muttered, frustrated.

Asura paused several times as they walked, staring out across the glacier, pursued by an unsettling feeling that something was eluding her.

There was *something* here, something mysterious, suffusing the place and yet impossible to discern. It was growing thicker, wrapping more closely around them as they walked.

The light from the sky still streamed down onto the ice, reflecting off the cliffs with such intensity it was nearly painful to their eyes.

At length, they came to the base of the cliffs. Siddhārtha hesitated to study the wall of ice; then he released the safety switch on the maser in his arm. Orionae continued walking, still muttering formulae to himself. The strangely shaped coil he carried on his shoulder bobbed and swayed as though it were part of his body.

Asura stopped. She could feel something sweep across her body—a readiness for battle that came not from within, but from without.

"What is it, Asura?" Siddhārtha asked, following the line of her gaze. He stared in shock.

A giant city stood buried deep behind the crystalline surface of the icy cliffs. At first, they thought it was only a trick of the shadows created by light refracted through the wall of ice—but with all of the light on this world, there were no shadows.

Roughly two hundred meters beyond the surface of the ice, rectangular buildings, some hundreds of stories in height, stood so close together they almost touched. Beltways ran through translucent pipes that wove between the buildings' enormous walls. Every surface in the city reflected prismatic sprays of light.

More surprisingly, the city was approaching them at roughly the speed of a man walking. It seemed to stretch all the way to the horizon on either side, and it was impossible to gauge how far back it might go. The glacier was as quiet as a coffin beneath the piercingly bright curtain of the sky. The phantasmal city approached without a sound, moving the way a tide sweeps in at sea, suggesting nothing so much as the approach of certain death.

"Asura! Maitreya knew we would come here—we've walked into his trap!" Siddhārtha cried, his voice ringing out from the bottom of his throat. A chill colder than ice ran down Asura's back. She detected something far more dangerous in the advancing city than Maitreya's assaults.

Turning back to Orionae, she shouted, "Quick—create a barrier with that coil! This is not one of Maitreya's psychic attacks! Quickly, Orionae!"

In one smooth motion Orionae lowered the coil from his shoulder onto the ice. He manipulated the deflector until the instrument began to emit a calm blue light. The space around the three travelers grew keen with a noise like vibrating silver wire. Immediately, the shining sky dimmed, and an ultramarine shadow fell over the glacier. Wrapped in the barrier's curtain, the three travelers shimmered like a mirage.

"Now, we each need to make our own barriers," Asura said. "Orionae wrapped the coil in several gravitationally sealed spaces. You have to maintain the link to the Dirac sea via an imaginary numeric circuit."

Standing in the middle of the shimmering blue light, the three companions shone with tremendous intensity. The heat entropy inside their barrier shot up rapidly before reaching a balance point.

Moments later, the moving city slid over the dome of their barrier.

The giant carved faces of the buildings, the countless rows of windows, beltways, and spires, passed soundlessly through their bodies, over their heads, and beneath their feet, continuing on to disappear behind them.

Beyond the city, the ice cliffs stretched like a dark shadow across the glacier. The translucent city continued to spill forth from the wall of ice, passing through them, gliding on and away until the buildings disappeared into the distance.

"What is this, Asura?" Siddhārtha asked from within the incandescence of his personal barrier. Asura was hanging upside down in her own sequestered space, looking like a minnow inside a shell.

"My guess, Siddhārtha, is that this planet is a gravitationally sealed imaginary numeric space. A 'negative energy world.' I'm sure you have a record of Noya's Formula somewhere in your neural memory web."

"Ah! You're referring to the event in 3005, when Noya Clark of Jupiter suddenly found himself inescapably trapped in what appeared to be a two-dimensional space, like a screen. There were others present, but though they could see a path within the 'screen,' when they tried to enter it, they simply passed through."

Orionae sat hunched over the coil's diffraction grating, apparently not listening. A strange light gleamed in his eyes as he murmured to himself.

"What is it, Orionae?" Asura asked.

"Don't tell me we're trapped inside this barrier or something like that," Siddhārtha grumbled.

"That's it, I've got it!" Orionae shouted. "There's been a terrible mistake!"

"What kind of mistake?"

"Asura. We must leave this place at once. I must find a safe location where I can repair the coil."

"I see," Asura said. "But, Orionae, in order to move, we will have to drop the barrier on that coil, and the barriers around each of us, and our external barrier as well—but, surrounded by imaginary numeric space as we apparently are, I'm afraid that's impossible."

Orionae held his head in his hands and moaned.

"What happens if you touch imaginary numeric space, Asura?" Siddhārtha asked.

"You generate a perfect void at the point of contact. Energy is consumed in order to create the void, and then *negative* energy will wrap around the void like a shell, spreading almost instantaneously into a limitless pool the ancients called 'Dirac's sea' . . ."

The city flowed on through them without the slightest break, buildings and streets appearing like phantasms, then disappearing into the distance.

"Look! The city is alive!" Siddhārtha spread his arms wide, as if to push the cityscape that surrounded them off to one side. The corner of a building passed through one of his hands. They saw buildings and hallways and beltways, then many men and women wearing outlandish clothes, walking through the streets. No one seemed to notice the three travelers at all. Nor did they notice that they were passing through the side of a cliff on top of a gigantic glacier. Their city was grand and beautiful, protected from all unhappiness and decay.

Orionae abruptly lifted his face. "If we combine our energy together, I wonder how much we could generate?"

"Roughly 1.1 billion megawatts, I should guess," Siddhārtha replied.

"Ah! If we truly can generate that much, then, for a very short period of time, we could control the flow of negative energy through the diffraction grating."

"I see. And how long would this very short period of time be?"

A shadow crossed Orionae's face. "At most, 0.08 seconds. We could not hold it much longer."

"Will we be able to move far enough in 0.08 seconds?"

"It shouldn't be a problem," Orionae said.

"What if it is?"

"Then all of the energy we've used will convert into a massive amount of heat radiation from the surface of the diffraction grating . . . I think."

"And all of us will be swallowed in a sea of negative energy."

"I could set it up so that, in the case that we did overstay our allotted time, the circuit would automatically collapse. However, quite a bit of energy will have already been consumed by that point, so I think it would be best to arrange it in such a way that the very first recovery circuit to activate will absorb any excess radiation. Then at least one of us will be able to recover their original form."

Siddhārtha shook his head. It seemed their options were limited. "All right, Orionae. Let's go with that plan."

"Orionae," Asura spoke up. "What was that you said a moment ago about a mistake? Whose mistake?"

Orionae looked back at the coil. "Do you know of a material called orichalcum?"

"I do! You've spoken of it—the special alloy used in creating the royal palace and other grand structures of Atlantis."

"When I was still in Atlantis, I once looked into the origins of that mysterious alloy. I discovered a few fairly interesting properties, and by far the most interesting was that orichalcum is an incredibly stable substance. Reflecting back on it now, I realize that each element of the alloy must contain a perfectly sealed heat-entropy world. Each segment of the orichalcum alloy would be able to contain a massive amount of energy. Furthermore, it could be used as a filter for negative energy."

"So what brings this up now?" Siddhārtha asked, growing impatient.

"As it so happens," Orionae said, "this coil is made out of orichalcum."

Asura and Siddhārtha stood for a long while in silence, watching the phantasmal city flow through them.

"So," Asura said at last, "we can imagine that at some point in the distant past, someone brought a bit of that strange metal to Earth and tried to explain its miraculous properties to humankind—perhaps even gave them the technology to understand it. Then when those bent on destroying our world arrived, they eventually discovered the orichalcum and took great pains to completely remove it from the planet, wiping mankind's collective memory as they did so. Siddhārtha, Orionae . . . it's very possible that there were other such materials on Earth that were subsequently removed by an external force. In fact, roughly three thousand years ago, a fragment of pure tin was discovered on Earth. One hundred percent pure tin does not occur naturally on that planet. Perhaps this too bore some great meaning, and yet the tin and all records of it have been entirely lost. And there was another material, tektite, that resembled obsidian. This too has been entirely lost. Our enemy is nothing if not a perfectionist."

"I only wish I had looked into the matter more closely back then or discovered the truth behind this destruction earlier. It is most unfortunate," Orionae said, sighing.

"No," Siddhārtha said solemnly. "I believe it was our world's destiny to walk this long road to ruin."

"Well . . . let's continue on then, shall we?" Orionae said, moving the secondary coil deflector to the zero mark, then withdrawing an impressive number of imaginary numeric circuits from the diffraction grating. These he wrapped around another pipe, creating a new induction coil.

"This is a response circuit—a fourth dimensional circuit, you might call it. In an emergency, this should absorb any excess energy generated." Orionae adjusted the sliding cover, closing off the diffraction grating. "All right, I'll go in last again, after which I'll open the imaginary numeric circuit. I've set our time window to 0.076 seconds. Now, quickly!"

First Asura, then Siddhārtha, then finally Orionae dived into the darkness inside the coil. A fraction of a moment later, the imaginary numeric circuit connected. The space linked to the coil emitted a tremendous burst of light, turning the icy glacier into a sea of incandescent flames. Quite suddenly, the buildings of the phantasmal city nearest to the blast broke into a million glowing fragments and scattered in all directions. A massive wave of energy crashed into the remainder of the city, and it burned, exploded, shrank, faded, then disappeared altogether. In the wavering blaze, light from the sky pierced through, swirling with imaginary space.

Another city, another civilization destroyed. It was meant to happen, as the three travelers had been meant to come to that place.

)

Asura stood on a vast plain where blue light fell like a silent rain of death. There was no atmosphere, no air to protect the exposed rocky surface. Though the lack of wind meant that there was minimal erosion, cracks formed over millennia crisscrossed the surface of the rock; some had grown large enough to be called crevices. The trickling of small fragments of rock down into those crevices appeared to provide the only movement in this world.

Everywhere there were signs that this planet had been subjected to incredibly strong radiation over a very long period of time. The radiation alert system on Asura's necklace had been sounding at maximum danger level since she arrived. The discordant clamor of the alarm shrieked in her ears, an unwelcome call to action.

She took a step, and her foot sank to the ankle as the surface soundlessly crumbled beneath her. All the way to the horizon, the conditions looked the same. In every direction there was nothing but the faint curve of the horizon—no indicators to say which way was north or south. Asura knew that even if she did cross over the horizon she would find no remaining mountain ridges or deep valleys.

Over the long years, the powerful radiation had transformed the very material composition of the rock, grinding down mountains until they were nothing more than dust that filled the valleys and the ancient seabeds.

Even death had no shape in this place.

Peering around, Asura realized that no one else was there. With blue light streaming down across her shoulders, she stood alone at the end of the world.

Neither Siddhārtha nor Orionae had been able to reconstitute themselves on the other side of the conduit. For reasons Orionae clearly had not foreseen, it had taken longer than the coil could withstand for them to pass through the region of space filled with negative energy. Either that, or their transit had used more energy than expected. As Orionae had suggested, it seemed that at the last instant the circuit breaker had tripped, dumping the remaining energy into Asura, who was already passing beyond the negative energy zone. As for her companions—

She remembered Siddhārtha's prediction of the sea of negative energy and shuddered.

This was what she was witnessing now: utter ruin made manifest.

Siddhārtha's energy and Orionae's energy—and whatever was left of Asura's—had combined to power their last, desperate effort, and now she was left to discover for herself what her final objective should be. *I could not have predicted that this would happen,* she told herself. Nor could she ignore the terrible loneliness she felt in her heart when she considered her chances of fighting and defeating a transcendent, godlike being alone.

The glacier and the phantasmal city that had appeared within it were gone and would never be found again.

Orionae had mentioned a mistake, but could it be that this devastation was, in fact, what they should have been seeking? *Is this our final destination, this small planet in the outer arm of the eighth quadrant of the Andromeda galaxy?* With great unease, Asura set out across the crumbling surface, feeling as though she were walking not on matter, but on pure light.

She contemplated the blue light that suffused the surface of the planet and looked up toward the sky to find its source. First she saw the stardust, countless billions of swirling fragments in an endless dance above her. Then beyond it she saw that there was something more, pulsing behind the stars like an aurora there in the remote vastness of space—a great spiral of timeless light turning in the center of the sky.

For a brief moment, Asura stared, the brightness burning into her visual cortex, not understanding what she was witnessing. She felt herself part of a tableau, a tiny figure standing on a devastated planet beneath a white-hot whirling spiral—a perfect portrait of the end of the world.

I know what that is!

An icy tremor passed through Asura's heart.

It was a massive spiral galaxy, coming from the depths of space directly toward the galaxy of Andromeda. Already the interstellar material of both galaxies were intermingling, each invading the other's territory, emitting powerful electron radiation. Eventually, the heat trapped in the gradually thickening cloud created by the collision would rise to tens of thousands of degrees, then hundreds of thousands, burning away stars and spewing out vast nebulae. In time, the two spiral galaxies would combine entirely, and release all of their energy at once.

Later, once that energy had dispersed, all that would be left behind would be a faintly radioactive nebula and the slightest dusting of interstellar material. The tremendous volume of heat released into space would radiate in every direction, eventually vanishing into the far reaches of the universe altogether. Existence becoming nonexistence. Being becoming nonbeing. The simplest process of all.

Of course, the dispersed energy would not truly become *nothing*. But how much effect on the rest of space could such energy have—even if it came from so potent a source as the collision of two galaxies? What could you call its long-term result, if not "nothing"?

The residents of this planet had wrapped their great city in a near-perfect gravitationally sealed space, after creating another such space that surrounded the entire planet—effectively girding themselves in a double layer of protection. And yet, Asura mused, their gravitational fortress relied on a planet to anchor it. How long could this fastness last within the torrent of energy released when two galaxies collided?

The giant spiral galaxy above her was making its final descent, pitching off-balance with the weight of entropic death it carried, raining radiation down on its Andromedan rival.

Asura wished she could show this quiet world to Siddhārtha and Orionae. She now realized the nature of the mistake that Orionae had spoken of. The mysterious blue light shining on the glacier they had visited was filtered light coming through a gravitational barrier constructed around the planet—a barrier that should have protected and preserved its civilization. Yet nothing had been living there. What could live at minus two hundred degrees and below? The mistake had been a faint warping in the gravitational seal, or perhaps a slight error in their gravitational field generators that had allowed heat to leak out over a long period of time. By the time the planet's residents realized what was happening, it had already been too late, and their home world was lost, buried beneath a thick layer of ice. And so the survivors had acted, raising another line of resistance, an even stronger gravitational barrier around their capital. It was they who had appeared, walking the streets of their phantasmal city. She wondered how long *that* civilization had lasted.

Did it even really matter? Was there any difference between being trapped in an endlessly reiterating city and being stamped onto a metal plate—the fate the citizens of Astarta 50 had chosen in an attempt to evade their approaching destruction? Asura thought she could hear Siddhārtha laughing somewhere, perhaps inside herself . . . A smile rose on her lips, but it was a pitiful thing with no purpose, not the sort of smile that could be mistaken for happiness. Mankind had first developed civilization less than ten thousand years ago. She wondered how it had gone here in Andromeda. On this planet.

She saw no signs of a transcendent being attempting to stave off the destruction here. Even with *his* power and *his* plans, had the three of them not been awakened too late, to find Earth already transformed into a dead planet, nothing but a wasteland to greet them?

We should never have awoken. Her memories went back to that day when she had first met the man of Nazareth in that cold, wasted desert.

Asura.

She heard a faint voice that seemed to come from inside her own body. Asura spun around, looking for the speaker. The surface of the planet was as still and silent as it had ever been.

Asura.

Now it seemed to her as if the voice were coming from somewhere far beyond the surface, carried to her along rays of blue light through the barrier above.

"Who's there?" she shouted into the distance.

"I have been waiting for you, Asura, but you did not arrive in time. Still, this is not your fault."

She thought she detected the ring of deep sadness in the voice.

"Who are you? Where are you?"

Asura linked the brainwave detector embedded behind her right ear into her entire nervous system, scanning. She found nothing. The planet's surface remained as featureless as a calm lake around her. She sensed that the level of the ground was slightly slanted toward the left—perhaps the remnant elevation of what had once been the tallest ridgeline on this world.

"Asura."

This time it sounded as if the voice originated right next to her. Reflexively she jumped to a spot several meters away. "What are you?" Asura squinted but saw not even a shadow of anything around her, only the suffusing blue light.

"I did not imagine that we would meet in a place like this, in this way. For I am sure the record will show that we have never met before."

Asura did not know how to respond to that. After a short silence, she heard the voice again:

"Asura. Do you think Siddhārtha understood the meaning of the 'other shore'—the place to which the dead must pass? I was pleased when he sensed something lacking in the teachings of the Brahmin and harbored doubts about several of their doctrines. Follow the threads of those doubts, and they lead here. I chose you three, placed you in a long sleep, and kept you until such a time as I would require your services. I also placed within your minds several words, several concepts, you would need. Asura: 'All' is existence. 'Void' is Dirac's sea. 'All is void' means nothing other than the fact that the sea of negative energy is the true mother of all existence. Asura, the 'other shore' is none other than a transcendent being or the world where that transcendent being exists. I wonder how you, Asura, understood the sense of separation, that desperate division we hear in the word 'other.' Siddhārtha was a signpost along the path. Orionae had memorized the letters written upon that sign. And you—"

"Yes?"

". . . I regret now that ultimately, I have been little more than a bystander, observing the change passing through this universe, unable to affect it. I wonder how many people paid attention to those words I whispered into the collective heart of humanity, warning them of the destruction that would come? I regret that I was not able to take more decisive action."

Asura screamed into the blue-soaked waste. "Why didn't you just come out and tell us the truth?"

"I could not reveal myself, lest those powers who have always manipulated your world with the intent to bring it to ruin should take notice of me."

"Yet they did notice, and in short order."

"And so they worked to erase all signs of my warning. It is in mankind's nature not to believe that misfortune and tragedy are approaching and to forget calamity after it has occurred. Ultimately, my passive strategy did not help prolong their lives by one minute. While the sun shone, they prayed for a good harvest in the coming year and adorned their altars, and when the storms and the floods came they thought only to raise their levees and protect their fields. When plague spread, they nurtured physicians and synthesized ever more medicines. Eventually, the land dried and the desert covered all, so they moved their cities below ground. When there was no longer any place on land or in the sea to support the growing of food, these places became wastelands and passed away, unmourned and forgotten. Humanity spread to Mars, Venus, and beyond, throughout the solar system, yet in the end their productive capacity always failed.

"Eventually, humanity became aware of the coming fall. They crafted robots and enhanced their own bodies with cybernetics—they searched for ways to escape to the outer reaches of the solar system. Yet what came of that, Asura? In the end, those bent on the destruction of the human worlds were victorious. Indeed, perhaps their victory was predetermined from the start."

Asura stood on the slight swell in the earth that was the ghost of a former ridge, looking out across plains that now appeared to her as a seabed at the bottom of an ocean of blue light. This place seemed a poor destination for someone who had traveled so far, but in a sudden rush of resignation she accepted that she would have to make do.

"Asura."

Asura shook her head. "What are you? *What are you?*"

The voice seemed to pierce her chest. "I am the Reincarnation King. I am the cakravarti-rājan."

It took several seconds for the words to sink into Asura's weary mind. "The cakravarti-rājan?"

"Yes. That is what the Brahmin monks once called me."

The cakravarti-rājan—King of Kings who moves the world. Asura had once described the cakravarti-rājan to Siddhārtha. The details of that night were still vivid in her mind.

)

Siddhārtha had appeared behind Asura where she stood on an outcrop of stone.

"*And what is this cakravarti-rājan of which you speak?*"

"*The Brahmins can tell you as well as I. He is the King of Kings, the master of karma. He stands outside this world and has viewed its life and growth for more than one trillion years.*"

"*And have you ever met this cakravarti-rājan?*"

"*My prince. No one has seen the cakravarti-rājan. Nor do we know where he might be. Yet all who know his name know that, not long from now, the cakravarti-rājan will appear among us. And when he does he will rule over all as the one great God, the Creator, he who transcends karma.*"

)

Now she faced not Siddhārtha, but the King of Kings himself.

"My king," Asura said, "am I to understand that you have existed here, upon this single planet in the Andromeda galaxy, and that from this place you presided over the rise and fall of many, many other planets?"

"My schemes and structures have all crumbled and scattered. I have stood here on this ancient slope, devoid of all life, watching the universe transform into something beyond the ability of my power to contain. I watched those who believed that Maitreya would come to their world and save them . . . I watched them build a statue to their supposed savior within the Pearl Palace, as I watched Maitreya himself assume direct authority over the kingdom of Atlantis. He caused the man Jesus of Nazareth to believe that he, Maitreya, was a god in heaven above, and from here I watched Jesus perform miracles in his name. Asura, even among my best and brightest followers, there were some who believed Maitreya's words and laid the blame for the ruination of the world at your feet.

"Śakra, Vajra, all fought against the wasting of your world—your universe, believing in the Pure Land promised them by Maitreya. Yet they never once thought to seek that which gives birth to ruination in the first place."

Asura thought back on the long road she had traveled, the vast span of time during which all of these events had taken place. It all seemed part of an even longer voyage, one with no beginning and no end.

"Let me ask you one thing, my king."

"Yes?"

"What exactly are these beings that desire the destruction of our universe? From whence did they come?"

"Before I explain, I must ask you whether you have ever thought about the limits of your reality."

"I have. I would assume they lie at the edge of the expanding universe, where the rate of expansion has reached the speed of light, forming a single, defined space, like an enormous sphere."

"True—but this is not a complete explanation. If we speak of a finite space, no matter how large, we must also accept a larger, infinitely vast space outside it, of which your universe is only a part."

The universe encompassed billions upon billions of galaxies. What did it matter if it was expanding or contracting, or doing something else entirely? What was the *use* of such knowledge?

"Time is the same, you know. The time that defines the reality inside those expanding limits of space is just a part of the time that exists in the infinity beyond. The flow of time began at the origin point of the universe you know, two hundred billion years ago, and its flow ceases two hundred billion light-years in the distance. Yet that is merely a fragment of the transcendent time stretching out into infinity."

The voice of the cakravarti-rājan was filled with the regret of one who had watched the entirety of the universe's long journey and knew its eventual fate.

"So, King of Kings, perhaps then you can tell me who *Shi* is? The absolute being who controls this transcendent time of which you speak?"

A long silence followed. The blue light falling on the bleak landscape around her, the great unbroken stillness, seemed increasingly bizarre, like something that belonged to another universe entirely. If this truly was the place from which the cakravarti-rājan had observed all change in the vastness of space she knew, then here, she thought, even a god would be little more than one aspect of that change.

Again, she heard the cakravarti-rājan's voice within her mind.

"Once, Asura, I had a vision. Though I do not know if it was a true vision, or just a shadow drawn in my weary mind . . . Perhaps I never saw it at all. I am no longer sure. Yet I remember the contents of this vision quite clearly. I will show it to you now, Asura—I will give it into your mind directly. I'm sure its meaning will be very different for you than it was for me. But that is to be expected. You, who have already traveled so far, will have to choose for yourself whether you will return whence you came or continue along a far more difficult path than any you have known."

As the words of the King of Kings ended, the vision began:

Wrapped in incandescent light, two spiral galaxies quietly devoured a third. Then the three galaxies became one, advancing toward the heart of another galactic cluster. Radioactive nebulae—the remnants of other galactic encounters—shimmered with light, moving through the full spectrum of colors as they gradually faded.

The scale grew greater and greater still. Now, several thousand galactic clusters swarmed in every direction, drifting at near the speed of light. The radiation they emitted destroyed other clusters billions of light-years distant.

The darkness of intergalactic space gradually lost its hue, as the drifting galactic clusters lost their shape and transformed into flowing bands of light. Coruscating bands of brightness twisted in the darkness, amid occasional blasts of brilliance. Again the darkness and light reclaimed their territories, then all began to brighten rapidly. Still the light was organized into bands . . .

Eventually, the true darkness came. All light was extinguished, making it hard for Asura to tell whether her point of view was in motion or completely still.

An immeasurably long time passed—the kind of time span during which the Milky Way could have emerged from the energy at the center of the universe and formed into a massive spiral galaxy, which then expended all of its energy and faded to nothing.

Asura herself became a spiral galaxy, adrift in the void. She sensed that she had already lost most of her interstellar material, and the vast majority of her stars had released all their energy, subsiding into cold, hard shells.

Suddenly, she felt herself flying through space at a frightening speed. It was unclear whether she was actually traveling faster than the speed of light, or whether the entire universe was moving. She could sense that Siddhārtha and Orionae had joined her in this changed reality.

So they made it after all.

Asura realized that they were watching over her, protecting her.

She heard their voices.

Here is the beginning of all existence.

)

Asura blinked. She found that she was in a place suffused with a curious thin light, like twilight, and a crystalline stillness that seeped into her heart. Life and death, even the flow of time, were encompassed within her. She understood that while she was still taking part in a change immeasurably vast, she had transcended far beyond that change as well.

Asura realized that now she was the cakravarti-rājan.

It was at that moment that she heard voices talking far off in the distance. The sound was fainter than the wind, yet it crept inside Asura's mind. Though she had no way of telling whether these voices were actually speaking or communicating by some other means, the words were intelligible inside her.

Asura stilled her mind and listened intently.

"*It was a failure.*"

"*A great failure. In order to destroy an agglomeration of high-energy particles, it is necessary to add another factor—one that enables the collapse that is a necessary part of the process of creation and transformation. Yet because particulate clouds are quick to react to change, and the reactions can sometimes be quite violent, we would have to be doubly cautious how and where we inserted this collapse factor.*"

Another voice interjected.

"*Yet if we made a mistake in our elimination procedures, the high-energy clouds generated within the reactor would eventually permeate the reactor walls and escape into the world.*"

"*I did not expect such strange reactive structures to emerge from this cyclical energy state.*"

"Reactive structures—should we not call them life-forms?"

"Extremely primitive life-forms."

The voices grew gradually fainter and more distant until they left Asura's mind altogether.

)

"Wait! Who are you?" Asura called out into the streaming blue light. But there was no answer, no sign or shadow of response in that blank landscape as far as she could see.

The cakravarti-rājan too was gone.

She wondered what it all meant. Was all the change she had witnessed just part of a greater change, which was in turn a miniscule revolution in an even larger transformation? It seemed to Asura that no matter what its scale, change had one face only.

A sudden feeling of tremendous loss descended upon Asura. Now she must face the truth of her situation—wherever she turned, however she advanced or retreated, she would be alone. There was no way back to what had been, and in front of her stretched another ten billion days and one hundred billion nights.

)

Surging and receding . . .

Surging and receding . . .

The sound of the waves rolling in and rolling back out has echoed across this world for hundreds of millions of years, a long reach toward eternity.

Not once in that span has it ceased rocking and crossing this blue world, sometimes gently, sometimes powerfully; stormy as the morning, calm as the deep of night.

Surging and receding . . .

Surging and receding . . .

The sea rolls in and rolls back out. One hundred billion shimmering stars rise between the wave crests, only to sink back into the vastness of the waves with the first dim light of dawn.

Surging and receding . . .

Surging and receding . . .

Time that knows no haste flows over the waves as they roll in and roll back out, through night and into day and into night again.

Ah. Those many hundred billion days and nights.

How I long to return—

The peace and tranquility Asura had known there seemed painfully distant now.

Yet there was no way back to what had been, and in front of her stretched only another ten billion days and one hundred billion nights.

"**N**ame the science fiction novels that have influenced you the most."

When I am asked this question, which is fairly often, I count them off on my fingers:

Childhood's End by Arthur C. Clarke

The Martian Chronicles by Ray Bradbury

The Door into Summer by Robert A. Heinlein

City by Clifford D. Simak

To that list I would also add *The Voyage of the Space Beagle* by A. E. van Vogt and *The Astronauts* by Stanisław Lem.

All of these were books I read in the late 1950s and early '60s. I was reared a product of imperial wartime Japan and educated by a militarist regime. Still, I eagerly adapted to the changes in public thought after the war and believed I understood my world. Yet nothing could have prepared me for the intense culture shock I experienced from these works of science fiction. I could feel the scales fall from my eyes.

From *Childhood's End* I learned about the heart of Western culture. From *The Martian Chronicles* I learned about the art of the novel. From *City* I learned about the beauty of decay.

For me, the concept of the "Absolute" was the key to the world of SF. I found it tremendously enjoyable to ponder what the Absolute, or an Absolute Being, meant in the West, in the East, to the world, and to the universe.

Around the same time, I discovered the beauty of the Big Bang theory.

Time, formerly a simple absolute that stretched from the infinite past to the infinite future in an endless stream, was understood now as something relative: a limited change that stretched only from point in time A to point in time B. If the borders of time's existence are the borders of our universe, what then was the universe before time began and after it ended? If we try to explain this by saying nothing exists outside our universe (not even nothingness!), we fall into the darkness of epistemological nihilism.

So what do we do? We could stop thinking about it altogether at that point, or we could try to find some answers to these primal questions, which is where SF comes in.

In retrospect, the mid-1950s found me planted in some very fertile SF mind-soil. The news and the excitement were fresh, and there was limitless material for writing.

Ten Billion Days and One Hundred Billion Nights sprang from the elation and confusion inside me. It is, to me, my most important work, while also being a work I never want to touch again. I can barely stand even to look at it.

(Oddly enough, I fear my own internal SF mindset has grown even bleaker since those days. No laughing matter, to be sure.)

With this edition of *Ten Billion Days and One Hundred Billion Nights*, I took the liberty of adding several new lines in places that had always bothered me . . . because I could.

Ryu Mitsuse
April 1973

Mamoru Oshii
Director, Ghost in the Shell

There is such a thing as passion without a focus.
    And because that passion lacks a focus—precisely because its focus has been lost—it burns hotter still.
This I believe.

I'd like to talk about another time; a time when the passion of youth was for revolution—before the word *revolution* itself lost its luster—when political forces such as the New Left Wing and the Zenkyoto existed in Japan.

A high school student operating in the lowest levels of this revolutionary movement (i.e. myself) in his role as reporter for the *Library News*—the official publication of a high school library committee in Tokyo—found himself paying a visit to author Ryu Mitsuse.

It might require a little explanation to understand the tangled series of events that led to a high school activist interviewing an SF author as a reporter for a library newspaper.

One doesn't hear people under fifty talking about "infiltration tactics" and "parasitic tactics" much, but back in the day these were commonly enough used terms describing ways of entering an organization so as to use legal methods of information dissemination and political maneuvering to eventually take over said organization. Surrounded by the insurmountable forces of the school administration, this student and his friends followed orders from the student "war committee" (i.e. themselves) to infiltrate the school-approved student groups and were in the process of actually making that happen.

This student dared to choose (i.e. no one else wanted to join) the rather unglamorous library committee as his infiltration target, and as the person in charge of acquisitions immediately began purchasing New Left texts. But as he was an activist, so he was also a fan of SF, and began purchasing many new works in that genre as well. Eventually, he was elevated to the role of reporter for the library newspaper and, under the pretense of an interview, tried to score a meeting with one of his heroes, the SF author Ryu Mitsuse—a truly revolutionary abuse of public office for personal gain.

Of course, the school was wise to these sophomoric tactics and only overlooked them because these activities were legal within the framework of the student association. However, the combination of New Left political thought and SF must have struck the teachers in charge of student activities as very curious indeed, for the advisor of this particular student once asked him rather plainly what was wrong with his head.

Anyway, back to the subject at hand.

When this student came to visit Ryu Mitsuse at the author's home, Mr. Mitsuse greeted him warmly and fed him dinner, after which they discussed SF, history, literature, and so on until it was time for the last train to leave—amazingly the author treated this cheeky high school lad as an *individual.*

Despite the fact that Mr. Mitsuse was, at the time, a card-carrying member of the faculty at a girls' high school and thus a *de facto* member of the opposition.

It goes without saying that when the author invited this high school student to "visit again when you have the chance," the student interpreted this in the most literal and favorable way possible and was at the author's door again within the space of a few days.

Of course, the student was ecstatic to have this opportunity to not just meet but actually hold a conversation with his idol. Not that he remembers much of what was actually said—other than a discussion about Asura, king of the *asura*, which I will relate here.

As the Brahmins explained, Asura was driven by former karma to invade Tuṣita and had already been fighting with Śakra's armies for four hundred million years. What, the student wondered, was this karma that motivated such a lengthy war?

The student detected the faintest trace of a smile about the author's lips as he explained that Asura had loved a girl, and that Śakra, the girl's father, had forbade them from marrying.

So an endless war had been waged against Śakra, king of the world, for the love of a girl.

The activist who, at the end of the day, was just a high school student in the throes of puberty, found his brain paralyzed by this new vision of Asura—a character who has since become a lifetime love.

I also remember seeing the author's wife bringing us tea now and then, and thinking, *Here is the woman upon whom all the female characters he writes are based.* But I digress.

So was Asura's war against Śakra really the result of an unrequited, yet never abandoned love, for a girl?

Another thought occurs to the student now, forty years since that mind-numbing night:

What if Asura's war didn't have a reason?

I wonder if the motivation, the whole purpose of the endless war hadn't, in fact, been lost—and in being lost, perhaps it drew even more people to its ferocious nature.

Perhaps the story the author told of unrequited love was merely what he *wanted* the war to be about, the symptom of a keenly felt need for meaning.

This might be why the high school activist found himself believing less and less in the goals of the "battle for Tokyo" and the "70s war" in which he was ostensibly involved. Because in addition to his student activities, he was steeped in SF, and not just any SF, but the ballad-like epic

SF of destruction, or more simply put, the deep mystery that was *Ten Billion Days and One Hundred Billion Nights*. He, too, had lost his purpose for fighting—at least, that's how it seems to me now.

A sense of loss is capable of engendering the most passionately felt emotions.

> A sudden feeling of tremendous loss descended upon Asura. Now she must face the truth of her situation—wherever she turned, however she advanced or retreated, she would be alone. There was no way back to what had been, and in front of her stretched another ten billion days and one hundred billion nights.

The "loss" presented to the readers at the end of this glorious tale is, to those who share these feelings, a declaration of passion like no other.

This, I believe.

March 10, 2010

RYU MITSUSE

Born in Tokyo in 1928, Ryu Mitsuse graduated from Tokyo University of Education with a degree in the sciences, after which he took up the study of philosophy. He debuted with "Sunny Sea 1979" in 1962, and his work—which often combines Eastern philosophy and hard science fiction—includes *Tasogare ni kaeru* (Returns in the Twilight) and *Ushinawareta toshi no kiroku* (The Chronicle of a Lost City). Mitsuse made SF history when his short story "The Sunset, 2217 A.D." was translated into English for inclusion in *Best Science Fiction for 1972*. With artist Keiko Takemiya, he created the manga *Andromeda Stories*. Ryu Mitsuse died in 1999.

HAIKASORU
THE FUTURE IS JAPANESE

THE FUTURE IS JAPANESE
EDITED BY NICK MAMATAS AND MASUMI WASHINGTON

A web browser that threatens to conquer the world. The longest, loneliest railroad on Earth. A North Korean nuke hitting Tokyo, a hollow asteroid full of automated rice paddies, and a specialist in breaking up "virtual" marriages. And yes, giant robots. These thirteen stories from and about the Land of the Rising Sun run the gamut from fantasy to cyberpunk, and will leave you knowing that the future is Japanese! Includes stories by Bruce Sterling, Catherynne M. Valente, Project Itoh, and Hideyuki Kikuchi.

GENOCIDAL ORGAN BY PROJECT ITOH

The war on terror exploded, literally, the day Sarajevo was destroyed by a homemade nuclear device. The leading democracies have transformed into total surveillance states, and the developing world has drowned under a wave of genocides. The mysterious American John Paul seems to be behind the collapse of the world system, and it's up to intelligence agent Clavis Shepherd to track John Paul across the wreckage of civilizations and to find the true heart of darkness—a genocidal organ.

BELKA, WHY DON'T YOU BARK? BY HIDEO FURUKAWA

In 1943, when Japanese troops retreat from the Aleutian island of Kiska, they leave behind four military dogs. One of them dies in isolation, and the others are taken under the protection of US troops. Meanwhile, in the USSR, a KGB military dog handler kidnaps the daughter of a Japanese yakuza. Named after the Russian astronaut dog Strelka, the girl develops a psychic connection with canines. In this multigenerational epic as seen through the eyes of man's best friend, the dogs who are used as mere tools for the benefit of humankind gradually discover their true selves and learn something about humanity as well.

VISIT US AT WWW.HAIKASORU.COM